Legion

Southern Watch, Book 5

Robert J. Crane

Legion
Southern Watch, Book 5
Copyright © 2016 Revelen Press
All Rights Reserved.

1st Edition

This book is a work of fiction. Names, characters, places and incidents are products of the author's imagination or are used fictitiously. Any resemblance to actual events or locales or persons, living or dead, is entirely coincidental.

The scanning, uploading and distribution of this book via the internet or any other means without the permission of the publisher is illegal and punishable by law. Please purchase only authorized electronic editions, and do not participate in or encourage electronic piracy of copyrighted materials. Your support of the author's rights is appreciated.

No part of this publication may be reproduced in whole or in part without the written permission of the publisher. For information regarding permission, please email cyrusdavidon@gmail.com

Mark 5:1 *And they came over unto the other side of the sea, into the country of the Gadarenes.* **2** *And when he was come out of the ship, immediately there met him out of the tombs a man with an unclean spirit,* **3** *Who had his dwelling among the tombs; and no man could bind him, no, not with chains:* **4** *Because that he had been often bound with fetters and chains, and the chains had been plucked asunder by him, and the fetters broken in pieces: neither could any man tame him.* **5** *And always, night and day, he was in the mountains, and in the tombs, crying, and cutting himself with stones.*

6 *But when he saw Jesus afar off, he ran and worshipped him,* **7** *And cried with a loud voice, and said, What have I to do with thee, Jesus, thou Son of the most high God? I adjure thee by God, that thou torment me not.* **8** *For he said unto him, Come out of the man, thou unclean spirit.*

9 *And he asked him, What is thy name?*

And he answered, saying, My name is Legion: for we are many.

Prologue

Yavapai County, Arizona Territory
1907

Franklin Dewitt was not a man prone to caution. When it came to charging in or hanging back, he was in up to his neck before you could say boo. He was fully aware of this fact about himself and had long ago reconciled himself to it. During the Spanish-American War it had been muchly to his credit, carrying him up Kettle Hill with Teddy Roosevelt and the Rough Riders.

Now, a few years later, it had carried him through the long, dry deserts of Arizona and into a red canyon where he'd spent the last week digging with his partner, excavating their way through tons of rock that they hauled out of a cave by hand, sweating in the summer heat as they tried to find what they'd come here to make their fortunes on.

"Gall-damn, it's warm," Arthur MacFee said, sweat rolling down his unshaven face. MacFee's upper lip was covered with a good mustache, but the rest of his cheeks and throat was catching up fast after all these days in the wilderness on their hunt. The taste of old beans was a familiar fixture on Franklin's tongue by now, that and rough jerky they'd bought in Flagstaff when they'd gotten off the train before heading south.

"Just like every other day." Franklin looked over at Arthur with a grin. Arthur was most assuredly the opposite of Franklin in nearly every way. Franklin had heard it said that this reason was why they were such a good fit, the two of them. Arthur wasn't a coward by any means, but the man was cautious, feeling it was always better safe than sorry. Choosing routes for travel between the two of them was practically an adventure on its own—where Arthur would say, "It's too steep, let's go around," Franklin would already have leapt off, dragging his screaming horse behind him.

"The days are getting mighty long, too," Arthur said, mopping at his face with a soiled handkerchief. He'd washed in the nearby stream where they made their camp only last night. Franklin had watched him, bent over the cold, clear water, wringing the cloth out over and over with a brow furrowed in dissatisfaction. "Hotter and hotter."

"That is what summer does to them, generally." Franklin just kept a-grinnin'.

"Well, it can just go ahead and stop any time now," Arthur said, balling up the handkerchief and shoving it back in his pocket. He stood, announcing his intent to return to work.

Franklin got up as well; it wouldn't do to be idle while Arthur was working. Resentments tended to build that way, and Franklin liked keeping things between the two of them on a real even plane. It was probably why they'd been able to work together so well after all these years, that fair division of labor between the two of them. Franklin went out of his way to try and keep things even-steven between them.

Arthur sighed, his mustache askew from his wiping, all the bristles running to the left. Franklin knew he'd developed something of a beard at this point as well, but he hadn't seen it even in the creek. The water ran too fast down there.

Franklin hurried to lead the way back into the cave where they were digging. Arthur sighed, lagging behind him and letting Franklin get out in front. They'd hung lamps every few feet to give them some light to work with. The cave was a natural formation, but it'd been blocked up real good less than twenty feet in. The rough walls bore marks that had been aged away with time and weathering and maybe even the efforts of man to destroy them. The marks were those of the Indians, or maybe even someone before the Yavapai tribe came to this area. Franklin wasn't sure, but he knew what he was looking for, and they were getting mighty close, he reckoned.

Arthur went to work with his pickaxe next to Franklin, and they pulled their bandanas up as the dust filled the air from their efforts. Whoever had blocked this cave had done it proper, big rocks all piled up so that not even air could pass through. It didn't look natural at all to Franklin, no sir, it looked like purposeful work, like someone meant to hide something here in this cave. That was what he was counting on, anyway. Why, he and Arthur had come all the way from Missouri on that very assumption.

"Gall-damned dust," Arthur complained again, eyes wrinkling around the edges as he squinted, the lamp catching the particles of broken rock that were drifting in the cave atmosphere around them from their labors. He stopped and wiped his eyes with his sleeve, which was not nearly so recently clean as his handkerchief. He paused, looking at Franklin through narrowed eyes. "How does this not bother you?"

"Why, it does bother me." Franklin kept tapping away at a small rock with his pickaxe. It finally shattered under his steady efforts, and he scooped up four handfuls of stone, throwing them back into the wooden barrow behind him that they used to cart the detritus of their dig to the surface for dumping. "I just don't moan about it all the time." He said it good-naturedly enough that Arthur just grunted and turned back to his work.

The steady tapping of the pickaxes was a maddening sound, Franklin supposed, if one were predisposed to be driven batty by it. It didn't really bother him, though Arthur had complained often enough about them that Franklin was certainly aware of the noise, the echo down the long cave toward the bright sunlight above. Even down here in the canyon, the Arizona sun beat down hard during the hours it was overhead. He couldn't rightly recall seeing the sun brighter anywhere he'd ever been, save perhaps in Cuba, but the thin air in this part of the world was very unlike that heavy, tropical place.

"Oh," Arthur said, as a rock shattered beneath his labors. He turned his head and spat, and Franklin knew by experience that it was due to his mouth being utterly filled with the dust that hung in the air. It was thick and chalky, and he himself spat what felt like a thousand times a day trying to get rid of it. Arthur stopped and was staring in intense concentration at the place where he'd been striking only a moment before. "I think I—why, yes, I did—I broke through, Franklin."

Franklin straightened up, nearly dropping his pickaxe as Arthur's words echoed through the cave's cool darkness. The heat of the Arizona summer didn't quite reach down this far, though he could feel it making an attempt at the back of his collar, a little breath of heat. He shuffled in the darkness, pulling the nearest lamp hung on the cave wall off its hook and making his way over to Arthur, who was stooped over and running his dirty fingers over what appeared to be a gap in the rocks in front of them.

Franklin knelt down and looked, lifting the lantern and trying to position it. Arthur took a step back out of his way, plainly content to let Franklin go first, once more. Franklin peered into the gap, trying to discern whether or not there was another rock hiding back there, perhaps wedged beneath the ones above so tightly that he just couldn't see it. The lantern shone through, though, and it looked like nothing but darkness in the gap that Arthur had created.

"Well, dang," Franklin said, staring into the black. "I think you did it."

"We did it," Arthur said, inching up behind him and placing a dirty hand on his shoulder. He knelt down just behind Franklin, and Franklin could feel his warm, fetid breath on the back of his neck as Arthur peered into the dark himself. "Well, this might just be it." Franklin looked back and caught his compatriot's more cautious grin, and by mutual accord they immediately went back to work.

They worked without a break, without hauling away the broken rock, just focused on tearing up the last obstacles between themselves and the darkness beyond the rock wall. They did not speak, barely even spat the chalky rock dust out, as though they feared somehow that any noise might cause another wall of rock to fall and block their efforts.

It took most of the day, and by the time that Franklin looked back to see the mouth of the cave turning red with sunset, they'd cleared enough of a space for a man to squeeze through at the top. Franklin ran his fingers over the cave roof and found it appropriately rough. Bringing his palm down to the top of the rock wall that remained between them and the open darkness ahead, he paused. There was no air stirring, and they had not once felt any breeze in their faces as they worked to clear their new path.

To Franklin, that suggested this cavern was utterly sealed off, no hidden chimneys that might lead to the surface, no spur routes that would let an animal sneak in, nothing. He sniffed; beyond the scent of the rock dust was nothing but still, stale air.

He looked into the dark, through the little window they'd carved. "I'm going in," he decided.

Arthur just sighed behind him. "That doesn't seem wise. What if the roof caves in?"

"You felt it, didn't you?" Franklin asked. "The ceiling of this cave has been standing just like it is for thousands of years, maybe longer. All this," he indicated the remainder of the barrier between them and the darkness ahead, "was put here, it didn't collapse. If the ceiling's going to come down now, I reckon it's just my time, and there's nothing for it." He grinned again.

Arthur sighed once more. "I'll wait here."

"Bully for you, then." Franklin didn't even wait for a reply; he plunged through the gap in the rock, wriggling his way through. The last two buttons of his coat caught and tore free on the rough rock below as Arthur let out a sound of disapproval mingled with worry. Franklin wormed his way through, writhing against the places where his hips caught the sides of their carved entry. With a last ripping of fabric, he dropped, landing clumsily on his hands on the dusty cave floor and thumping his head on a poorly placed stone.

It felt like someone had thrown a boulder against the top of his head, maybe dropped one on him from the top of the canyon. His vision went wavy, and the darkness flashed with red and amber as Franklin clutched at his head. Warm liquid trickled between his fingers, and he could feel the parting of the skin, a little crevice an inch long that had carved its way into the crown of his head, a river of blood overrunning its banks.

"You all right in there?" Arthur called. There was a clink and light shone in. Franklin looked up to see his lantern shoved into the ovoid hole he'd just crammed himself through. *Thank you, Arthur.*

"Just landed a bit poorly," Franklin said, mopping the blood with his sleeve as his vision cleared. He stood and grabbed the lantern by its wire handle, swinging it around slowly in the dark.

Dark was all there was ahead of him, nothing but blackness as he stood there, peering into its inky depths. He blinked a few times, but that didn't help. The pain in his head was not receding much, persisting as a reminder not to take his own skull for granted.

"What are you going to do?" Arthur asked tentatively. "You going to come back so we can dig out the rest—"

"No." Franklin shook his head, making it feel like he'd loosed a rock slide inside, and every boulder hurt as it moved. "Just hang on. I'm going to go take a look around."

"I won't dig while you're gone," Arthur said. "Don't want to cause a cave-in."

"Why don't you just lay your worrying head aside for once and come join me in here, Arthur?" Franklin asked as he took his first step forward.

"I ... well ..."

"Yeah, you give it some thought," Franklin said, easing forward again. He could see the outline of the cave itself around him, the light from the lantern giving off just enough illumination to allow him to see a few steps ahead. He peered at the uneven footing and took each step carefully. "I'll be back before you finish thinking it over."

Without waiting for Arthur to answer, Franklin started taking longer, more ambitious steps. Letting the light guide him, he swung the lantern back and forth in front of his face. The stone walls of the cave were a light red in this light. It reminded him of a small town they'd passed through on the way here, situated in the end of a long canyon with red rocks all around it.

His boots scuffed along on the dusty floor, the cool air prickling at his skin up his back and around his shoulders. Franklin licked his dry lips and kept steadily on, the cave widening into a larger chamber ahead. He listened, but could not hear anything except the faint drip of water somewhere ahead.

The cave widened into a larger circular chamber, lines of strata in the rock making it look like it had been shaped by a pottery wheel. Franklin leaned close to the nearest wall and frowned as he traced a bare hand over the rock wall. He felt the bumps beneath his fingers, so different than the tunnel he'd been working in up until this point. He brought the lantern around slowly and saw half a circle of the chamber illuminated and something sitting right in its center.

Franklin's breath caught in his throat. The lantern's handle creaked as it swung gently from his movement. He eased closer to the center of the chamber, the lamplight casting the object at the middle in brighter relief. The other side of the chamber was visible now, smooth and stratified like the one he'd just examined; the whole room was only twenty feet across, but his attention was entirely on the centerpiece.

"Arthur!" Franklin called toward the gaping darkness through which he'd come. He did not look back to see if Arthur was making his way through the gap. "I think we found it!"

Arthur did not answer, and Franklin did not wait for his reply. He moved closer to the center of the chamber, where a pedestal stood, just as shaped as the rest of the chamber, with its smooth lines as it extended out of the floor. He had a suspicion he knew what kind of power had shaped this cave to its purpose, and it caused his stomach to quiver.

Atop the small pedestal of red rock sat a vase. Franklin stared at its utterly smooth sides, its very plain clay construction. A breath escaped his lungs quietly as he crept closer, now less than a foot away. This was what they'd been tunneling for, what they'd been looking for. Franklin took his free hand and let it creep down to the chain around his neck. He pulled up the crucifix hidden beneath his shirt and ran his fingers over the smooth silver, then brought it up to his lips and gave it a quick kiss before letting it fall, this time landing outside his shirt.

Franklin licked his lips dryly once more, wishing he'd brought his canteen through with him. "Arthur ..." he called, but there was no answer.

He looked back, just once, and saw nothing from down the tunnel. No light, no sign of Arthur in the distance. He'd probably gone back to the creek to refill the canteens, ever-practical Arthur. It wasn't as though they had cause to worry, after all. This was just a vessel, just a clay pot that was worth a lot of money to the right buyer.

Franklin didn't fully believe that. He never had, and neither had Arthur. He peered at the vase, deciding what to do. Franklin never allotted too much time for a decision. He simply didn't believe in pondering, because the first course of action was almost always the right one, he'd found. The snap decision turned out to be better in hindsight than the carefully considered one, at least in his experience.

Franklin flexed his fingers in the cool air and set the lantern at his feet. There was a clatter as its metal bottom clanked against the circular grooves that lined the chamber from floor to ceiling, extending out in perfectly symmetrical circles from the pedestal. The lantern rattled as it found its balance, and Franklin shed his coat. It was old and worn, had seen more miles than he cared to consider. It was due for replacing in any case, and for now it would serve him better than trying to climb back out to get a blanket with which to lift the vase from its resting place.

Franklin took a breath of the cool cave air, the still, stale smell permeating his nostrils and the taste of dust still hanging in his mouth, unspat. He took a step forward, his coat hanging from his hands like a protective shield before him as he advanced on the object in the middle of the room.

The vase looked delicate, and it probably was. Franklin Dewitt was no archaeologist, but it looked to his eyes like a very old thing. How old, he wouldn't even have cared to speculate, but along with old he associated "delicate," and so he took his time approaching it—at least as much as Franklin ever took his time approaching anything.

He wrapped the coat slowly around the neck of the vase, then tucked it around the wide middle and the smaller base. Whether it was some sort of Indian artifact or simply something that had somehow made its way to Indian country, he did not know. He treated it as though it were older still and more valuable than a Biblical scroll, cradling it in his arms as he lifted it from the pedestal.

He waited in the quiet as he held it in his arms, listening for something, anything—a rumble in the mountain, skies to darken outside, rivers of blood to start running. Franklin's breath caught in his throat for a second and he listened—

Nothing.

There was not a sound, not a whisper, no cataclysm at hand. Shrugging, he stooped, carefully snagging the wire handle of the lantern with his ring and pinky finger as he rose and started back toward the way out.

"Arthur!" he shouted into the darkness ahead, "I think I got it!" Franklin could feel his eyes subtly bulge, his pulse quickening with the thrill of discovery after long weeks of digging. He had listened to the clink of the pickaxes against the rock with unceasing patience, over and over, and this was the moment of reward. He held the bundle of the vase in his hands, wrapped in his coat, the scratchy fabric between his fingers and the smooth pottery.

Between him and what rested within the object itself.

"Arthur!" Franklin called again. He stared straight ahead, wondering when the small passage they had carved would be illuminated. The sides of the cave tunnel crowded in around him as he made his way slowly, choosing his steps with care once more, the passage nowhere near as smooth as the carved circular chamber where he'd found the vase. "Arthur, I found it, damn your eyes! Tell me you didn't choose this moment to go outside to relieve yourself."

The outline of the small passage he'd squeezed through appeared before him, faint shadows the only thing visible beyond. He peered but could not see, could not discern anything beyond a vague pinprick of light that suggested a lantern somewhere on the wall in the distance. The air was getting fresher as he drew closer to the hole in the rock barrier. The lantern light showed it plainly now; it was a pile of stones that was far wider at the base than at the top where Arthur had broken through and he'd climbed in.

"Arthur!" Franklin called, struggling under the awkward heft of the bundle in front of him. "I've found it, Arthur, found the—curse you, you old dog." He dropped his voice at the last, almost disbelieving. It was just like Arthur to choose this very moment, this very climactic moment, to take his leave for a break. The dust hung heavier in the air here than it had in the chamber behind him, and he stuck out his tongue once more and spat over the top of the bundle in his arms. The dusty, chalky taste in his mouth did not depart, though. But then, it never did, did it?

Franklin reached the rise of the rocks ahead of him and paused, minding his footing even more carefully now. He felt unbalanced even though the vase only weighed a scant few pounds. He shifted it against his chest, the pottery pressed against his coat. The chilly cave air was still causing him to break out in goose pimples as though it were the first of morning.

Franklin looked into the dark gap in the rock wall, trying to decide what to do next. "Arthur!" he snapped, raising his voice. "Arthur, I have it, will you come down here and—" He paused, listening, but heard nothing from beyond.

For a moment he considered waiting, but that simply would not do.

With great care, he climbed as far as he could up the incline of rocks that he'd slid down to land upon his head only moments earlier. He chose his steps carefully, and when he could go no further with the vase in his hands, he pondered how best to approach taking it the last few feet and writhing his way out the other side.

"There's nothing for it but to do it," he said, feeling that itching sensation up and down his chest and back, that tickling fire within that urged him to action. He took a breath and then slipped a foot into the narrow passage awkwardly, bending his other knee.

Franklin thumped his head on the ceiling of the cave and grunted as it reawakened the pain he'd inspired upon his landing. "Almighty!" he cursed, cringing, holding himself still as the warm blood trickled back down his scalp. His eyes were half-closed at this point from the stinging. A drip of sweat fell into his eyes and it burned.

Franklin bent double, clutching the vase against his chest, the coat placed carefully between him and his prize. He felt a stab of fear as a rock shifted beneath his feet and he dropped an inch. There was a tearing feeling in his groin and he took a sharp breath, but his balance came back and he caught his breath again. His heart still hammered in his ears, though.

"Arthur, I must warn you, I am of a mind to kill you when I get out of here," Franklin said, holding himself still for a second before readjusting. He was reminded of climbing to the top of a church bell tower and then squeezing back down the hatch to the ladder, save for this was a horizontal maneuver, and he did not have gravity on his side nor the benefit of free hands.

Franklin hugged the vase tight and backed himself even closer to the hole, sliding his leg through awkwardly. He hooked the leg on a rock inside the small tunnel and then gradually applied his weight. He felt more than a little foolhardy; it was not exactly a given that the rock would hold him, and should it fail in the midst of his efforts, it might well roll onto him, causing injury or death.

Still, he tested it, slowly. It held, and he put a little more weight behind it, until finally he was entirely committed to it. Taking another slow breath, he shouted, "Arthur!" and waited five seconds without response before deciding to go on with it.

Franklin bent entirely double and rested his left elbow on a rock. It pushed at his bone uncomfortably, and now he was half standing, half kneeling, with his left leg extended behind him to climb backward through the hole in the rock barrier. His right leg was aching at the groin where it creased to bend unnaturally far. He was practically in a position to eat his right kneecap if he wanted to, just give it a nibble through his dirty, scuffed-up breeches.

Putting his weight on his left side, both the elbow and the foot hooked against the large stone, Franklin lifted his right leg and pushed it behind him, the vase still cradled in his arms like a baby wrapped in the coat. When he'd managed to get his right foot braced in the hole, he lowered his right elbow and found a suitable place to brace it as well. That done, he very slowly began to worm his way backward.

"Oh, Arthur, you'd be so proud to see me now," Franklin grumbled, his voice thick with umbrage for his partner. "Here I am, crawling ass-backwards through the cave tunnel because you couldn't be bothered to follow after me or at least wait for me here, like a sensible person."

Franklin moved rearward an inch at a time, the sound of his clothes brushing hard against the rock and gravel. There was a sudden rattling as he set loose a small avalanche of pebbles down his left side. He took a breath that stuck in his lungs and halted his progress for a second, then exhaled and pushed back again, still clutching the vase tightly. It shifted in his arms and he held still for a long second, waiting for it to stabilize before moving again.

The rough fabric of his coat was rubbing against his wrists, the coarse material like rough grains of sand pushed against Franklin's skin. He couldn't wait to get through this, to finish his crawl. His mind was already on loading up the vase, on getting on their mules and getting back to Flagstaff, where they could catch a train to the east. They could be in Chicago in just a few days. After that, it'd be on to New York to deliver the thing, at which point they could get paid and consider this whole expedition behind them.

That'd be a banner day. Franklin was certainly looking forward to it. Perhaps a little too much, in fact, because while his mind was on that, the side of the vase bumped against a rock that jutted out in the hole.

The sound of pottery shattering stopped Franklin's motion completely. He held utterly still, listening as the clay broke where it had hit the jutting piece of stone. He held it cradled in his arms, but the vase shifted, and he stared into the dark, barely lit by the lamp he'd left on the other side of the rock wall, as the pottery cracked and collapsed in on itself within the bounds of his coat.

"No! NO!" Franklin screamed in the dark, and shifted in a

frenzied hurry to try and stop what could no longer be stopped. The vase was broken, the damage done enough to completely destroy the entire structure of the thing, and it fell to pieces even as he tried his hardest to keep it together.

Franklin shifted on the right and one of the larger pieces, the neck and mouth of the vase, freed from the weighty middle, came tumbling out of his coat. Franklin could feel it shift, and acted instinctively to try and save it. Working entirely from reaction rather than thought, he let go of the coat and grasped with bare fingers, dread and panic cramping his heart and stomach as he moved without consideration to catch the pieces that remained—

And his fingertips brushed the cool pottery, unobstructed by the coat that had kept him from it before.

The world went suddenly black around Franklin, and he could not see anything. The light that had been gleaming from the two lamps on either side of the tight passage in which he was trapped vanished as though they'd been snuffed suddenly by a stiff wind. The chill air grew suddenly warmer, and Franklin took a sharp intake of breath. He'd been on his belly a moment earlier, but now he had the disconcerting sense that he'd been suddenly turned upright without warning, that he was standing again, all the blood rushing out of his head.

"Lord a-mighty," Franklin breathed into the darkness.

"Quite the opposite, in fact," came a voice from the black, a faint pulsating light glimmering with each spoken word. The accent was peculiar, reminding him Franklin of a British fellow he'd once met in New York City. The cadence was slow, steady, and with a hint of drawl to put emphasis on some syllables. The effect was strange, but it gave the speaker's voice a quality of ponderous thought, carefully punctuated.

"Don't go scaring the poor man," came a second voice, this one almost mirthful. "He's just had quite the jolt to his constitution."

"Who are you?" Franklin spoke into the dark, his skin feeling suddenly warm, almost flushed.

"Mmm," came the first voice, the sterner one. "Names. I think ours are nearly unpronounceable in English, aren't they?"

"As though we'd freely give them in any case," said the second, amused. "Perhaps we should just go with the old standards."

"Perhaps, indeed."

"Very well, then," the second voice said. "You may call me … William."

"I suppose then I shall once again go with Chester," said the more serious, ponderous voice. Both sounded indubitably male, though.

"Who in the blazes are you?" Franklin asked, feeling as though he were spinning around, trying to catch sight of the speakers, their words still pulsing with light.

"I'm Chester."

"And I am William."

"That doesn't help at all," Franklin whispered under his breath, the prickle of fear dusting him.

"How do we explain it, Chester?" came the more youthful voice, filled with genuine curiosity.

"Hmmm …" Chester said, clearly giving it serious thought. "I think … well, there is a rather classical way that he'll be able to understand, but I don't think you'll find it favorable given you don't want to scare him."

"Ah, yes." William's voice seemed resigned, the light dimming. "That will have to do, I suppose, though it feels as though it could be a bit … cruel."

"Leaving him ignorant seems crueler, especially when things are now so radically different for the man," Chester said.

"Who are you?" Franklin asked, spinning in the dark, the world whirling around him, the light spots indicating Chester and William blurring in front of his eyes. It was getting harder to see, other spots seemed to be popping out like stars in the Arizona sky.

"We are the speakers," Chester said, "for a great congress of—"

"You said you were going to explain it in the classical way." William cut him off suddenly and with a hint of rudeness.

"Being aware of your distaste for anything traditional, I was trying to be more accommodating," Chester said primly.

"Well, that would be a first," William said. "And while I appreciate it—"

"Speaking of firsts." Chester said.

"Just go with what we agreed on," William said.

Chester made a harrumphing sound in the darkness, the light vibrating. "Very well, then, have it your way—"

"I'm asking you to do it your way, not mine—"

"And I was willing to do it more like yours—"

"What the blazes is going on here?" Franklin asked, feeling as though he might break out in a cold sweat at any moment.

"You know the answer to that, don't you?" Chester asked. "You touched a piece of the vase." Franklin began to feel that sweat coursing down him, even though there was no temperature change to prompt it. "You know what that means to you, do you not?"

"I—I don't—" Franklin began.

"Come now, my good man," William said in a friendly manner, "you're not some Johnny-Come-Lately, new to this sort of digging. You knew what you came for, after a fashion. You knew what the vase was, why not to touch it—or at least part of the reason not to." The voice paused. "What was in the vase, Franklin?"

"In its center?" Franklin asked, his own voice wavering. "Nothing."

"What was in the pottery?" Chester asked, drawling. "Come now, denial will fetch no favor here."

Franklin felt his hands shake, the spots of light penetrating the dark around him. "It was ... said a ..." his voice shook to match his hands, "... a demon was imprisoned in the clay."

"Don't believe everything you hear," William said.

"Indeed not," Chester said in obvious agreement. "And you need not fear, Franklin, old boy."

"But you're—you're a demon," Franklin said, bowing his head, his eyes closing in despair of their own accord. "And you're—you're here in my mind, now ... in my body ..."

"I think you mean '*we*' are," Chester said sedately.

"Very important to understand the distinction," William said.

"Two demons, then," Franklin said, and the despair rose; he'd been careful, but plainly not careful enough. The desire to hurry through and secure the vase without Arthur's help had cost him now. And it had cost him dear, for he knew that there was no easy way to remove—

"Oh, heavens, no," Chester said, lightly chuckling.

"Two of us?" William asked. "Good grief." The darkness pulsated with light as he crackled with airy laughter.

Franklin stared into the dark, looking at the tiny pinpricks of light that suddenly started to grow larger. They truly did remind him of the stars in the sky, of the darkness of the night in the canyon, the cloudless sky beset by the faint glow of the heavens. "How … how many are you?"

"I think this is the moment," William said. "Go on, 'Chester' … with your tradition and all that …"

"Your names are not Chester and William," Franklin said with a sense that his mouth had gone as dry as the desert plains.

"Goodness no," William said. "Tell the poor man."

"'My name is Legion,'" Chester said, repeating the old verse that even Franklin knew, "'for we are many.'" And the light blazed around him, the infinite stars shining brighter in the darkness.

"We are the speakers for all of these," William said. "The voice to the many."

"He doesn't understand," Chester said.

"He doesn't need to, at least not immediately," William said.

"What do you want with me?" Franklin asked.

"I didn't want anything with you," Chester said, sounding more than a little cross. "But you broke our vessel, our home, and left us nowhere else to go. I would have been quite content to remain in the vase."

"I wasn't content," William said with what sounded like barely contained glee. "I consider it a blessing that you fumbled, that you rushed in where angels fear to tread."

"Why did you have to mention *them*?" Chester grumbled.

"I wasn't thinking," William said, "and do try to stop being so sensitive. I can't steer away from every word and common phrase that might offend your delicate self—"

"Well, you could try—"

"I do try, but it feels as though you're getting touchier by the day—"

"Oh, dear God, deliver me from evil," Franklin mumbled. The light of both speakers seemed to swivel to him, as though they pivoted and covered him with lamplight.

"'Evil'?" Chester rumbled.

"See, now even that offends you," William said, "and you just quoted a verse to him whilst proclaiming our identity that's in their holy book and clearly associates us with what they consider the 'bad side.'"

"What are you people?" Franklin moaned.

"We are not people at all," Chester said.

"There you go getting offended again," William said.

"WHAT THE TARNATION IS GOING ON HERE?" Franklin burst out of the darkness, lamplight flooding in all around him, suddenly once more aware of pressure on his hips, his belly, rocks poking up at him and a jagged piece of pottery clenched in his hand. He let it spill from his limp fingers and crawled without conscious thought, his body pushing him backward until he rolled down the slope and into the cave, shedding the coat and the pottery fragments as he went. Blood welled up on his right hand where he'd grabbed hold of a shard, and he wiped it on his breeches, fingers against the rough cotton, without thinking about it.

"What are you doing?" Arthur said, stalking up to him, the faint light of day mingling with the lantern hanging on a nearby hook. Arthur had his handkerchief out in his hand, probably from just finishing mopping his forehead again beneath his hairline. "Franklin ... what did you find?"

"You weren't listening?" Franklin asked, voice coming in a croak.

"I was outside filling the canteen at the creek," Arthur said, edging closer to him. "I thought about what you said, and I was all set to climb in after you when I came back." He looked Franklin up and down. "But you're already out. Did you find anything?" He stiffened. "Did you find ... it?"

"I ..." Franklin's mouth was dry, exactly as he'd felt it in his dream, or delusion, or whatever it had been. "I don't know."

Arthur stood straight in front of him, and the handkerchief slowly fluttered out of his grasp. "Franklin ... did you find the vase?" His fingers inched slowly down toward his hip, where his revolver waited in a beaten-up leather holster. "Did you ... touch it?"

"I didn't even say I found it," Franklin said, angry and watching his friend's hand move cautiously toward his gun. Franklin didn't have one on his hip; he'd left it in the bundle on the back of his mule. "But thanks for the trust."

Arthur's hand didn't move, hovering above his holster. "Did you find it, then?"

Franklin swallowed hard. "I ..."

Arthur's gaze was hard as the stone walls of the cave. "Did you find it?"

"There is nothing to fear," Chester said, speaking through Franklin's mouth. Franklin, for his part, felt shock as the voice burst out of his lips unasked.

Arthur's eyebrows rose, even in the low light. "Franklin …"

"We mean you no harm," William said, taking hold of Franklin's tongue and using it to speak. "There's no need to reach for your weapon, Arthur. Let us pass, and go on about your business."

"Oh, Franklin," Arthur said, and his finger twitched where he held it above the holster.

"Please don't," Chester said, Franklin's eyes fixed on Arthur's hand.

Arthur couldn't help it; he was not bold but he was no fool, either. Had it been Franklin in his shoes, he would have made it to the holster before Franklin covered the ground between them, before Franklin's fingers, with newfound strength, wrapped themselves around Arthur's neck and throttled him, staying his hand from drawing his gun all the while.

"Let it be merciful," Chester said. "He has little ability to harm us, William."

"Yet still he tries," William said, straining, forcing Franklin's fingers to dig into Arthur's throat. "He's a hateful little man, isn't he? Hates us with all he has. And here I go, hating him right back."

"It is unnecessary," Chester said, sounding faintly regretful.

It felt as though it took days, or an age; Arthur's eyes bulged from their sockets, shining in the dark like stars until they went glassy and his neck and wrist went suddenly limp. The eyes rolled, a final breath came out in a rattle, and Franklin's hands let Arthur go, and his old partner tumbled to the floor of the cave.

"This was truly a shame," Chester said, shaking Franklin's head for him. "It did not need to come to this."

"Protecting the many is our highest duty," William said, then was silent for a moment. "I make no apologies for that."

"What … have I done …?" Franklin croaked, his own voice leaking out like air from a hot teakettle.

"You haven't done anything," William said.

"That was entirely us," Chester said with muted agreement. "And … I hate to say it, but for this to work, I think it's going to have to be entirely us going forward."

"For the greater good, I quite agree," William said. "Terribly sorry, Franklin."

"What ... what are you going to do to me?" Franklin asked, frozen in the darkness, standing in the middle of the cave, Arthur's body at his feet. "Are you ... going to kill me?"

"Good gracious, no," Chester said.

"You're going to be one of us, now, Franklin," William said, and the light started to recede from Franklin's eyes, the cave fading around him. "One of the many, you see. As Chester told you, we are Legion—"

The smells of dust, the taste of chalky broken rock receded into the depths of memory, and the stars that had pulsed in the blackness around Franklin grew brighter. He could hear other voices now, a thousand, a million of them, and it reminded him of a New York night, the avenues all alive with conversation and laughter. Some among them were happy, some were sad, but the feeling of being in the cave with Arthur's body at his feet began to grow distant, like an old memory of those city nights. He could hear conversations behind William's voice, behind Chester's, and he receded into the midst of all of it like sinking into a warm bath.

"That's the spirit, old chap," Chester said as Franklin Dewitt dipped into the depths of the many. "Part of the crew, then."

"I suppose that's an appropriate analogy," William said, "as it seems we've press-ganged him into joining us." He turned Franklin's eyes toward the light at the end of the tunnel—

No, not Franklin's eyes. Not anymore.

"Come on, then," Chester said, and they started to move. Daylight was waiting. The world was waiting. "I may not want to be here, but there's little choice now."

"Well, try and enjoy it just a bit," William said, and he split the lips of their new body in a smile. "You know, if you wanted to try to be accommodating once more."

"Don't think I'll go along with you on every occasion," Chester said, smoothing his hands down the cotton shirt that they wore on their new body. "But perhaps just this once, again ..." And he went along with the smile, stepping over Arthur's body as they all walked out to join the world that they had been cut off from for oh so long.

1.

Midian, Tennessee
Present Day

"Same shit, different day. That's what you Marines call this, isn't it?"

"I think we generally just call it being outnumbered," Lafayette Hendricks said from beneath the brim of his wide cowboy hat, staring out at the dozen demons that were stacked up in front of him.

"Simple, yet descriptive." The demon named Duncan had shed the suit that he had so typically worn in the past. Now he was clad in a t-shirt with the words "I'm Not With Stupid Anymore" plastered across the front. Hendricks approved, but then he hadn't been the biggest fan of Duncan's last sidekick. That guy had been a dick.

Dusk was settling over the quiet neighborhood in Midian, Tennessee, the sky a bright orange as Hendricks and Duncan stood on a playground, a bevy of demons lined up between them and a grade-school-aged kid who the dirty dozen had been encircling before the two of them had rolled up in Hendricks's SUV to square off. The kid looked scared shitless, face half-hidden behind a thin, circular piece of jungle gym that he was peering out from behind, his normal world having taken a detour right off the fucking track.

"I thought it captured the feeling of the moment pretty well," Hendricks said, fingering the sword in his hand. It was a thin, sharp piece of metal a couple feet long, no more than an inch across. Every single one of the demons hanging out on the playground was staring at it. Well, it or Duncan's baton, which the demon had in his hand, a little cylinder six inches long, spring-loaded, Hendricks knew by experience, and not deployed just yet.

"It smells like fear up in this piece," the lead demon said, sniffing the air. Probably theatrically, Hendricks figured. When they'd pulled up, he'd been looking like a twenty-something grunge guitarist who'd washed up from Seattle or somewhere, lank brown hair coruscating down in messy tangles, tattoos spilling out of his short-sleeved shirt. He had a little bit of a smell about him, too, like he was trying to articulate "grunge" in a very literal sort of way.

"Really?" Hendricks asked. "Because to me it smells like unwashed, too-old broc'aminn playing like he's trying to get himself a piece of something too young for him." The lead guitarist's face rippled, revealing darkness behind it, like his skin had turned liquid and dark, a pond disturbed by a thrown rock at the surface. Broc'aminn were one of the nastiest kinds of demons Hendricks had ever run across. Lots of demons liked children, but broc'aminn weren't shy about all the nasty things they did with them. Most kinds would just eat the kids and get on with it. Not a broc'aminn, though.

Also, they were pack hunters, which Hendricks acknowledged with a look around at the guitarist's fellows. The fact that there were an even dozen was mildly worrisome.

"You're doing the math, aren't you, demon hunter?" Lead Guitar asked with a smirk on his demon face. "It's not in your favor."

"Yes, I do math," Hendricks said, nodding, fingers on the leather hilt of his sword, running a finger along the metal crossguard. "It's a thing we humans have spent time on, like evolution. Helps keep us out of trouble. You don't meet too many graduate physicists that are cannibals, after all. Mostly idiots like you, really."

Lead Guitar looked around, smirking with those ugly extended lips, revealing a mouth full of way, way too many teeth. He breathed, and Hendricks almost had to take a step back from the smell. "I'm not a cannibal. I'm a meat eater." He ran a long tongue around his mouth like a lizard, lasciviously. "I'm a meat lover, in all the ways you can imagine." His eyes blinked sideways. "But I like my meat tender, so if you and your empty shell will just motor along … me and my buddies will give you a pass, just this once."

Hendricks didn't take to sentimentality too easily, but he threw a glance at the kid hiding behind the jungle gym. "Hey, you. What's your name?"

The kid flinched, frozen like he'd been in the perfect hiding spot. "J-Jacob."

"Jacob," Hendricks said. "You doing all right over there, Jacob? You're scared, aren't you?" Jacob could only nod. "That's good," Hendricks said. "That's smart. Because these are very bad guys, and they mean to do very bad things. My friends and I are going to help you, but Jacob, I need you to listen." Hendricks looked him right in the eye, talked past the herd of broc'aminn like they weren't there. "When you get your chance, Jacob, I need you to run. Don't be afraid they're going to catch you. Just run when you get a chance. Okay?"

"What chance do you think this little lamb has got?" Lead Guitar asked, laughing, brushing his hair out of his eyes. "We're demons. We can run him down."

"My friends are going to help you, okay, Jacob?" Hendricks asked, not breaking eye contact. He received a small, terrified nod in return. "Okay, then." And Hendricks shifted his attention back to Lead Guitar. "All right. You ready to get this gig underway?"

Lead Guitar just chuckled low. "You got a real death wish here, demon hunter. Maybe I'll just leave you half-alive for some scavengers to come collect. Maybe it'll be one of the yargraad nesting in the hills. I could open up your belly, tear up your vocal chords, leave you rotting in the night for them. They eat you insides-first, you know."

Hendricks glanced at Duncan. "I think I've heard that about them. Did you know there were yargraad in them thar hills?"

Duncan shook his head, his features softening in the waning light of day, all orange and glorious through the clouds on the horizon. "I did not. Someone should write that down. We could go after them next."

"Oh, bro, you guys are suffering from serious false confidence," Lead Guitar said, and a few of his cronies chortled behind him. "It's like you don't understand the lay of the land, the state of things."

"And it's like you don't understand the meaning of words," Hendricks said, shrugging lightly. Lead Guitar cocked his head. "I mean," Hendricks went on, letting a slight smirk bleed out, "you didn't even notice I said *friends*, plural ... ANGEL, you ready?"

The roar of a fifty-caliber rifle rocked the quiet night, and one of the Dirty-Ass Dozen, as Hendricks had already taken to thinking of this little band of shitters, took a hit to the chest that slammed his back into the ground like he'd been hit by a missile. He snapped, his legs folding and knees nearly hitting him in the face as he made hard contact with the grassy park ground.

"I guess she's ready. And that's our cue," Hendricks said, charging into battle, Duncan a half-step ahead, his sword raised and ready, the Dirty-Ass Dozen's wide demon eyes looking around in shock as the two of them came in fighting.

*

"ANGEL has two breaking off to go after the kid," Alison Longholt Stan said into the Bluetooth headset in her ear. The microphone was unobtrusive fortunately, because she needed wires interfering with her shooting like she needed a kick to the ass from a mule. She drew a bead through the scope on the massive Barrett rifle, leading her target by a little bit, and gently squeezed the trigger after blowing out her breath slowly. She watched through the scope as one of the broc'aminn was launched sideways. She figured she'd pegged him in the shoulder pretty good by the way he flipped and hit the dirt. She was actually impressed she'd hit him; the twilight hour didn't exactly lend itself to great lighting. It was too dim to see well at a distance, and too light for her to switch to the night scope. "Make that one."

Alison took a sniff of the late October air as she readjusted to try and draw a bead on the other runner. Looking through the scope, she didn't have the faintest idea what was going on with Hendricks and Duncan at the moment. She hoped it was going well, but she didn't have the mental space to give it much thought. She had one mission, and it was to stop any strays from eating or killing Jacob Arnold while Hendricks and Duncan distracted the others. It was a mission that had been assigned in a hell of a hurry, with a conferencing phone call as they'd rushed to the site, warned by Duncan's strange sense of things. She'd heard Hendricks call it "an op laid on a little too quickly," and that seemed to fit her conception of how it was all going. She figured her daddy or Arch would have called it a "hurry-up offense," and that also worked.

"This is not going so good," Hendricks called through the headset, and Alison could hear the muffled sounds of a struggle, heavy breathing that could only belong to the cowboy, through her earpiece. "Any chance we can get a little help here?"

Alison fired again, the reverberation of the fifty-cal shot running through her whole body. She was perched on a roof across from the park, lying prone on the flat roof of an open carport. Pebbles were eating into her chest through her shirt and jeans, but they were a minor discomfort compared to what she knew would happen to Jacob Arnold if they failed. She watched the demon in her sights take the bullet to the shoulder and buckle, tossed like he'd just performed a gymnastics maneuver into a flip, landing hard on his back. She gave it a second to be sure both her targets were at least down before she swung the rifle around to where Duncan and Hendricks were up to their balls in the other nine or so bandmates, and it took her less than a second to make her assessment.

"No shot here, COWBOY," Alison said tightly, taking her finger away from the trigger, pointing it up at a forty-five degree angle. "ANGEL can't do anything without hitting you." She felt a numb sense of worry settle over her. "OOC?"

"I'm a little busy!" Duncan shouted, and Alison watched through the scope as one of the six demons piling onto Duncan turned into a blast of black hellfire as he disappeared back from whence he'd come.

"Don't sweat it, COWBOY," came a cool voice breaking into the line, one as familiar to her as any she'd ever heard in her life, "We wouldn't leave you out to dry. BULLDOG and SOCRATES are in play, which means the Army is coming to save your ass again, Marine."

A pickup truck thumped as it mounted the curb and churned up the park grass, speeding toward the fight. It slammed into a small knot of the broc'aminn as Hendricks threw himself out of the way just in time. Alison counted at least three of the demons hit by the old pickup as the doors flew open and her father and brother leapt out to join the fight.

*

"I still say your brother's code name should have been BONG HIT," Hendricks muttered as he got back to his feet, sweeping his long black drover coat behind him as he lashed out with his sword and struck down one of the broc'aminn while its back was turned and it was gawking at Brian Longholt's stumbling dismount from the passenger side of the truck.

"You got a real gratitude problem," Brian Longholt said, his faux-hawk looking particularly pointy today. He moved sideways awkwardly, raising his Roman gladius to parry a demon attack. The broc'aminn that came at him seemed even more awkward than he, which worked in the stoner's favor; Hendricks watched the dumbass cut himself on Brian's sword and then dissolve into a black burst of hellfire tinted slightly orange by the sunset.

"It's not that I'm not glad to see you," Hendricks said as Bill Longholt came out swinging from around the driver's side, the older man with a cavalry saber clenched in his fingers. It looked old, like maybe Civil War vintage. He vaped a demon with it as he stalked off toward Jacob, who was still hiding in the shadow of the jungle gym, peering out in stunned horror at the battle going on in front of him. Hendricks watched Bill end the dreams and lives of the three broc'aminn that his daughter had knocked down with the fifty out of the corner of his eye as three more of the damned demons came at him and Brian. "It's more like ... SOCRATES? Really?"

"I realize it's not a deeply thought-out code name like COWBOY," Brian muttered, breaking off from Hendricks as two of the broc'aminn came at him, their arms blurring with speed, their wide mouths hissing as they spit, "but I feel like it fits!"

"Yeah, you're a real deep thinker," Hendricks said, the aching crawl of weariness running across his muscles from the hard exertion of the last few minutes and the half-dozen glancing demon attacks he'd taken. He lashed out hard at one of Brian's attackers, taking his eye off his own targets for a beat as he vaped one of the fuckers. The damned kid wouldn't stand a chance against two of them. Hell, he probably wouldn't stand a chance against one, but Hendricks figured he had about a second to help the sonofabitch before he'd be forced to deal with his own problems again ...

When he came around, Hendricks realized that his second estimate had been a little too generous. Lead Guitar was about an inch from his face, his mouth opened wide, arms spread, closing in like he was all set to give Hendricks a big hug. Hendricks had no doubt about his intentions, though, and he knew a hug was not in the offing. Not that he'd want one anyway; the smell was even worse up close.

As if in answer to the prayers he never bothered with, little droplets of water splashed all over Hendricks's face like spittle from the open mouth of the demon. It was not spittle, though. It was refracted off the demon's cheeks and nose by the sheer power of the stream of water being shot. The sound of an electric motor ran under the noise of battle, and Lead Guitar halted in his tracks.

Hendricks just took a stumbling step back in reaction, free hand coming up to wipe the liquid off his cheek and eyebrow. He stared at the clear liquid there, like sweat on his fingertips, and broke into a smile as Lead Guitar burst into black hellfire under the assault of the holy-water-filled squirt gun.

"DOCTOR is on the field," Alison announced in his ear. Like he didn't already fucking know that.

"Nice to see you, Dr. Darlington," Hendricks said as Lauren Darlington, MD, came jogging up with her mechanized squirt gun clenched in her hands. She looked like one of the new Ghostbusters, actually, dark hair shining in the fading light.

"Looked like you needed an assist," Darlington said with a smile of her own, turning loose a hard stream of water over Duncan's opponents and setting the four of them to dancing in pain like they'd just had acid run over their backs.

"I see what you did there," Hendricks said and wheeled off to help Brian Longholt with his demon.

"Ayup," Dr. Darlington said and advanced with her squirt gun's engine running full blast. Hendricks had rolled his eyes when she'd first brought it out, but after he'd seen it work the first time, he'd kinda kicked himself for not thinking of it first. Its effectiveness was undeniable, like a flamethrower for these hell beasts, but without the danger of explosion those things brought.

"Is that everyone?" Hendricks asked, as Brian's demon started to fall back, caught between the two of them and Bill, who was moving to cut off the damned broc'aminn's retreat. "Are we all on the field?"

"Everyone that was available for the fight," Alison called. "Everyone else is—well, you know." Her voice carried a certain solemnity. "They've got their own fight tonight."

Hendricks blanched at that. This right here was his sort of fight. The one that Arch and the others were involved in? It wasn't a fight he wanted any part of, he reflected as Bill plunged his cavalry saber into the broc'aminn's exposed shoulder. It cracked the shell and after a subtle hiss of what sounded like escaping air, the demon burst into black, shadowy flames and disappeared back to hell. "How do you reckon they're doing?" he asked. It might not have been his fight, but it was damned sure gonna have big fucking consequences for all of them.

"If I had to guess?" Bill Longholt let out a sigh, his large frame slumping slightly as his broad shoulders came down. "Not well," the big man said, and Hendricks caught the apprehension on his face. "Not well at all."

*

"This is bad," Arch Stan said, looking out on what they faced with barely concealed panic. The atmosphere in the room was tense, and the tension stretched down into his own chest, where it felt like every muscle in his body had contracted at once. Pucker time, that was how his high school football coach had described it, though he was referring rather inartfully to a different muscle. From Arch's point of view, though, it made sense, his knuckles clenched, his skin crawling with the urge to be somewhere, anywhere other than this.

"You're wishing you'd gone with the others when they bailed out to go fight that demon, aren't you?" Erin Harris whispered in his ear. Her voice was low and soft, and it was plain that she didn't mean for anyone else to hear her.

It wouldn't have mattered. There was far too much commotion around them for anyone to have picked up on what they were saying anyway.

"Please," Sheriff Nicholas Reeve said from the podium at the front of the Community Meeting room in the municipal building near the town square. "Please, if I could just get a minute to say what I came here to—"

There was a dull roar in the meeting room, loud enough it felt like someone had switched on one of those white noise machines in Arch's ears. He could barely hear Sheriff Reeve over all the voices. Someone was shouting from the front row, loud enough to drown out any other conversation. "You're so full of shit, Reeve! You don't know what the hell you're talking about!" It took Arch a minute to figure out that was Eric Gronhoy doing the shouting.

"I'm trying to—" Sheriff Reeve bristled, clearly not deaf to what

Gronhoy had just shouted at him over the din. It made Arch itch a little to hear what the man had said. He and Erin were sitting on the dais, after all, decked out in their khaki uniforms, trying to present an image of strength, but Reeve's bombshell revelation that demons had been behind Midian's recent troubles had seemed to let all the reason out of the room. "For fuck's sake," Reeve said, a little lower but not nearly low enough for it to go unheard by the majority of the crowd, amplified as it was by the microphone sticking out of the podium.

"Let the man speak!" A voice like the crack of thunder in the heavens snapped in the middle of the room and hushed them all. It was a voice of authority, a voice that was used to being listened to, and it made Arch smile to hear it laid down in such a way. "I said let him speak!" Barnabas Jones shouted, hushing the hubbub further. Arch caught the eye of Jones; they'd known each other for nearly forever. Barnabas Jones—Barney as everyone called him—was a tall black man with an easy smile and a word of kindness for everyone. He was also the pastor at the Methodist Church. Arch's church. Arch had known Barney Jones since the man baptized him, and he was looking up at Arch, Erin, and Reeve, staring at them over the crowd with a knowing smile as the mob lost its enthusiasm and started to sit, casting fearful glances at Jones. Jones wasn't a man Arch would have cared to cross, even if he hadn't been one of the man's parishioners. "All right, then, Sheriff," Jones said. "You may continue."

"Thank you, Barney," Reeve said, nodding sincerely at the pastor. "I know this … is a lot to handle."

"It smells like bullshit!" Nathan McMinn shouted from the back of the room, and a grumble of discontent rippled through the room, threatening to toss the whole meeting into upheaval again. "You're covering up for your department's fuck-ups, Nick!"

"Well, thank you for the vote of confidence, Nate," Reeve said dryly. "I assure you, I'll be glad to accept your condemnations at the end of the meeting, but I got something to say, first." He paused only a second for effect before plunging ahead; Arch might have given it a second more, but then someone else might have interrupted. "Demons are real, they're here in Midian right now, and they're killing people—our people, dammit. I know that's hard to believe, but it's true—"

The cacophony rose once more, and this time a sharp whistle

screeched, causing almost everyone in the packed meeting to blanch at the high noise. "Excuse me, darlings," Melina Cherry said in her European accent, standing up in the third row. The madam of the local brothel was decked out, wearing a very nice suit that looked like it wouldn't have been out of place on a catwalk in Milan, in Arch's opinion. It was black, which matched her raven hair, and though it was a little low cut for his taste, he couldn't deny that she looked classy. He could have sworn he could smell her perfume if she hadn't been a few rows back. "I believe the sheriff, and if you had seen what happened to Colleen Hudson in my own house, you would, too. Her murder—no human did this."

That provided a moment of quiet. "Yes, that was done by a demon," Reeve said, giving Melina Cherry a nod. Arch tried to quell his surprise; the local madam standing up and supporting the sheriff in a moment of need was not something he'd ever anticipated.

"I had some boys come bust up my bar," Michael McInness stood up, taking off his old baseball cap to reveal hair that was desperately thinning. "I know not many of you come up my way and visit the Charnel House, but lemme tell you something—my patrons may be rough as cobs, but they ain't the sort to back down from or lose a fight. Well, we got these three city slickers up in there one night, and they started some shit that—I'm telling you right now—it wasn't human what they did. Ain't no way some skinny hipster shitbird in girl's jeans can knock out one of my boys like that—"

"Oh, come on!" Keith Drumlin called out from somewhere near the back.

"He's telling the truth!" Molly Darlington stood up in the first row. Arch locked his gaze on her, a little surprised. He hadn't even noticed she'd come to the meeting; she was sixteen or so, after all. Weren't all the kids that age supposed to be out drinking milkshakes or painting graffiti or something? "I know y'all heard about what happened to me at the Summer Lights Festival. Well, that guy that ... that tried what he tried ..." Her face flushed at the attention. "He was a demon. And when he got stabbed, he just ... swirled away in a black storm of hellfire—"

"I believe it!" Chauncey Watson cried out, coming to his feet, his skinny body hidden underneath polyester pants and short-sleeved dress shirt that looked like he'd been wearing it for twenty years. Arch could almost smell the mothballs on the man from here. "There was some demons holed up on Mount Horeb, too, and we heard 'em. They came down and killed Tim Connor and—"

"All right, I get it," Gina Carras stood up, drawing every eye in the room to her. She was the head of the PTA at the local elementary school, Greenbriar, and had a red face to match her dark hair. "All these people are standing up and saying you're right, it's demons, Nick," she nodded at Reeve. "Then we got all these other folk," a rumble went through the crowd, "gonna shout at the top of their lungs that it's all malarkey, that you're making this up." She held up a hand to keep that contingent from breaking loose with their disgruntlement. "I think we see how the room is divided up, right?" She turned her attention to Reeve. "What I want to know is—assuming things are as you say they are, and I know that's a mighty big 'if'—what are you suggesting we do, Nick?" There was a light chorus of nods and agreement across the whole room. "I mean, do you have a solution? Or is this just gonna get worse?"

Reeve stood in the middle of the stage. "I know this ain't what y'all want to hear ... but we have a start to a solution ... but all the experts we've talked to seem to suggest ... yeah, it's going to get worse."

That threatened to send the room into chaos again, but Gina Carras held up her hand. "All right, all right, just wait, y'all. How much worse are we talking here? Because a lot people have already died ... I mean, you've already lost one of your deputies and—"

"Look, there's not a scale for demonic destruction," Reeve said, sounding a little calm and a lot exasperated.

"If you want us to buy this bullshit, you better square with us!" Eric Gronhoy called out. "How bad do you think it's gonna get? Are we talking, like, *Smokey and the Bandit 2*, here?"

Reeve thought about it for a second. "More like *Smokey and the Bandit 3*."

A mutter ran through the crowd, and Nate McMinn spoke loudest of all. "That movie sucked. It just killed the whole franchise."

"Yeah," Mike McInness said, "Burt Reynolds saw that meteor coming and dodged it."

"He blew it later, though," Chauncey Watson piped up, "in that one movie he was in, the one with Demi Moore naked—"

"It was called *Striptease*," Casey Meacham, the local taxidermist answered. Arch was unsurprised that Meacham would have known this; the man was a pervert by any standard, proving it less than a second after he had this thought. "She looked mighty damned good dancing naked, too."

Reeve sighed at the podium, dipping his head low. Arch had worked with the man for years, and could practically see the quiet desperation was radiating off of him. He hadn't wanted to do this meeting, none of them had. But the sheriff knew it was necessary, and Arch could see he was paying for it now. Yeah, Arch had a sense the sheriff was strained, that the man was just about nearing the explosion point. And having seen him go off before, he didn't much fancy the thought of what would happen if he blew up right here in the middle of any meeting, let alone this very important one.

*

Nicholas Reeve had been working in law enforcement long enough to feel like he'd run across damned near every scenario. Only a week or so before, if asked, he would have confidently answered that while things were always changing in the world, especially in the realm of new and different drugs gaining popularity, he'd seen just about everything under the sun.

Then Erin and Arch had gone and blown his mind with the revelation that demons were real and that they were invading the town because it had become something of a hotspot for their activities. Midian, Tennessee, hadn't had a murder in years, and now they had more files open than he could count. It wasn't the sort of stuff you'd see in a normal crime blotter, either—not gang-related killings, domestic gone wrong to murder, child abuse—no, this was a grotesque clump of crime stories, the kind even the most depraved serial-killer writer wouldn't have dreamed of.

"Can we focus on the problem at hand?" Reeve asked, trying to draw his clearly wandering audience back from discussions of *Smokey and the Bandit* movies and where Burt Reynolds' career had gone wrong. He looked right at Gina Carras, since she seemed to be a pretty good focus for his attention. She had asked some pretty good questions so far, after all, and she seemed to be keeping some of the less responsible parties in line, holding them off from disrupting the damned meeting.

"Maybe you can give us a little insight on how you came to this ... uh ... conclusion, Nick?" Gina asked, folding her arms over her broad chest. She was not a small lady, Gina Carras. She had a perfect build for a linebacker, but she was a little short.

"That's a good idea," Reeve said, nodding along. He tried to ignore that desperate sense that was burgeoning inside of him; he hadn't exactly wanted things to go this way, after all. He'd kind of planned for them to, but he had hoped the townspeople would see reason. "So ... most of you know Arch Stan—"

"Best player our town ever produced!" Keith Drumlin called out.

"No doubt about that," Mike McInness agreed, adjusting his old SM Lines hat. It was from one of the local trucking concerns.

"Well, Arch actually stumbled across this stuff himself when Old Man MacGruder went missing," Reeve said, feeling a little catch inside as he spoke about it. He hadn't quite forgiven Arch yet for keeping him in the dark for so long. "He crossed paths with a demon hunter that showed him what was what—"

"You getting high on the taxpayer's dollar, Arch?" Eric Gronhoy asked, his big face showing plain hostility.

"Oh, get your head out of your hindparts, Gronhoy," Barney Jones said, standing up at his place on the aisle. The big black preacher looked more than a little perturbed. "If you knew Arch, you'd know the man barely touches a drink, let alone anything illicit."

Arch, for his part, shot Gronhoy a steely look that Reeve caught out of the corner of his eye. Gronhoy nodded a grudging acknowledgment of that point, and Reeve went on. "Since the day the MacGruders disappeared, we've had quite a few incidents. Some of them were small—a meteoric rise in assaults and some robberies, break-ins." He let out a slow breath. "Others, like the massacre on Crosser Street and Colleen Hudson's murder at Ms. Cherry's, uh ... place of ..." He struggled, trying to find the right word, "... residence ..." he got a nod from the madam at that, "... as well as the incident at the Summer Lights Festival," he caught Molly Darlington reddening in the front row at that, her grandmother sitting next to her, peering intently at Reeve, "and finally what happened when a full-sized demon got unleashed and tore through town—"

"I thought that was a bear?" Scott Karshman asked, staring up at Reeve in undisguised curiosity. Karshman never was sleekest car in the show.

"You heard of a lot of bears ripping right through the middle of houses and blowing up propane tanks?" Mike McInness asked with undisguised scorn. "Because me, I ain't ever even heard of people doing that, let alone animals. That oughta be a clue to any one of y'all skeptics that things ain't right here and that Reeve's got the explanation that makes sense."

"You telling me all this crap is connected?" Nathan McMinn asked, looking out through his glasses. McMinn was a skinny fella and had been unemployed for as long as Reeve could remember. "Like ... the freeway accident, even?"

"That wasn't an accident," Reeve said, "and yes, it's all connected, from start to finish."

"What about the turds I been finding on my doorstep?" Keith Drumlin shouted out. "They're all smoky and long and unnatural—"

"Are you shitting me?" McInness bellowed.

"No, people are shitting him," Chauncey Watson said with a low chortle.

"Hey, uhm, Keith," Nathan McMinn said, "that ... that was me. I was just fucking with you, dropping deuces on your doorstep ..."

"You asshole!" Keith shouted. "You cost me three doormats, and I want—I want satisfaction! I demand it!"

"And I can't get any," Reeve said, shaking his head. "Demons, people. We're besieged, all right? Is anyone—?" It felt like the meeting was spinning out of his control, on stranger and stranger axes. "Does anyone really think that what's going on here is a natural phenomenon?"

"I don't think it's a natural phenomenon," came a voice from the back of the room. Reeve looked and saw a tall, lanky figure in a suit standing there in the doorway, arms folded confidently, his sandy blond hair perfectly coiffed. "I think we're dealing with something truly strange, in fact," the man went on, stepping into the aisle and walking slowly to the front of the room. He looked up, and his eyes sparkled, as if he were sharing a joke with everyone in the room. "But that doesn't mean I automatically jump to the assumption that demons are behind all the troubles we've been experiencing in this town—and this county."

Reeve just stood there standing at the podium, feeling all the air rush out of the room with the man's entry. He'd been hoping to avoid this by making it a town meeting, but apparently that little gambit had failed, and failed royally. "Hello there, County Administrator Pike." He tried not to sigh, but failed. "Nice of you to show up."

*

Watching County Administrator Pike stride up the aisle of the meeting room like the second coming felt a little blasphemous to Arch. He'd tried to reserve his judgment on the man, but it was difficult; every time he'd met him, Pike had set Arch's teeth on edge. He was a consummate political operator, the sort who ought to have been a senator somewhere, gladhanding constituents and kissing babies. He certainly did all that, but he did it here in Calhoun County and on a local level rather than at the state or national one that Arch felt his skills deserved. He gave Arch the willies, but in Arch's capacity as deputy sheriff, newly reinstated, it was his job to sit down and shut up, and he did his dangdest to do just that.

"Throwing around words like 'demons from hell' seems a little extreme," Pike said with a smirk as he worked his way up the aisle toward the podium, where Reeve was standing stiff as a post, gripping the edges of the wood with white knuckles. Arch couldn't see his face, but he had to guess the sheriff was biting his lip pretty hard. "In tough times, cool heads prevail, and giving in to panic doesn't reward anyone but … well, there ain't no easy way to say this … but an extreme statement like this would tend to benefit only the speaker."

"You calling me a liar?" Reeve asked, at least twice as cool as Arch would have been were their positions reversed.

"I'm just saying that an unprovable explanation like 'demons' would seem to be quite the life preserver for a department sinking under your leadership," Pike said with that same insufferable smirk.

"Jesus," Melina Cherry said, drawing to her feet. "And they call me a whore, but we sit here silently and watch this man," she pointed at Pike, "trying to sell the sheriff downriver to make himself look good."

"Whoa, whoa," Pike said, holding up hands. "Using the phrase 'sell downriver' in this context is … well, it's racist."

"Oh, fuck you," Melina Cherry said, snorting at him.

"Well, I think we know where she stands," Pike said, swiveling away to look back at Reeve. "But there's an awful lot of people in this room, and a great many of them seem to be holding their tongues presently. Now, if I had to calculate, it's because they think you're out of your damned tree, Reeve, but as good southerners, they're too polite to say so—"

A new voice came from the back row. "The fact that you'd come here from across the county and level those accusations when you don't have a blessed clue what you're talking about just shows that like with every other bit of trouble we've had lately, outside help ain't no help at all."

The whole room turned, and Arch craned his neck to try and get a look at the speaker. He knew that voice, and he was almost positive who was doing the talking by the whiplash, commonsense tone that he'd heard maybe a little too often, especially of late.

Addison Rutherford Longholt—Addy to those who knew her, and woe to those who didn't but called her that—stood up in the back of the meeting hall, removing any last doubt of Arch's that she was the speaker. It wasn't as though he hadn't heard his mother-in-law speak a million times before, not to mention that her daughter had adopted many of the same characteristics and demonstrated them to Arch every day of their married life. He stared with the others as Addy rose, her purse clenched in her hands. She was white-knuckling the black handbag like Reeve was holding on to the podium, less like a lifeline and more like a squeezable outlet for the rage she wasn't entirely managing to keep out of her voice.

"County Administrator Pike," she said, putting hard emphasis on the title, "have you been to any of the crime scenes where these people have died?"

There was an unpleasant hum from the crowd during the pause. "Why, no, I haven't," Pike said, still smirking, though it relaxed a little, more in the territory of a gentle smile now that he was focused on her rather than Reeve. "But I have been to countless funerals over the last few weeks—"

"That's nice," Addy cut him off. "So have we. Some of us have maybe even seen an open casket or two, but that's beside the point." She was like hardened steel, and she went right back after him. "Have you seen the crime scenes? The places where these people died?"

Pike's smile didn't lose its luster. "Of course not. But that doesn't I mean don't know—"

"Let me tell you what I know, *County Administrator*," Addy said, "because my son, my husband, my daughter, and my son-in-law have all been fighting these things over the last few weeks. Some of y'all maybe want to tune me out right now, and you're free to do so, even though I've known most of you either your whole life or mine." She gestured to Reeve with the bag she still clutched in her hand. "We've all known Nick for years, just the same. We've all known each other for years, those of us who have been here our whole lives. We trusted him," she pointed the finger at Reeve, "before this all happened, but now we've got this fancy county administrator here—"

"Who is a whore," Melina Cherry snarled.

"—coming in and telling us who to trust when things have gone wrong," Addy went on, ignoring her. "We've got people we've trusted for years telling us something incredible is happening when we know—we *know*—something incredible is happening, and we just reject the explanation of these people we've trusted for years out of hand? Like we don't know them at all? Like some jackass from Nashville that just blew into town last week?"

"I think we should trust the evidence of our reason," Pike started.

"I think reason'd work a lot better if we were in *reasonable* times," Addy said. "If we had a *reasonable* explanation for people being eaten and torn apart and burnt up and all else. If we weren't being presented with an explanation by people we trusted before all this came down, people who we knew, that would have given us the shirts off their backs in a crisis. Yes, it's a wild story, I'll grant you." There was another uncomfortable hum across the crowd, but Pike watched in silence, still smiling, but the smile seemed to be frozen on his face. "But if anyone else has a better one … I'm all ears. I think we all are. Because this ain't nothing we asked for to come to Midian. It's just something we're stuck with trying muddle through, and all I hear so far from you and yours, Mr. Pike, is shouting down what's being said, no alternative presented, no solution—"

"Oh, I have a solution," Pike said with a faint glimmer in his eyes, and he looked straight at Reeve as Arch felt like he was in a spiral, a lurching feeling striking him a moment before the shotgun blast of

Pike's pronouncement hit and silenced the room in its wake. "A recall election for the position of sheriff of Calhoun County."

*

Alison had come off the roof when she knew things were pretty well mopped up, lugging the big Barrett rifle on her shoulder. It wasn't light, but if she carried it right it wasn't the world's biggest imposition, either, just hella-awkward. The damned thing was thirty pounds, though, so it was like carrying a good-sized toddler around, which she didn't have a ton of experience with.

She'd wanted to, though.

Alison had a vague recollection of the way things had been before the demons came to town, before the shit exploded all over, before she'd had her own home's door busted in and dark-faced demons had swarmed all over her and ripped her back to a time when she'd been older than a child but scared like one as she and her daddy had run from demon dogs in Alabama. Before all this, she and Arch had been planning to have a baby. They'd been trying, practicing real hard, as Arch would have said. That was a while ago, though, and they hadn't had much in the way of luck before that door came crashing in.

Ever since, Alison hadn't given babies much thought. When your whole world was collapsing around you like Midian was, it didn't seem a time to give much thought to baby-making. Or at least it wasn't on her mind, that was for sure. She and Arch were still doing a fair amount of practicing, but to her, that's all it was now, practice. Before all this, having a baby and being a momma had consumed her waking hours like nothing else.

Now she was consumed with making sure the Barrett was ready, that she was ready, in case a call like this one came in and she had to scoot. They were coming fast and furious, too, though typically not from Duncan. The OOC was trying his damnedest to put down the last broc'aminn, who was flaming, waving his hands around somewhere between rage and panic, until Duncan got past one of the burning limbs and stuffed his baton right in the demon's face. It just halted, all motion stopped, and the black fire crawled out from its face and sucked it back to hell with a pop and a faint whiff of sulfur that caused Alison to upturn her nose even yards away.

"Yay, team," Lauren Darlington said, letting the squirt gun nozzle point toward the earth, weariness showing through on the doctor's face, which looked a little flushed.

"How'd you get the sense of these, Duncan?" Hendricks asked, still gripping his sword.

"No runes," the OOC said, pushing his baton closed. When it wasn't deployed, it was just a cylinder of metal that he could slide into his belt, looking a little like a bomb detonator from an old movie, except surrounded in black rubber for traction. Duncan pushed up his t-shirt and stuck the baton back where it belonged, revealing a pale, hairless belly in the process. "I guess they didn't get the memo. Or at least they didn't see any ads for Spellman before they started preying."

"Yes," Brian muttered under his breath, pumping his hand once in victory. "Maybe it worked."

"Maybe," Alison's daddy said, wandering up to stand in the loosely formed circle with the rest of them. His pickup was still sitting on the park's grass, looking damned out of place. "But don't let one isolated incident lead you down the path of thinking we've won this."

"What the fuck are you people talking about?" Hendricks asked, sheathing the sword finally. It glinted in the orange glow of sunset as he put it away.

"We've been doing some ad-buys for Rogerson's lately on the web, seeing if I could displace some of those targeted ads Spellman's been using to drum up business for those runes," Brian said. "Not the easiest thing to crack, I must say, trying to determine the demographic criteria he was picking."

"This all sounds like foreign language stuff," Dr. Darlington said, brushing her dark hair back behind her with her free hand.

"Wren Spellman," Duncan said patiently, trying to clue the doctor in. "He's a demon doing business in these parts. He's selling these runes that make demons untraceable to my abilities. Almost every demon in town has been picking them up, and it's making our job harder. The demons have been finding out about him through—"

"Web ads," Darlington said with a nod. "Okay, got it now." She was sharp, Alison would give her that. The doctor frowned. "How do you target a demon with a web ad?"

"We don't know," Brian said with a little smug glee, like he used to have when he'd just rubbed Alison's face in being wrong. He used to do that shit all the time just to annoy her. "So we've been trying to just blanket the area with internet ads, figuring maybe we can push him out a little bit." He smiled. "I think maybe we can chalk this one up to the plan."

"Or we could chalk it up to luck and demons being too stupid to check their email or whatever when they got to town," Hendricks said, plainly unimpressed, arms folded.

"Doesn't work like that," Brian said, bristling a little. "It'd be in the ad bars, not direct mailings to—"

"Hey," Alison said, passing by him and thrusting the rifle into his arms. Her brother *oof'd* at the weight as she held it for a second longer to make sure he had it. He fumbled it a little but didn't drop it or his weapon, so she moved on, heading toward her goal, approaching real slow so as not to scare him. "Jacob," Alison said, talking to the scared kid still hiding behind the jungle gym on the playground, quivering with fear, his pants wet, plainly trying to hide it by clutching tight to the bars. Jacob Arnold was still standing there, his shoulders so tight he almost looked like a hunchback. "How you doing over there?" she asked, stopping at the sandy playground's edge. He didn't answer, and the conversation behind her had ground to a halt as everyone finally remembered that the kid they'd just come to save was still there, and still scared shitless. "Hey, Jacob?"

Jacob finally blinked, big tears in the corners of his eyes, wet as the front of his pants that he was trying to hide from her, from them. He didn't speak, just nodded in frightened acknowledgment of her presence.

"Jacob, how are you doing?" Alison asked, lowering her voice, taking another step toward him. "You all right?"

Jacob didn't seem to know how to answer that. He looked around, dazed, then his eyes crawled back to her. "I'm ..." he croaked when spoke, like he had a big old frog in his throat. "... I'm okay, I think." He was shaking.

"That's good," she said, taking a few more steps onto the playground. The sand warred against her sense of balance. She could smell the pee in the wind now, strong, like he'd been holding it for a while before this happened and scared it out of him. Clearly he hadn't meant for it to come out, and by the way he was holding himself he was just as aware and ashamed of it as she would have expected a nine-year-old to be even if he hadn't had damned good reason for it. "It's going to be okay, Jacob. You want to come out to me, so we can get you home?" She squatted down, trying to come more to his level, be as non-threatening as possible.

He looked around, and the tears in his eyes sparkled as the light caught them. He looked absolutely stricken, his freckled complexion disturbed by the tracks of already fallen tears that had made their way silently down his cheeks. If he'd made noise during the fight, she hadn't heard it, and it would have been whimpers, not screams.

With slow effort, Jacob Arnold pried himself loose of the jungle gym and took halting steps toward her, looking sick all the time. He put one hand over his crotch like he could hide what he'd done in fear, and self-consciously wiped at his eyes with the back of the other.

"It's all right," she said quietly, looking him in the eyes, trying to communicate with him over the ten feet between them. She knew Jacob, knew his mom and dad, talked to his momma every time she came into Rogerson's. They lived not three minutes' walk from the park, and she was of a mind to make sure he got home safely. He was taking steps like a wind-up toy, like he was gonna miss one and come tumbling down, his balance all shot to shit by fear.

She caught him when he got close and he pressed up against her and wrapped his arms tight around her neck. She felt the cool wetness against her skin and knew he weighed more than the Barrett. She picked him up anyway, like a child, like a baby. Even though he was heavy, it wasn't that much of a strain. The wetness on her neck and seeping through her shirt at her belly didn't bother her one whit, not one, and she lifted with her back and got to her feet. "I'm gonna take Jacob home to his momma and daddy," she said and started walking away. "Y'all keep a watch, will you?" She said it lightly, knowing they'd take her meaning: *Make sure we get there safely.* And she heard them all following behind, even with Jacob whimpering in her ear the whole way, and her whispering, reassuring him the entire time that it was gonna be okay.

*

Braeden Tarley hadn't really wanted to come to the meeting that Sheriff Reeve had called. Braeden Tarley was a diesel mechanic by trade, a father by the grace of God, and single father by shit-ass misfortune. Between work and parenthood, he had plenty enough on his mind and on his plate without involving himself in local governance. But it would have taken a man with a lot more on his mind, and maybe a head buried not just in sand but solid concrete to fail to notice the shit going on around him in Midian, and so he'd come to this meet figuring maybe there'd be an answer or two. But the answer he'd gotten had not been much to his satisfaction, and now the whole damned thing had become some sort of fucked-up shitshow from Tijuana, like watching a donkey burst out of its enclosure and start fucking everyone in the audience. He hadn't been to one of those shows, but he'd heard about them.

After Administrator Pike—who, no matter what words were coming out of his mouth, Braeden thought was a pencilneck prick—had dropped that little bomb about Reeve and a recall election, it seemed to snuff the air out of the room for what felt like a full minute. The administrator was just sitting there with a prickish smile on his face, and Braeden didn't really know how to feel. He'd had run-ins with Reeve and wasn't a fan of the man, kind of a dictator son of a bitch as an officer, and his pitch about demons being responsible for their current dismal state didn't ring true with Braeden at all. Braeden sat watching the thing unfold coolly, not really sure where his allegiance, if he had any, lay.

"Almighty," Barney Jones said into the breach, and all hell followed the pastor's words.

"You can't—"

"Damned right, oughta drag his ass outta office right this second—"

"Crazy as shit—"

"I ain't even joking about them doormats, Nathan, you asshole, I want—"

"Like trying to change horses in the middle of jumping the Grand Canyon."

"What do you reckon?" Sam Allen leaned over to Braeden as shit sluiced on toward the fan and parliamentary procedure went right out the window again and everybody started yelling at once.

"Hell, I don't know," Braeden said, trying to figure it all out. He looked down at his hands, covered in black stains that even the normal helping of Zep TKO couldn't quite get out, and sighed. "Maybe this is too much to hope for, but I'd just like the murdering to stop."

"You said it," Sam agreed. "Though there's other funny stuff going on here, too." He nodded at Erin Harris up on the stage, on her feet, face red, shouting at the top of her lungs. Braeden couldn't hear what she was saying over the chaos, but he didn't need to. He could read lips well enough to tell when someone was dropping the f-word every two seconds. "She went down Mount Horeb not that long ago, did you know? I hauled off the cruiser after she fucked it up."

"Did you?" Braeden didn't look at Sam, switching his attention to Arch Stan, who was on his feet as well, behind Erin Harris, but about a hundred times calmer. Braeden had kinda had an eye on Erin lately. She was cute, seemed nice, but he didn't exactly get a lot of opportunities to date. Hell, he wasn't even sure he was ready to date. His daughter was only four, after all—Abilene Tarley, though he called her Abi—and her mother had only been gone a couple years. Still, a man in his position tended to notice things like a pretty girl crossing his path, couldn't help it, really, especially when he worked with two other guys and a woman who was more like one of the guys than the guys themselves. Braeden had his own business to focus on. "I think you showed me that cruiser when I came to your junkyard, Sam."

"I did," Sam said. "It was pretty fouled up, huh?"

Braeden could vaguely recall. "Looked like it fell down a mountain, yeah." The pretty deputy bellowing from the stage in front of him was at odds with the state of that cruiser he'd seen. It was the sort of wreck that nobody walked away from, he would have figured.

Jennifer, his wife, certainly hadn't, and her car hadn't looked nearly as bad as that cruiser. She died anyway, though.

"Weird shit going on around here, man." Sam was observing the chaos unfold around him, and that donkey was sure making his way through the audience. Braeden watched it all with mix of fascination and disgust, but he couldn't tell which was stronger.

*

Reeve met County Administrator Pike's eyes as the yelling fest raged on. The man stared straight at him, cool as cucumber, with nothing like the face he'd presented to the sheriff only a week or so ago when he'd come to the office to offer his support. Reeve looked at him, watched the man push some of his perfectly coifed hair back, even though it was wet with enough gel to hold in place against a tornado, or that demon that had come through the town last week.

Pike looked like he was the only one that hadn't been completely blown away by his own pronouncement, though Reeve felt like he was doing a reasonable job of holding his cool. He just stared the man down, a sense of resignation papering over his anger, which was definitely present. He didn't feel too blindsided, even though he definitely hadn't seen this coming. This was the politician for you, working in the shadows to stab you in the back, or maybe the sack.

The roar of all the talking was drowning out the individual voices. Reeve didn't even know sixty people could be this damned loud. Everyone in the place was on their feet, some howling for his blood, others yelling at their neighbors about why they shouldn't be so goddamned stupid. There was, of course, yelling back being done, and he figured shots were going to be fired for real in the next few minutes as this got louder and more acrimonious. They might even be fired by him, a round in the air to shut everyone up.

"How do we make peace in the midst of all this?" Arch leaned in and shouted toward his ear. It was the first clear statement Reeve had heard since the war of words had started with Pike's pronouncement.

"I don't suspect it'll be quite as peaceable as how it was done at Appomattox Courthouse, but we'll need to come up with something," Reeve said, sure his deputy wasn't going to hear him. He didn't really need to, because it wasn't the sort of answer that was going to elucidate anything. More like amuse for a quarter second at best. Maybe shooting a gun in the air was the right idea.

Barney Jones slammed a Bible down on the back of the chair in front of him, producing a sound like a gunshot, and a couple people went diving for cover. Pike didn't, Reeve noticed, but he did snap around like everyone else to look for the source of the sound. "Well, all right, then," Jones said.

"Let's wrap this up," Reeve said, taking advantage of the moment of silence offered to jump right in. "One thing, and then we're done with this meeting." He shrugged, by now just worn out from the realization that an awful lot of people he'd known and trusted now thought he was out of his damned mind. That was probably how Arch felt a few weeks ago, though Reeve didn't much care to admit it right this moment. "I can see there's a division here, and obviously the county administrator has his own plan in place to make things right as he reckons them. I expect we'll see that election in the next couple weeks." He held up a hand to stay any over-exuberant protestations or exultations, and for once, it worked. "I got my own plan, of course, but I don't see any reason to waste any more of y'all's time if you're firmly in the camp of 'Get Reeve the fuck outta here.'" He took a deep breath. "So ... if you just want to raise your hand if you believe me, and are willing to try and help in some way ... well, I'd greatly appreciate it."

He stopped talking, and the room fell into what felt like a real reluctant silence. Barney Jones raised his hand immediately, as high as he could, and so did Melina Cherry, God bless her soul, as well as Casey Meacham, the little pervert. Molly Darlington was practically standing on her tip-toes with her hand high, like she was trying to get chosen to give the answer in class, and Mike McInness was standing with his hand raised as well, though more sedately. There were others of course, but a lot of sullen faces in between, a lot of suspicion from people he would have invited to a barbecue only a week ago. Addison Longholt had her hand up, but next to her Pat from the Surrey Diner was sitting with his arms crossed, looking like someone had pissed in every kind of breakfast cereal on his menu. Gunther Sweeney was stroking his grey mustache without a hand raised anywhere, and Sam Allen was whispering right in Braeden Tarley's ear, both of 'em with arms folded.

"Thanks, y'all," Reeve said, giving 'em a nod even though he damned sure didn't feel grateful to see more than half the crowd thought he was off his nut. "If those of you interested in helping would please stay for a minute, those of y'all who think I'm out of my goddamned mind can go on about your lives now."

And so the meeting broke up, and thankfully not with nearly the acrimony it had started and nearly ended with. Part of that, he figured, was down to the fact that Pike was out the door before everybody, before Reeve almost even saw his back. That was a politician for you, though, wasn't it? Like a goddamned snake slithering off into the high grass.

*

Lauren followed at the back of the line of them, demon hunters all now, as they escorted the kid home through the deserted streets of Midian, Tennessee, at sundown. It was a hell of a spectacle, she would have guessed, especially with her carrying a super squirt gun complete with tanks of holy water on her back like she was in the ultimate teenager water battle. The water sloshed behind her with every step, and goddamn, was it heavy. She was bringing up the rear of their little procession, Alison Stan at the fore with the little boy clutched in her arms, his tears visible to Lauren on his petrified face whenever they'd cross into her view. He was a pretty big kid, maybe ten or so, and Alison was plainly struggling some under the burden, but she was too tough to make a peep. Lauren had the measure of her, she thought—but then, she'd thought she had the measure of life before a goddamned passel of fucking demons had leapt out like a jack in the box. Now here she was, wandering through the streets in a little parade with a tank of holy water sloshing on her back, which was not exactly something that had been on her bucket list.

"Thanks for the assist," Brian Longholt said, easing up to her, his gladius slung back over his shoulder, flat against his t-shirt. She eyed him as he nodded at her, bringing down that pointed faux-hawk 'do he was wearing as he glanced away from her eyes. "That was going pretty bad before you showed up."

"I'm sure you had it under control," Lauren said coolly. She had gotten a whiff of interest from Brian Longholt and she didn't want to squirt any gasoline on that brushfire. She thought about squirting him with the gun, but decided against it. While holy water was not a precious resource, it was a useful one, and dousing some geek stoner with it preemptively felt wasteful.

"Maybe," Brian conceded, "but you coming in with the heavy artillery and just burning the herd out sure helped."

"Uh huh," Lauren said, focusing on Jacob, whose head was still perched on Alison's shoulder. He was crying quietly, sobbing almost without sound.

She could vaguely recall Molly being that young, but only barely. It was almost like a disconnect, like she could sorta remember her that size, but not exactly. She tried to recall the photographs she had of

Molly from third grade, but it was kind of a jumble since she'd had one every year, and Lauren had been pretty much up to her neck in med school at that time. She did remember picking Molly up like that, a thousand times, a million times, but she couldn't recall if her body was ever exactly that size; likely as not, Molly at age ten or so hadn't expected to be picked up and carried any more than she came running into Lauren's room in the middle of the night, scared and looking to creep under the covers.

Then again, Jacob Arnold probably hadn't expected it until he'd had his evening and maybe his youthful life ruined by a bunch of demons that wanted him for supper and worse.

"You really do some good work in these fights," Brian said, stirring Lauren out of her little reverie, and she detected a note of self-pity in the way he said it.

She looked over at the faux-hawked young man, and her mouth came open and stuck there. What the hell was she supposed to say to that? *Good job, champ, with that little peeny sword?* She hadn't watched him closely this round, but she'd seen him go charging into battle with it before, and it looked like someone was always having to run in and save his ass like a damsel in distress. Come to think of it, when she'd rolled up it looked like Hendricks the cowboy was fulfilling the role of knight in dull canvas coat to the poor bastard. "Thanks," she finally said, in lieu of anything complimentary.

It wasn't like there wasn't anything good about Brian Longholt, she reflected as she looked away in embarrassment. But if everyone had their specific purpose in life, she imagined his was about as far from an actual fight as his penis likely was from actual vagina at this stage in the game. He belonged on a college campus, arguing in the philosophy department over a snifter of brandy or something, lecturing a class in one of those tweed jackets with the stupid-looking patches on the elbows, maybe speaking in an English accent for extra hoity-toityness.

Not in the middle of a demon fight in a backwater town in Tennessee. Lauren sighed. Hell, she didn't even belong here, though, did she?

"Thanks," she muttered again, still not looking at Brian Longholt, and she tucked her head down and stared at her feet, the water sloshing in the tanks behind her in a steady rhythm, like the wash of the water on ocean shores as they made their way to getting Jacob Arnold home safely.

*

The meeting had broken up slowly and awkwardly but fortunately still hadn't degenerated into anything unpleasant twenty minutes after it was officially over. Reeve was making his way through, talking to everyone who'd remained behind one by one, doing his best to solidify the support he knew he'd need here pretty quick. The air conditioner that had been turned up to account for all the excess bodies in the room hadn't been dialed back when a whole ton of said bodies had left, probably to the parking lot to bitch and moan about how much he sucked—not that he was dwelling on that overmuch—and now Reeve was starting to feel the chill.

"I sure do appreciate your support, Miss Cherry," Reeve said, surprised the words were coming out of his mouth. In the long list of things he'd set out to accomplish when he'd been elected sheriff, nowhere among them was getting the support of the local brothel owner to help wage a war on demons.

"We do what we can in these troubling times, darling," Melina Cherry said with that accent of hers, rubbing a hand down his uniform sleeve. He eyed her as she did it and she yanked the hand back. "So sorry. Force of habit."

"Yeah," Reeve said. "Well …"

"Call upon me if you can think of anything I can do to help," she said, giving him the nod as she headed toward the exit. She walked with a sway that he had to jerk his eyes away from. She might have been getting up there, but Melina Cherry was still younger than him, and she could seduce a schoolboy right out of his lunch money with minimal effort.

"Sheriff," Molly Darlington came up to him, burbling a little with excitement, like she'd had a cup or two of coffee before she'd come to the meeting. Reeve caught a glimpse of her grandmother across the room, talking to Addison Longholt but casting glances at Molly all the while, furtively watching her like Molly was going to evaporate or something. Reeve expected he might have kept a watchful eye on her in Mrs. Darlington's shoes, too, considering what Molly had already been through.

"Molly," Reeve said, glancing around the room again. He'd worked his way through most everybody. Braeden Tarley was lurking back a little ways, scowling. Nothing too terrible, but Tarley had always been kind of a problem kid for him, a pain in his ass back when he'd been on patrol and written the little bastard more speeding tickets than anyone else in the county. There was a mutual antipathy there, so the fact that he was standing ten feet away, scowling only lightly, suggested to Reeve that talking to the man might not be the worst idea. He looked more open and less hostile than Reeve could ever recall seeing him, actually, and it had been a year or two since he'd had to write him a ticket. Maybe he'd grown up after having a kid. Most people did.

"Sheriff, I need to ask you some things," Molly said, following along as Reeve started toward Braeden Tarley. He met the man's eyes and they didn't waver, so Reeve nodded politely as he threaded through the chairs toward where the diesel mechanic stood.

"What things?" Reeve asked absentmindedly, crossing the aisle in the middle of the meeting room. He hadn't eaten dinner and it was catching up to him, stomach rumbling, taste of the turkey sandwich he'd had for lunch kind of bubbling up behind the coffee he'd drunk pre-meeting. It wasn't having the same effect on him as whatever Molly Darlington had taken, though. Maybe she'd downed one of those energy drinks the kids were taking these days or something.

"Demon questions," Molly said, and Reeve halted about three feet from Braeden Tarley, who had shifted his attention to Molly trailing in Reeve's wake.

"The hell …?" Tarley muttered under his breath.

Reeve swiveled slightly to the teenager standing behind him, looking up at him earnestly. "Can this wait?"

"I've just got questions that my mom hasn't been able to answer," Molly said.

Reeve looked back at Braeden Tarley, who was still scowling a little, but splitting it between Molly and himself. "Like?"

"Lots of them," Molly said confidently. "Like, are demons responsible for the rapid explosion of portmanteau-ing?"

"Port-man-what-ing?" Reeve asked, breaking off from Braeden Tarley, who was now sharing his confused look.

"Portmanteau-ing," Molly said, plowing along, twitching with energy as she spoke. "You know, like combining two words together to form a new one, like when you take a couple's names and merge them into one. Like, Brad Pitt and Angelina Jolie are 'Brangelina,' Ben Affleck plus Batman equals 'Batffleck'—"

"How the fuck should I know if demons are responsible for that?" Reeve asked, bewilderment running together with irritation to whistle out.

"Fair enough, sure, that's a tough one," Molly said, like she was checking off a list. "What about Martin Shkreli? Is he a demon?"

"Martin who?" Reeve frowned at her. "Molly ... not now, okay?"

"Okay, okay," she said and lapsed into silence, still standing there behind him, bouncing slightly on the balls of her feet.

"Braeden," Reeve said, turning back to Tarley, who was looking just about as put off as Reeve was at Molly Darlington. At least he'd kept his quiet while she was running off at the mouth with geysers of verbal diarrhea.

"Sheriff," Tarley said gruffly.

"You got any questions, Braeden?" Reeve asked, probing gently as he could.

Tarley took a long breath, looking sideways. "Nothing quite as sophisticated as, uh, port-towing or whatever the hell she said—"

"Portmanteau-ing," Molly said. "It's French."

Reeve looked at her with resignation, wondering how exactly his life had gotten this colossally fucked. Nowhere on his list was figuring out if demons were making up new words, no sir. That had not figured into his goals for being sheriff. Lowering the rate of property crimes, yes. Answering the questions of a sixteen-year-old regarding demon habits and behaviors ... no. Just no.

"Who the hell are you, exactly?" Braeden Tarley asked.

"Molly Darlington," Molly said, smiling slightly. "Dr. Darlington is my mom."

"Yeah, okay," Braeden said with a deep frown, like Molly had a disease or had just come down from Mars.

"Braeden's got a daughter, too," Reeve said, trying to figure out how to make Molly go torment someone else for a while.

"Oh?" Molly brightened, if that was possible. "What's her name?"

"Abilene," Tarley said, softening slightly. "We call her Abi."

Molly blinked. "Abilene is a city in Texas."

Tarley stiffened, and Reeve watched him get just as defensive as he'd seen the man on every occasion they'd gotten into squall. "We wanted something unique," Tarley said. "Something nobody else named their kid."

"But it's a city in Texas," Molly said, frowning. "I'm sure other people have named their kid Abilene."

Tarley looked at Reeve, and the sheriff saw the embarrassment burn for a second before the anger took over. "This from a girl who's named after a club drug," Reeve said weakly, trying to give Tarley a little bit of covering fire.

Tarley recovered in a second or so. "Ain't never met anyone named Abilene, have you?" Molly shrugged, and Tarley got a little self-righteous, clearly vindicated. "Thought not."

"I'm actually glad we got to talking about Abi," Reeve said, not at all glad the conversation had gone this way, and even less so that he'd opened the door for Molly Darlington to just jump right in and make a mess of things further. "Because, really, this meeting, and everything that's going on—it concerns, you know, the children—"

Tarley reached up to scratch his face with a filthy-looking hand. "Sorry, sheriff," he said, plainly not at all sorry, "I have a hard time swallowing this stuff about demons."

"That's fair," Reeve said, trying to dodge around this semi before it clobbered him, "but you gotta admit some terrible things are happening. And no matter what the cause is, people are worried for their families, their kids—"

Tarley's eyes lit up. "Damned right we are."

"Of course you are," Reeve said, watching the anger smolder in Braeden Tarley's eyes, "because you're a good parent—"

"How the hell would you know?" Tarley fired off.

Reeve stopped dead in his rhetorical tracks. "Well, Braeden, I assume since you're a single father now—"

"What happened to Abi's mom?" Molly asked, then suddenly seemed to realize she'd blundered and clapped her hands over her mouth. She looked contrite, for which Reeve felt blessed, though it was about five minutes too late. "I'm so sorry," she said.

"No, it's all right," Tarley said, still smoking from the ears. "She died in a car crash when Abi was young." He was wound tight as a spool of thread, string eating into the cork. Reeve wanted to grimace, because he suspected this was about to go nowhere real good. Tarley's gaze whirled around to Reeve. "You're right, I'm trying to be a good father to my daughter. And you're right, too, crap is going real wrong around here." He raised a finger and pointed it right in Reeve's face, something that would have earned him a disorderly conduct or worse if it had happened in a traffic stop and not here at a meeting about demons gone shitshow wrong. "I don't buy your line, though. Maybe you know what's going on here, or maybe you're just out of your depths or maybe you're just blaming others for your own screw-ups."

Reeve took a breath, then two. "If that's how you want to see it, Braeden."

Tarley's eyes burned, not like a demon, but like a man reaching the end of his rope. "That's how I see it." He drew his finger back. "Reckon I'm not the only one, either." He turned and started to walk away.

"Reckon you're not," Reeve agreed as Braeden Tarley walked out. "And I hope you don't have cause to change your mind anytime soon."

*

The name on her driver's license said Amanda Guthrie, but no one really called her that. No one really called her anything, except maybe "ma'am," or "lady," if they were trying to get her attention. That was rare, though, she reflected as she steered the car up the interstate off-ramp. It was an SUV, a rental from Atlanta, where she'd flown in this afternoon. It had been a few hours' drive through Atlanta rush hour—that town felt like it was always in rush hour to her—and now she was here, pulling past the *Welcome to Calhoun County* sign. Seeing it didn't prompt a smile or a frown or much of anything, really. It was just a sign of the times, a sign of where she was now, and how she felt about it was pretty well irrelevant.

She turned right on the off-ramp and headed toward town, the SUV's headlights illuminating the road even though the sun hadn't fully set yet. Everything was in shadow, dusky and dark, the sun hidden behind the horizon, buried beneath the trees to the west.

Amanda Guthrie, as no one called her, took a steady few breaths and focused her rapt attention on the road. She was passing places now—"Fast Freddie's," read a glaring neon sign. There was a diner, a Wal-Mart Supercenter, a fireworks outlet. She took it all in, then turned her gaze back to the blacktop, the neon sheen of the bar's sign lending a little more color to her life.

She brought the vehicle to a squealing halt as someone staggered out in front of her, reeling and clutching their midsection. She applied the brakes judiciously, not wanting to run someone over only a minute after entering this town. That wouldn't make a very good impression, and it'd surely draw attention.

The poor soul in front of her stumbled, clutching his belly. She could tell he was a he now, by the hair and the beard. He was wearing a coat, too, protection against the cool fall air she'd felt when she'd fueled up outside Chattanooga. The bastard hit all fours in the middle of the road and Amanda Guthrie rolled her eyes, staring past her dark chocolate-colored hands where they gripped the steering wheel tightly.

A pack of them were on the man in the middle of the road in a hot second, three guys in coats, rough-looking, like they'd come up from the Gulf after rough-necking for a while. Amanda watched out her front windshield, cocking an eyebrow at the spectacle, watching it all coolly.

"It was a mistake to try and run," the lead roughneck said, a black man talking in a South London accent. She knew that accent, all cockney. "Now you're in Barney. Lads?"

The Brit and his compatriots surrounded the fallen man and proceeded to beat him for a spell. Amanda just watched calmly, waiting. After a few seconds she honked her horn.

The Brit looked up and held a single finger aloft, and fortunately for him it was the index finger and not a ruder one. "Just a minute, there. We'll be out of your way in a jiffy. Or you could just drive around," he made a motion suggesting she steer her car into the other lane, "if you're in a hurry." He smiled with what he probably regarded as charm.

Amanda just hit the horn again, longer this time. She wasn't going to steer out of her way for this trash, no damned way.

"Oh, all right, then," the Brit said, lit by her headlamps, "have it your way." He spread his arms wide, grinning. "Gentlemen."

One of the other two behind him drew a knife and stabbed down, penetrating the fallen man's back just above the kidney. Guthrie saw his face as the blow struck, pain and surprise flashing in his eyes for a hot second before—

Black fire crawled up his back and devoured him whole, ripping out of this plane and back to hell.

The Brit and his two friends eyed Amanda in her car, and she honked again, briefly, watching them and none too impressed.

"All right, all right," the Brit said, not smiling quite as broadly. "Let's get out of the bird's way, lads. Give right of way and all that." He retreated from the road slowly, looking back at her all the while. She wondered if he could see her face through the headlight's gleam, but she didn't wonder too hard.

As soon as he was clear, she put foot to accelerator again, bringing the SUV back up to speed. She watched the three men in her rearview as she drove away, shaking her head, still rolling her eyes, for all the good it did.

"Fucking demon hunters," she said, with nothing but contempt as she headed into Midian, Tennessee. The road looked nothing but clear ahead.

*

"Why in the bloody hell would we leave everything we've worked so hard for behind in order to go to Midian, Tennessee, at the height of a hotspot?" Chester asked the empty air in front of him, the slow curve of Interstate 75 wrapping around a bend in the distance. They passed a sign telling them Knoxville was ahead.

"Apparently you're seeing things somewhat rosier than I was," William replied. He'd changed his name to Bill some time ago, but Chester did not adapt easily to this change, nor any other. He waved the body's left hand, taking it off the wheel for a second to make his florid point. "We were working in a factory, Chester, for a damnably low wage, living in a one-bedroom apartment in Queens."

"We were carving a life out for ourselves, William," Chester said, losing patience. He kept the hand he retained control of firmly gripped upon the wheel. "Through steady effort we were making headway—"

"Well, perhaps my brethren are sick of your definition of 'headway,'" Bill said, a little of his irritability seeping out with his unease. "If you like what we had going in Queens so damned much, maybe I should find a new body and—"

"Why do you always threaten that?" Chester asked, shaking the head as best he could on his own. It caused a mild, spasmodic jerk since he did not have full control over the neck, and being in a spat they were not sharing well at the moment. "We've all been together for longer than any of us can even measure. I know you and yours are growing ... restless ..."

"Restless, yes," Bill said with a nod. "Oh, indeed, my people and I are quite sick of this stagnation you and yours seem determined to foist on us. More and more of your voices are trickling over to my side."

"Your little grouping is determined to get us killed like some new rathtala, thirsty for blood," Chester said, the head jerking in another attempted shake. "We have proven we can live beneath attention for over a century—"

"Except for all those times we were forced to pull up stakes abruptly," William said, his part of the lips curling in a half-smile.

"Perhaps if we were to work in slightly better harmony," Chester suggested, starting to lose his patience.

"Perhaps if we were to go somewhere that demons are more expected," William said, not really suggesting it since they were clearly already on the way, "we might have a better chance."

"A better chance at what?" Chester asked quietly, the panel van steering heavily. They'd had it for a long time, and it was no joy to drive, but it was theirs, wholly. "To have opportunities to kill humans? To stand in a place where there are surely OOCs who would love nothing more than to find us and send us back in one large, blessed bundle to the pits?"

"You're very black and white about these things," William said with some humor, probably because he and his faction had already won the argument; they were on their way, after all. "As though the only alternatives are to continue to scratch out a living in New York or meet our tragic end at the hands of the Office of Occultic Concordance. Countless demons live their lives without fear of a consecrated baton sending them back, and a great many do it at hotspots—which is why we're going. To seek better fortunes."

"Go west, young man," Chester muttered under their breath.

"We tried west," Bill said, smiling his half of the smile. "We ended up stuck in a vase for a thousand years, biting and clawing at each other over the most trivial things imaginable. The inner life of a legion of demon souls trapped together is hardly more thrilling than that of a quiet, blending-in factory-working demon, and, as we have argued, considerably less honest, since we're hiding who we are all the time. Though, I suppose, at least in the vase we could be ourselves."

"And in the vase we never had sensory stimuli," Chester said. "No feel of the wind on our skin, no warmth of a summer night to make us sweat in this vessel. No sound of music—"

"Your taste and mine veer considerably from each other in this, Chester—"

"—nor the smell of good coffee on a morning, or a television to watch—"

"Try to remember that not only did you hate the television when first we saw it," William said, still pushing his part of the smile, "but you also didn't want to leave the vase when this body first crossed our path."

Chester was silent for a moment as the road straightened ahead of them; the sky was dark, and the stars were coming out. "I don't recall that at all."

"Your collective has a very selective memory, then," William said. "Though I think I've noted that before during our arguments."

"And yours has no temperance," Chester snapped back.

"Yet we have enough votes to win this particular day," William said, the half-smile fading as his annoyance rose. He was well tired of this battle, tired of all the battles with Chester, really.

"Don't think that means you will win forever, as you constantly proclaim at every decision that goes your way."

William's eye twitched, and the next sign shone under the van's headlights. Knoxville was only thirty miles away now, and he knew the hotspot was less than thirty from there. "I'll be quite content just winning this one, I think." And they fell into silence as they drove through the Tennessee night toward their destination.

*

Hendricks unlocked the door to his room at the Sinbad Motel, feeling a couple little aches and pains, nothing that couldn't be solved with an

Advil or two and a night of sleep, probably. He'd come out of this fight considerably better than some of the others, that was certain. Still, this town hadn't been kind to him, and neither had this particular hotspot. Less kind than any he'd been to, really, and that was saying something since he'd broken his arm a year or so ago in a small town in Wyoming.

He clicked the light before he walked in. It was a habit he was getting into, that and sleeping with a light on. Lafayette Jackson Hendricks didn't consider himself a 'fraidy cat—a tour in Iraq that had included busting down doors in Ramadi precluded such possibilities from his mind—but all the same, he didn't mind sleeping in light or walking in it wherever possible.

This time, again, the light revealed that his room wasn't as empty as it should have been. He took a long breath, then stepped over the threshold, shutting the door behind him. "Why am I not surprised it's you that's here to greet me like a dog at the door?"

"I am not standing at your door," Starling said, red hair gleaming in the motel weak lamps. "Nor have I greeted you yet." Her voice was dull and flat as the paint on the walls, but it didn't crack as much.

Hendricks took off his hat, taking care to check that the consecrated switchblade didn't fall out and whack him across the nose. It had happened a time or two, and it hurt enough to make him wary. He placed both carefully on the dresser that stretched across the side of the room, working his way through the narrow channel between the furniture and the shitty bed. "Well, you're here, and that's about like a sweet greeting for as cool a customer as you. Like Arch saying 'ass' or something, it carries more weight because he just doesn't do that."

Starling cocked her head in that way she did. "This is hardly the first time you've found me waiting in your room."

"No, you're making a right habit of it lately," Hendricks said, peeling off his drover coat. Even though the late October air had been cool during the fight with the broc'aminn, he'd still sweated considerably. Probably not as much as he had waiting outside that kid Jacob's house while Alison dropped him off and explained what was what to his parents, though. He'd heard some of the conversation and it was enough to give him night sweats, thinking about what those people were about to go through.

Starling stared at him. "You are troubled."

"I'm living in a cheap hotel in the heart of demon country at the moment." Hendricks flashed her a smile. "There's nothing but trouble around me right now."

"Something happened. Something unpleasant."

He raised an eyebrow at that. "Something unpleasant is the very definition of a hotspot. Someone's dying here practically every day, and that's with us doing our level best to prevent it."

She took a couple steps closer to him while he drifted around her, hanging the drover coat up on the old metal rack in the bathroom area. No closet in this shithole, but at least they had HBO. "What happened tonight?" she asked, lower than her usual tone.

"You seem to know everything around here," Hendricks said, shrugging as he wrapped the heavy shoulders of the canvas coat around the wooden hanger and listened to it clink against the rack like a bell ringing in the distance. "Why don't you tell me?"

"A child was attacked," Starling said, cool as a Canadian lumberjack in January. "It bothers you."

"Yeah, people get antsy when children start getting attacked," Hendricks agreed. "Even a heart of stone like mine cracks a little when a defenseless kid gets surrounded by a pack of broc'aminn." He made a face, because he suddenly had a very bad taste in his mouth, like the thought of what could have been made his stomach spit acid up his esophagus.

"But it was not your child," Starling said.

"I don't have a child," Hendricks said, working his belt buckle. If she was going to talk all night, he wasn't really in the mood. He just wanted to shower and collapse for a little while, maybe catch a *Game of Thrones* rerun until he fell asleep. "Never did."

"Yet you feel called to protect those of others," Starling said.

Hendricks made his way into the bathroom, taking his 1911 out of his holster and setting it on the back of the toilet. Then he unsheathed his sword and leaned it against the reserve tank. He always did this lately, his little routine before getting in the shower. He hadn't used to, but ever since—

"You worry," Starling said, eyeing his preparations.

"I've kinda gotten my ass beat a few times since I got here," he said, letting the belt buckle clank on the floor, tossing the scabbard and holster past the redhead who was just hanging out in the doorway of his bathroom, being of no particular use to anyone, least of all him. "Better safe than sorry, as they say."

"But this is new," Starling said, still staring at him with those dusky, impenetrable eyes.

"Every other hotspot I've been to, you know how many times demons have tracked me down to do me harm?" He held up a hand with his index finger pressed to his thumb in the international sign of zero. "Nada. As in, 'not a one.'"

She cocked her head in confusion once more. "But this didn't come about after any of the attacks on the places where you stayed—"

Hendricks just froze, holding himself upright, hands clenching the bottom of his t-shirt, ready to strip it off. His back locked into place and he couldn't move his arms for a second, like a combat freeze, like his animal brain took over for a few beats of the heart and he was playing dead right there in front of his toilet.

"—it came after—"

"I damned well know what it came after," Hendricks said, hands still stuck at the bottom of his t-shirt. He swallowed hard and wiped at his mouth with the back of his hand, suddenly struck by nausea. He gagged, looking down at the toilet. At least he was close if he chucked.

It took a moment but the nausea passed, and he stared at the white porcelain, stained all around the bowl, and at the dull gunmetal of his 1911 on top of the reserve tank, then the sword beside the throne. They reassured him, at least a little, and he looked at the redhead framed in the door out of the corner of his eye. "I know very damned well what it came after," he finished.

"Do you want to hear something?" Starling asked.

"Is it a cryptic warning about shit yet to roll my way?" Hendricks asked, the scent of bile wafting out of his mouth, infecting his taste buds.

"The blood-dimmed tide is about to be loosed." She stared at him, those impossible eyes fixed on him, and he didn't know quite what to say.

"You make that up?" he asked at last.

"It is a quote from a poem by William Butler Yates," she said. "It is called the *Second Coming*."

"I don't really acknowledge a first coming," Hendricks muttered, mostly to himself, staring at the stained toilet bowl. "You trying to change up your routine? Because even with the hints of poetry, it still sounds like a cryptic warning."

"There is always danger afoot," she said, "always something to be wary of, as we move toward the end of all things."

Hendricks listened to her as he stared into the toilet. His skin felt dirty, sticky, disgusting, like he'd been marked somehow, slimed. He felt filthy and wanted to climb into the shower, to let the hot water burn his flesh for a while as he scrubbed himself clean. "I need to shower," he announced suddenly.

"Do you want me to stay?" she asked, staring at him.

He didn't look at her. "You can if you want. It's a free country."

"I will watch over you, then," she said.

He shrugged, still feeling that transient hint of nausea. "I don't reckon you'll see anything you haven't seen here before, given your profession when you're not whooping demon ass and making apocalyptic announcements of doom." But the words rang hollow even in his own ears, and he undressed a lot slower than usual. That sick feeling didn't quite leave him, even after he was under the hot water, the shower curtain between him and the redhead who was standing guard at his bathroom door.

2.

Braeden Tarley made it home just in time for his favorite part of the night. He'd been worried he wouldn't get back from the meeting earlier enough, but as soon as he walked in the door and caught the smile and nod from the babysitter, he hurried and fumbled for his wallet to pay her and ushered her out so he could get down to the most important business at hand.

"Daddy!" Abi squealed as he came into her room. She was already in bed, covers twisted from clearly playing when she was supposed to be sleeping. The hall light behind him cast his shadow long across the toys strewn across her floor, dolls and a mini-kitchen and a little shopping cart. There was a noise machine making sound like waves crashing against rocks, like music to his ears, sitting there on the dresser across the room from her bed, and he slid the knob lower as he came into the room.

Abilene Harlequin Tarley (he'd wanted to call her Harley, because owning one of those motorcycles had been Braeden's ultimate ambition, but his wife was having none of her being Harley Tarley) was the most beautiful girl in the entire world, Braeden was damned convinced, and had been since he'd first laid eyes on her. She had these perfect little blond pigtails that it had taken him months to master, a beautiful button nose that was a little round at the end, and a smile that was like someone turned on a tractor-trailer's headlamps in your face without the covers. She gave him one of those right then, and he couldn't help but forget everything that had happened at that stupid meeting, breaking an idiot grin of his own.

"How's my girl?" Braeden said, sliding in next to her on the little day bed tucked into the corner of her room. It doubled as a sofa, and its cushions were a little too thin for his taste, but he didn't have to sleep on it. If she got scared, she always just came and got in his bed anyway.

"Daddy, today at Miss Creek's we learned about the states," Abi said, eyes all excited. She didn't look tired, which was a mite vexing considering it was at least half an hour past her bedtime. "Do you know how many states I know?"

"How many states do you know?" Braeden asked, stooping low so that he could put his elbows on the edge of the day bed.

"All of them," she said, smiling broadly. "Arizona, Alaska, Texas, Tennessee, West Carolina—"

"I don't think there's a West Carolina," Braeden said, barely suppressing a grin. "North and South, I recall, but no East or West Carolina."

Abi frowned at this, looking toward the ceiling as she pondered it. "No, there's a West Carolina."

"Sure you're not thinking of West Virginia?"

She considered this a little further. "No, you're wrong. Miss Creek says there's a West Carolina."

He barely held it in. "Either Miss Creek failed geography or you're not recalling it right."

"What did you do today, Daddy?" Abi asked, clearly just moving right on past.

"I fixed engines, just like every day," he said with his best smile. He brought up one of his hands and she grabbed it, pressing it to her nose. She liked the citrus smell of the Zep TKO hand cleaner, and she made a big production of drinking it in, holding his hand up there and then smiling, her eyes closed as she let it drop away from her face.

"Mmmm," she said, resting her head back on her pillow, eyes opening just a slit to peer out at him while trying to act like she was sleeping. "Sing me a song."

"What do you want me to sing?" he asked, leaning his elbow on the hard wood at the edge of the bed.

"Something pretty."

"That's a broad category," Braeden said, thinking it over. "How about 'I'm So Lonesome I Could Cry'?"

Her eyes popped open. "No." She squinted them shut again.

"It's a great song, a classic—"

"No."

He thought about it again. "How about, 'Bartender Blues' by—"

"I want 'Do You Want to Build a Snowman'," she said, easing those eyes open again for a second.

Braeden thought about mounting a half-hearted protest but gave it right up and launched into the song. Whatever Abi wanted that he could give her, he gave her. He figured that since she was missing one parent that could say yes to her, he kinda had to do double duty on that, too.

*

"So that's how it went," Reeve said to his wife, Donna, sitting in their kitchen. The dark, thin wooden wall panels were the height of seventies and eighties style, and he'd been meaning to tear them out and paint, but his priority list of projects had taken a backseat ever since he'd gotten elected sheriff. He and Donna had been married for umpteen million years, together for a little while before that, so she was used to the honey-do list getting put off. "Not exactly the biggest success of my political career," he finished.

"You're a lousy politician, sweetheart," Donna said, full of sympathy, her steel hair cut short around her ears in a little bit of a bob. It was a classy look for a classy lady, and Reeve didn't mind it at all. She'd done a hell of a great job raising their kids while he was working his ass off for the department and a succession of sheriffs. Now the kids were all grown, and he and Donna were in their sunset years, and he was in the big job, the one he'd always wanted. "You're too straight a shooter to deal with people like Pike."

"Oh, if it was down to me actually shooting him, I reckon I'd do all right—because of the straight nature of my shooting." Reeve mimed drawing a pistol, making one out of his finger. He smiled, but it faded in an instant.

"What are you thinking about right now?" She reached across the table and took his hand. He stared down at it; both of them had their fair share of wrinkles, and their hair was a hell of a lot shorter than when they'd met, but he had a hard time imagining her any different than she was now.

"I'm thinking ..." he said slowly, "I can imagine what some of these people in our town are going through. The ones I've had to deliver the news to." He squeezed her hand gently. "One of the things I've always loved about Calhoun County was how tight we pull together when things go bad. How many times have we gone over to sit with someone when they lost kin? And you get there, and the house is all filled up with casseroles and deviled eggs and sandwich plates and food brought in by people who are feeling the sympathy." He shook his head. "We've lost so many folks lately ... I wonder if the people seeing their kin die now are getting ... less, you know? I wonder if we're starting to hit the point where our community is jaded enough that they feel like they've given enough."

"I don't think so," Donna said, shaking her head. "I went over to Marge Rosalind's daughter's place—you know her husband got killed when the big demon came stomping through, and they lost the house—she's living with them for a bit. Well, they were stocked up, Nick, I tell you." She scooted a little closer to him, put a hand on his shoulder and started to rub. "The people around here care about each other. They trust each other, are neighborly for the most part. It's just who we are." She gave him a faint smile. "Whatever happened tonight, just know that before the end of this, they'll come back 'round to you."

"I shudder to think what it'll take to convince some of these folks I'm not a lying sack of shit, making this crap up to cover what an incompetent fucking idiot I am," Reeve said with a weak smile. He leaned forward and gave his wife a peck, and she turned to take it on the lips. He halted before pulling away, and gave her a deeper kiss, the kind they didn't really exchange very often any more. She returned it, and he scooted his chair a little closer, the leg scuffing on the linoleum floor as he hopped over.

They kissed like that for a few minutes, like they used to. The longer it went on, though, the more Reeve felt his internal temperature rising, a peculiar kind of worry setting in.

Finally, his wife broke from him, hand on his cheek. "What's wrong, Nick?"

Reeve didn't know quite how to say it. "This ... this ain't never happened before."

It took her a second to get it, but when she did, she was steely calm. "It ain't no big deal. We can fix this in a hot second."

She unzipped his pants, reaching on in there, taking his penis out as she pressed her mouth back to his lips. She worked him good, just the way he liked, but after another ten minutes of her making every effort she could, it was as clear as day to him that this particular battle was a loss, and not a pretty one.

"Sonofabitch," Reeve said breathlessly as Donna settled back into the chair next to him, limp dick just sitting there are folded and ashamed—as it damned well should have been. Donna bent to put her head on his shoulder, stroking his back gently.

"It's all right, Nick."

"The hell it is," Reeve said, disgust threatening to give him an ulcer. Hell, if he had an ulcer, at least that would have been a reasonable excuse for the disgrace that had just happened here. "This—I mean, this doesn't happen."

"Those commercials for Cialis say differently."

"Well, it don't happen to me," Reeve said, indignant. A moment later he regretted turning his hostility to his wife. "Not to me," he said, lower and little contrite. He felt little reassurance from her there at his side. "There are demons invading Midian, more than half the town turned against me tonight, and now this. Shit."

She rubbed at his shoulder again. "Well, at least you know it can't get any worse."

He narrowed his eyes, looking down at her, head on his shoulder. "Don't you go tempting fate, now."

*

Arch rolled off Alison, breathless, his energy spent. He was sweating between the sheets, trying to mop it up off his forehead with the edge of the cotton. They were nice sheets, nicer than anything he'd owned. They were staying in Alison's old bedroom at her parents' house, and that meant they had to keep quiet, which was easier for Arch than Alison. He was habitually quiet anyway, to the point where she teased him by asking him if he was afraid the Good Lord would hear him if he made any sound louder than a whisper. She, on the other hand, didn't mind getting embarrassingly loud, even when they were in an apartment that had a common wall with an elderly lady. Fortunately, she hadn't been able to hear. Even more fortunately, Alison had learned to tone down her enthusiasm slightly in her parents' house. If only she'd felt the same when they'd lived with Hendricks and Duncan. Arch hadn't been able to comfortably look either of them in the eye for the first few weeks in that farmhouse.

"I never get tired of that," Alison said, sheet resting just above her waist. He gave a look over at her pale nipples, almost glowing in the faint light breaking in past the curtains. The back porch light was just outside and shone right in the room. Time was, in the wee hours of the morning that gave Arch problems, but he doubted he'd have much trouble anymore. Not after they'd just spent weeks living in a country house, sleeping during the day without the benefit of curtains.

"It is one of the better rewards for us human beings," Arch said.

"Duncan says demons do it, too," Alison said. "Hell, you know they do."

"I have a hard time imagining them enjoying it as much," Arch said a little stiffly. "Duncan doesn't seem interested at all, for instance."

"Like we ain't never met human people that exact same way," Alison said with a frown in the dark. She got up and headed for the bathroom. Her parents' house was pretty nice, and Alison had an in-suite bathroom. Made it convenient, that was for sure. And it certainly didn't motivate him to go looking for an apartment at the moment, either. He heard the tinkle of her making water, wishing a little self-consciously she'd close the bathroom door. The sound the toilet paper roll squeaking followed a few seconds after it stopped, and then the loud flush.

She padded back into the room. "You have trouble thinking of demons as people, don't you?"

"Because they're not," Arch said, pulling the sheet up to just below his neck as she got back into the bed. The whole thing shook under her light weight.

"Duncan's people." She sounded certain. "Don't you remember that whole argument with Hendricks we had out in the barn at the other house where—"

"Duncan strikes me as different than most of the demons I've driven a sword point through," Arch said. "For one, he's not interested in hurting human people. For another, he is interested in stopping the demons who do."

Alison shifted uncomfortably, grunting in bed next to him, fanning herself with the sheet. "Good God, it's hot in here, isn't it?"

Arch arched his eyebrows. "I was thinking it was fairly cool, myself."

"You're crazy," Alison said. "But I suppose it shouldn't surprise me that you're not really willing to think of a demon as a person until they're part of the cause or whatever."

"Well, a large portion of the ones I've met had ill intent, so I'll admit it might be coloring my perspective a bit."

"Lerner wasn't interested in hurting people, either," she said.

Arch didn't respond to that one. Lerner, Duncan's old partner, had been sucked back to hell after he'd gone flying over the side of Mount Horeb in a police cruiser during a chase. Before he'd gone, though, he'd been a sarcastic bastard, the sort with a personality like sandpaper, rubbing everyone around him the wrong way. Rather than saying so, though, Arch tried to make like he was heading to sleep, closing his eyes and letting the fight that one would open up pass him right on by.

"We're meeting tomorrow, aren't we?" Alison asked, jarring Arch slightly.

He cracked an eye open. "The watch? Yeah. In the morning. Gonna talk about what happened at the meeting tonight for the benefit of those who weren't there to witness it go all to heck."

She let that rest in silence for a second. "All to hell, Arch." When he looked over at her quizzically, she elaborated. "Fits better." He didn't agree verbally, just closed his eyes. But she was right.

*

Brian lay on his bed down in the basement, eyeing the ceiling balefully. He'd heard Arch and Alison going at it upstairs, and it didn't exactly thrill him. "Picked a bad month to quit smoking weed," he said to the empty basement room.

And he had, on both accounts. Hunting demons would have been a lot easier to tolerate if he were stoned, and stewing in the fact that he didn't really know what the hell he was doing would probably also be easier if he were fucking lit.

But no, he'd decided to do the responsible thing and swear it off, because all he needed was for everyone to start rushing out to a demon attack and have him baked out of his fucking mind, swinging a sword and not really in command of himself fully. He'd probably be fine, but when throwing hurt with a Roman gladius, "sorry" probably wouldn't cover the damage if he fucked up.

So now he was sitting in his basement bedroom, rubbing lightly against the too-soft sheets his mom bought, staring at the smooth, fog-textured knockdown ceiling, trying to figure out where he fit in on this whole thing. He knew he could swing a sword about as well as he could swing a baseball bat at a fastball—terribly, bordering on not at all. He wasn't blind to this fact, and that people had had to come save his ass from demons every time they'd gotten overwhelmed was pretty prominent in his mind. It was a worry, even, and Brian didn't typically do worries. The weed helped with that.

He took a breath of non-smoky air and longed, just longed for a chance to light up. No, he wasn't going to do that. Everyone already thought he was some useless stoner, he could see it when they looked at him. But he'd done that ad thing, and that might have made it possible for them to take down those kid-eating demons tonight. Maybe. It was possible he'd saved little Jacob Arnold's life by his effort.

Maybe.

Possibly.

Ehh, who knew?

Brian had considered asking the cowboy for sword fighting lessons, or for his dad to teach him how to shoot better. The pride stuck in his craw, though. He could maybe ask Arch to take him shooting, but that took time to learn, didn't it? He'd given up on shooting a long time ago, like probably when his age was still in the single digits.

When he thought about the contributions he'd made since joining this little watch, as he'd heard them call it, he had to admit that driving a tractor trailer into that demon had probably been right at the top of the list. But it wasn't like he owned a truck he could just drive into demons in every fight, so that wasn't even a valid option.

Brian took another breath in the faint light of the bedroom, and now, a few days removed from his last smoke, even he could smell the faint residue on everything. He had to do something. He couldn't just stand idly by, after all. He had a degree from Brown, dammit. There was bound to be something he could contribute to this war. He just had to find it.

*

Lauren Darlington came home wanting to toss her keys across the room. It was a weird desire, wanting to toss her keys, but somehow it felt more compelling than putting them on the usual hook or placing them on the table, so she chucked 'em. They skidded unsatisfactorily against the surface of the kitchen table.

"What is the *matter* with you?" her mother screeched from the kitchen.

"I don't know," Lauren admitted, mea culpa right out of the gate. "I just ... wanted to throw my keys."

"You're killing demons now," her mother said, rushing over to the table at top speed, which, for her, was something akin to a hobbling walk. "Can't you just pitch a holy knife at them or something and spare the finish on my home furnishings?"

"Find me a demon and I'll do just that," Lauren agreed, shrugging out of her light fall coat and hanging it on the hook beside the door. She thought about tossing that, too, but figured her mother would just lose her shit again, even though it was improbable a leather coat would do much damage to anything but a sensitive vegan's self-image.

"Mom!" Molly called, streaming across the room toward her, peppy as all get out.

"You've been in the Red Bull again, haven't you?" Lauren asked, peering at her daughter with undisguised suspicion.

Molly hung her head. "I had a moment of weakness."

"Oh, daughter. How bad was it?"

Molly's lips curled upward at the side. "It has been three hours since I mainlined two Red Bulls." She hung her head dramatically. "I need absolution. And probably some sleep, sometime next year, maybe."

"I'm gonna need you to say twelve 'Our Mothers' and perform an act of contrition—which will probably be vacuuming and cleaning your room." Lauren shook her head.

"Y'all are so strange," Vera said, just shaking her head at it all.

"You missed the meeting. I hope it was important."

"Emergency calls usually are," Lauren said, stepping into the kitchen. Why did they always gravitate toward the kitchen? "We got a bunch of demons on a playground, about to ... I dunno, do stuff to Jacob Arnold."

"Why do you say 'do stuff?'" Molly was frowning. "Why not just say they were going to kill him and eat him?"

Lauren's stomach rumbled unpleasantly. "Because that's not all this breed of demon does to their victims, apparently."

Molly's pupils dilated slightly. "Oh. Oh!" She made a face. "Gross, I'm assuming."

"Can't get much grosser," Lauren agreed.

"Why do we have to talk about this?" Vera asked, shuddering all the way down her body while opening the refrigerator door and pulling out a caffeine-free Diet Coke. "It's not proper, it's not natural, and it's enough to give a body nightmares."

"Mom, you say that about everything you don't understand," Lauren said. "It's a long list that includes music made after 1981 and bedazzling."

"I get it about the bedazzling, I really do," Molly said. "I mean, I thought we'd seen the worst, and then it mutated like airborne ebola into vajazzling—"

Vera stood up straight, slamming the door to the fridge and spinning around, looking like a bee had flown up her bathrobe. "How do you even know about 'vajazzling'?"

"Because I have a pulse?" Molly asked carefully. "And an internet connection? And go to school in these modern times—"

"Lord ah-mighty," Vera breathed. "The things they teach you these days, I swear ..."

"I doubt that's part of the official curriculum of the school," Lauren said.

"Oh, no, they totally have a class on it," Molly deadpanned. "Self-Destruction 101. We also practice other forms of self-harm, like listening to Nickelback on repeat."

"Cheap shot," Lauren said. "You know I like Nickelback. Also, hasn't everybody made that joke by now?"

"I try not to hold your bad habits against you, since you did incubate me for nine months," Molly said with a nod. "But between that and the rhinestone-covered shirt in your closet, I have begun to question my parentage."

"I question whether either of you are related to me, even tangentially, all the time," Vera muttered. "I hold out hope that the nurses switched my daughter with the offspring of a baboon that snuck into the ward. Someday my real daughter will come rescue me from this nut house, maybe take me off to live with her wealthy husband and his aging single father, who is actually Rob Lowe's twin brother."

"Ugh, Mom, you're a cougar swooping in on a member of the Brat Pack," Lauren said with undisguised horror.

"I would also accept Judd Nelson's twin," Vera said, staring off into space.

"So, how'd the meeting go?" Lauren put her arm around Molly's shoulder and led her out of the room, just trying desperately to escape the last thought promulgated into the air.

"It got ugly," Molly said.

"How ugly?"

"Like if Adam Driver had a baby with Josh Gad," Molly said.

"Ooh, that's ugly," Lauren said. "And harsh. They'd have to hope some recessive grandparent genes saved the day. What happened?"

"Sheriff Reeve got threatened with a recall election," Molly said.

"I feel like there's a joke about recall elections and that if I were Mom's age, I would make it," Lauren said, looking back to see if Vera was following them.

She was, and she gave her daughter a scalding look. "I can both hear you and recall the twenty-two hours of painful labor I spent squirting your ungrateful backside into this world."

"And thanks for electing to." Lauren looked back at Molly. "Who did the threatening?"

"County Administrator Pike," Vera answered before Molly could. "I never did like him."

"I like him," Lauren said, a little defensively. But then she and her mother had probably never once voted for the same candidate on the ballot. "He really threatened Reeve with a recall election?"

"Yeah," Molly said. "It was pretty grim. He called for a show of hands for who supported Reeve, and I bet two-thirds of the crowd were all Luke Skywalker in that moment."

"Blond hair, smug face?" Lauren asked. "Whining about power converters?"

Molly shook her head. "Their hands were not in the air. Because … he lost his hand, you know."

"Hmmm, that one was not obvious, and kind of dated. Maybe if you'd gone with a Jamie Lannister joke—"

"You don't think the *Star Wars* reference is mainstream enough? I mean—"

"Well, *Game of Thrones* is more modern and topical—"

"I would have said Lindsay, the lawyer from *Angel*," Vera said, sipping her Diet Coke like a boss.

Lauren and Molly exchanged a look. "That one's better," Lauren said.

"We all would have gotten it," Molly said. "Anyway, the meeting kind of death-spiraled after that. But you might have some new members of the watch." She puffed herself up a little but looked away, which Lauren knew was her attempt to act casual. "Speaking of new people in the watch, maybe I could—"

"No," Lauren said.

"Fuck no," Vera said, drawing Molly and Lauren's gazes in a comical whip-around.

"Jesus, Mom," Lauren said, looking a little aghast at her, "is there one of those Jack Daniels add-ons attached to your Coke can?"

"Oh, I'm sorry if I feel strongly about keeping my sixteen-year-old granddaughter away from meetings where townsfolk discuss fighting the demon scourge that's invading our home," Vera said.

"It wasn't that you feel strongly about it," Molly said, "it was more that you threw out the f-word. I didn't even know you knew that word."

"I hear it from your mother all the time," Vera said.

"I wasn't sure you knew what it meant," Lauren said snidely.

"I have an Oxford dictionary, and surprisingly, as your daughter figured out about a decade ago, all the naughty words are listed in it," Vera said.

"It was very helpful in furthering my education," Molly said with a nod.

"I'm with grandmother on this one," Lauren said.

"Use of the f-word?" Molly asked, frowning.

"Well, fuck yeah, that too," Lauren said, "but I meant about you going to watch meetings."

"Mommmmmmmm," Molly said, dropping her shoulders, teenage look of frustrated disgust all over her face. "I want to help."

"Help me by staying way the fuck out of trouble," Lauren said, patting her on the shoulder. "Hmm?"

"Ughhhh," Molly said, going seemingly boneless and turning away, like her upper body was composed of slime, shoulders all down and her head back.

"That's a very flattering posture," Lauren told her as she moped out of the room. "I like it. It's like a feminist antidote to all those old exercises at finishing schools where they made you sit with a book on the top of your head." Another disgusted grunt issued from Molly as she headed for the stairs and up to her room.

"That girl wants to get herself in trouble," Vera said, sipping again from her Coke can.

"At least this kind of trouble doesn't involve teenage pregnancy," Lauren said.

Vera waited a second before replying. "No, it involves death, which, last I checked, is worse than teenage pregnancy. Or, at least, less survivable."

Lauren waited a second, relishing her impending reply. "But, Mommmmm," she said, barely holding back the grin, "when I got pregnant at sixteen, you and dad said it was the worst thing that could have happened to meeeeee—"

"Oh—oh, get the fuck outta here."

Lauren paused, mildly surprised "There's that word again. Twice in one night, Mom?"

"Yes, there it is again," Vera agreed, turning away from her. "If you're going to fail to be ladylike, you might as well go all out, not half-ass it."

"Did you learn what 'ass' meant from the dictionary, too? Because it has more than one meaning—"

"Get out of here and go to bed, you damned donkey—and I mean that in more than one way, too."

*

Amanda Guthrie pulled her rental SUV into the hotel parking lot, under the glaring, bright lamps hanging overhead. Stopping the car, she put it in park, looking around before she got out. She grabbed a travel bag out of the back and rolled it along over the rough, pebbled pavement, the wheels making noise every step of the way.

As she walked into the lobby, she looked around for a moment before heading to the front desk. The place seemed calm, sedate, and fully made up in the Southern style. It had lush red curtains over the windows, fancy couches set up for people to just hang out and chill, and ice water with orange peels floating in it in the corner, a remnant of the summer which was now gone.

She strolled up to the counter and looked right at the clerk, a young bearded guy on night duty who squinted at her through thick glasses. "Checking in," she said, her voice clipped and to the point.

"Got a reservation?" the bearded clerk asked.

"Do I need one?" She didn't take any shit from anybody.

"No," he said, backpedaling a little. Probably didn't want to chance her going 'angry black woman' on him. She wasn't tall enough to be physically imposing, but she knew for a fact that her Resting Bitch Face game was on point, as the kids said. "Uhh, what kind of room do you want?"

"King bed," she said. He looked up, like he wanted to protest or suggest or something, but he must have decided this was a bad idea because he returned to typing without voicing a damned thing.

"Okay, you're up on the third floor, room 309," he said, pulling up a couple key cards and practically throwing them at her. He hadn't even asked how many guests or for her license plate. They probably didn't do too many tow-aways for improper parking in Midian, Tennessee, anyway. Likely as not the police and property owners had plenty of other things to worry about right now.

Amanda Guthrie didn't bother to say thank you, just gave the clerk a stony look, grabbed the door key cards and headed for the elevator. He may have started to tell her where it was, but when he saw her heading in the right direction, he shut up quick. Didn't even say when check-out was.

Didn't matter. She wasn't checking out for a long time, anyway.

The elevator dinged immediately, opening for her without needing to make her wait. She got in and pushed the button for the third floor, listening to it hum as it went to the top.

When it opened, she stepped out into a long beige-yellow hallway. It seemed a little summery, but she supposed it had been painted to appeal to the hotel's guests, not to play to her personal proclivities, which were somewhat offended by such a damned ugly color. She took a right and headed down the hallway, pausing in front of room 309.

She caught motion out of the corner of her eye and looked up.

There was a man standing there—no, not a man, an Officer of Occultic Concordance. He was fumbling with a key card, hadn't even noticed her. She knew he wouldn't, but it was fascinating to see him going about his business without even realizing she was there, standing in front of her door, watching him. He got the key card to work finally, and opened his door, his ice bucket rattling and full. He was wearing a t-shirt, one of the ones with writing on it, but she couldn't see what it said before he closed the room door behind him, leaving her out there, still clueless that she was watching him.

She stared after the OOC for another minute after he'd shut the door, thinking about what to do. She smiled slightly as she pondered it; she had plans for that OOC, but making any kind of disturbance here in the hotel wasn't among them. She finally just used her key card to open the door and step inside the room.

It took Amanda less than ten minutes to unpack, putting her things exactly where she wanted them. First she hung the clothes in the closet provided, making sure they didn't get wrinkled, and setting aside a few of her suits for ironing. Then she undressed, peeling her current suit off and placing it inside the dry cleaning bag provided by the hotel. She was down to bra and panties, and once she shed the former, she felt like she could breathe worlds easier through her shell. That damned tight-fitting thing was like a strap around her chest, like someone had tied a rope around her and squeezed the whole damned while.

After all that was done, and now that she was infinitely more comfortable, Amanda spent five minutes just setting things up in the bathroom, looking at her own eyes and face in the mirror, and even occasionally letting her gaze wander further down. Her skin was a dark chestnut and her nipples were darker still. She paused in her labors and stared, just briefly, running a hand over the smooth, flat skin between her breasts and the top of her panties. Losing interest quickly, she finished her labors, and then wandered back out to the room and turned the bed down, slipping between the sheets.

She could feel the cloth under her shell, above her shell, a nice little tent that covered her body from top to bottom. She listened to her own rhythmic breathing as she stared at the ceiling, the light still on next to the bed. She didn't need to turn it off; it wasn't like she actually slept, after all. No, she didn't need to. She had a lot on her mind, anyway.

Like what was going to happen tomorrow. So much to do. She stared at the ceiling for the rest of the night, just thinking about it all, and smiling just a little bit.

*

When they reached Midian, Tennessee, it was a surprisingly simple matter for Chester and William to agree on the next course of action. Night was hanging overhead, after all, countless stars in the sky, which was not a sight they were familiar with from their time in New York.

"Quite impressive," Chester said, looking out the windshield. They craned their neck together to lean forward and see as the van coasted down the road at twenty miles an hour.

"I forget what it looks like sometimes after we've been in a city for a while," William said. He had his hand gripped firmly on the steering wheel. They pressed the brake together.

"Shall we find a quiet road, a nice place to park for the evening?" Chester asked, still blinking up at the sight of all those stars. Without as much light out here, it was an impressive spectacle, pinpricks of light across the black veil of the sky. So numerous, like the souls contained within their body.

"Indubitably," William agreed, and they took the panel van down a side road. They chanced a quick look back; the two back windows had curtains that could be shut over them, and there were no windows along the side. A bedroll lay in the rear in lieu of seats, because it wasn't as though they ever had guests or passengers.

The van's engine rumbled in the quiet night. Finding a suitable street was an easy matter. They came across a public park in a neighborhood not ten minutes off the exit ramp, a half dozen cars parked all along the avenues adjacent, and settled the van in for the night.

Chester pulled the keys out of the ignition and pocketed them as they stretched, rising out of the seat, the light still on overhead, timing its way until it shut off. "Shall we lie for a bit?" he asked.

"So that we can indulge in the rich inner life of a demon colony?" William asked with amusement. "I think we can accommodate you and yours in this, Chester."

"I do thank you," Chester said stiffly as they lay down, the hard rubber floor of the van's back padded by the roll of foam they'd laid down with a sheet over it. They fought with the pillow until it was positioned just so for the maximum comfort of all involved in the decision—not an easy matter—and then lay there, still.

"I wish it could be like this all the time," Chester said, and a chorus of quiet agreement rose from within them, his side speaking their feelings.

"And you know we don't," William said, and this time it was his turn to be stiff. A cacophony began, voices shouting each other down inside.

"Let us discuss it for a time," Chester said.

"Because you wish to end the evening in acrimony?" William asked with a half-sigh. "On this matter I'm not certain we are so accommodating." He paused. "Do you not ever grow … tired of argument?"

"No," Chester said quietly. "Of course not. Argument is a necessary part of any debate—"

"Perhaps I grow weary of having a debate," William said. "Perhaps some things we see should just be done—"

"Without discussion?" Chester asked. "Just—just do them? Without asking, consulting, deciding—"

"Yes," William said. "Yes, exactly."

"That sounds rather like … a dictatorship, William," Chester said.

"You always default to that," William said. "And I've asked you to call me Bill." The voices inside them were raging at one another again, as they always did. Those who spoke in reasoned tones were drowned out in the noise of argument. Those who spoke the loudest were barely even heard. "Every moment of our lives, every piece of progress we try to make can't simply dissolve into argumentative committee meetings or a poll to see what needs to happen next. Sometimes, things need to be done—"

"And if they are done without any of that consultation," Chester said, and his staid voice broke into the closest thing he ever showed to compassion, "if they are merely decided on by us, by philosopher kings with their hands on the levers of power ... what makes us wise enough, righteous enough to claim that mantle?" He paused, and his voice grew brittle. "What makes us *right*?"

"We are right because we are right," Bill said. "Because we know right when we see it."

"Every man thinks he is right in his heart," Chester said. "And he would argue it to his dying breath—"

"Well, you're the one who wants to argue, not I."

"I do," Chester said. "I want to argue. I want to discuss, to poll, to have us talk about the things we do. I do not want to lurch blindly in the direction of whatever desire crosses my face, to lunge toward the next 'right thing' without even considering first what makes it right for now and for all the moments after now—"

"I said I don't wish to argue it anymore," William said and shut his eye. The cacophony did not die within, not nearly, but William—Bill—simply diminished.

"I do not wish this to become the making of an Ambrose Bierce quote," Chester said into the silence at the fore. He could still hear the rumbling, angry argument roiling within, but he barely listened to that anymore. He wanted to hear William's voice, but nothing but silence came to him. "William?"

No more argument came to him that night, and so Chester spent the dark hours staring through his open eye at the shadowy lines of the roof of the van, counting the hours until morning, when he hoped all would be well again.

3.

Hendricks pulled up to the sheriff's station off Old Jackson Highway in his purloined SUV, dropped it into park, and let go of the wheel, staring out at the highway rolling along in front of him. It was just after sunrise and the traffic was minimal. A couple cars in a row came past, making a little noise that was mostly dissipated over the ditch between the lot and the road, leaving Hendricks to just stare out at them as they went.

Part of him wished he could be in a car getting the hell away from here, but they had a meeting, and so here he was. He hadn't had the greatest night of sleep, but neither had it been the worst in recent memory, so he just sort of yawned and rubbed at his eyes for a minute before shutting off the car and getting out.

Meetings were not a usual thing for the demon-hunting crowd. It was kinda like being back in the Corps again, except worse somehow. Civilian oversight had never been a real joy for him or any other Marine he'd known, and this was all civilians, all the time. It hadn't been too bad when it was just him and Arch, but with every addition it felt more and more like they were having circle time in kindergarten rather than getting to the shit that needed to be done with a cold and efficient eye to fucking up demons with maximum impact.

He pulled on the handle to the door, staring in through the clear Plexiglas to see an already full room waiting for him. No joy there. He'd hoped maybe the action last night would cause some people to skip this one, but it didn't look like his hopes and dreams had been answered any better this time than they ever had in the past.

"Same shit, different day," he muttered on his way through the open counter into the back bullpen area. It was nothing but open air dividing the waiting space from where the entirety of the watch was waiting for him.

"So you do say that." Duncan greeted him with a smirk, sitting on a desk at the far side of the room. Today's t-shirt had the words "Naked Prozac" written in lush, multicolored letters. Hendricks frowned. He'd seen that somewhere before, but couldn't recall where.

"Morning," Arch said, standing near the front of the room with Sheriff Reeve, who was looking a little more tired than he had when Hendricks had seen him yesterday. Hendricks's impression of the sheriff was that he was a ball buster but probably a decent guy, just way out of his depth.

"You're late," Alison ragged him as he went past. She was sitting at the back of the class, eye fixed on the door, her momma and daddy arranged around her, her hair all wavy and wet like she'd just got out of the shower. He'd lived with her and Arch for a month or so, and given what he knew about how they fucked every night, he figured she had probably needed to shower this morning.

"Jesus, it's like you're trying to be his personal assistant," Brian Longholt said, standing uncomfortably a dozen paces from his parents and sister, his arms folded, because he had to be cool and distance himself from his uncool family. Nope, Hendricks did not care for the stoner smart boy at all.

"At least he showed up," Erin Harris said a little stiffly, kinda toward the front of the room, sitting next to that pervy taxidermist, Casey Meacham. Him, Hendricks kinda liked, in spite of him seeming dumb enough to try catching a bullet with his forehead. Hendricks had him pegged as first man down if he ever stepped up to the combat side of the watch. He was support corps all the way, if anyone with half a brainpan was running things here.

Hendricks felt about the same about the sheriff's wife, who was sitting up front like the favorite pupil, a little notepad in hand. They were gonna have minutes for their meeting and everything, it looked like. Hendricks buried a sigh so deep it would have taken the entire Army Corps of Engineers to find it, but of course only one Marine to do the work of digging it out. "Sorry," he said, not really meaning it. "Overslept."

"It's all right, you're not the last one here," Sheriff Reeve said with a surprising magnanimity that Hendricks wondered about until he realized who was missing. There were actually two people who hadn't showed yet, but then one of them appeared at the door and Hendricks felt like he'd wriggled loose of the hook.

"Father Nguyen," Sheriff Reeve said as the priest came in the door. Nguyen wasn't a very tall guy, and he greeted all the crew waiting with a thin smile.

Nguyen came inside the counter, but only just, leaning himself against it and placing his palms on its edge. "Did I miss anything?" he asked with a vague hint of an accent.

"You missed the cowboy showing up late, too," Brian Longholt said with his customary smartassery. That guy was a pain in the dick, and he didn't even have the social grace to do it playfully, like Alison.

"So we gonna get started now?" Casey Meacham asked, looking around. "That's everybody, right?"

"Not exactly," Reeve said, a little tightly. There was a sound of tires squealing in the parking lot and silence fell for a second. "That's probably the last of us, right there."

They all waited in the quiet and a second later the door swung open and Dr. Darlington came in, out of breath and carrying a cup of coffee big enough to caffeinate one MEF. "Sorry, sorry," she said, a big fucking donut with a few bites out of it in the other hand. "I am so sorry."

"Now that we're all here," Reeve said, clearly not gonna call the doctor out on her tardiness, "we can start." That burned Hendricks's ass like a ghost pepper sandwich with jalapeno dressing on cayenne-peppered bread. If he'd been the last to arrive, the old bastard probably would have ripped a good chunk out of his rectum. Nothing like a Marine drill sergeant would have in the same position, but enough to raise his eyebrow, at least.

Duncan caught Hendricks's gaze from across the bullpen and nodded once. The demon was probably reading his mind again, or his essence, or whatever. That was an annoying damned thing, but at this point just another on an endless pile.

"Gonna deal with the urgent and sudden first," Reeve said, looking at his one page of notes for the meeting. "We got an emergency call last night just after the meeting—three guys attacking a third out near the freeway."

"And we're just hearing about this now why?" Hendricks asked, hands sweating on the sleeves of his coat, arms folded in front of him. "I live like two seconds from there. I coulda checked it out."

"Ed Fries took the call," Reeve said, meeting his gaze steadily, which annoyed Hendricks further. Stare downs were a fun game, but the sheriff was plainly old enough that an uncomfortable gaze didn't bother him at all. Hendricks would have bet that little bitch Brian Longholt would have melted under it, though. "He went out for a look, didn't see any sign of anything—"

"Where was he coming from?" Hendricks asked.

"I think what my colleague means," Arch said, stepping in between Hendricks and the sheriff to gentle things up, "is that if he was that close and Ed was across town, it might have made more sense to have Hendricks take a peek first."

"Yeah, it would have," Reeve agreed, pretty brusquely, "but unfortunately, I don't have a contact number for Mr. Hendricks."

"Just Hendricks is fine," Hendricks said for the umpteen billionth time.

"I don't have a contact number for Just Hendricks," the sheriff went on, the prick. "So Fries took the call. If things had gone wrong, I'm sure we would have gotten in touch somehow."

"Yeah, why do you not have a cellphone again?" Brian Longholt, of course, asked this question.

"My motel room has a phone." Hendricks felt his jaw tighten. "And power, and running water, before you ask." He gave a sidelong look at Brian again, whose face fell as Hendricks ripped the obvious follow-ups right out of him before he could set absolutely nobody to laughing with his butter-knife sharp wit. "HBO, too."

"This brings up a point," Reeve said, still all serious and shit. "Our current method of communication is pretty inadequate to the task before us."

"Group text messaging and the conference calls have carried us this far," Bill Longholt said from the back of the room. "You looking to change?"

"It is a pain in the ass to try and do group conference calls," Duncan said, looking once more at Hendricks. "Especially since I'm carrying the burner that stupid over there uses." He nodded at Hendricks.

Hendricks made a kissy face. "Is that why you're not with stupid anymore? You tired of holding my purse?"

"Yeah," Duncan said, "I can't figure out for the life of me why you can't carry your own phone in that big coat of yours." He held up the little burner phone that Hendricks used to wire himself with a mic for some of the battles they'd done lately.

"I don't like those things," Hendricks said, shrugging. "It beeps off at the wrong time, maybe a demon eats your ass."

"Ain't a demon out there wants to eat your filthy ass, Marine," Bill piped up from the back of the room.

"Yeah, they're all interested in my—" Hendricks started, before a sudden, violent sense of unease rolled over him.

"Ain't a soul interested in that, either," Brian said, once again taking a pretty decent gag and dragging it dead over the line. Maybe it was just Hendricks, but every time that shit spoke it was like roofing nails on a chalkboard.

"What were you thinking in terms of changing up our communication?" Bill Longholt said, dragging 'em back on track.

"Some kind of radio system," Reeve said. "Cell phones don't work in some of the hollers in Calhoun County, and I'd like something that doesn't necessarily beep loud, to Mr. Just Hendricks's point. We've had to go some places lately where quiet is needed, and having something blaring out with a ringtone isn't a great option."

"We could just treat it like the theater and put our cell phones on vibrate," Dr. Darlington suggested.

"That sounds like fun," Casey Meacham said, and Hendricks thanked a God he didn't even believe in that nobody asked him why that sounded like fun.

"Anyone want to look into some options for us?" Reeve asked. "Maybe figure things out?"

"I can do that," Brian Longholt leapt into the fray. Sadly, he didn't strike Hendricks as the sort who'd ever catch a bullet with his forehead. He was more the sort that would get friendly fire right into his back. Accidentally, of course. "I can read Amazon reviews with the best of them. I'll see if I can find us something that'll work, that's got some range to it."

"Make sure it can take a headset," Alison said. "And it's gotta be small. I've got enough shit to carry as it is." She made a face and her hand went to her stomach, like something she'd eaten was disagreeing with her.

"Okay, that's two things out of the way, then," Reeve said, eyes moving down his list.

"Speaking of your other deputy," Hendricks said, inserting himself right into the gap in the conversation like he was punching a hole in the enemy lines, "where is that guy?"

Reeve exchanged a look with Arch then with Erin. "Ed's sleeping. He had a long patrol last night."

Hendricks enjoyed that look enough that he decided to go back for more, just to see what happened. "I noticed he's never been to any of our meetings."

Reeve went back to stare-down mode and Hendricks knew he'd found a bullet hole. "Well, let's just say that Ed might not be philosophically predisposed to join up with our plans."

"You mean his sympathies are with the people who didn't raise their hands at the meeting last night?" Addison Longholt asked. Hendricks hadn't seen much of Brian and Alison's mom, but what he had seen, he liked. He also felt like he now knew where Alison got her "take no shit" attitude.

"I don't know if I'd go that far, but Ed's having a hard time wrapping his head around the idea of demons in Midian," Reeve said, voice fraught with tension. Apparently shit-talking his underling in this meeting was not his idea of fun. Hendricks could respect that, but at the same time, it tickled him a little to watch the man squirm.

"So how did that meeting go?" Hendricks asked, pretty damned sure he knew but keen to toss another grenade to liven things up. The last meeting had been damned dull; he'd thought about gouging his ears out with his own sword to end it.

"Swimmingly," Reeve answered with just the appropriate amount of pissed off to tell Hendricks he'd not only hit the mark, he might have punched well past it.

*

Reeve had had about enough of that ornery, salty, black-clad fucking demon hunter to last him for a decade or twelve. As if it hadn't been bad enough facing a room of people last night that were about two steps shy of hunting down pitchforks and lighting up torches, now he had to deal with this blamed outsider coming in and stirring the shit pot Reeve was presently boiling in. And boiling was the right word, because for some damned reason the building's heat had just kicked on, and the vent above him was pouring out hot air.

"So it went super well, then?" Brian Longholt asked with the sarcasm he was learning to expect from that little punk. Reeve could smell the marijuana on the little bastard, and he knew for a fact that he could make a case for possession just based on how he wafted. But Reeve was playing nice, and honestly, none of them needed this right now.

Reeve tried to keep his tone mellow as he responded. "You walk out of every town meeting knowing at least somebody's bitching in the parking lot about how everything you just said was bullshit, but this was probably a higher proportion of that than usual." Donna caught his eye in the front row, trying to give him a reassuring smile. Reeve forced one onto his face and pointed it back at her while he waited for the inevitable return of fire from the cowboy and the stoner.

"I hear you're going to be facing a recall election soon, Nick," Bill Longholt said, quiet and serious, as the man always was. Reeve liked Bill; he was a good man. "You got a plan for how to deal with that?"

"Other than kick County Administrator Pike right in the ass?" Reeve asked, only half joking. "Not really. Didn't exactly see it coming until the possibility reared its ugly head last night."

"Are we sure he's not a demon?" Casey Meacham asked, causing Erin Harris to swivel her head to look at him in a double take. Reeve couldn't blame her; it did sound a little stupid.

"He's a politician, so I don't rule it out," Reeve said dryly. "But no, I don't think he's a demon." He caught a flash of resentment from Lauren Darlington. "Probably." He glanced at their resident demon, the bland guy with the t-shirt in the corner. "You think?"

Duncan spoke after a moment's thought. "Some demons do tend to gravitate toward places where they can exercise some power, but typically they'd want to remain out of the spotlight for fear of being discovered or revealed. A county administrator in a place like this wouldn't be so famous as to discourage a demon from taking the office."

"So you're saying none of our presidents have been demons?" Brian Longholt snarked. "Because I was pretty confident that—"

"Just shut up," Hendricks said, rolling his eyes. When Brian blinked in surprise at him, the cowboy unfolded his hands to spread them in a very "don't give a damn," gesture. "We all know which president you're going to say, so just go ahead and stow it and save those of us in the audience who voted for him from an ugly argument, all right?"

"I was gonna say William Henry Harrison," Brian said, almost under his breath, like he couldn't bear to let the moment pass without comment.

"Tippecanoe and Tyler, too," Casey said, crowing just a little.

"Speaking of pointless discord," Reeve said, leveling his gaze at Lauren Darlington, who was cramming the last bite of a glazed donut in her mouth, "I got a bone to pick with you about Molly."

*

Lauren had the donut almost fully in her mouth, sweet sugary goodness embarrassingly perched between her lips like she was trying to—well, it didn't look good, and she damned well knew it. She'd been trying to finish her breakfast on the go in a rush so she could better participate in the discussion, but then, like a kid daydreaming in class, Reeve had gone and called on her when she had a mouth full of dough and icing and couldn't speak for herself. "Mmmbrummph!" she managed to get out around the donut.

"Molly came up to me at the meeting last night," Reeve began, apparently undeterred by her biting off more than she could chew. Lauren just sat there, mouth full, cheeks burning, and not just from the overwhelming heat that had just shifted on in the otherwise pretty comfortable sheriff's station. "Right as I was trying to have a conversation with Braeden Tarley, who looked like he might have been otherwise amenable to listening—"

"Who the hell is Braeden Tarley?" Hendricks asked. Lauren's eyes darted toward the cowboy as she frantically tried to chew her food. He'd been piping up all meeting so far, kind of obnoxiously, but now she was glad he was taking a little bit of the heat off her. It gave her a chance to finish her donut without everyone watching her cheeks move.

"He runs a diesel engine repair shop here in town," Reeve said, and Lauren could see him barely holding back his contempt for Hendricks in his answer. She suspected that holding it all in probably wasn't too good for the man's health, but she didn't have either the inclination or a mouth free of donut to be able to give voice to that opinion. "Young guy, probably one of the more successful examples of someone turning his life around after a rough start. It would have been nice to have him on our side."

"Did anyone else actually come over to our side?" Father Nguyen spoke up from his place at the counter.

"They did, and we'll get to that in a minute," Reeve said, turning his attention back to Lauren. "Please keep Molly away from the next meeting, if we have one."

Lauren swallowed the last bite heavily, still feeling red in the face. "Sorry. She just has questions."

"Maybe Hendricks can answer them," Reeve suggested, almost earnestly enough to get away with it. He pointed the notes in his hand toward the cowboy, top edge first. "He's the expert in demons, after all. I don't even know who Martha Shelly is."

Lauren took a second to decode that. "You mean Martin Shkreli, don't you?"

"I don't mean a damned thing, it was your daughter that was asking me if he was a demon or not," Reeve said with a classic buffoon's exaggerated shrug. He looked back to Duncan.

Duncan gave it a moment's thought. "He could be. I wouldn't know without either reading him or striking him with a holy implement."

"If it comes to it," Lauren said, "I vote for the latter."

"Great, we'll add him to the list of people to do that to," Reeve said.

"Along with—" Brian started.

"No," Hendricks cut him off.

"I was going to say Fred Phelps," Brian finished, surly as hell at being stomped on again.

"No, you weren't," Alison said with a roll of her eyes. She paused halfway through her eye roll and paled for a second. "Ugh."

"Brian, while you're adding your two cents," Reeve said, focusing on the young man, "did you and Casey get that Rog'tausch or whatever it was disposed of?"

Lauren turned to look at Brian Longholt, and she could tell by the stricken look on his face that he hadn't. Even though it was wrong, she felt a sense of relief, like her part in being called out during the meeting was over, and whew.

*

"Uh, yeah," Brian said after a suitable pause, after the first dumbstruck moment passed him by. It was almost like he'd zoned out for a five count after Reeve had drawn attention to him, and blinking stupidly wasn't doing him any favors. "No, we, uh, haven't gotten rid of the, uh, bones yet."

Sheriff Reeve just stood there, staring at him, and Brian got that feeling in his stomach like he'd had on the first day of school every year. Hell, he'd probably had it on the second and third and fourth days, too, but it was the lesser version of the same—the sense that he had no idea what was about to happen, but he knew it wasn't good.

Reeve held his tongue for another few crucial seconds, allowing the tension to twist and ratchet in Brian's gut. For all the sense of ornery arguing he did with most of the authority figures in his life, he still felt a need to quail away from the guy in uniform. It wasn't something he was proud of, and he was pretty sure if it came down to it, he could get into a hell of an argument with the sheriff. But his instinct was not to, like his uniform was some kind of mind-warping thing that shut him down, like Duncan's badge or something. "You had one job," Reeve said, his face twitching a little.

Brian looked over at Casey, who looked dully back at him. Casey hadn't exactly offered to spearhead this whole disposal of the last big bad they'd faced, after all, he'd just been stuck with it because the bones of the thing were still sitting in terrariums in his taxidermy shop. "I was trying to figure out the best place to put them," Brian said at last.

"Who gives a shit?" Reeve didn't sound like he was buying it, and that made Brian tense even further; he knew for a fact that the sheriff wasn't going to buy his explanation for what was taking so long. Well, not on its face, anyway.

"Look," Brian said, steadying himself for fire, "we're talking about disposing of a big, bad demon corpse here—"

"Yeah, and I'm asking why it ain't done yet," Reeve said.

Brian opened his mouth and faltered, then stumbled backasswards into an answer that would satisfy most of the room. "Because of the goddamned EPA," he answered, and that was pretty close to the truth, if phrased in a way that he thought would appeal to his audience.

Reeve frowned, lines deepening between his brows. "Excuse me?"

"We don't know if the ... Rog'tausch is toxic or not," Brian said, not really embarrassed to admit it so much as embarrassed that he was having to couch his concerns in a way that felt foreign to him.

"It's a demon corpse," Reeve said.

"It could be emitting radiation, chemicals, toxicity ... anything," Brian said. "If we dump it and the EPA finds out ..." He shrugged and did not allow himself to think about how that didn't sound half bad.

Reeve melted into a state somewhere between annoyance and resignation, one of his eyeballs fluttering and the other shooting skyward. "Goddammit. You might just have a point there." He looked to Duncan. "Is that thing toxic?"

Duncan's answer was immediate and sarcastic. "Do I look like a portable chemical and radiological testing lab to you?"

"Well, are there any toxic or radioactive demons?" Arch asked, stepping in and becoming Brian's knight in shining khaki.

"Possibly," Duncan said with a shrug. "There are definitely toxic ones. Radioactive ... maybe. It's not like they measure rads in the underworld. It's pretty much, 'Hey, does that burn like acid? Why yes, yes, it does. Let's not mess with that demon, then, except maybe at a distance. Stick a baton on a ten foot pole and give him a poke from way back there.'"

"Brian brings up a decent point about the EPA," Lauren Darlington said. "If you think you have trouble with the voters over a recall election, try and imagine how much worse it would be with the EPA up your ass like a ham-handed proctologist." Brian watched his dad shudder silently and Reeve make a face. Even Arch cocked an eyebrow at that one. Casey Meacham, on the other hand, seemed to be smiling faintly. "I might be able to take a bone sample from the Rog'tausch and see if we can get it tested in the lab down at Red Cedar. If it comes back negative, you can split the pieces up and bury them all over hell and gone."

"What if it comes back positive?" Reeve asked.

"Then any of us who handled the pieces that survive the live-action series finale of *Buffy the Vampire Slayer* are probably going to die of cancer," Lauren said, completely serious. "But since surviving this demon invasion is a long shot, I'm not too worried about it."

"Cute," Reeve said, giving her an icy look.

Lauren just smiled and snuck a glance at Brian. He caught it and gave her a grateful one in return.

*

"One last thing," Reeve said, looking down at his sheet. "Halloween is tomorrow."

Arch stood there thinking that one over for a minute. He'd just about forgotten it, truthfully, and would have been happier still if he could forget it for even longer. All Hallow's Eve wasn't exactly his favorite holiday, even absent their current crisis.

"Good God, already?" Casey said, staring off into space. "Man, time just flies. It ain't gonna be too much longer and we'll all be down at Moody's Roadhouse singing, 'Oh, by gosh by golly, check out the camel toe on Holly'—"

"You're a real pervert, Casey," Erin said from next to him as the whole room just sat there in silence.

"Thankee kindly," Casey said.

"Wasn't a compliment," Erin said, inching away from Casey by sliding down the desk a little.

Arch caught another shared look between Reeve and his wife. He'd caught a few of them throughout the meeting, and he considered them a good sign. Reeve had been confronted first with demons and now with the distrust of many of one-time constituents; at least his biggest supporter was on board.

"Halloween, people," Reeve said, more patient than Arch would have been in his shoes. "Kids in the streets. This is something we need to think about."

"I don't mean to settle you down in the middle of what I'm sure is about to be a grand old worry fest," Duncan said, "but I wouldn't worry too much about Halloween."

Arch felt a couple eyes fall on him, and he sighed, figuring he might as well ask the question, since it was on his mind anyway. "Isn't Halloween traditionally something of a demon-related holiday?"

Duncan frowned. "No."

Everyone waited a second, and then Hendricks spoke. "Was anyone else expecting more of an explanation than we just got?" A loose round of murmurs of assent broke loose.

"It's not," Duncan said. "There's not even any history there for us, just the significance you meatbags attach to it. Different demons with different belief systems have their own holidays, and none of them coincide with Halloween."

"There's still going to be kids in the streets, I expect," Reeve said. "Even with all that's happened."

"Well, I'd expect there's going to be a lot of adults in the streets as well," Duncan said with a shrug. "If this hotspot was closer to the tipping point of disorder, you maybe could expect some preying on the part of demons, but since it's not—"

"What the hell hotspot are you at?" Addy Longholt said, bristling. "This place is entirely in chaos."

"It's really not, comparatively speaking," Duncan said flatly.

"What my demon friend means to say," Hendricks jumped in, and for once he sounded conciliatory instead of like he was ready to add some gas to the fire, "is that there's not a total societal breakdown here yet. Midian's not a free-for-all zone without any law and order. People are still living here, still going about their jobs, still abiding by the law for the most part. Demons, even when they're killing, are mostly doing it very quietly, not blatantly and in the open."

"Except for when that giant demon went crashing through the streets of town," Brian snarked.

"It was kind of an isolated incident," Duncan said. "It's certainly been noisy around here, but nothing big and bold and obviously, blatantly destructive has happened right in the public eye other than that."

"So we still haven't hit the 'tipping point of disorder,'" Bill said, patting his wife on the back gently.

"No, which surprises me," Duncan said. "We—I—predicted it weeks ago based on how quickly this place heated up."

That hung for a second. "Why hasn't it, then?" Lauren Darlington finally asked.

"Us, probably," Duncan said. "Demons who have come here have been opposed in a way they wouldn't have been, given the fact there's only one professional demon hunter in town at the moment. The early showings suggested things would spiral faster, and although some ugly stuff—"

"Shit," Hendricks said.

"—has happened," Duncan went on, shooting him a frown, "it's not been all chaos, all the time in the way that hotspots tend to go before a town turns to ground zero. So, anyway, I think Halloween will probably be fine, as long as there are adults everywhere. Most demons won't want to risk the chance of all-out wrath. I'd expect a backlash on November 1st, though. Pent-up desires coming to the surface and all that."

"You make it sound like no one's got the balls to come out on Halloween night," Brian Longholt said, frowning.

"Maybe some onesie-twosie demons, working independently," Duncan said with another shrug. "But in order to face down all the adults in the streets during a trick-or-treating of the sort I've seen, it'd take—to use your criteria—a demon with balls bigger than the small-timers we've got operating here right now. Maybe if Kitty Elizabeth or some of the other royals riding her coattails were still in town, I'd worry. As it is, nobody's here that draws enough water to concern me."

"Every other time some giant douche has come to town, it's blindsided you, hasn't it?" Hendricks asked, much less pointedly than when he'd been needling Reeve. A quick glance told Arch that Reeve had noticed it, too, and was scowling. "I mean, you and Lerner didn't even know about Hollywood and Ygrusibas, and Gideon with the acid-jizz took you by surprise—"

"Says the demon hunter who was living next door to him," Duncan poked right back.

"—not to mention the guy with the fire-dog impregnation powers on the Ferris wheel," Hendricks said.

"Wait, the *what?*" Lauren Darlington asked. "I thought he was just a rapey carnie demon!"

"And the Rog'tausch," Hendricks said, shrugging while Duncan stared at him neutrally. "I mean, some big nasty could be here right now and you probably wouldn't even know about it given how many of those runes Spellman seems to be selling. Talk about the must-have demon accessory for the year—"

"You have a point," Duncan said nodding. "Yes, there could be something nasty hiding around here, something with a terrible plan to kill all your children. I doubt it, because they probably would have shown some sign, but it could be so."

"Well, gosh," Father Nguyen said, "that's not very reassuring for the safety of the children."

"Oh, the irony," Brian Longholt said.

"Predictable," Hendricks snapped at him. "Goddamn, why are you so fucking predictable?"

Brian stared at the cowboy, his mouth slightly agape. "I—excuse me?"

"Hold your fire on each other until after we wrap this up, all right?" Reeve said. "Let's just … keep Halloween in mind, then. Plan to be on the streets in bigger numbers, and uh, keep our ears to the ground, all right?" He looked around, but nobody said much of anything. "Adjourned, then."

Arch frowned as Hendricks took off for the door before anyone else had even started to move. He was out of it before Arch could even make the counter.

*

Hendricks was halfway across the parking lot when he heard his name called and stopped, mostly out of politeness to the person who'd called it. He turned slowly back to see Arch standing at the station door, all cleaned up in his khakis like when Hendricks had first met him. He even had his holster back on his hip, though now he was wearing his sword on the other side, which was a weird look on a Southern lawman, even to Hendricks.

Hendricks drew his coat in close around him, listening to the canvas make noise as he did so. The air was chilly as he breathed it in through his nose, the smell of diesel exhaust from the nearby highway wafting over him. "What's up, Arch?" he called back, thrusting his hands in his pockets.

"I was wondering the same about you," Arch said, sauntering his way over to Hendricks in that stiff-ass way he had. Hendricks always did think he moved a little funny, but then Arch wasn't exactly the type to fit any mold. "How are you doing?" Arch asked, lowering his voice now that they were only a few feet away from each other.

"Why I'm just fine," Hendricks said. "Fine as a frog's hair, in fact."

"I believe that'd make you 'nothing' rather than 'fine.'"

"Well, nothing's better than something," Hendricks said before realizing he didn't have a damned clue what that even meant and shaking his head.

"You got a burr in your saddle?" Arch asked, easing a little closer.

"I don't love meetings," Hendricks said, letting that explanation do for an answer. It wasn't untrue; it just wasn't the answer to the question asked.

"We need to organize," Arch said.

"Well, I'm glad I'm not in charge of that," Hendricks said, adjusting his hat.

"You could be a little more helpful, though," Arch said, clearly trying to be as tactful as he could.

"Probably," Hendricks said.

"You come off ornery, you know."

Hendricks paused before answering that one. "When's it gonna be just you and me again, Arch?"

Arch raised an eyebrow. "When everyone else is dead, I expect, and since I don't favor that outcome—"

"It was easier when it was the two of us," Hendricks said without enthusiasm. "Or when it was us plus Bill and Alison and Duncan. Now we've got all these goddamned people, and half of them I don't know, and your brother-in-law I can't fucking stand—" Hendricks made a noise deep in his throat, guttural and angry. "Your old boss, who made our lives miserable and drove us out into the country, is now giving the orders—"

"He's the sheriff," Arch said. "And it's not his fault I didn't square with him, or he might have been in all along—"

"I don't give a fuck," Hendricks said, frowning. "I lived years of my life taking orders. Forgive me for not jumping up and down with cheerleader-like excitement when they start coming my way again."

"What's wrong with cheerleaders?" Alison said, emerging from the station door with her arms folded in front of her over her flannel shirt. She hadn't been wearing it a minute ago, so Hendricks concluded it must be some sort of half-ass jacket she put on to block the cold.

"Nothing," Hendricks said, shrugging. "They're perfectly fine, fuckable people in most cases. I just don't feel like being one."

"Because you don't want to be a fine, fuckable person?" Alison asked, jabbing him as she smiled slyly. Arch just cringed at her use of profanity, which was always hilarious to Hendricks.

"Darling, we were just having a conversation here," Arch started.

"Were you asking Hendricks what got up his ass?" Alison asked.

"Definitely not a ham-handed proctologist," Hendricks fired back.

"That's good to know," she said coolly. "What are you up to for the rest of the day?"

"I got my exercises to do," Hendricks said. "Gotta keep in shape, you know."

The door to the station opened again, and out stepped Erin Harris. She locked eyes with Hendricks on her way out the door and froze just a second. He didn't want to look away first, but he did, turning to get back to his car.

"See you later," Alison said, overly loud.

"I'm sure," Hendricks spun to deliver his reply, walking backward all the while so he could get away as soon as possible.

*

No sooner was Hendricks in his car than he fired it up, the rental SUV he'd taken from Kitty Elizabeth belching a cloud of mist as it started. Alison was watching. He jacked the damned thing in gear like a second later and she heard the transmission do a power drop, not quite fully in gear before he hit the accelerator. It made a little noise, and he gunned it backwards, then floored it out of the parking lot in a squeal of tires that left the scent of burning rubber in a cloud that almost made Alison sicker than she was already feeling.

She coughed weakly and slapped Arch on the shoulder. "Dammit, what were you thinking?"

Arch let a little cough of his own, his expression sour, and not just from the smell of rubber. "I was thinking I'd ask him what was wrong."

"You know damned well what's wrong with him," Alison said,

shaking her head at her husband's unbelievable denseness.

"Really?" Erin interjected, stepping into the conversation. "Because I don't know what's wrong with him, but I'm wondering if it might be something a speeding ticket could fix, since he looked like he was heading for one."

"I wouldn't do that if I were you," Alison said.

"If you were me as a sheriff's deputy?" Erin asked, cocking a faded blond eyebrow at her. "Or me as—"

"You as the person he was screwing most recently," Alison said, just giving it to her straight. "Hendricks is damaged right now."

"He's been damaged since I've met him," Erin scoffed. There was plainly some real bad blood there, Alison saw.

"Well, he's a lot more damaged since Kitty Elizabeth got her immaculately-done nails sunk into his ass," Alison said, watching Arch's near-inscrutable expression all the while. "He's fucked up in ways that he wasn't before, which probably took some doing."

"I like how every time you say 'fuck,' Arch acts like you've just said 'Voldemort' in the wizarding world," Erin said, a dry sort of nastiness to her tone that Alison couldn't remember hearing from her before the accident.

"Yeah, it's really funny how I don't like the sound of my wife swearing," Arch said under his breath.

"It *is* funny," Erin said.

"What do you think, Erin?" Alison asked, more to see if she guessed right on the deputy's read of Hendricks than because she really cared what the girl thought.

"Hendricks is just a boy," Erin said, shrugging it off like it meant nothing. Alison caught a glimpse of the pain behind the eyes, though, and if she'd been feeling a little less sickly and a bit more ornery, she might have told her so. That wasn't likely to do much good, though, so she just let it pass. "Boys do what boys do, and then they go off and fuss and moan about it all afterward."

"You don't think he took some damage from Kitty Elizabeth?" Arch asked.

"What'd she do, cut his balls off?" Erin scoffed.

"Tortured him for sure. And likely raped him," Alison answered for Arch, who'd gotten his stony face.

"Gross," Erin said, making a face like she'd just had shit rammed right up to her lips. She paused for a second. "Like, made him—"

"Does it matter?" Alison asked.

Erin's gears spun around a couple more times, but she didn't speak until they stopped. "So you think he's chugging along, even more angsty and damaged than before?"

"Yeah," Alison said. "I think it's—I think she's—in his head. All the time, maybe. Not sure if he knows it or if she's just lurking in the shadows, but she's there. He's not saying anything, so it'd be tough to tell."

"Feels like that'd be the sort of thing to stick with a man for a while," Arch said in solemn agreement.

"Like he wasn't fucked up enough already," Erin said, kind of regretfully as she stared after the SUV that was now long, long gone.

*

It was more than a little bit of a relief to Reeve when he called the meeting to a close. While this one hadn't gone as bad as the one last night, he couldn't exactly chalk it up in the success column, either. Between the cowboy on PMS, the stoner who couldn't even do his one job, and the discord about what exactly defined a town in chaos … On second thought, Reeve wasn't sure if this meeting actually had been any better than the one last night.

"You did fine, Nick," Donna said, sliding up to him as soon as the meeting was done. She always did know what to say, and she said it with a little smile on her face.

"Hey, Duncan," Reeve said, trying to get the attention of the demon. He said the name awkwardly, like he didn't even really know how to pronounce it. It wasn't his fault; Nicholas Reeve couldn't recall a time he'd ever really talked with an actual demon before, unless he counted Lex Deivrel, the lawyer. Which he mostly guessed he did.

"Sheriff," Duncan said, coming up to him with his black 'Naked Prozac' t-shirt bunched up around his slightly protruding belly. Reeve wouldn't have known what the hell 'Naked Prozac' even was, but thanks to Alison Stan and a similar shirt, he knew it was a band that played music that even Warren Buffett couldn't have paid him enough money to listen to.

"I appreciate your help during all this," Reeve said, "assisting us unskilled rubes in how to, uh, kill your people and all."

Duncan didn't react to that. "Demons as a whole aren't really a thing. There's hundreds of species, and while we're all theoretically bound by the laws of the Pact and subject to the Office of Occultic Concordance, thinking of us as the same people would be just as erroneous as assuming you and Martians were the same."

Jesus, there are Martians? Reeve didn't say, but only because he caught himself at the last second. "Still, as a fellow lawman, your help is appreciated," he said instead.

"There are no Martians that I know of," Duncan offered helpfully. "It was obvious as the nose on your face," the demon answered after giving Reeve a second to experience the cold, clutching fear of wondering if his mind had just been read.

"So we don't have to worry about Halloween?" Reeve asked again. That was a nagging thought for him, the idea that all hell would break loose in the streets of Midian while there were kids out there. It was bad enough losing the few kids to this shit that they already had.

"I don't think so," Duncan said. "Things could change between now and then, but for now, just so long as there are plenty of adults and we're watching, I think we'll be okay. Any demon who wanted to start shit in the middle of all that would have to have a death wish, and whatever else you might think of us—and I'm actually speaking of pretty much every species here—we're not really that into glorious, pointless, self-destruction."

"Best news I've heard all day," Reeve said, and suddenly he realized that Casey Meacham had cornered Father Nguyen. The priest had his eyes open wide, and his lips were a thin line. Reed just stared over Duncan's shoulder at them, wondering what was being said. "Shit. That can't be good."

*

"And this other time, there were these three hookers, one male and two female—" Casey Meacham said as Father Nguyen just stood there, listening as the horror rose within him.

"Wait, wait," Nguyen managed to get out, cutting him off. "Why are you telling me these things? There's no confessional here." He paused. "Wait. Are you even Catholic?"

"What? No," Casey said. "I just figured you might like a good story." The taxidermist broke into a grin. "Thought this might be the sort of thing you wouldn't have heard before."

*

"Thanks for the assist back there," Brian said, wandering over to Dr. Darlington, who was standing back, watching Casey Meacham appall the hell out of Father Nguyen with something approaching amusement. When she looked up at him quizzically, he elaborated. "On the dumping the remains thing. I was worried about how that was going to go over."

"Yeah, well," Lauren said, shrugging, bringing the coffee cup up to her lips. "Just speak your piece next time."

Brian felt the hot flush run across his cheeks. "I don't know if you've noticed," he said, leaning in a little closer as Casey Meacham burst into a cackling laugh behind him, "but that's not the sort of argument that goes over real well around here."

Lauren just stared at him blankly. "You don't think anyone would give a shit if you dumped a radioactive corpse near the reservoir and killed the whole town?" Her meaning was plain: Are you out of your goddamned mind?

"I think they'd care if I killed all the fish in the Caledonia River," Brian said with a smirk.

She rolled her eyes. "Listen ... Brian ..." It was amazing how much patronization she could cram into his name and one other word.

"What?" He leaned in closer, trying to look as concerned as he could.

Her eye roll came down to meet his. "I know you're probably used to being a really smart person in an environment of really smart people at Princeton or Columbia or wherever you were—"

"Brown," he said, a little self-consciously.

"—but there's a difference between not being in the Ivy League anymore," she went on, "and assuming everyone around you is a fucking idiot."

"I ..." He stuttered, fishing for a response. "I—I don't assume everyone is an idiot, I just, y'know, try to approach my audience—"

"Like they're idiots," Lauren finished for him. She showed not one trace of humor, and it definitely put him off his game. "I get it, I do. You've spent years at loggerheads with the people in this town over God knows how many things. You go off out into the world, you connect with people who totally get you, who believe the same things you do, and it's like you were born into the wrong family and now you've found the right one, and all is good. Then you leave that and have to come back." She shrugged. "I understand that, probably better than you know—"

"I'm sure you—"

"Still talking here," Lauren interrupted him. "But just because you've disagreed with these people or some of them have done you wrong or most of them didn't understand your gentle, brilliant philosopher's soul—" that one stung, he had to admit, "—you're carrying all that baggage into these meetings, and everywhere else in your life. It's gotta be exhausting." She took a sip of coffee. "I mean, it's exhausting for me to watch you try and interact with people while doing it, so I would guess it's worse for you."

"That's ... there's a difference between baggage and experience," Brian said, trying to shape his umbrage into an argument rather than sputtering in pure outrage. "I mean, you can't deny that this town—"

"Is being attacked by demons," she said, pulling the coffee cup away from her lips. "I had all the same problems you did. With my mom. With the town. I have a list of people who were shitty to me when I was a pregnant, unwed teenage mother. It's long. But the day my daughter almost got raped by a demon and I found out people were being murdered by these things, my list, my issues with people around here started to look a lot pettier than usual. It's like the difference between seeing someone's face at an inch and at half a mile—"

"You're just airbrushing away your problems, then."

"I'm overlooking them for now and focusing on bigger ones," Lauren said. "This isn't a *Cosmo* cover shoot, all right? If the problems I have are still there once the demons have been driven out of Midian, cool, I'll pick my baggage up just like you and go back to whapping people upside the head for this shit. I've got grievances aplenty." She shrugged, keeping careful command of her coffee. "But they're not gonna mean anything if all the people that I have them with are dead, because the likelihood is the people I don't have them with are going to be lined up right beside them. Demons don't care who they kill or hurt. I care, though. Even about the people who pissed me off back in the day."

"Well …" Brian paused, trying to figure out how to respond to that. "How do you do that?"

"Look past the flaws of the people in this room," Lauren said, pushing off the counter where she was leaning. "Maybe focus on your own for a while. Or just stop being a smug dick when you can't swing a sword for shit." She pointed at the gladius on his belt.

He stood there, open-jawed. "Yeah. Maybe."

She edged a little closer. "There's no shame in admitting that being out in the fight isn't for you."

"So I'm supposed to just join Felicity Smoak as Overwatch?" Brian asked. "Because I think you'll find very few cameras or doors to hack around Midian, and I suck at computer science-y stuff anyway."

"Yeah, I don't know who that is."

Brian settled back, his anger having piped out a little. "I just … don't know how I can stand back and be of any damned use at all in this fight."

"Better trying to be of use from the outside than being out there in the thick of things and accidentally getting someone killed while they're trying to cover your ass. You know?" She brushed his shoulder lightly with a hand as she went past, and any other arguments he might have made were deader than a demon with a holy sword through it.

*

Braeden Tarley was in the middle of a repair to a big rig when a quiet car came pulling up outside his shop. He tended to work with the garage doors open all the damned time when he could, though that got more difficult in the worst parts of winter. Fortunately that was a pretty small sliver of time, and it sure wasn't here yet, so he had them open and could see the Toyota Camry drive up and park just outside one of the garage stalls. He even saw who got out, and though he was surprised, he wasn't as surprised as he might have been only a day earlier.

Braeden hopped down from what he was doing, grabbing a rag and wiping at his hands. It didn't do much, but he wasn't much of a mind to care about that. He could still smell it in the shop air, anyway, that scent of petroleum, of metal, and he liked it. This was part of the reason he'd gotten into this gig.

"Holee-shit," Tucker said from where he was working on Lester McQuaid's diesel Ford pickup. "Lookee what we got here."

"Why don't you just keep on working, Tucker," Braeden said as he walked toward the open garage door. He paused, laying a dirty hand on the door's rail. "How do you do today, County Administrator Pike?"

"Why, Braeden, I am doing marvelously," Pike said with that wide smile. He was holding a briefcase in front of his nuts with both hands, like Braeden might kick him right in the boys otherwise. Braeden wouldn't have, not at this age, because that would be felony assault. Braeden of a different age might have, but probably not. His younger self had been more into self-directed mischief. He hadn't given many fucks about what was going on in county politics back in those days. "How's your little one?"

"She's fine." Braeden gave his hands a once over again with the rag he was holding. It didn't do much to improve the situation, but he wasn't really eager to try at this point. He had figured out that Pike was carrying the briefcase as a different sort of shield, to keep from shaking his dirty hands, and Braeden was of a mind to try and force the issue. "What brings you out here today, sir?" He added the sir to be respectful. His natural inclination was not to trust the man, but he'd rarely had cause to encounter Pike. His impression of the man might have been limited, but what he had seen suggested to him that this guy was a world champion bullshitter with a silver tongue. That didn't necessarily make him a liar, but it did make Braeden aware and wary.

"I know you're a busy man, Braeden, so I don't want to take up too much of your time," Pike said. "I'm here to talk to you about the meeting last night. I know you were there."

"I was." Braeden didn't see any point in lying about that; Pike had probably laid eyes on him, and as much fun as it might have been for him to be contentious about it, he didn't want to waste time giving the man a chance to beat around the bush.

"I recall seeing you with your hand down at that point toward the end of the meeting," Pike said. Now he was fishing, though poorly.

"That's what you're here to talk about?" Braeden asked.

"It is," Pike said, smiling. "If you aren't familiar with how a recall election works, it requires signatures from people in the county in order to kick one of them off—to remove Sheriff Reeve from office." He lifted the briefcase that he'd been using to protect his nuts and his hands. "I've got just such a petition here. I was wondering if you might be willing to sign." He indicated the rest of the shop carefully. "If any of your employees might be willing, that'd be just fine, too."

"What are you gonna do if you kick Reeve out of office?" Braeden asked, tossing the dirty rag behind him. Pike had piqued his interest a little.

"We're gonna bring it before the people to elect a new sheriff," Pike said without hesitation. "We're going to find someone who'll actually do the job, put an end to this wave of bullshit instead of just spinning around making excuses about demons to cover up what's actually going on."

"What do you think is actually going on here?" Braeden asked. He heard Tucker behind him, listening. He knew the fucker was because he wasn't making a sound.

"Well, I don't think it's a big secret," Pike said. "Some real bad characters have come to town, and the sheriff don't know how to investigate or deal with them. That's not a demon problem, that's a leadership issue. Our town's under concentrated attack from criminal elements, not some shady otherworldly underworld. Could be Russian mafia here, or the cartels, but whatever the case, Reeve's decided to go and make up cockamamie bullshit to cover his failures." Pike straightened. "I don't know about you, but my momma taught me that when I screw up, I should take responsibility for it, and if I'm not up to the job at hand, maybe be a man, admit it, and step aside for someone who can do it."

Braeden chewed on that for a minute. "That all sounds real pretty. But what are you gonna do if you get Reeve out of there? Who you gonna bring in to replace him?"

"That's up to the people," Pike said, smile fading a little.

"So you don't want the job?"

"Jesus, no," Pike said. "Ain't my territory, policing. Like I said, it's up to the people, but I got a couple ideas to float—either we bring in a big-city police chief or sheriff that's had experience with this sort of shit or we go local with someone like Ed Fries." He shrugged. "Can't hardly get any worse than what we got going now, what with half of Midian getting wrecked."

Braeden thought about it for a minute. "You might have a point there. I just can't swallow this demon stuff." He motioned Pike forward. "Come on in here, I'll sign your petition." He looked behind him. "Tucker, you want to sign this?"

"No sir, not me," Tucker said, and the sound of a wrench turning came clicking over to Braeden. "I'm sorry, but this shit happening in Midian don't sound like anything I've ever even heard the Russian mafia or the cartels doing, and they are some nasty bastards, I tell ya. I'll buy demons on that."

"Pshhh," Braeden said, shaking his head. "You are out of your mind, son. Go get Haskins and Tracy out here, see if they want to sign."

"I thought you wanted me to repair this Ford?"

"You can't take ten seconds away to help me out here?" Braeden tossed back with a frown. Goddamned Tucker being a shitdick. He always was, but he'd never looked for an excuse to put down his wrench and fuck around before.

The sound of the ratcheting stopped for a second. "HASKINS! TRACY! Come on out here," Tucker's voice reverberated within the garage. "Braeden wants you to toss Sheriff Reeve out of office so we can all get fucked up by the shit tearing up this town quicker. Guess enough people ain't died yet or something—"

"Fuck you, Tucker," Braeden spat at him.

"Be a cold day in hell before I'm that desperate, Braeden."

"You just can't hire good help these days, can you?" Pike asked with a knowing smile.

Braeden seethed a little as he heard Haskins and Tracy coming out from the office. Tucker always was a pain in the ass, but this was a new low, doing it in front of Pike like this. "No, you can't," Braeden said. "You really can't."

*

Hendricks was almost back to the Sinbad, the sun hanging high overhead on a cloudless day, sky blue as Babe the Ox, and he was still pissed as hell in his stolen SUV. He had his hand hanging out the window a little as he came up on the freeway overpass, lost in his own thoughts, when he saw them.

There were three of them, dressed pretty funny, walking out of the diner. His first thought was demons, so he slowed the SUV, trying to get a better look as he cruised on up. They were walking along, looking like they were heading out to a car, a beat-up old thing that looked like it might have crept out of the seventies, one of those big-framed steel monstrosities Detroit used to make. It was big and grey and had rust spots all over, and Hendricks knew that fucking car just like he knew its fucking driver.

Hendricks jerked the wheel, cutting off a Volkswagen Golf that honked furiously at him as he hit the gravel parking lot of the diner at almost fifty. He adjusted the wheel to keep from sliding, but his move made enough noise that the triad walking toward the big damned car spun to look at him, and he whipped around so he could present his driver's side window to them as he came up.

"You're late, fuckers," Hendricks announced after he'd slid to a stop. "Just like every time."

"Fuck my mother, is that Cowboy Lafayette?" The leader spoke, a black man with a British accent, ducking his head down like that would help him peer into Hendricks's face. His accent was thick, heavy, and it didn't sound a goddamn thing like Dick Van Dyke in *Mary Poppins*.

"Is that Martin Lonsdale?" Hendricks fired back. The Brit sagged a little more; he liked being called Mart, Hendricks knew. He always called Hendricks Lafayette to be a giant, douchy Brit. One night in a bar he'd accused Hendricks of being French, and they'd had a hell of a tussle over it. It ended fair, no knives, swords, or guns pulled.

"Oh, that's how it is, is it?" Lonsdale said with something between irritation and a grin.

"You keep calling me a Frenchman, and see if I don't beat your ass again," Hendricks said.

"It was a Jaffa Cake, that one," Lonsdale said. "The last time you and I went 'round, I felt like I'd been skull-fucked by Ron Jeremy the next day."

"So you're saying you enjoyed it, then?" Hendricks asked.

"I forgot how much fun it is to be around you, Hendricks," Lonsdale said, smiling weakly. "Have you met my associates, Mr. Grass and Mr. Sky?"

Hendricks looked at the guys with Lonsdale. They were both medium height, medium build, brown-haired generic dudes. "What the hell, are you working with OOCs now?"

Lonsdale looked at both of them for a second, a little alarmed. "They're—no, they're not OOCs."

"I'm not an OOC," Grass said, frowning. He had an English accent, too.

"I don't even know what an OOC is," Sky said, with a blunt face that looked like he'd never had an expression in his life.

Lonsdale eased up to the car window. "They're not terribly bright, these boys," he whispered to Hendricks. "But they're Robin Hood in a spot of bother, they are."

"Where'd you come in from?" Hendricks asked, ignoring the parts of what Lonsdale said that he didn't understand, as usual.

"Eastern Washington, if you can believe it," Lonsdale said. "Spent the last six weeks in the high desert. I didn't even bloody know you had a desert in Washington. Thought it was all redwoods and rain, like England but with more of your tree huggers and the correspondingly larger trees for them to hug."

Hendricks let out a low guffaw. "Where were you before that?"

"Croatia," Lonsdale said. "What about you? Been here long?"

"Since early September, I think," Hendricks said, nodding.

"Seen any others of us?" Lonsdale asked.

Hendricks shook his head. "Only you, now. Everyone else was chasing other hotspots, I think."

"Well, they'll be rolling in now." Lonsdale rubbed his hands together. "Word's getting out. Plus, nine of the eighteen are burned out. I heard Tredegar is coming this way from Poland."

"Fuck," Hendricks said. Tredegar made a mess everywhere he went, and not quietly, either. "We need him around here like we need the rest of the town knocked down."

"Tell me about it," Lonsdale said in quiet agreement. "Next time we hoist a pint, remind me to tell you what happened with him when we crossed paths out in Missouri last year. I have never been so knackered, before or since." He stood up a little straighter. "So you've been here a while, then? All by yourself? What's it like?"

"One of the worst I've seen," Hendricks said. "This town is having a hard time catching a break. But we've been holding back the rolling brownouts so far."

"Oh, he went there, ladies and gentlemen," Lonsdale said with a laugh, looking back at Mr. Grass and Mr. Sky and seeing nothing but blank looks. He lowered his voice. "You can't tell a joke around this lot, either. They just stand there and guffaw if they know it's a joke, but they don't get it at all. It's terrible." He went back to speaking normally. "I suppose that's not a problem for you, though, Mr. 'I Work Alone.'"

"Time are changing," Hendricks said. "I've got a crew now."

"You're a Dunlop, mate," Lonsdale said, looking at him in studied disbelief.

"I never know exactly what you mean with that cockney bullshit, Lonsdale," Hendricks said, "but it's true. There's a local group that's been helping me hold back the night."

"Look at you, Cowboy Hendricks, assembling your posse." Lonsdale grinned. "You're like Shalako or something, you are."

"Again, I have no idea what that is," Hendricks said. Sounded like calico with a "sh" at the front.

"It's a classic western," Lonsdale said. "Very disappointed you wouldn't know it, being an American cowboy. My grandfather used to watch them on Sunday afternoons, with cold chocolate from the fridge in hand, and—"

"Been good catching up with you, Lonsdale," Hendricks said, tipping his hat to Grass and Sky behind the demon hunter.

"Wait, wait," Lonsdale said, holding up his hands. "How's the state of things here?"

Hendricks made a show of looking around the sun-drenched parking lot around the diner. "Bright, I'd say."

"The demon state, fucking git. You said it's bad a minute ago."

"Demons? They're here," Hendricks said simply, aiming for infuriating and pretty damned sure he'd hit his mark by the way Lonsdale's face fell. "Lots and lots of 'em."

"Well, I know that, too, you twat, as we managed to vape one just last night right over there." Lonsdale pointed to the edge of the highway. "Merkroth, I think."

Hendricks glanced back, realizing that was probably the call Reeve had got. No wonder that other deputy hadn't found anything; by the time he'd gotten his pudding ass moving, the demon was already in the atmosphere. "Merkroth, huh? Hadn't seen any of those around here yet."

"I'm not entirely certain I saw it now," Lonsdale said. "It ran like a little bitch at the sight of me and my boys." He puffed up with pride.

"If you ran it down on foot, it wasn't a merkroth," Hendricks said, glancing back.

"Doesn't matter," Lonsdale said. "Got a line on any others? We haven't quite made it into the town proper yet. Is there pandemonium in the streets?"

"Neither pan nor ium, but quite a few demons when the sun goes down," Hendricks said. "They're still lurking below the surface. We've turned back a few big moves that might have opened the season on their end. It's keeping a lid on things, letting it simmer." Hendricks had a sudden memory of his mother fixing food in a pressure cooker.

"So if I go strolling down the streets of this little hamlet, I'm not going to be confronting demons at every turn? Like that one village outside Amsterdam?"

"I don't think I was there for that one," Hendricks said. "How about that one in Wyoming, where—"

"Oh, yeah, I forgot about that. That was similarly bad," Lonsdale agreed. "Is it like that?"

"No, but they're here," Hendricks said. "Like I said, still in the shadows. You walk around at night, you'll see some warpaint."

"Well, I think the boys and me will go do a little looking 'round," Lonsdale said, brightening. "Get the lay of the land."

"There's also a whorehouse on Water Street, since I know by lay of the land you mean—"

"Oh, you are saucy James Hunt, Hendricks."

"Just trying to help," Hendricks said, adjusting his hat once more. "Stay out of trouble, Lonsdale."

"Why would I ever do that?" Lonsdale said with a grin as Hendricks pulled away from him. That was just a little too damned close to the truth, wasn't it?

Since when had a demon hunter ever avoided trouble? Hell, it was their reason for being here.

*

When the office cleared out, the only ones left were Reeve and Donna, and Reeve had to admit he liked it better that way. Arch and Erin were heading off on patrol, and he'd finally pushed Casey Meacham out the front door in the middle of a damned story. It hadn't been a good story, either; more like the kind that *Penthouse Letters* wouldn't have printed even if they had a hard kink issue. Not that Reeve had read that sort of material in years.

"It's quite a group you've got there," Donna said in the quiet bullpen as Reeve leaned against the edge of his door. He glanced at the white-faced clock hanging high on the wall, watched the minute hand tick over. "It's a good team, Nick."

"I didn't put 'em together," Reeve said.

"You hired Arch," Donna said. "Your predecessor wouldn't have done even that."

"And I've got cause to be glad of that now," Reeve said, coming off the doorframe and sauntering over to Erin's desk, where he pulled out the chair and sat. "A week ago I wouldn't have thought so, but here we are." He smiled wanly and widened his eyes. "Imagine where we'll be in another week."

"In a better place, I hope," Donna said.

"I'd settle for that bastard Hendricks going to a better place."

"That's not very Christian, Nick."

"I'm pretty lousy at that, lately," Reeve said. He furrowed his brow. "I wonder what happened to that reporter that came into town before the Rog'tausch busted through everything." Even thinking the name of that damned demon almost gave him reflux. He followed that train of thought down its track. "I can't believe they ain't got rid of that damned thing, yet." He idly felt the place where the giant demon had burned him on his arm. It was mostly healed, still a little tender.

"I'd settle for this recall election business to go by the wayside by next week," Donna said, thinking real hard.

"Yeah, that'd be mighty nice," Reeve said, folding his arms. "I'd settle for Pike not cutting the increased funding levels he promised me to staff up. I was all set to start paying these people, too."

"Money's not everything right now," Donna said gently.

"Only because Bill Longholt is paying the bills when we need something," Reeve said, getting a little sour. "I don't know where we'd be without him. Or Casey, come down to it. That little weasel may be sicker than shit when it comes to the stuff he's into, but without his bugs I don't know what we would have done with the pieces of that big demon bastard."

"Like I said, it's a good team." Donna smiled again and reached out to put her hand on his wrist. He got a little inkling of pity from her, and some of the relief ran out of him as he realized where it was stemming from.

Goddamn. Of all the things to feel sorry for him about ...

*

Arch pulled into the parking lot of the Methodist Church of Midian and killed the ignition, looking over at Alison. "You want to wait here or come in?"

"I'll wait," she said, pulling out her phone. "I was going into Rogerson's later to try and work, and I got a couple emails to catch up on."

"Okay," Arch said, stepping out of the Explorer and shutting the door behind him. He wasn't too worried about Alison fending for herself at the moment. It was a church parking lot in the middle of the day, the sun was bright overhead, and she not only had a Glock on her hip but she had a holy dagger she'd collected from Duchess Kitty on the other side of her belt. She'd put it to use a couple times that Arch had seen, too, and it gave him some comfort to know she had it.

He walked across the parking lot, gravel crunching under his feet. The church wasn't so wealthy that they had gone for a paved lot, not yet anyway. They were growing, albeit slowly. Barney Jones's preaching style was attracting some folk in, but Arch had heard the church elders do nothing but complain. They were all old, and his exuberance didn't quite fit with what they were looking for, which Arch presumed was a place to fall asleep on Sunday mornings.

He opened the enormous white front door of the church. The church was a big brick building, with a towering spire up top. Not a bell tower, because there wasn't a bell, but it was a lovely building. They'd had one before this that was a historical site with roots dating back to the Civil War. There was actually a bell, just not in the bell tower. The cord to pull it was hanging in the narthex where he stood, just to the right. Arch had pulled that bell a great many times as a child, almost all of them without permission.

"Arch Stan, as I live and breathe," Barney Jones said, catching sight of him from up on the pulpit. Jones looked like he was practicing for something, either a sermon a few days hence or a funeral, and it was hard to tell which it might be. Jones descended from the raised platform at the front of the church as Arch kept walking, through the big doors that separated the narthex from the sanctuary with its rows of pews. He and Jones met down the middle of the aisle that ran through the center, where the acolytes carried their brass candle lighters into the church to light the candles at the beginning of service. Arch had done that once upon a time. It had started fun and turned serious as time went on and he got more faithful. "What can I do for you, good sir?" Jones said, shaking his hand in a firm grip.

"I think you know I've been out of town for a bit," Arch said, looking the church over like it might have changed in the weeks he'd been gone. He had attended services every week he was able, unless he was working. Heck, he'd even gone to Wednesday nights most of the time, so long as he wasn't working. At least until Lafayette Hendricks had crossed the county line. "Just figured I'd stop in."

"Trying to assuage a guilty conscience?" Barney Jones had a twinkle in his eye, like he had a great joke in mind. "Being wrongly pursued by the law while chasing down demons is probably an excuse that the Almighty would accept for missing church for a few weeks, especially from you, Arch."

"Mmhmm," Arch said, not really putting any thought to it. "Well, I have missed this."

"I doubt you've missed an empty building," Jones said. "What you've missed is the fellowship."

Arch stumbled over that one for a second. "Of course." Jones was a clever man, always knew how to sneak one up on him.

"You didn't just come to make apologies for missing church while you were fighting demons and running, did you?" Barney asked, surveying him cannily, like he knew. "You got a guilty conscience about something, Archibald Stan?"

"I got something I'm working through my mind," Arch said, checking around them to make sure they were alone.

"Oh, this ought to be good," Jones said, beckoning him over to sit in one of the pews. "You've been out on the front lines of a fight against the devil's own. I can't wait to hear what's going on in your head right now."

Arch took a seat in the pew behind Pastor Jones, and the preacher turned around to look back at him. "I don't know how to say this," Arch realized after a moment of trying.

"Just say it."

"It ain't right," Arch said, looking away from Jones, "but before I found out about demons ... there was an empty feeling in me that ought not have been there. Not in relation to—to my daily prayers or anything, I mean I was—I was on—I was all right there, I think."

"You getting complacent?" After a pause, Jones brushed it off like he hadn't meant to say that. "Never mind. Keep going."

"It was my job," Arch said, struggling to find the words. "My marriage. We were trying for a baby, and, uh ... I mean, I knew, spiritually—or I thought I did—where I was going, what my place was. But as a lawman, I ... I felt like I was butting up against a great purposelessness." He looked the pastor in the eyes. "I was writing tickets and responding to accident scenes and ... doing what I thought I was supposed to be doing. But when the demons came to town—and I started to fight them—everything else clicked in place in a way it hadn't before. My prayers seemed more ... full of feeling when I'd thank God for his blessings. My love for my wife felt more real and genuine instead of being forced and stretched to try and fit the ... the boredom? I don't even know? The rut I was in?"

"You found your calling," Jones said, nodding. "That's a powerful thing. It's not usually a good sign when your life starts to get stale, Arch, not your marriage, not your job, not your prayer life ... it's all a symptom of something real wrong."

"I know that, and it bothered me for a long time," Arch said. "And when I was out there these last few weeks ... I didn't step foot here one time, but I prayed every day, and I felt more alive in my heart and in my faith than I can recall being in, well, a long time. I mean, I'm not saying I'm not coming back, I'm just saying—"

"I see what you're saying," Jones nodded his head, mock concern.

"You're saying my sermons aren't enough to push your stubborn butt through a whole week. That my one hour a week of trying to get your head right with the Lord isn't nearly enough to make sure it stays screwed on straight for the seven days before you come back and sit in these pews again. Well, Arch, there's a hundred and sixty-seven hours a week I don't have you in front of me, so, no, this isn't exactly a surprise. You're a faithful man and all, but if your head wasn't dwelling regularly in Scripture, then you're falling away from God." Jones made a clicking noise. "Far be it from me to lecture you about falling, especially after what you've seen lately."

"No sermon necessary there," Arch said. "I guess I just … I don't know if I realized how hollow I'd gotten. Things on the surface, they were … I was, I was doing all right, I thought—"

"If the center of the fruit is rotten, Arch, the whole fruit is rotten," Jones said. "And what you're telling me here is—you got rid of the rot. And that's a good thing. It's easy for a Christian to pat himself on the back and compare himself to the world, thinking he's doing all right. And that's the wrong message. The world is blighted, filled with people who cut themselves off from love. It's harsh sometimes, and there's a temptation to bend to that. Comparing yourself to the world is a recipe for heartbreak." Jones wagged a finger at him. "Don't you go comparing yourself to other people and thinking you're 'doing all right.' Ain't no perfect people left in this world, Arch. I guess I don't have to tell you that … but maybe I do. Maybe we all need a reminder sometimes." Jones smiled. "So … you going to be at church on Sunday?"

"So long as there ain't a demon attack taking place at nine on Sunday morning," Arch said, taking the cue to stand. He proffered a hand and Barney shook it, smiling at him genuinely all the while.

"Always an excuse," Jones said, giving him a poke as he headed back to the pulpit. "I'm talking to your sheriff later today, going to see what I can do to help y'all out." He paused. "He didn't get a chance to finish in the meeting last night, what with all the shouting … But it's going to get worse, huh?"

"Seems that way," Arch said.

"How bad? Pretend I ain't seen *Smokey and the Bandit 3*, because I haven't. Sensible folk would have stopped after *2*."

"Well, we've already nearly lost the town a few times," Arch said, starting to make his way back down the aisle. He glanced at the big cross hanging at the front of the room. "So ... pretty bad, I'd say."

Jones let out a whistle. "Reckon I ought to be praying harder, then. And working harder, too, if it's that bad."

"We could use both," Arch said with a nod as he passed back into the narthex on his way out the door. "We sure could use both."

*

Amanda Guthrie cracked the door and went out into the hotel's hallway, ice bucket in hand. She didn't really need ice, it not being much of a requirement for her, but she needed an excuse to wander the carpeted halls while she waited for the OOC to come back. And wander she did, up and down the hall, padding along in her bare feet, pressing against the hard floors, barely covered with the thin carpet. She wandered up to the ice machine near the elevator and then back again a few times, listening. Every time she heard the elevator ding she would turn and act like she was heading to the machine once more, waiting to see if the OOC was coming. Every time it had been a disappointment so far.

Until now.

She was halfway down the hall when she heard the ding, and she spun, trying to get around before whoever was arriving could get out of the elevator and see her. She'd taken some time on this, straightening her hair, making up her face. She'd fallen a little flat in dressing up, sticking with a tank top and sweatpants, but she figured that was what a person would wear when wandering around a hotel to get ice.

She saw him coming as soon as he stepped out of the elevator. His head was down; he didn't appear to be watching. She knew looks were very deceiving in this case, though, because OOCs were demons, and demons didn't have irises or lenses in their eyes that pointed in one direction. They could see the entirety of their field of vision, all at once, and this OOC was a senser, which meant he could detect things that others couldn't.

Of course, he couldn't detect her, and that was half the fun of doing this.

The OOC shuffled his way down the hall, wearing a t-shirt that said "Naked Prozac," whatever the hell that was, looking like he wasn't paying attention to a damned thing. He was, though, she knew.

"Morning," she said in greeting, all smooth and velvety.

The OOC raised his head to acknowledge her, just barely, with a grunt to go with it. It was the perfect response of someone who was trying not to be rude enough to garner notice but who didn't want to talk.

She debated whether or not to stop him now, as they passed. He steered wide around her, and she thought about just darting toward him, starting this thing off, but when the moment came, she let him go on. He didn't even look back. It wasn't as though he needed to. She did, but she wasn't sure if he noticed this time.

She'd come close to doing it this time. It had been hard not to, but she'd stopped herself at the last minute. This wasn't the time or the place. But the time and place would come, she thought as she ducked into the little alcove room with the ice machine. She could hear his door open and shut down the hall. Yeah, that time was coming fast.

*

If the administrative part of being sheriff of Calhoun County had been hell before demons rolled in, now it was enough to bury a full-sized bureaucracy, which Reeve did not have at hand. What he had was himself and three deputies, his wife, and some new auxiliaries, at least in the main station, which was where all the action seemed to be lately. He ran a hand over his bald head and it came back a little oily. He hadn't showered this morning, having woken up a little late. He'd shaved, though, as a concession to not looking like hell, for whatever good that would do him. With a mountain of paperwork as his present adversary, he had to concede that it wasn't going to do much.

The phone rang out in the bullpen, interrupting an otherwise quiet morning. Sun was shining in from the window behind him, and it had been a nice sort of quiet, the kind not filled with repeated 911 calls. He'd considered having the outsourced call center that was fielding at night right now take up the job all day long, but that was back when Pike was promising additional funds rather than an election to haul his ass out of office.

The ring that echoed in the bullpen was distinctive, and it told him that it was, in fact, a 911 call. Donna picked it up and he could hear her say, "911, what is your emergency?"

He waited, listening through the pause, hoping that when she replied, her voice wouldn't be absolute panic, the kind that denoted something really terrible. If he had his druthers, it'd be a heart attack or a crash on some winding road with no fatalities. Those he could deal with, and fairly easily. They sure beat the hell out of someone calling to say they found an entire family massacred in their own house or a hooker burnt up from the inside or one of his deputies dead on the side of the road with his neck stretched out like taffy.

"Uh huh," Donna said, and he could hear the frown in her voice without being able to see her face. She was outside and around the corner, with her back turned so that even if he'd had x-ray vision, he wouldn't have been able to see her face right now. "Well, we should be able to send someone out to check here in the next few minutes, Lyle. Thanks for calling." She hung up the phone with a click of the plastic receiver against the base.

"What was that?" He didn't wait for her to shout it out. He figured it was minor, but he was dying of curiosity.

"Lyle Schmidt," Donna said. "He said there's some kind of argument going on out on Fleer Street, a bunch of strangers he's never seen before, bickering around a brown panel van. Sounded like it was turning ugly."

Reeve got to his feet. Strangers in town? Now? Probably not tourists. "Start making some calls," he said, grabbing his coat off the back of his chair. "Might as well start getting everyone moving, because odds are this ain't going to be some innocuous thing, not with strangers involved."

"You are turning into quite the xenophobe," Donna said as he went past her, headed for the gap in the counter.

"You been calling me that ever since I told you I wasn't going to eat that raw fish you wanted me to try."

"It's called sushi, Nick, and it's really good."

"I prefer my fish cooked," Reeve said, pushing against the Plexiglas door. "Maybe some men don't, and that's their business, but I know what I like."

"I'd like you to be careful," Donna called after him, sounding awfully hopeful.

"I'd like that, too," Reeve said as he headed across the parking lot to Reyes's old car. "I'd like that real well."

*

Chester had finally roused William into some form of speaking and action after about nine. It hadn't been easy, and he recognized the surliness present in William as a sort of long-held resentment that bubbled to the surface every now and again. Chester knew that its source was in William's constituency, though; those voices were as loud as his own, perhaps louder even, but William was more passionate, more given to going in the direction his people suggested. Chester considered himself a bulwark; his role was careful action and diligence even when a course appeared clear. Long experience had taught him that seldom were things as simple as they seemed.

"I need fresh air," William had insisted as soon as they'd gotten up, and Chester had gone because it was necessary. He felt in a mood to appease his counterpart, to give him a breath of morning. The mornings in Queens of late had lacked the peaceful tranquility he expected they would find here in Tennessee. Too many noises, too many cars, too many people. That city had become a cacophony of its own, less a suburb than it used to be.

They slid open the panel van's side door, and together drew a deep breath of the quiet air. Here there were fewer noises. The sound of cars in the distance was still present, of course, but not nearly as loud as where they had lived in Queens.

"Nothing like a change of scenery," William said into the morning quiet. It was hardly early; the sun was already high in the sky. In truth, Chester could have remained in quiet in the van for considerably longer, but not with William ignoring him. That was a sort of pox of its own, and one he did not care for. Silence of mutual, respectful accord was one thing. The silence resulting from a bitter argument was quite another, and one Chester was eager to put behind them. All of them, he hoped.

"It is an altogether pleasant experience for the constitution," Chester agreed.

A squeal of tires on pavement halted their conversation. They turned their head and looked down the street; an SUV was stopped in the middle of the main road just down the way. When they had parked, they had searched for a side street, and had pulled off it only a hundred yards or so. Back on that main road, the SUV reversed, then went into gear again and headed toward them, speeding up as it came their way.

"What is this?" Chester asked, peering through his eye at the oncoming car.

William answered with that mix of resentment and anger that was becoming all too familiar from him. "Demon hunters."

*

Hendricks was in the SUV inside of a minute of his motel phone ringing, heading toward Fleer Street, though he wasn't exactly sure where that was. He'd gotten the general description from Arch, that it was somewhere off the Jackson Highway, and it was only five minutes or so from him, and he figured that was all he'd need. Besides, the sheriff, Arch, and Alison were already on their way, with Erin and some of the others gearing up in case shit went down. Hendricks figured that was enough for daylight hours. How bad could it be, after all?

*

"Well, lookee what we've got 'ere," the dark-skinned man said in a British accent that, to Chester's ears, sounded terribly unsophisticated. "I think this is a demon, it is."

There were two others with him, both squat creatures that reminded Chester of pit bulls following a master. "I think you are mistaken," Chester managed to get out.

"I suspect it's been a long time since this piece of lumbtwaa has had an actual thought of his own," William said, and the anger was audible in his voice.

The demon hunter's eyes widened, and he took a step back. "Did you 'ear that?" He seemed to be speaking to his two associates. "That was two separate voices, it was."

"I suppose you would have to 'ear' it,'" Chester said dryly. "As your entire race seems incapable of listening beyond the sound of things."

"Think that's funny, do you?" the demon hunter asked, his good humor disappearing. "I knew da moment I laid my mince pies on you that you weren't normal for around here. I got a nose for these things, don't I?"

"Ears, eyes, nose, yes, you have them all," William said dryly. "But not for much longer unless you take a pass at us." He waved his hand at the demon hunter.

"You have never faced our sort before, old boy," Chester said, trying to step up and defuse the situation before it escalated into violence, which he did not care for. Why, the last time they'd had to take a life had been over a hundred years ago, in that cave, when that other excavator had tried to shoot them. "We mean you no harm, but if you intend to visit it upon us, you will end up regretting it."

"More than you know," William vowed, and there was something about the way he said it that set Chester's side of the stomach to churning.

"Well, see, 'ere's how it is, boys, girls, whoever's in there," the demon hunter said. "My name's Mart Lonsdale, and I've got a reputation."

"Do you?" William asked. "Can't say I've heard of you."

"I don't let demons walk away," Lonsdale said, smirking. "Dat's why you've never 'eard of me."

"And I thought it was because you were an inconsequential sort of gnat," William said, adding, in Chester's opinion, unnecessary fuel to the fire.

"There is no need for this to become a fight," Chester said, putting his own hand up. William, however did not raise his. "You are, I presume, here to keep the dangerous elements in check in this hotspot, and I do not begrudge you nor any of your sort that right. I, am, however, entirely peaceful unless provoked, as you can tell by the fact that I have yet to show you my true face nor attacked you in spite of your provocation."

"That's a bit of a head scratcher," Lonsdale said. "I just assumed it was because you were a Frankie Howerd."

"That we are … a comedian?" Chester asked.

"Oh, for fuck's sake," Lonsdale muttered. "That you were yellow of the belly. Chicken, you see."

"We are restrained in the face of stupidity that is now bordering on incredible folly," William said.

"Your appended labels are of little consequence to us," Chester said, trying to speak reason in this. "You may think what you wish; we mean no harm to others unless they intend harm upon us—"

"Well, lad," Lonsdale, said, drawing what was surely a holy blade out of his coat as the two behind him did the same, "I am here to tell you ... harm is intended."

"You fool," Chester whispered.

"Now it is settled," William said, and there was a hint of triumph in his voice. "Shall we, Chester?"

With nothing but regret, Chester had to agree. "Yes. We shall."

*

"What do you think it is?" Alison asked as Arch kept a lead foot on the gas pedal, sirens blaring as they shot down Old Jackson Highway. The sun was in his eyes but not too bad, just a general overhead glare that was outside the reach of the visors above him.

Arch pondered his response as the heavy heat blew out of the vents right in his face, drying his already parched sinuses. That was the problem with fall and winter for him. "I don't know. Could just be strangers picking a bad time to get in a scuffle."

"You don't believe that." She sounded so sure.

"I really don't," Arch agreed, subtly adding a little more pressure to the gas in hopes that he could get to the answer just a little quicker.

*

Chester abhorred violence, finding it just a step above the feral savagery of animals. If they were meant to do things this way, then what was the point of civilization? What was the point of all those years of climbing out of the mud, of going from using stone tools to build things and defend against wild predators to creating a civilized society with electricity and factories and progress if the desire to violently harm others was still the first resort?

He knew for a fact that this demon hunter and his ghoulish associates meant both he and William and all their many fellows harm. The leering, the drawn sword proved it beyond a doubt, and inspired a sense of caution in him that William apparently did not feel. To split their efforts was not simply foolhardy in this case; it would be suicidal.

Although they had inhabited this human body for the last century and more, Chester was acutely aware that a holy blade applied to the flesh could still drive them out in exactly the same manner as any of their shelled brethren. A cut to the arm, and they would, all of them, be dragged back to the bowels of darkness and fire.

Not there! came thousands, millions of voices within. Chester heard them, a unified chorus, and he knew William heard them from his as well. It was a raging uproar, the fury of their entire constituency given voice, and Chester had no wish to disappoint any of them, even those he found personally irritating.

"You're not going to fight me on this?" William asked, steeling them both.

"Oh, I'm going to fight you," Lonsdale said, stepping forward. "Make no mistake. I'm gonna end you—"

"Do as necessary," Chester said, and they sprang into motion, William at the helm.

The demon hunter Lonsdale did not see them coming; he had his sword raised in a pathetic guard, low and ill-suited to anything but someone jumping and impaling themselves upon it. William had learned swordcraft in its early days. Chester had lost his taste for such fighting after the Battle of Hastings, before they'd been imprisoned in the vase. He knew how to move, how to fight, but leaving it to William ensured a continuity, allowing him to fully control every function, every maneuver. And as William slapped aside the ill-placed sword and jabbed Lonsdale in the throat hard enough to stun the man and set him choking, Chester felt assured his decision was right.

The other two seemed taken aback by the suddenness of the attack. William did not leave them long to form that impression. Chester watched as William struck the first in the throat, but harder than he had Lonsdale. This time, there was a distinct sound of cartilage failing under pressure. He slapped away the demon hunter's blade and shoved the dying man to the ground to meet his fate.

The last of the trio managed to spur himself into action while William was dealing with the second. He came in with a low thrust, the sword gleaming in the sunlight, shining with danger on its holy edges. William spun like a dancer, moving inside the demon hunter's defense and well past the point where the blade would be able to harm him. He lashed out with a hard palm strike to the hunter's forehead, and the snapping vertebra echoed over the cold morning.

The last demon hunter's eyes died, rolling back in his head as he lost all bodily control. William whirled to a stop, taking a deep breath. Their body was tired; the sudden exertion of demon power through human flesh always took a toll. Chester kept mute, watching in some small amazement; William had dealt with all three within five seconds.

"You didn't have to kill those two, you know," Chester said quietly.

"They weren't the sort to leave us alone after a simple thrashing," William said, breathing hard, breath fogging the cool morning air.

Chester could not deny the likely truth of this. "Then why leave the last alive?"

William's answer, when it came, was pained, as they both stared down at the felled demon hunter, on all fours, his sword knocked aside. Lonsdale was choking, trying to get his breath after the hard strike to his neck. "Because I'm not done with him yet."

"No, William," Chester said, reasserting his control over his half of the body. "We will not stoop to torture."

"I didn't intend torture of any sort," William said, his anger rising. "And I tell you this for the last time—my name is Bill now."

Chester's slow curiosity suddenly gave way to a stark sense of terror. It alerted the other voices, his constituency, who had descended to revelry after the battle was won. "William ... Bill ... what do you mean to—"

But the answer came more quickly than Chester could ask the question, for William dragged him down with all the strength of his half of the body—and seized the demon hunter Lonsdale by the ankle.

*

Arch turned onto Fleer Street and saw Hendricks coming up over the hill a quarter mile away, heading toward him fast. The cowboy looked like he'd be getting to the scene about thirty seconds behind them, and that suited Arch just fine. He reckoned Reeve wouldn't be too far behind, which was another reassurance.

Fleer Street was a mostly residential street in the older part of Midian. The houses had a mishmash feel to them, some from back in the antebellum days, maybe, others from the 1900s sometime. It was hard to tell which was which, because he knew at least one of the houses on the block was new yet constructed in a very gothic style, with high gables and a turret.

"Right there," Alison said, pointing through the windshield at the van parked on the side of the road. There were four guys littered around it, only one of them standing, and he was all leaned over grabbing another one, who was holding a sword and screaming to the heavens like he'd just gotten kicked in the nuts.

*

"Don't do this, William," Chester said, but he already knew in the moment that it was too late. Pain surged down his hand and suddenly Chester found himself utterly in control of the body that they'd shared for the last century and more. He stared down at the demon hunter's bared ankle, and considered throwing himself down into it as well, following William on to his new digs, but—

William, taking over Lonsdale's body, kicked loose of his grip and got to his feet, the sword in hand. "I know you would have preferred to keep going as we were, Chester … but really, we've reached a parting of the ways. Somebody had to leave."

"I don't believe that for a second, William," Chester said, then, lowering his voice, wounded, said, "Bill."

"It took us leaving for you to remember that," Bill said with a faint smile. "Chester … we want different things. Now you can go back to Queens. Your lot can have things your way, and we can have things ours. No more bones of contention, no more argument and anger."

"No more of each other, either," Chester said, staring in muted shock at him. "We've been together for tens of thousands of years, the whole lot of us … to just … cast it asunder like that without even saying—"

"You weren't listening," Bill said, still smiling faintly. "We've been talking about this for years. You had things your way for a long time, and now that we've finally managed to move along somewhat, to stir you out of this rut and make progress, we realize that your hearts aren't in it." He lowered his voice. "Go home, Chester. All of you. You never wanted to be here to begin with. You wanted a nice, quiet life, with—"

Squealing tires interrupted them, forcing them both to look up as a police SUV came bouncing up, mounting the curb. The door flew open and a black man came out in a rush. "Nobody move!" he called.

*

Reeve saw Hendricks turn onto Fleer Street just ahead of him, and sped up a little on the turn, causing his tires to screech in protest at the bare hold on the asphalt blacktop. Reeve didn't like to drive this fast, even with his lights on, but in this case he didn't want to leave his people high and dry without backup, either. He knew Arch was likely first on scene, and that was confirmed when he finished his tight turn, the Explorer he'd given back to the man parked up on a lawn. He couldn't see much of anything else, though, between the Explorer and Hendricks's SUV, so he just hurried on up behind the cowboy.

*

Chester watched the new arrivals with a rising sense of frustration that felt like a welling tide within. There was an anger burning at him like the wind when it whipped through, chilly and raw. He stared at the back of William's new head, where he'd taken over Lonsdale's body. The hair was different than his own, curlier by far, and Chester felt an urge to reach out, to expel himself and the others with him into it, unasked. It felt wrong to be without William and his lot, even though Chester disagreed, most violently, with almost every decision they thought right.

"Just keep it cool!" the lawman shouted, his khaki uniform a garish display against the black and white police SUV. When he came out from behind the car door, Chester saw the sword hanging on his belt, and it took his breath away.

"William," Chester said.

"There's no need for violence, officer," William said, dangling the sword gently from his fingertips, letting it hang down as though ready to surrender it, "I mean you no harm."

"Is that so?" the lawman asked. Chester could see his nameplate from here, and it said STAN in etched letters along its front. "Then drop the sword, lace your fingers, and place them atop your head."

"As you wish," William said, and Chester knew in that moment that he was lying to buy time, "sir." He dropped the blade and it plunged an inch or two into the soft grass and stood there, tilted just a bit.

"On your knees," Deputy Stan said, advancing from behind his car door. Chester already had his hands up and was unarmed. He started to sink to his own knees, worry about what William planned to do enveloping him. Either one of them, acting alone, could remove this deputy from being any sort of problem. Chester had a sneaking suspicion that William intended just that, but Chester felt frozen in place, unable to move or cry out.

William got down on his knees and laced his hands behind his head as another car came screaming up, and another still. Men poured out of them, and for the first Chester realized a woman had arrived with Deputy Stan. She had been standing behind the hood of his SUV quietly the entire time, a gun drawn and covering them both.

*

Alison got the feeling something was real wrong with these guys from the jump, but she didn't have much to say about it until Arch started to advance on them, gun in one hand and the other hovering over his blade. "Arch!" she said, loud enough and commanding enough that he stopped, but didn't take his eyes off them to look at her. "Just hang on. Hendricks and Reeve are pulling up."

"All right," Arch said. Her husband was a real terse man, but he got a lot across in those two words, and the message she got out of them was, *Yep, best to wait, you're right.*

"What the fuck is going on here?" Reeve shouted out over the scene. He'd parked on the other side of the panel van, out in the middle of Fleer Street, cutting the non-existent flow of traffic and circling around the front of the van to come up behind the two guys left standing. Alison hadn't gotten a real clear look at the two that were down, but she knew by the tongue hanging out that at least one of them was dead as a barbecued pig.

"The hell are you doing, Lonsdale?" Hendricks asked, coming around the Explorer behind Arch.

"You know this guy?" Arch asked, keeping his distance from the two suspects.

"Yeah, this is Mart Lonsdale," Hendricks said, nodding at the black guy up front. "He's a demon hunter."

"Explains the sword," Reeve tossed in from where he stood behind the suspects. "Doesn't explain the corpses, though, does it?"

*

Chester was feeling the strains of panic. He and William were both on their knees, clearly somewhat at the mercy of a police department armed with what was almost certainly anti-demon weaponry. "Officers," Chester said, hoping desperately to explain, "we mean you no harm."

"That's a lovely sentiment," said the man coming up behind him. Chester looked back and caught a glimpse of his nameplate, which read REEVE.

Chester's mind raced, the voices within him screaming suggestions so loudly that he could not concentrate on any one of them, or indeed, even his own mind to form an idea. *We came here at the behest of our brethren to find a peaceful life*, Chester said within, trying to quell the dissension. "Please," he said aloud. "There is no need for violence."

"Come along with us peacefully and there won't be," the man named Reeve said from behind him. "We're going to have to take you back to the jail, though, and you're going to have to do some explaining about these dead men here."

"That will be just fine," Chester said, offering his hands. "Won't that be just fine, Bill?"

"Who the hell is Bill?" the cowboy asked.

"You want to put us in your jail?" William asked quietly, his hands still fastened atop his head. "To ... imprison us? To keep us from our freedom?"

"That's generally what happens when you murder someone, yes," Reeve said.

"We did not come looking for this fight," Chester said, the strain building within. He could hear the desperation, closer to action, with William, and feared for where the emotion might lead him. "These men attacked us."

"Well, we'll sort it all out," Reeve said, advancing on him. It had the air of a promise, and the sound of the handcuff clicking closed on his wrist, the cold bite of the metal against Chester's flesh, was the promise fulfilled. "Down at the station." He pulled Chester's hand down and clicked the other cuff in place behind him, and Chester let him willingly.

"Something is not right here," the cowboy mumbled. "Lonsdale's talking funnier than usual."

"Who the fuck is Lonsdale?" Reeve asked, his voice right in Chester's ear.

"Him," Hendricks said, pointing right at William's new host body. "He talks in this Cockney accent, always saying shit you couldn't understand if you had a damned dictionary handy."

"Something is not right here," the woman covering them with the gun agreed.

"You mean to deprive us of our freedom," William said and started to rise to his feet. "That is what is wrong here."

"That's not a Cockney accent," Reeve said. "More like a Queen of England type, but with a drawl—"

"I know, that's what I'm saying," the cowboy spoke with measured irritation.

"Get back on your knees," Deputy Stan warned, keeping his pistol up, matching it to aim at William.

"Let's get out of the firing line," Reeve said and jerked Chester back toward the front of the van.

"Bill, don't do anything foolish," Chester warned, letting himself be led backward. "This is a temporary situation—"

But William was not listening. He started to move, and it took no more than a lurching step forward before a gunshot rang out and William staggered from the impact of a bullet.

"No!" Chester said, but he knew it was far, far too late.

*

Alison fired as soon as she saw that peckerwood move. Friend of Hendricks or not, she knew something was whacked about this guy, and when he took a bullet to the chest without falling down, it just confirmed it for her. She stroked the Glock's trigger twice more in rapid succession and watched this Lonsdale guy jerk a couple times, like he'd had a finger stuck up his ass by surprise maybe, but he didn't slump and he didn't fall down, and to her, that was a real bad sign.

*

"We got a demon!" Arch crowed, holstering his gun after Alison's third shot failed to drop this Lonsdale guy. It wasn't just that, though, it was the fact that the man's eyes turned yellow in a flash of anger, and there was a subtle ripple across his face that told Arch everything he needed to know about what lay beneath the surface of this Lonsdale's skin.

*

"Bill!" Chester shouted as he was dragged back around the front of the van—their van, his and William's. His voice sounded unduly harsh and high, ringing out over the quiet suburban street. The lawns were green and wide, rolling, no fences between the houses.

It was peaceful.

Idyllic.

This was why William had wanted to come here, because it was the opposite of Queens, where everything was tightly packed, where people nearly stumbled over one another, where the houses were close enough to touch between them and the streets were crowded.

Chester resisted the pull of Reeve against his handcuffs, even without leverage. He yanked himself free of the man's grip and came around the side of the van in time to see what happened.

*

Hendricks wasn't going to let Lonsdale, however hopped up or fucked up or whatever he was take a run at Arch, not a chance. He was already moving as the guy came forward again, but Alison was acting, too, blasting Lonsdale with shot after shot that had no effect on the man other than to stagger him, rip his clothing, and start bringing a demon face to the surface.

Hendricks had known Lonsdale in passing for a long fucking time, and of all the things he might have guessed about that shithead Brit, demon would not have been among them. He'd never shown demon face, not ever, not even the time they'd battled it out hand to hand. And if ever there'd been a time for Lonsdale to show himself, that would have been it, especially since Hendricks had beat the living hell out of him.

Lonsdale lunged through the gunfire, his face totally consumed by enormous, jagged demon teeth and yellow eyes now, the feral look of a predator appearing as the skin blurred away. The fury of what lay beneath came to the surface, and Hendricks damned near shat a brick. He'd never seen a face quite like that before, and the fact that the bullet holes made by Alison in the man's clothes were swirling with the same kind of flesh-toned rippling was something else new to him.

Lonsdale came in fast, and Arch didn't even have his sword out yet. Lonsdale was going to catch him flat-footed, with the big man still trying to holster his pistol and draw his other weapon, the one more applicable to this current fight.

Hendricks was ready, though, as Lonsdale came flying at Arch, and although the bastard was moving at demon speed, he was still charging forward, and there was only one thing to be done for it.

Hendricks thrust his sword past Arch, aiming hard for Lonsdale as the man came surging ahead. Lonsdale was fast, but he was enraged, focused on the nearest target, Arch, and the sword clipped him neatly across the wrist as he came in with a hard swipe.

It was like the moment went to slow motion and took on a life of its own. Hendricks could smell the sweat, the stress, from where he stood a foot or so behind Arch's left shoulder. The sun was up but it was fucking useless at dispelling the autumn chill in the air, as Hendricks planted his free hand on Arch's shoulder to yank the man back while he tried to thrust forward and stop the attack.

A grunt came hard from in front of him, and Hendricks couldn't tell whether it was from Lonsdale or Arch as he made his move. Could have been either, a deep, throaty sound. Hendricks pushed the sword forward but it caught on something, hit something, bounced a little to the side—

And suddenly everything was happening at once again. Arch stumbled back with Hendricks, knocking him off balance with his superior height and much heavier weight. Hendricks tried to maintain his footing but failed; he'd put too much into thrusting the sword with one hand and yanking on Arch with the other, and he spilled over onto his ass, hitting the ground and rolling, pain stinging him through his coat on his right elbow and his left asscheek, cool grass stroking his face as his hat fell in front of his eyes.

By the time he got the hat off, he found Lonsdale on his knees in front of him ... and then he saw something he'd damned sure never seen before.

*

Chester stood in silence as William surged forward on the attack. Bullets did not stop him, as Chester knew they would not. They bounced off the demonic alteration to his flesh like rubber pellets off the side of a house. Chester blanched at the sound of the shots. Each one was like a slap upon his own jaw, though he knew they would do no harm to William, the sound of each crack still caused him almost physical pain.

The smell of grass, of the rubber from the tires that had burned upon the pavement as the cars had squealed up to the scene, all of those were present, filtering their way into Chester's consciousness, burning themselves into his memory. There was a faint prickling on his skin as the breeze stirred his hair ...

And William charged forward into the cowboy and deputy Stan.

Chester couldn't see terribly well from in front of the van; its size obscured his view of the developing situation. William was nearly to the back, not far from the Explorer with the sheriff's markings on the side. His back was turned and he was charging them down. It all unfolded so quickly and yet so slowly.

A hard tug on Chester's handcuffs sent a shock of pain surging through his wrists. "Get back here!" the man named Reeve barked in his ear as he jerked him away from even watching the unfolding conflict.

Chester did not obey, panic beating its drum in his essence, throbbing through him. Handcuffs were nothing but metal, at a thickness meant for holding humans. Whatever body he and his brethren might have inhabited at the moment, Chester was far from human, and so when he twisted on the cuffs, they tore as easily as if they had been constructed out of cooked pasta.

He broke free and started a charge around the van's hood, which jutted slightly from the front passenger compartment. It was less than a plan, more than instinct. He would get to William, and together they would fight their way out of this—carefully, without harming these men or the woman. They could take the bullets, could dodge the swords. There was no need to reprise the deaths of the two demon hunters. They could knock all of these people out and escape in the van, or even flee on foot and they would not be caught.

They would go north, or south, or in whatever direction that William wanted. Chester did not care anymore. Queens and the factory and where they lived were a distant memory already. The wide yards and open spaces of the road and of this place had convinced him. Or perhaps William had convinced him. Either way, he did not want to stay here but he would go wherever William and his brethren wanted to go. Chester could hear the other voices, alarmed, diminished by the fearful thoughts of what was happening, of the disappearance of so many of their fellows in the space of a heartbeat.

He was past the hood when he saw it happen. It was a subtle thing, a stirring in the air. It did not remain subtle, however, and it took only a second to reach that higher level. A howling rose out of William's new mouth, pain and fear that jarred a chord in Chester's soul. It was the sound of agony, of terror, and it frightened Chester in a way that nothing had in many millennia.

William looked back over his shoulder with a hard jerk, and the terror present in his cry was right there, for the reading, in his eyes. They were the true eyes, not the ones of his human host, the eyes that Chester had known from so many conversations. The fear the sight of those emotions in them stirred was like nothing that Chester could remember since the days before they entered their imprisonment in the vase.

"Chester!" William screamed, his voice fading already as the eyes swirled with yellow light, suddenly replaced by black, swirling darkness sweeping through.

Chester stumbled as William reached out, an outstretched hand grasping for Chester, a storm of dark twisting around him. "WILLIAM!" Chester shouted, lunging forward on hands and knees, trying to reach him before—

The black fire disappeared within a second, William's yellow eyes replaced by the human Lonsdale's brown ones. William's voice faded into a bleating cough as the demon hunter sagged.

And the outstretched hands missed each other by inches as William's essence, and all those precious essences of his brethren were dragged away from Chester and his own, the silence following as raw and painful to Chester as the sound of William's last scream.

*

Arch saw something he'd never quite seen before as he came back up from where Hendricks had pulled him out of the way of that charging demon. He saw a demon ripped plainly right back to hell while the body he was in stayed just where it was. "What the dickens was that?" Arch asked, getting back to his feet.

"Fuck," said Hendricks picking himself up and dusting off. "What the *fuck* was that?"

"You say it your way, I'll say it mine," Arch said, glancing down at the man in front of him, who looked like he was shrugging off one heck of a headache.

"I think it was a demon leaving a human body," Hendricks said. "Lonsdale, you in there?"

"Oh," the man called Lonsdale grunted, sounding far different than he had before, "you know how before, I said last time we tangled, I felt like Ron Jeremy skull-fucked me?" He brought up a hand with a prominent cut across its back where Hendricks had caught him with the sword. "Well, now I really feel that way, except it's also true of my kingdom come."

"Your ... what?" Arch asked.

"That's Lonsdale, all right," Hendricks said. "I think he might have been possessed."

"What the fuck does that mean?" This came from Reeve, who was standing just behind the other guy who'd been involved in the altercation. Arch hadn't looked too hard at him before, because he'd been quiet and followed commands, but now he was just sitting on his knees, looking like he was in a state of real shock.

"I *was* fucking possessed," Lonsdale said. "And not nicely, either, like say a pretty voice in your ear talking dirty to you about sucking your Blackpool Rock. It was like a thousand harpies shrieking in my head."

"What's a Blackpool Rock?" Reeve asked, exasperated. "What the hell is this guy talking about?"

"Later," Hendricks said, and pointed at the other guy, the one that was left alive. "We got a survivor."

Arch looked at the guy; he was on the short side, heavily tanned, and a little stocky. "Hey," Arch said, barking the command as he went for his sword. The guy looked dazed, staring at Lonsdale the demon hunter prostrate on the ground like he was about to cry over him. "You need to put your hands back behind your head and—"

He stopped mid-sentence, because he realized that the guy he was talking to, that was looking so longingly at Lonsdale, had broken handcuffs still hanging from his wrists, the chains dangling and catching the sun's light as they hung there.

*

Chester was not prone to sentiment. Not now, not ever. But he could feel the strange tear at his heartstrings, something William—Bill, he would have to remember—accused him of not even having. Yet he felt those heartstrings, in that moment, that tear at his chest, that hole where it felt as though something very great had been torn out. He took a hard breath, and another. There was a low buzz around him, as though a bee had wandered through this wide-open neighborhood with its rolling lawns and glistening blades of grass, still wet with dew.

"—you need to put your hands up," the man named Reeve said behind him, and he ignored it. Words broke through as he remembered—remembered William. Bill.

"That's a demon, he broke those handcuffs like they were nothing."

The vase that had been hell for William had been perfect for him. Chester could adapt; William couldn't, even though he professed the opposite. William's rigidity to circumstance had been all the more ironic given how hard he tried to push for change. But inevitably, when it happened—

"He's just standing there, not doing a damned thing."

—he was always left standing there, wondering how to adapt. The time they'd been discovered in Hutchinson, Kansas, found out in the dead of night by a group of home invaders, Chester had been moving in an instant after they'd scared the bastards off with a solid beating or two. William had been left clinging to the uncertainty, to their rental house, even though he had been steadfastly pushing to leave for six years—

"I bet that doesn't last long."

—and now he was in the pits, surely, he and all of his raucous, aggravating, hypocritical, loud-voiced, push-for-change-but-scream-like-children-when-it-came-time-to-cope-with-it followers, burning with the rest of those sent back.

"Sir, please place your hands behind your head."

William was not coming back.

"You really think that's going to work? He's a demon."

William was in torment.

"Fine, let's just vape this bastard and be done with it."

Forever.

"Do you know what you have done?" Chester asked quietly. The sound of footsteps behind him paused as he spoke. "Do you have any idea?" His voice was hushed and muted, quiet in the day, the sound of a car passing by on the main road the only noise.

"Sir," Reeve said from behind him, "you need to get down on your knees and cross your hands behind your head before this gets out of control—"

"This is already out of control," Chester said, the heat of anger bubbling up as he imagined William and his brethren, burning in anguish. "Out of your control. But not out of mine."

"He's gonna—" Deputy Stan started to say.

Chester slung a hand backward clumsily. He knew the man named Reeve was behind him, could hear him breathing. He hit him squarely in the chest and the lawman was flung backward. He landed with a hard "Oof!" on the lawn, and Chester felt the rich satisfaction of knowing that he'd transferred some of the pain coursing through him into someone else.

"Shit," the cowboy said.

"Shit is what you say when you crash your car and damage the fender," Chester said, looking up at the demon hunters before him. They'd done something so vile, so horrible, so objectionable—he needed to kill them. "They have not invented a curse in your pathetic bug languages that expresses what horror you have just visited upon this place, upon ... William."

The cowboy and the black lawman both had their swords out and were splitting from each other, both preparing to circle around him. Chester knew that the third, Reeve, was probably out of the fight for now, but he was surely armed, as was the woman still covering behind the car, her pistol aimed at him. They could not stop him, but they could slow him enough to keep him from ripping the skin from the demon hunters.

And keep him from avenging William before he joined him.

"This doesn't have to get any worse," Deputy Stan said.

Chester fixed on him, staring him down, etching every line of his face down into memory. He heard the angry barks of his constituents, furious, wanting to rip this man apart in a way they had not ever.

"This cannot get any worse," Chester said simply.

"I don't know if I'd agree with that," the cowboy said.

Chester stared at the cowboy. He had always regarded the humans they lived among as peculiar and often tragic figures. They could not know the joy of the collective; isolated, alone, there was a wide gulf between them and even their supposedly closest compatriots. Chester and William had argued it most vociferously, Chester taking the perspective that it was a difficult challenge to overcome in order to remain as functional as these people were and to build such an advanced society in spite of this handicap; William had not lacked admiration for humans, at least not at first; but he had spun from adoring the way they overcame their shortcomings to becoming jaded and angrier with them as the centuries rolled on.

The one thing that living among humans and learning from them had taught Chester was that much like their saying about babes' mouths, some occasional wisdom could be drawn from their words.

He stared at the cowboy, pondering the thought spewed forth from the man, and it was as though someone had replaced a missing gear in the machine of Chester's mind. "Of course it can get worse," Chester said, thinking aloud. "For you. And it *should* get worse. So ... very much ... worse."

William and his fellows were in unspeakable torment, and would be for all eternity. Reciprocity—justice—demanded a similar price be exacted, as best as it could, from those responsible for his agony.

"I don't much care for the sound of that," Deputy Stan said as they inched closer to Chester.

Chester shot a look toward the van that he and William had shared. If he fought his way through them and took it, it would give these lawmen something to look for, an identifying mark to focus their search on. It was baggage, of a sort, and he didn't need it anymore. He could run faster than the van could carry him over these streets, and all that was left for him was the sentiment, the memories of William that remained with it. His decision was made with startling speed and practicality. William would have labored with it, but Chester did not.

"You will not much care for the sound of your own screams, either, especially by the end," Chester said. There was fury in his voice, but he tempered it with cold as he considered the voices within, agitating for vengeance. He had a better plan, though, or at least one that would guarantee that these bastards suffered as they should for William's fate.

"Uh-oh," the cowboy said.

"You have made an enemy today," Chester said, "and when you look back on this moment ... remember that it was your failings that drove us to this inescapable moment of destiny, for I would have been content to leave this place in peace. But you have done me grievous harm, and that ... I cannot merely let pass."

With that, Chester leapt into the air, using his full strength for the first time in a century, and landed atop a nearby house. Another leap carried him farther away, and the sound of gunshots behind him ceased quickly as he left his new enemies far behind him—for now.

*

"Goddammit," Hendricks said, watching the demon leap out of sight, going up in a hard jump as Alison's pistol barked one last time and then fell silent. He sheathed his sword, pretty sure that this guy, whoever he was, wasn't doubling back right away.

"Did that sound particularly ominous to anyone else?" Arch asked, still gripping his sword. He had the blade gripped so tight that the tip was wavering back and forth as he stared off into the sky, toward the horizon where the trouble had fled.

"Yep," Alison said, coming out from behind the Explorer's hood. Hendricks watched her step past Lonsdale, who was still grunting lightly on the ground, to head for Reeve, who was doing some grunting of his own, flat on his back. "It sounds bad."

"Shit," Hendricks said, bowing his head. "Well, Arch, I think you better get on the horn to Mrs. Reeve. Might want to tell her to assemble the watch because I'm guessing this new guy in town—he ain't the sort that's just going to duck out after making a vow like *that*."

4.

Lauren was pulling up to Red Cedar Medical Center in Chattanooga, her place of work, when the phone rang. It jangled discordantly through the car, causing her to cringe and let off the brake a little too much. Her front tires bumped the block at the front of the parking space, jarring her as she fumbled to answer it.

She saw it was the sheriff's station and answered immediately. Part of her had hoped it would be Molly's dad, so she could delight in sending him straight to voicemail. As soon as she answered and heard what was said, part of her wished she'd done it anyway.

"Right now? Are you shitting me?" She closed her eyes and listened to Mrs. Reeve, a couple notes shy of panic, lay it out for a few seconds before she sighed. She'd just gotten here, dammit, and after getting someone to cover for her for an hour so she could go to the watch meeting this morning. "Fine, fine. I'll be right there."

Tossing the phone onto the passenger seat, she put her car in reverse and backed out of her spot. She'd need to wait a few minutes before she called in sick for the day. If she did it now, she'd sound so goddamned pissed that faking sick wouldn't be a viable option.

*

Alison wasn't much of the nursing type, but she did what she could, getting Hendricks and Arch to help Sheriff Reeve into the station while she trailed behind. She'd driven the man's car while he rode with Arch. A little bit of her wished she could have been a fly on the window of that car as they drove back, but as soon as she saw her husband's face, she knew it was all swearing and pretty much of nothing else, just by the scowl he worse.

"Set him down on the cot over here," Mrs. Reeve said, about two steps shy of wringing her hands, Alison figured. She would have been in about the same boat if Arch had been in Reeve's shoes, maybe a little better off but not much. Hendricks and Arch helped the sheriff over to the cot Mrs. Reeve had set up in the corner of the bullpen, a blanket draped over it. She had it figured for something from emergency supplies, but it looked old, maybe World War II era castoffs.

"I should go get Lonsdale," Hendricks said, glancing out the door as the bell jangled. "Or not, since he seems to have crawled his way in."

Alison looked over her shoulder to see the other demon hunter hunched over, dragging himself along with a surly look on his face. She'd never heard of anyone being actually possessed before, and this guy didn't look like he was taking it real well.

"How are you, Nick?" Mrs. Reeve asked, all sad and solicitous.

"Feel like Stuntman Jake tried to drive a damned school bus through me," Reeve said, clutching his side. Alison chortled; Stuntman Jake did exactly that sort of thing, driving a retired school bus through old, stripped down campers and other "fun" obstacles at the Calhoun County Fair.

"Where's Duncan?" Arch asked, looking around like he'd be able to see the OOC through the walls, or lurking in the cells or something.

"Saw him pass on the way here," Hendricks said, keeping his eye on Lonsdale, who was shuffling back behind the counter like he'd been the one who'd had a demon play enthusiastic xylophone on his ribs. "I expect he wanted to meet Erin at the scene, maybe take a look before he joins us here."

Arch frowned. "Why wasn't he there right off?"

Hendricks shrugged. "I saw him turn behind us as we were getting back on the main drag. He waved and everything. He was probably five minutes behind you getting there, since he started about five minutes farther away."

"What the hell was that thing?" Reeve asked through gritted teeth. He started to sit up, but Alison saw him cringe and then take about five seconds to mentally write that off as a bad idea. If things weren't presently going somewhat shitty, she might have found the process funny.

"Looked like a demon in a human body to me," Arch said, looking at Hendricks. She saw her husband's eyes burning as he looked at the demon hunter, and she suspected this had potential to get kinda ugly. "Would have been nice to know such a thing was possible before this happened."

"I agree," Hendricks said, coolly and smartass as ever, "since I didn't have a fucking clue that it was anything other than a whispered joke among us demon hunters."

"Like demon royalty?" Arch asked.

"Seems there's another something Duncan failed to mention to us," Hendricks said, with a little ire of his own. "Might want to take a chunk out of his ass when he gets here instead of trying to turn your teeth at me."

"Sorry," Arch said, sounding genuinely contrite for a second. "So it is real? Demon possession of a human host?"

"Fucking right it's real," Lonsdale said, collapsing in a chair nearby. "I fucking felt it, didn't I?"

That drew a moment's attention. "What did it feel like?" Alison asked, because no one else probably would.

"Like I said before, a thousand screams in your ear," Lonsdale said, rubbing his head. "A skull-fucking with a big fucking hickory-dickory-dock."

"Does he have Tourette's?" Reeve asked with loud frustration. "What the hell is he saying?"

"It's Cockney rhyming slang." Duncan breezed in, jangling the bell atop the door as he entered. "They rhyme what they really mean with something else in order to obscure the meaning."

"From who?" Reeve asked. "Anyone trying understand them?"

"When it first started, it was to hide what they were saying from the cops," Duncan said, rounding the counter. He paused then smiled faintly. "And right this minute, looks it's being used for the same purpose."

"Son of a ..." Reeve drawled in pain.

"Duncan," Hendricks said, and Alison recognized him reining himself in, "why didn't you mention demon possession being a thing?"

Duncan didn't really show surprise, but Alison could have sworn she saw a little nonetheless. "Because there isn't, not anymore. It's been consigned to history books and horror movies. The type of demons that can do that sort of thing were all wiped out and sent back to—well, you know."

"Hades?" Arch offered.

"Hell?" Alison corrected.

"The Flying Spaghetti Monster's Ship?" Hendricks asked with a huge fucking grin. Arch grimaced visibly at both their added answers.

"However you want to spell it, the Office of Occultic Concordance solved this problem for you." Duncan looked around. "You're welcome."

"Well, you didn't solve it very fucking well, did you?" Lonsdale asked, sounding pretty put out about it.

Duncan looked right at him, frowning. "You … you've been possessed recently."

Lonsdale's face darkened. "I fucking know that, I do. Just said it, too."

"That's impossible," Duncan said, and now he was actually frowning, bending at the waist and looking at Lonsdale like he was peering into a dark well, trying to see the water at the bottom.

"Like Ygrusibas rising was impossible?" Hendricks asked.

"Yeah, like that," Duncan said without appearing to notice he was even saying it.

"So then it's totally just happened," Hendricks said.

"What?" Duncan snapped upright again, breaking his gaze away from Lonsdale, who had been looking at him with a hefty amount of suspicion. "No, it's not possible. We accounted for—"

"I'm here to tell you that you didn't," Arch said, and strolled over to Lonsdale, lifting his wounded arm and prompting the demon hunter to say, "Ow!" when Arch exposed the bleeding wound on his wrist. "Hendricks cut him here, the demon face went away, leaving nothing but a—"

"Incoherent whiner," Reeve finished.

"Oh, you're a right Moby Dick," Lonsdale fired back.

"That means 'prick,'" Duncan said. "And—this," he grabbed Lonsdale by the hand, tearing it away from Arch and causing the demon hunter to let out another cry of pain, "this could be anything. He could have cut himself masturbating, or whatever it is you people do with sharp objects."

"Generally not masturbate," Alison said. "Not with sharp objects."

"Yeah, that'd be hard objects," Hendricks said with a smirk. He didn't say it as quick as he would have before Kitty Elizabeth, though, Alison knew, and his smirk was pretty hollow, fading after less than a second.

"Oh, Lordy," Mrs. Reeve said under her breath.

"The point is, this is not necessarily possession," Duncan said, but to Alison it sounded like he was trying real hard to convince himself.

"Look at the holes in his shirt, Duncan," Alison said, trying to cut right through the bullshit and self-denial. "I shot him a half-dozen times."

Duncan paused, looking down. "Could have been that serum from Spellman at work here."

"He didn't even take damage, man," Arch said. "Skin just rippled. And he had himself a demon face."

Duncan stood there, frozen, and let Lonsdale's arm fall from his grip. "Well … shit, then."

The door opened, bell jangling, and everyone turned to see who walked in.

"Just us," Brian said, smirking at his sister. Alison could see her mom and dad following behind, back in the glass entry. Brian hadn't bothered to hold the door for them, because why would he? "What's the haps?" He nodded at Lonsdale. "Another new face."

"Same one I've always had," Lonsdale said, scowling, "though the mind behind it was almost recently changed out like a Longmire."

"Tire," Duncan said absently, his mind or essence or whatever clearly elsewhere.

"Ali," her mother said, coming around the counter and giving her a big hug. Her mother was about her height, but Alison felt like she'd gotten frail recently. Addy rubbed the back of Alison's arms after she finished giving her a peck on the cheek. "I was worried."

"I'm fine," Alison said, trying her best to act like it was nothing. She was fighting demons now all the time, after all. She caught the look from her mom, though, that told her that there was a struggle still going on in there—moms were going to mom, after all, Alison thought as the phone rang loud in the station.

*

Chester only leapt twice, for that was all that was needed. Leaping high was a conspicuous activity and tended to draw undue attention, so after he landed he settled into a jog, making his way quickly through backyards until he found one with an immense clothesline hung with clothing from one end to the other.

The internal debate was going quite loudly, but Chester was ignoring it for the most part. It was pure anger and venom, and all of it directed at those they viewed as the responsible parties for William's departure. He had all those feelings himself, and listening to the others was rather like running a knife blade across a newly healed scab. He had no interest in that at the moment, and so he stayed in command of himself and considered the next priority.

And the next priority was to formulate a plan.

They would be looking for him, which suggested that he needed to get out of sight. His body was not so unusual as to cause people in this town to take immediate notice, but he was a stranger and this was not a large place. They would surely notice him by his clothing first, and so that needed to change. Chester stole a flannel shirt and a pair of old jeans from the clothesline and made the switch, balling up his old clothes and tossing them in a drainage ditch as he made his way across several backyards to another street.

He walked along the street focused on his next steps. He would need a place to lie low, to hide. He would need food, and currency, for after the drive he had little money remaining. None of these problems were particularly difficult to deal with, and so he continued his walk unworried, cool air rushing against his cheeks.

He stopped in front of a playground, casting a wary eye over the scene. Children were at play, small ones, chasing each other around in circles. Sitting on a bench, watching it all, he saw his first humans since he had fled the encounter that had cost him William.

Two women sat talking, one dark-haired, one blond, both of them with similar hairstyles that reached their shoulder blades. Chester had not done this in quite a long time, centuries, in fact, and he felt awkward as he made his way across the grass toward them.

He walked as silently as he could, their backs turned to him, a peal of laughter causing them both to shake with the hilarity of whatever one had just said to the other. They both paused mid-laugh and turned their heads; the dark haired one shouted, "Abi—don't you do that! Leave Charlie alone."

Chester's gaze followed over to the playground, where one of the girls was guiltily clutching a small shovel filled with sand, poised to dump it on one of the younger children, one so small Chester doubted he could walk yet. Chester's experience with children was limited, but the answer came from his fellows—the girl child looked about four, the baby she was about to dump sand on seemed to be closer to one. There were two others laughing and frolicking as well—aged three or four according to those within him who knew.

Chester took that little into account as he swooped in behind the women. He had his plan already set and had received more than enough concord to make it happen. He took the last steps at demon speed and landed his hands on the back of the women's necks before they had a chance to turn around. He touched them gently, and a wash of five of his fellows poured into each of them. Plenty enough to keep their human minds under control while the collective did their work.

Both of the women stood, their eyes focused, and each gave him a nod. Bentley was the duly elected speaker for the blond, Charity was in charge of the dark-haired one.

"This one has an empty house at present," Charity said, staring right at Chester.

"This one doesn't," Bentley said, shaking the blond head. "An older child is home, a male, fifteen or so."

Chester pondered that for a second. "We will need all the ears we can get." He reached out a hand and touched Bentley, who raised the woman's to meet his. He poured twenty-five more volunteers into Bentley's new body, and the body sighed as it received the bounty. "Take the older child, learn what he knows, and spread yourselves around wisely. Then come to—" He looked to Charity's dark-haired vessel.

"538 Cokeworth Lane," Charity said. "It's two blocks from here, and only across the street from that one's home." She nodded her head at Bentley.

"Very well," Chester said, nodding once, crisply. "We won't have much time in a town this small."

"We would have more if we dealt with these," Bentley said, nodding at the children playing on the playground. Another light laugh reached Chester's ears.

"We have no time for those bodies," Chester said, leading his two new additions away from the playground and away from the children, who played without noticing their guardians leaving. "We have much to do."

*

"Nine one one," Arch said, answering the phone. This wasn't his job, but with Mrs. Reeve looking like she was ready to fret herself right to madness over the sheriff, he reckoned he was the next person in charge of it. "What's your—"

"Is that you, Arch?" It was a woman's voice on the other end of the line, but he didn't recognize it straight away.

"Yeah," Arch said, frowning. "Who is this?"

"It's Lucy Prater." Arch knew it after the lady spoke again. She had a real husky sound to her. "Hey, Arch, I was just watching TV in the living room, and you know how my house is right across from the playground on Church Street?"

"Yes'm." Hendricks gave Arch a funny look for that one.

"Well, I just saw Evelyn Creek and Brenda Matthews go strolling away with some man I ain't never seen before, and they left their precious little babies behind. They been gone for about five minutes now, and I stepped outside and there ain't no sign of them at all. Now, that Evelyn, she watches Abilene Tarley during the day while her daddy works, so we got—"

"Oh, Lordy," Arch said and took the phone away from his ear. "Lucy Prater's saying some man just convinced Brenda Matthews and Evelyn Creek to walk away from their kids at the playground on Church Street." He could hear Miss Prater still talking, but he was already snapping to get things done.

"You think it's our possession demon?" Reeve said, pained, from his place on the cot.

"Didn't seem to indicate there was any struggling when they walked off," Arch said, half-listening to the faint buzz of Miss Prater's voice in the earpiece.

"No, there weren't no struggling, Arch," Lucy said, loud enough he could pick it out. "They just walked off pretty as you please."

"We're on our way," Arch said and hung up on her. He glanced at

Alison. "You want to come along with me?"

She was still tangled up with her mother, though she looked none too happy about it. "Sure," Alison said, pulling free. "Let's go."

"I'll go with you," Hendricks said, moving toward the end of the counter in a hurry.

"Me too," Duncan said, casting one last look at Lonsdale like he was going to burst into flames or something.

"I'll come—" Bill Longholt started to say.

"Maybe you ought to stay here, Bill," Arch said, nodding to the man and meeting his eyes as he headed out. He didn't say it, but he caught Bill's nod that said he'd figured it out. Fact was, Arch didn't want to leave the sheriff or any of the others here helpless in case this new demon came calling, looking for his revenge while they were out.

*

"We need basics," Chester said as he and Charity stepped into the woman's home. "Food, money, whatever means she has available."

"Food in the pantry," Charity said, clearly skimming through the brain. "There are guns upstairs, in the closet. I'll get them."

"I will see to the sustenance needs," Chester said, breaking off and heading toward the kitchen. "How shall we—?"

"There are bags upstairs, I will bring them along with the weapons," Charity said, already on her way up.

Chester nodded and broke off to go to the kitchen. It was pleasant to be like this once more, as in the days of old when they would freely break apart for a time and then reconstitute later with new experiences. It had not been possible in recent years, especially in light of the purging that had gone on in the days before they had been trapped in the vase. Chester and William had watched with horror as many of their kind, their communities given flesh, had been sent back.

But their number had escaped it. They had been free. He and William had led them out of—

Out of danger.

Chester ransacked the pantry and refrigerator at demon speed, careful not to break anything. He heard footsteps upstairs and knew that Charity was taking care of her part. That was the beauty of sending five or more into a new body; one, alone, tended to regain a certain individuality, and might develop their own ideas about different courses of action available to them. Five or more allowed for control not only of the body and the mind they inhabited, but a certain resistance to individual thinking. They remained a collective, a team, dedicated to a goal.

In this case, to taking everything they could of value and getting out of this house before the police arrived.

Charity came thumping down the stairs with a camouflage bag that clearly held some sort of long gun, and two small duffels the size of gym bags. The smell of old sweat wafting from one indicated to Chester what function it had served previously. No matter now, though; he loaded the food into it while Charity opened a cupboard and extracted a cup filled with dollars.

A squeak of a door behind them heralded the arrival of Bentley, and Chester turned to see the blond body there, along with a male that was slightly taller. He knew it was Mary inhabiting the boy, and a simple nod from each of them was all that was needed before they sprang into action helping to gather up the supplies.

*

Brian had watched his mother's worried exchange with Alison with something just short of the desire to roll both his eyes back in his head for all eternity. She'd been fawning over her precious baby daughter ever since she'd gotten back from her exile trip to the country to fight demons. Brian had been surprised when his mother hadn't utterly excoriated his dad for lying about knowing where Alison had been, but maybe that had happened sometime when he wasn't watching. They'd certainly shared a few furtive looks now and again, and not of the good sort.

Brian watched his dad's eyes follow Arch, Hendricks, Duncan, and Alison as they headed out to pick up some abandoned kids on the playground. He had heard something said about a possession demon. Bill was watching the departing group with a pretty close eye, and then Brian realized he was really watching Alison, who didn't seem to take any note of her parents' anxious gazes. It was about enough to make even him jealous—in addition to making him want to roll his eyes yet again until he died.

"So … possession demon?" Brian asked, figuring he'd get the ball rolling. "I'm assuming it's not one that's been arrested for carrying a dime bag." He leaned on the counter and smirked, looking across at Sheriff Reeve, who looked awfully pained where he was half-lying, half-sitting on an old cot.

"Hardly," Reeve said, cringing from some pain and clutching his side. "We watched a demon that seemed to be able to take over a human body this morning." He nodded at the new guy, a black man who looked like he was dressed to be an extra on *Arrow* during a fight scene. "This is Lonsdale. He's a demon hunter. Oh, and don't expect to understand what he's saying."

"It's a real treasure to make your acquaintance," Lonsdale said.

There was a moment's pause, and then Brian laid on the sarcasm. "I think I understood that just fine."

*

Braeden was up to his elbows in his second engine of the day when Tracy came up with the phone. He had her tuck it between his shoulder and neck, mostly as a courtesy to her, because Tracy was going to have to take it and hang it up later. Braeden didn't give a damn if his shop phone had grease stains all over it, because it was bound to happen at some point, but he didn't care to fuck up the one in the office that Tracy had to use.

"Hello," he said, continuing to work while he was trying to have a conversation, twisting his wrench. Trying to talk while working didn't always go that well, depending on what was going on in the background of the shop. It was mostly quiet at the moment, though. Tucker had kept his mouth shut since Pike had left, surly as hell, and whatever he was working on wasn't causing any noise.

"Braeden, this is Lucy Prater," came the babbling voice on the other end of the phone. It was kinda low and husky, and Braeden knew who he was talking to immediately, though he hadn't the faintest why she'd be calling him.

"Yes, ma'am," Braeden said, trying to sound polite while he paused to gather his thoughts. It wasn't that he meant to stop; it was that the mystery of this call put him off for a second. "What can I do for you?"

"Well, I don't know if you know where I live, young man, but I'm across from the park, and I just watched Evelyn Creek walk off and leave your little girl behind—"

Braeden dropped his wrench and heard it clang its way down through the engine until it hit the concrete floor, completely blotting out whatever Lucy Prater might have said next. "Excuse me?" Braeden managed to squeeze out after the clatter of the wrench had died away.

"I said your little girl is here at the park and there ain't anyone watching her," Lucy Prater said. "I called the law to let them know, and Arch Stan is on his way, but I figured I'd let you know, too, since I know Evelyn watches your little girl for you—"

Braeden's head was swimming like he'd gone and taken a few real deep breaths over an open fuel line. This wasn't like Miss Creek. No way would she just walk away from Abi and leave her at the park.

Then again, a few weeks ago, it wouldn't have mattered much if she had, because it wasn't like anything bad happened in Midian up until now.

"Shit," Braeden said and dropped the phone. Tracy caught it in surprise, fumbling it slightly but managing not to drop it. "I gotta go to the park." And he ran right out under the door without even stopping to wash his hands first.

*

Arch pulled up against the curb on Church Street as Lucy Prater was walking across the lawn. Arch had her figured as the kind of lady that knew everyone in the neighborhood mostly so she could watch their business and stick her nose in it. She was in her early fifties but trying real hard not to look it, her hair dyed a lustrous shade of black. Only now, minutes after she'd called them, was she walking across the street to come check on the kids. Arch could hear some serious crying going on as he opened the door and got out, the sound of kids who'd realized that there was no one watching them and had started to panic. He figured it'd started with one of them and spread like a virus because now there were three of them wailing to the heavens, and one that was almost a baby that was just looking at the other three like they were crazy as all get out.

"Damn," Alison said, slamming her door behind her and taking off for the playground. She jumped the curb and Arch followed, not too quick on his part, since he wasn't looking forward to getting to the crying kids at all. He kept his eyes peeled for danger, though, and saw pretty much of nothing lurking.

"This isn't a real good sign," Duncan said, calling out to Arch from where he'd parked behind the Explorer. Hendricks had gotten out of his SUV, too, and they were both standing with their doors open, watching Alison head for the kids and clearly not in much hurry to join her. Hendricks, in particular, had a look on his face that was bordering on disgust.

"Who the fuck leaves an infant to play in a playground like this?" Hendricks threw up a hand to indicate the youngest child. Alison was almost to them now, and Arch could hear her speaking in soothing tones to the kids. The one Hendricks pointed to was the only one not crying. He was sitting in the sand holding a little pail in tiny fingers, alternating his attention between the others and whatever project he was working on. "Cats and dogs shit in that sand, you know."

Arch gave that a moment's thought. "I never thought of that before."

Hendricks was moving fast to revulsion. "Even before these ladies took off, they weren't exactly Mom of the Year."

"I hear digging in the dirt is good for your immune systems," Duncan said, still hanging back. "Makes you less likely to develop asthma. So maybe they're better than you think."

"It's really fascinating to hear the two of you chuckleheads argue about parenting strategies," Arch said, trying to keep his eyes nailed to Alison in case something came jumping out at her, "when it's clear as day neither one of you wants to go over there and pick up a kid to soothe."

"We're gonna go look for the suddenly negligent parents," Hendricks said, sounding like he was doing some fast thinking.

"I don't see you sprinting over there to pick up a tricycle motor and give it a burping, either," Duncan fired back.

"Alison needs cover," Arch said, but he couldn't help feeling a little ashamed. Kids weren't quite his thing.

*

"Hey," Alison said, kneeling down in the sand. There were three kids crying in front of her, big sobbing wails, loud as if they'd just had a thunderstorm happen in their ears or found a monster under their beds. "It's okay."

She knew in passing all but one of the kids in front of her. The baby was Charlie Creek and his older sister was Tammi, and standing in front of her in a dress covered in sand with an adorable pair of pigtails was Abi Tarley. She'd seen them all in the store since they were babies. She did the whole mingling-with-the-shoppers thing, trying to be an effervescent personality like her dad. She wasn't nearly as good at it as he was, but she had gotten to know almost all the town that way. She had her own opinions about Evelyn Creek and Brenda Matthews, especially after she'd heard they both got drunk as hell in Fast Freddie's last year and needed to be escorted home, but bad parents to the point of abandoning their children? That wasn't anywhere in what she knew of the two.

"Miss Cweek left us," Abi Tarley said, her little face dripping with tears and her frame racking with uncontrollable sobs. She seemed like the spokesperson of the group, and the other two kids let out a wave of whimpering following her pronouncement.

"Abi, I called your daddy and he's on his way," Lucy Prater called out from twenty feet away. She was just hovering over there, apparently trying to keep at a safe distance. Alison looked back and saw Arch doing much the same but keeping it to an extreme that even gossipy old Lucy Prater wasn't carrying it.

Abi Tarley stopped crying and made a little sniffling noise instead. "R-really?"

"I doubt Miss Prater would lie about that," Alison said, trying to be reassuring and yet still firing a shot at Lucy Prater in the process. She couldn't help it; she'd never liked that old biddy much. It sailed over Lucy Prater's head anyway.

"But ... but ... where'd my mom go?" Tammi Creek asked, tears streaming down. Alison was wondering exactly why it was she was suddenly having to deal with so many crying, upset, lonely kids. These things happened in threes, though, didn't they? Hell, that wasn't going to be any fun if she had another of these crying kid incidents coming up.

"Sweety, it's okay," Alison said, soothing. "My husband's over there, and he's a policeman." She waved Arch over frantically, and he started to walk toward her, though a heck of a lot slower than she would have preferred. "We're going to find your mommy. We think she just went to check on something and figured she'd be back real quick." How were you supposed to tell a pre-school kid that their parent got possessed by a demon, anyway?

Alison listened to the sobs fade and picked up Charlie Creek under his armpits. He let her quite willingly, staring right into her face with interest, his big brown eyes looking into hers, his cheeks as red as if she'd given him a good pinch before she'd picked him up. She lifted him up on her hip and braced him there, against her side. It felt pretty natural once she got the weight balanced right, and she wondered why Arch and Hendricks were working so hard to keep their distance from this.

*

Arch started across the playground when he saw his wife beckon. "You oughta join me over there," he said over his shoulder to Duncan and Hendricks. "Do your share."

He didn't bother to watch for the answer, knowing it was coming. When it did, it was chock full of the discomfort he'd expected from Hendricks when he'd raised the possibility: "We should ... go investigate the address you gave us. See if we can find the mothers of these kids," the cowboy said, and Arch could practically hear Duncan nodding along without even turning around.

*

"That's all we should take for now," Chester said, looking at his little de facto army around him. They had loaded up a few big bags, and were now across the street at the other house, the one Bentley had cleared with the fifteen year-old. They were loaded with many burdens, and Chester already had a solution in mind for what should be done about it.

"We could use a few more things," Charity said, shooting him a glance that he knew instantly how to interpret—quiet suggestion with an utter willingness to throw out that option without ego or reserve should the collective decide to.

"We can pick them up later," Chester said, agreeing without agreeing. "We need to secure transportation." He looked over at the boy who was being controlled by Mary. "Does your teenage form know how to drive a car?" Mary shook her head and he immediately passed back to Bentley. "It's you, then. Try the neighbors behind this house." And he pointed out the kitchen window.

Bentley nodded and left without another word. The rest of them worked in the quiet of the kitchen to gather things together and start moving them out the back door. This would need to happen quickly.

*

Hendricks just rode with Duncan. "You getting any tingling on your spider-sense?" he asked the OOC, wondering if the demon actually ever felt anything these days. Time was, it had felt to Hendricks like Duncan had been able to read his damned mind. Now, he mostly seemed to crab about that guy Spellman and his runes. Surely this new player hadn't gotten runes from Spellman, had he?

Duncan stared straight ahead, steering the car onto a quiet street. Hendricks saw the green street sign flash by, the sun hitting it perfectly so he couldn't read it. Duncan probably could, though, and he knew where he was going. "My 'spider-sense,' as you call it … is not tingling, no. It's not so much a sense, either, as it is a—"

"Yeah, I don't really care how it works so long as it does," Hendricks said, easy and breezy. Maybe a little cranky. He'd had a couple plans for how he was going to spend this afternoon, and it mostly involved trying to sleep with the curtains wide open. Something about sleeping in the light felt better to him lately, though he wasn't under any illusions about the idea of monsters being somehow averse to the light. He'd seen them come in the day before.

"Well, it's not working real well right now," Duncan said, as close to tense as Hendricks had ever heard him get.

"Why's that?" Hendricks asked.

"Probably for the same reason that home office wanted demons with the ability to possess others sent back to the pits," Duncan said. "Because OOCs can't read them effectively. They get all churned up in whatever human they're possessing and it's almost impossible for us to see them. Like hiding a red ant in a carpenter ant's hill."

"You're not expert enough to pick 'em out?"

"It would take a lot more time and patience to sift than I've got at any given moment," Duncan said. "I'm still struggling with the idea that this thing, whatever it is, is a possession demon. Could just be strong with the power of suggestion, like a vardwall."

"The fuck is a vardwall?" Hendricks frowned. The tires bumped against the curb as Duncan parallel parked on a near-empty street.

"It's good you've never met one," Duncan said, throwing the door open and getting out. "They tell you to jump, you don't even ask how high before you go a-leaping."

Hendricks got out of the car, adjusting his brim against the cool, sunny day. "Seems to me a demon like that would be a pretty powerful nuisance." He fell into step next to Duncan as they started up toward what he assumed was the address Arch had given them. "Figure I would have heard about a demon doing mind control."

"Not mind control," Duncan said, shaking his head. "Suggestion. They can't make you do anything you don't already want to do at least a little. It's not like they could convince a perfectly healthy and normal person to go jump off a bridge or anything."

"Then what do they do with that pow—"

Duncan slapped a hand across Hendricks's chest and halted him in his tracks. The OOC was frozen there on the sidewalk, the smell of autumn briskness in the air, and he looked ahead at the door of the house they were walking up to. That sucker was open, and not just a little bit. Wide open, like a barn door. "Shit," Hendricks said.

"Yeah," Duncan said, and he pulled his baton out. "Follow behind me."

The made their way up onto the porch, the floorboards squeaking loudly under their weight. It made Hendricks cringe, standing there all exposed with a woodwind section announcing their arrival. He paused, listening for a second, and watched Duncan peer intently at the open door. "You think there's—" Hendricks started to ask.

He saw the shotgun barrel pop out the door less than a second before it fired, splitting the air on the quiet street and dragging his ass back to his time in Iraq in the most uncomfortable damned way possible.

*

Arch was helping Alison, leaning close to the kids as she talked to them, soothing, all quiet and pleasant. She was good at it, he thought as he watched her build a little rapport with them.

Then the sound of gunfire echoed across the playground and caused everyone to look up, Arch and Alison with a hell of a lot more alarm than the kids.

*

Hendricks saw Duncan catch the full load right in the face. He didn't stagger or fall over, but his t-shirt shredded in a hot second under the fire and the demon seemed to blink and raise his hands in surprise. Hendricks, for his part, didn't need any coaching on what to do. He drew and fired through the window into the house on pure instinct, emptying four rounds out of his 1911 before he even realized he was doing it.

"Get out of there!" Duncan said, shoving him backward off the porch. It came just in time, too, as the window he'd just fired into exploded over him. Someone was blasting out of it, and Hendricks could just about feel the bullets whistling over him as he landed in the bushes. A hard branch landed right around his kidney and a dozen other ancillary pains sprouted all across his ass and lower back, but he managed to keep his legs low and flip out of the shrub that had broken his fall and just about busted his anal cherry.

There was a wet slap of bullets hitting something and it took him a second to realize, face in the grass, that they were hitting Duncan as he stood there. Hendricks was keeping well out of the line of fire, head down, and when a pause came for their attackers to reload, he let off a couple rounds and then rolled hard to his right, back toward the stairs. No reason to wait around for return fire, after all.

*

"Shots fired," Arch said into his shoulder mic, staring transfixed into the distance. Whatever was happening, he was at least a minute's run away, and he felt frozen in place. Whatever kind of trouble Hendricks and Duncan had wandered into, he couldn't risk leaving Alison and these kids alone to try and intervene.

"Damn," Alison whispered, clutching Abi Tarley and that Creek baby close to her. The other two kids were shaking a few steps away, and Arch was torn between offering them some form of comfort and running off half-cocked, trying to get to Hendricks and Duncan before something bad happened. If it hadn't already.

*

Bentley came bursting up just as Chester was about to send Charity to see how things were coming for their retreat. The good news was that Bentley was not alone, and had two others with her, clearly now turned to their will. "We have an escape vehicle," Bentley announced as another round of gunfire exploded in front of the house. "I'm having someone bring it around now. We'll need to run these supplies over to—" She pointed past one of the houses behind them to a road running through the green lawns.

"Very well," Chester said with a curt nod. "Begin, and I will join you momentarily. I need to inform Charity and Mary to cover our retreat for another few moments before they withdraw."

Bentley nodded once and then sprung to action without a word, snatching up several bags and running them across the backyards, her new additions assisting her. This was the way it should be; all Chester needed to do was get the others and they could make good their escape—but perhaps do a bit of damage first.

*

Braeden Tarley heard the gunfire start when he was still about a block from the park, his windows down and his Ford F-150 growling as he kept his foot to the accelerator. He let off for a second, just to confirm for himself that it was gunfire he was hearing. He wasn't a stranger to it, having put a couple bucks on his wall as a young man, but it had been a year or two or more probably four since he'd gone hunting, and probably at least that long since he'd fired a gun. It was unmistakable, though, that staccato sound, and damned sure not fire crackers.

He pushed that accelerator down again and blew right through the four-way stop just before the park, screeching to a halt when he pulled up and tearing toward Abi and the other kids, who were all standing together next to the playground, Alison and Arch Stan right next to them, everyone looking off into the distance like they could see the guns being fired.

"Daddy!" Abi's gaze swung over to him and she slipped out of Alison Stan's grip without much of a fight. Ms. Stan gave him a quick once over and he turned his entire attention to Abi, dropping down to scoop her up, making a mess of her dress in the process. "Miss Cweek left me here," Abi said, very bluntly. She did that. She had red eyes and looked like she'd cried some recent tears down those big, adorable cheeks.

"I heard," Braeden said, trying to keep it cool in front of his kid.

"I just don't know what she was thinking," Abi said, sounding a little too grown up and precocious, or more likely playing parrot and spitting back something she'd heard an adult say.

"Neither do I," Braeden said, shifting his attention to Arch. "What the hell is going on here, Arch?" Braeden asked as he came up. He was in school with Arch and Alison both, and though he didn't know the man very well, he knew him well enough to ask a question like that.

"I don't know exactly," Arch said, quick and glib, and not really like him, so far as Braeden knew, "but I expect it's linked to the troubles we've been having around here lately."

"So that means demons to you, right?" Braeden asked, giving him a stinkeye. He wasn't being particular where he directed his grief at the moment.

"It means demons to all of us, whether you accept it or not," Arch said, and the sound of a couple more rounds popping off echoed down the street.

"Like demons from the devil, Daddy?" Abi asked in a hushed voice.

"Don't you worry about it, princess," Braeden said, meeting Arch's hard gaze with one of his own. He wanted to stroke her hair but he'd have a bear of a time getting the grease out of that later. He'd probably already ruined her dress.

*

"What do we do?" Brian asked, feeling like the whole world had started to shake around him. "What do we do?"

"Stop looking like you're going to pee yourself for one," Lauren Darlington said as she came in the door behind him. It damned near sent Brian through the white Styrofoam tile ceiling, because he had no idea she'd come in. Clearly he'd missed the bell in the excitement that came after Arch's breathless, "SHOTS FIRED!" call. "What's going on?" Lauren said, settling next to him at the counter for a second while she looked the place over.

"A little help here, please, Doctor," Reeve said, beckoning her over. She took heed and headed toward him, but Brian caught a flash of reluctance as she did so, like she didn't fancy being ordered around. "I got a cracked rib."

"If you're so sure about it, what do you need me for?" Dr. Darlington quipped, making her way around the counter. Brian watched her go, and it settled him down a little from the energized, frenetic state he'd been heading toward.

His dad stirred, catching his attention. "Not much we can do," Bill said, gaze catching Brian and calming him a little. Brian wouldn't have cared to admit it out loud, but hearing his father say so was a little reassuring. "We need to stay here."

"Seems we might need some of our new volunteers sooner than anticipated," Reeve said as Dr. Darlington crouched next to him and gave him a good push to the side. "GODDAMMIT!" he howled.

"Yep," Dr. Darlington said, cool as ice, "you've got a cracked rib there."

"I fucking told you that!"

Darlington shrugged her thin shoulders. "Had to be sure."

"God," Reeve said, plainly still feeling the pain, face red like he'd just had all the blood run to it, "I bet your malpractice insurance is through the roof."

"You're not wrong," Dr. Darlington said, "but you know what they say—malpractice is the best kind of practice." She looked up at him. "I'm going to need to tape these ribs."

"What about Arch and the rest?" Brian asked again. "Can we find some help to send them? In case they need it?"

Reeve looked pretty damned distressed, and Brian couldn't tell whether it was from the pain, the feeling of being utterly out of control of the situation, or both. "Bill ... I think you need to get on over there, now."

The next round of gunfire out of the front window came twice as hard as the last, and Hendricks had no damned idea where Duncan was. He'd rolled right past the front stairs and was behind the bushes on the other side of the porch, pretty sure the volume of fire coming out that front window was coming from not only the shotgun that had ripped Duncan's shirt apart, but also an AR-15, which meant there were at least two shooters. They were doing yeoman's work blanketing the front lawn with lead, too. Hendricks had doubts about exactly how many blades of grass were going to survive this massacre, but he would have laid odds that this house wasn't going to need a mowing in that area for a while.

Hendricks listened to a last round of rifle fire crack and then rolled hard to his left again. He had it in his mind to get to the side of the porch so he could peek up and take a look sideways. It wouldn't be a great angle to fire from, but it'd be a great place not to get shot by a demon with high-capacity rifle, and he was all about that. Besides, Duncan was probably fine. Bullets didn't hurt him.

Did they?

*

Alison heard round after round fired off and knew she was in the wrong place at the wrong time. She should have been over there with Hendricks and Duncan, rifle at the ready, but here she was holding a baby and trying to clutch two other kids around her legs while she and Arch listened helplessly as that rifle cracked off in the distance.

"You should get her out of here, Braeden," Arch said, standing restlessly, looking like he was ready to charge at any second.

"Not a bad idea," Braeden Tarley said, and he started hightailing it back to his truck, Abi clutched in his arms. She was peering over his shoulder like she could get a look at what all the adults were trying to see. It would have been cute if it hadn't been so terrifying to Alison, who was wondering if Hendricks was a couple blocks over, lying in a pool of blood.

"That's some sort of high-capacity rifle," Arch said.

"An AR-15, I think," Alison said, listening intently. It could have been other types of rifles, maybe an AK-47 knockoff, but the odds were good this was it. It chattered in the distance, round after round firing off.

Arch was in a state of high tension, and Alison could see him ratcheting up to do something about it. He wasn't the sort to abandon a teammate in trouble, that was sure. "Arch," she said, reaching out a hand and running it down his arm, from just below the khaki sleeve down to his hand, "we're playing defense right now, okay? Not offense."

That didn't exactly settle him, but she could tell it got through. He may have wanted to run, but he stayed there with her and the kids. It wasn't like there was any kind of safe ground presently, anyway, even if they'd had car seats to move the kids out of here.

*

"I don't think we should leave," Bill Longholt said, and it was like someone using a cheese grater on a steel rod next to Reeve's ears. Not that the man had an annoying voice; it was that Reeve was already irritated and in pain, so anything he didn't want to hear right now was bound to aggravate him. "Arch said—"

"Arch wanted you to watch me so this demon didn't come a calling and snuff me," Reeve said, holding his side as Dr. Darlington stared at it, probably trying to figure out exactly what she was going to do without a single medical supply. Reeve caught the slightly guilty look on Bill's face. "I know what he was up to, Bill. I'm not in trouble right now, and if I get in trouble, I got a sword that can be used to stop it." He pointed toward town, even though there were plainly walls between him and his target. "They need help right now. No maybes about it, unlike here."

"As you say," Bill said with a nod, and started for the door. Brian started to take off after him.

"Brian," Reeve said, just about grinding his teeth. "Maybe you should stay here."

Brian paused just outside the door and his dad stopped just ahead of him, shooting Reeve a relieved look. "I …"

"We might have some use for you here, son," Reeve said, and pointed at Donna's desk. "We could use someone to man dispatch."

"What about my mom?" Brian asked, nodding at Addy.

"Oh, darling, you know I don't know anything about technology," Addy said, demurring both quickly and effectively. She was, Reeve figured, lying a little bit, too. But it worked.

Brian Longholt had a chagrined look, to say the least. "I am become Felicity Smoak, the sitter of desks."

Reeve just stared at him. "I got no idea who that is." He nodded at Bill. "Give 'em hell. Or help. Give help where needed and hell everywhere else."

"I might be able to aid in that." That demon hunter Lonsdale came to his feet, still looking he'd been through a crap press, but a little better than he had right after they'd de-possessed him.

"I will do my best," Bill said. He cast Lonsdale a look. "You coming?"

"I'm on my Marvin," Lonsdale said, jumping up and sliding over the counter to join Bill.

"You're gonna have to speak better English if we're gonna work together," Bill said.

"What the fuck does 'gonna' mean?" Lonsdale asked. "That's proper English, is it?"

"More proper than replacing the word that means something with another phrase that means something else entirely," Bill said and disappeared beyond the glass doors.

"It's gonna be okay, Nick," Donna said, leaning closer to him. Brian Longholt was standing over Donna's desk frowning, like it was going to leap up and attack him.

"I need something to tape these ribs with," Dr. Darlington pronounced and got to her feet. She gave Donna a look. "Medical supplies?"

"With the other emergency gear in the closet over there." Donna pointed. "In the back, I think there's a box for first aid and a kit for first responders. There's a good chance it's been picked over, though, because we ain't had the budget to restock since—"

"I'll go take a look," Darlington said. She thrust a thin finger at him and Reeve noticed she had short nails. "Don't move."

"Oh, as soon as you're gone I'm going to be dancing the Macarena all around this place," Reeve said.

Darlington frowned. "Nobody has danced the Macarena since the nineties, and if you revive it now, you're going to drag half of hell back with it. I mean, we're talking the Charleston being done on every street corner, the—"

"I'm sure this is about to turn into a really instructional lesson on trendy dances of the last hundred years," Reeve said, "but my fuck count is at zero and rapidly dropping, so if you could just fix these ribs as best you can—"

"Nobody appreciates the healing power of wit," Darlington said as she moved away toward the supply closet.

"Nick," Donna whispered as soon as she was gone.

He looked right into his wife's eyes, her grey hair falling in bangs over her forehead. "Yes, dear?"

"Are you all right?" she asked, clearly concerned.

"Well, I got a busted rib—"

"I know that much," she said. "I'm asking if you're all right, though. Otherwise."

He peered at her, trying to figure out what she was getting at. Then he got it. "Oh, Lord, this is about last night again—"

"I'm just worried about your overall well-being, not just your ribs—"

"Well," Reeve said, raising his voice a little louder than he'd intended, "in addition being actually impotent last night, right now I got people in harm's way and can't do a thing about it, so I'm feeling figuratively impotent as well. Does that answer your question?"

Donna blushed, and her eyes darted around. He doubted she could see anything without moving her head to look at the rest of the room, but he followed where she was plainly trying to look without moving her head, and he realized—

Aw, shit.

"Don't worry, sheriff," Brian Longholt said, plainly trying to keep in a good laugh. His mother was looking in another direction until he started speaking and then shot him a flaming look. "I hear it happens to guys your age."

"This town really is going to hell," Reeve opined.

*

The sound of gunfire held steady, and Hendricks was along the side of the porch now, perpendicular to the line of fire and glad to be out of it. There was a window along the side of the house that could either give him a chance to return fire and surprise the demons or maybe even provide an entry point. Either way, he was finally able to look up on the porch without fear of getting hit by a stray bullet—

When he looked up he saw Duncan with his shirt in tatters, standing dazed against one of the porch columns. He wanted to shout, "What the hell are you doing?" but it would have given away his position. So instead he tried to figure out what to do, staring at the OOC as he took four more rounds directly in the chest. He didn't exactly shrug them off, more like took them hard, wavering a little, bouncing back against the porch column. The bullets were like little moles on his skin, flattened against the outside of the demon's shell. The whole area reeked of powder, like he was back on the firing range at basic.

Hendricks started toward the window and thought the better of it; he had just reloaded his last mag, and he had seven shots. Not one of them would do anything more than stun the demons firing out, and that was assuming he could peg them from across the house. He figured that was at least twenty, thirty feet. He was decent with a 1911, but in a combat situation where they could turn and hose him with 5.56 rounds? Adrenaline would bring that accuracy right down, making it unlikely he'd do much of anything.

"Shit," he whispered to himself, keeping his eyes on Duncan while he ran through plans. He could storm the back of the house, try and sneak up on the demons. They had to run out of bullets eventually, didn't they? The most recently fired shots peeled off Duncan's chest as he rose back to his feet from a hard lean, and Hendricks expected they clunked to the porch floor, though he couldn't hear it over the sound of shots firing.

Magazines. The demons couldn't have more than a few mags loaded, and even if they had a thousand rounds, they wouldn't be able to effectively reload the mags. But they had that shotgun, too, and that'd be a decent covering weapon while they did reload ... and with demon speed, they could probably get a mag reloaded in half the time it'd take a human, maybe a little more, given proficiencies ...

"Fuck," Hendricks said. There really was no good way to crack this particular nut. Duncan should have been able to just wade in and cause havoc, but he was lumbering like a robot or something, seemingly unable to control his body. Sneaking around the back was starting to sound like a better and better option to Hendricks. He'd have to do this up close and personal, though, getting the drop on them before they could turn and splatter him all over the wall with that shotgun ...

A screech of tires caused him to snap around as a vehicle mounted the curb and came to an abrupt stop on the front lawn. Hendricks cringed at the sound of the frame walloping concrete as it climbed onto the grass and bounced down hard against metal as it did so. Sounded like a car crash. He saw the sheriff's markings along the side of the Crown Vic and had a wicked suspicion he knew who'd just come charging into the party before he saw the blond hair catch the sunlight as she bailed out the driver's door and went around the side toward the trunk, which was wide open.

Erin was here.

*

Chester watched the sheriff's car jump the curb at forty miles an hour and rip to a halt on the front lawn, leaving torn-up sod and messy grass everywhere. He wondered if the homeowner was complaining within Charity's mind. What they had done today was so anathema, so different from what he would normally have done or endorsed or considered acceptable that Chester very much felt as though he had undergone some sort of dreamlike metamorphosis. It was as though he had fallen into a darkness that he could not escape.

"What should we do?" Charity asked, raising the rifle to her shoulder again. She pounded six shots in a row into the OOC that had been assaulting their front door through the window, which was more or less bereft of glass at this point. The OOC wavered, his essence doubtlessly compressed and jolted by the force of the rifle impacts. It wasn't quite unconsciousness, but it most certainly did not leave him at his best.

"I have one more load of supplies," Chester said. "Bentley is carrying them now. We can leave."

"If we do," Mary said through the mouth of the teenage boy, "this OOC will be on his feet and after us in seconds."

Chester thought about that for a moment. "Perhaps—"

"You should leave this with us," Charity said, firing again, the gun stopping after three rounds and producing a clicking noise that told

Chester it was empty of rounds.

"Chester bristled. "I will not leave you behind to—"

"We will be along shortly," Mary said, not deigning to look at him. "We cannot let this OOC pass. If he catches you and the rest—"

"He must not," Charity said, looking back as she ejected the empty magazine from the rifle and slapped another in. She pulled back on a lever and a loud clacking noise came from the rifle. She brought it around and fired straight into the OOC once more. He danced as though electrified, disoriented by all the hits to his shell. "All else is in your hands, but you must leave this in ours."

"We cannot lose any more," Chester said, whispering hoarsely.

"Lose us or lose the plan," Mary said. "We will all be together again, in the depths. There is no turning from that course now."

Chester closed his eyes for a moment. He had not said it yet, but he knew in that moment that it was true; there was no happiness without William and his fellows. They would never be whole again without them, and to believe otherwise was … foolish. Naive. There was an immense hole right through the middle of them, and Chester felt it acutely, as did the others, though their howls of rage belied their ocean-deep sense of loss.

"We will make good your escape," Charity said, firing again. "And we will join you if we can, if it is safe."

The howl of gunfire covered over a grave quiet as the collective fell into solemnity. "We will miss you," Chester said simply. "We will be together again, when this is all over."

"Hurt them for us," Charity said, her demon face leaking out from behind the human mask.

"Make them know pain as we have known pain," Mary said. "Visit it upon them a hundred, a thousandfold for what they have done to us and ours."

"This thing will be done," Chester said, and with a last nod at them, he sprinted out the back of the house and ran across the wide, green lawn to the waiting car. He heard the gunshots continue as he got in, and they pulled away with a squeal of tires, leaving behind yet another sacrifice in what was certain to be a bloody war. But one they would most assuredly win, Chester knew. For what other choice was there?

And who could stop them?

*

Braeden Tarley was damned happy to get Abi out of that mess, so happy he barely had her in her car seat before he was starting the truck and blazing out of there. He could still hear the chatter of rifle fire behind them, and he stomped that accelerator like in the old days. The cops clearly had better things to be doing than chasing him right now, anyway, and he meant to get the hell away from potential danger as fast as his truck would go.

"Daddy, why did Miss Cweek leave? Where did she go?" Abi's words all ran together, and she was still pronouncing her R's like W's.

"I don't know, baby," Braeden said, white-knuckling the wheel. He still had the window open, and it drowned Abi out as she said something else. He rolled up fast and said, "What, darlin'?"

"Where are we going?" Abi asked. "Are we going back to Miss Cweek's house?"

"No," Braeden said tightly. His brain was at war with itself, trying to fight through to an answer for what was happening. Demons didn't use rifles, did they? And didn't Arch and Alison sound like they were worried about someone getting shot? That made Braeden even more suspicious of this shit, like they were hiding something or not telling something that they knew. It'd just about figure for the cops to be lying, of course.

"Daddy ...?" Abi asked, and he paused because she sounded cute and a little worried.

"Yes, baby?"

"Are we going home?"

Braeden blinked. That was probably the best idea, wasn't it? They were out of Midian that way, a little outside town. That was safe enough, surely. "Yeah, baby," he said, taking the next turn as he adopted his daughter's very sensible suggestion. "Yeah, we are."

*

Hendricks figured out why Erin had popped the cruiser's trunk about ten seconds before she opened up with the department's AR-15, letting loose a volley of return fire that made him cringe. This wasn't a war zone, in spite of how it probably sounded at the moment, and as small as the 5.56 shells were, they still had a tendency to overpenetrate through walls. He had a brief vision of some poor old lady sitting in the house behind this one and catching a round in the back of the head, not even knowing what hit her.

"Shit," Hendricks muttered again. The demon's AR chattered back and hosed the side of Erin's car, puncturing holes all over the word "Sheriff." One of the tires popped, though he didn't hear it so much as see the sudden sag in the frame.

Hendricks decided his course pretty quick at that point. Duncan was still dazed on the front porch and didn't look to be coming out of it anytime soon. Whatever they were doing by splashing him with rifle fire was not doing him any favors. It was like they'd knocked out his brain or something, and all he could do was flail.

With a sigh, Hendricks popped up and started unloading through the side window. He hadn't wanted to do it, but if there was any hope of distracting these bastards long enough to make something happen, this was it.

*

Amanda Guthrie could feel something stirring in the wind. At least, that was what she told herself. It sounded better than the truth, which was that she could hear gunshots off in the distance, even through the hotel's walls.

She walked across the room, still in her pajamas, and put a hand on the windowpane. It was cool, and she figured the air outside was likely in the range of crisp. The parking lot below was sparsely populated, and she reached out with her essence through the hand and could feel the disruption of the bullets being fired, somewhere in the distance. It was nothing magical, just her senses being far more refined than those of a human or the other animals like them. In this case, it was the vibration the sound waves caused. She could feel it in her essence, even though it was probably happening half a mile from her.

The OOC was involved. She was almost certain of that. That was all right, though. He'd survive gunshots.

Survive so she could unleash what she had planned for him. And it was gonna be a doozy.

*

Hendricks didn't hear another car screech up because it was a street away, but he did see Bill Longholt come sneaking across the wide open space of the back lawn while Hendricks was belly-crawling his ass along the side of the house toward the back so he could perform a rear entry. He doubted the demons were going to enjoy that, but it looked to him like Bill was going to make it before he did, which suited him just fine. He'd heard the blast of the shotgun peppering the window he'd just shot into and knew he'd dodged that return fire. Of course, it had meant he only got off about three shots, not so well aimed, before he had thrown himself sideways and started his journey on his stomach, but that was a lot smarter than getting tapped in the head by a rifle round. He wouldn't just be struck dumb like Duncan, after all.

He waved to get Bill's attention, and the older man saw him. He didn't want to say anything in case the demons inside could hear over the thundering of their own shots and Erin's. They might be able to; Hendricks had seen demons detect some shit he would have considered well-nigh impossible.

Another shotgun blast behind him sent pieces of glass tinkling onto the sill. Fortunately, Hendricks was a good twenty feet away and opening the distance, but it distracted him for a second and when he looked back, Bill had already run into cover behind the house, out of his sight.

"Well, damn," Hendricks muttered, hurrying up. He was going to try and warn Bill about the fact that Erin was adding some pretty heavy fire to the equation, and all of it was heading through to where Bill was. There was only one thing for it, really. "INCOMING!" he shouted, figuring even an old Army guy would catch his meaning on that one. He heard the thump of the older man hitting the ground in a break between shots and reckoned he'd done right. Then he rolled sideways a few times to get close to the concrete foundation of the house, figuring it'd be a good defense in case one of the demons tried firing that AR through the floor to direct some bullets his way.

He made the corner as things started to heat up out front again, and this time it sounded like Erin was going all out, and like maybe the goddamned demons had finally run out of mags. That was a plus in his view, because it meant—

Hendricks heard a pitched scream and automatically turned to look, even though an entire house was between him and the screamer. It sounded like a woman but was muffled by the paneling and windows and all else. He dug in with his elbows and started crawling with even more fervor, wet grass brushing against his coat and the canvas dragging along behind him like a tail. He could feel a few rocks underneath his t-shirt, pushing against his belly and his johnson as he hurried along. He caught sight of Bill at the rear door, on his own belly.

The rear door was three concrete steps up from the ground, and Hendricks could see the grass was disturbed just outside, between him and the steps, like something heavy had been laying there real recently. He brushed that on out of his mind in a hurry, figuring he had way, way more important things to focus on at the moment. Bill peered up over the top step. Now he was crouched, using the concrete foundation of the house as cover against the shots, but wisely not busting in the back door just yet. A bullet burst out of the wall above Hendricks, showering his hat brim with wood splinters. Another reason to wear the thing, as far as he was concerned. He was hard-pressed to tell whether that was one of Erin's strays or one of the demons in the house getting wild with their weapon.

The sound of footsteps thumping hard on wood floors echoed in a gap in the fire. Hendricks's ears were surprisingly keen at the moment; he figured he had enough adrenaline going through his system that the gunfire wasn't bothering him—yet. It'd catch up later, though, sure as shit, and he'd hear the ringing of bells, that klaxon-like sound.

Hendricks figured out what was happening a second after Bill did. Someone was coming at the back door, and fast. Bill stuck out his consecrated cavalry saber just over the second step, and it caught the runner right at the shins, causing them to spill over and nicking them a little at the same time. Hendricks gave the man kudos for that; it was smarter than he would have figured an Army guy would be.

It was a blond-haired woman who went tripping down the second step and sprawled on the small concrete patio. She screamed as she flailed and landed hard, the sound of a demon being sucked back to hell crying out of her lips. A stink of brimstone blossomed over the area and hit Hendricks in the face, but it faded in a second. The woman landed hard on her wrist, and he heard the crack. That was going to hurt in the morning. And right now.

"Damn, Brenda," Bill said, on his feet way too soon for Hendricks's peace of mind. He would have let the woman writhe a bit, make sure nothing else was coming out that back door before he left cover. "I'm awful sorry about that."

The woman was clutching her wrist, moaning in pain, but she locked eyes with Bill. "Oh, thank God, Bill. You got those damned things out of my head. They were—I couldn't—oh, my God." Her voice got quiet. "I left my baby—"

"It's all right." Bill got down on one knee next to her. "Alison and Arch are with them right now, don't you worry. They're safe as houses."

Hendricks eyed the house next to them. There were about ten bullet holes in the back that he could see, just little pockmarks where Erin's gunfire had gone straight through. "Not sure I'd say it that way," Hendricks muttered.

"Clear!" came a voice from within the house. There was another noise of someone moaning in pain, but it sounded a little deeper, like it might be a guy. Hendricks realized it was Duncan that had called clear, and he figured that was good enough. The gunfire from Erin had stopped, too, so he got to his feet and straightened his hat. It was cool out, but he'd been sweating through this whole gunfight.

The neighborhood was quiet except for Brenda's stifled moans. The guy inside had shut up, maybe trying to keep a stiff upper lip about his pain. That left Hendricks free to hear Erin say, "Situation resolved," and get a short burst of radio static afterward. Everybody would know it was over now. At least for a little while.

*

Lauren was trying to do her best to align Reeve's busted ribs together when the call came in. "Situation resolved," Erin Harris's voice crackled through the radio in front of Brian Longholt. "Everyone's fine."

Brian was looking like he'd swallowed a lemon slice sideways. "What ... what do I even say?"

"Who gives a shit?" Reeve's reply came out about in line with where Lauren figured his pain was on the scale. "Just say we hear you, whatever." She couldn't tell if he was relieved at all under his agony, but she caught a flash of what Addison Longholt was thinking, and it was plainly, *Oh, thank God.*

*

Arch could barely believe it, standing where he was, body positioned between Alison and the kids and the sound of the shooting all those blocks away. They were all crouching, figuring that was the best move given that the sound of gunfire sometimes preceded bullets winging in one's direction.

"Thank God," Alison said, clutching baby Charlie right against her. She looked strained, and not just from trying to keep care of three kids.

"Thank Him, indeed," Arch said, and pulled at his mic. "Should we bring the kids over?"

There was a pause before Erin answered. "I think ..." Someone shouted in the background, and it sounded a little Hendricks. "Yeah, go ahead. Duncan says the house is clear and Hendricks and Bill are out back with Brenda."

"Shame on her, leaving these precious babies alone like that," Lucy Prater said. Arch had to look back, he'd forgotten the woman was even there. She was just standing, apparently oblivious to any danger, her arms folded and her lips pursed primly.

"I reckon she had a compelling reason," Arch said, "probably did it under duress given what just happened." In spite of Hendricks's constant ribbing, Arch did try his best not to be judgmental. Sometimes it was easier than others, such as now, because if he looked inside and was real honest with himself, he had formed a very definite judgment about Lucy Prater, and it was distinctly un-Christian of him, what he was thinking.

"It's a disgrace," Lucy Prater said. "There's just no excuse."

"Well," Alison said, and Arch could feel the quiet, sarcastic wrath about to descend before she even got more than that word out, "I expect that in twenty years these children will be more likely to talk to their mothers than your kids will be to talk to you." Arch blanched and blew out a little air; Lucy Prater's kids had grown up and moved away, and even Arch had heard the rumors about a family rift. He wouldn't have said anything, though, and that was a difference between him and Alison.

"Well, I never!" Lucy Prater huffed off back toward her house.

"I agree, you never should have opened your mouth," Alison tossed after her. Lucy Prater didn't turn around; she just sped up.

"Not sure that was needed," Arch said, watching her go.

"She's a mean old bitch," Alison said then put a hand over her mouth. "Biddy, I mean. Biddy."

"What's a bitch?" One of the older kids asked, eyes full of innocent wonder.

"Dang," Arch said, looking at his wife in time to catch her guilty expression. Hopefully like the rest of this experience, that little word would fade right into the recesses of their memories.

*

Hendricks went through the house again with Duncan after he'd called it clear, and what he'd seen—other than the teenage boy that Duncan had applied his baton to, evacuating demons and giving the kid what was bound to be a lovely bump on the head and maybe a concussion—concerned him. He'd seen demons go through a house or two in his time, and they tended to go about it like the dumbest of criminals, driven entirely by id. You'd find snack wrappers on the floor, broken glass everywhere from them turning over TVs and chucking plates, and empty bags of chips like the pantry had been sacked by a stoned-out college student.

This place had clearly been turned over, but it hadn't been done in a careless way. The only signs it had been done at all were open cupboards with spaces in the pantry where food had clearly been. In the upstairs bedroom, some stuff had been obviously removed from some of the closets. Not clothes, but suitcases or travel bags, and something from the top shelf of the closet that suggested to Hendricks it might be firearms of some sort.

Yeah, this house had been pillaged pretty good, and it had been done by someone who knew where everything was, knew exactly where to look, and who hadn't been driven one iota by their id. It was a robbery of calculation and care, and the stuff taken suggested that whoever had done the deed, they were looking to supply up for something.

Something bad, Hendricks figured.

"What the hell happened in here?" Erin asked, finally coming in the back door as Hendricks and Duncan were coming back down the stairs.

"Nothing good," Duncan said, glancing into the dining room, where the demons had been firing their weapons. There were shell casings everywhere on the floor, brass mostly but a few red shotgun empties for color and variety.

"Looks like this possession demon made off with enough shit to keep them fed for a while," Hendricks said, not looking at Erin.

"How do you know that?" Erin asked, holstering her gun. "I thought we got 'em."

"We got a couple of them," Duncan agreed.

"What were the names of the ladies that went missing from the park?" Hendricks asked, looking at the front door, which Duncan had apparently smashed off its hinges at some point between the time they approached and the time the confrontation had ended. Hendricks remembered it being open when they came up, which meant at some point they must have closed it, because it was damned sure opened by force, and not the human sort.

"Brenda Matthew and Evelyn Creek," Erin said, frowning. "Why?"

"Because Brenda is the only one here," Hendricks said. "Where'd that teenage boy go?"

"He's out back with Brenda and Bill," Erin said, and her frown was only deepening. "You're saying …"

"The original guy we fought it out with, the leaper," Hendricks said, "he's not here. And your other missing mommy isn't, either. That suggests—"

"They got away," Erin said, running a dirty, powder-blackened hand up over her brow, leaving traces of grey on her skin and in her hair. "Fuck."

"My sentiments exactly," Hendricks said. He nudged the busted door and it cracked loudly, the weight all resting on the bottom hinge. It split loose and came smashing down next to him, causing a hell of a noise through the house. It caused his ears to ring, but not loudly enough to blot out Erin's exclamation of, "Goddammit!"

He opened his mouth a few times, trying to clear the noise like he would a clog in his Eustachian tubes. It sorta worked, and he caught a little of Erin's heated anger being poured at him. It was funnier when he couldn't hear her, but he took it with an air of indifference even when he could. "—You really have to do that?" Hendricks just shrugged, and she sighed. "Well, what the hell do we do now?" Erin asked, apparently moving on.

"Probably ought to check nearby houses," Duncan said, his voice still a little drowned out by the ringing in Hendricks's ears. "Especially the one belonging to the other missing lady."

"I think they took whatever supplies they stole out the back," Hendricks said, pointing out toward the kitchen door where Bill was waiting with the survivors. "There's a spot on the grass that looks like they put some heavy shit there. Probably used their demon strength to hoof it out the rear while those two were keeping us in fear for our lives." He looked at Duncan. "By the way, what was your deal during all that? Because I doubt it was you fearing for your life."

Duncan looked like he'd gotten pinched. "They kept shooting me."

"That's not supposed to kill you, though, I thought?" Erin had enough alarm on her face that when she raised her voice to turn her statement into a question at the end, Hendricks wasn't surprised.

"No, it doesn't kill me, my shell's too thick for that," Duncan agreed. "But nailing me squarely in the shell with a rifle causes my essence to slosh around inside. Kinda like if you get hit in the head, it can cause a concussion?"

"Are you concussed?" Hendricks asked, being a real dick, even by his reckoning. "Should we have the doctor put on a glove and give you an exam up the rear?"

"Unlike you, she wouldn't find a lot of luck there with me," Duncan said, taking his shot in stride. "No, I'm not concussed. But when I take repeated hits to the shell, the world does spin and I have a hard time moving. It's like up becomes down and vice versa."

"You get vertigo?" Erin asked.

Duncan looked like he wanted to answer that, but after a thought he just shrugged. "Close enough. Makes it hard to charge the enemy when you can't figure out which direction you're supposed to go."

"I'd been wondering why a gun stuns demons," Erin said.

"Handguns don't produce quite that much effect, but a rifle fired repeatedly will." Duncan moved his body in a snakelike way. "The aftereffects … are also unpleasant."

"What do you mean, aftereffects?" Erin asked.

"Well, you know how I eat sometimes?" Duncan asked. Hendricks took a step back, suspecting what might be coming.

"No, but I'll take your word for it that you do," Erin said, edging away a little herself, like she caught on to him moving back. "Is it … is it gonna come back up?"

"Oh, no," Duncan said, shaking his head. "I mean, not yet. I've got it under control. But it will come out eventually, and it will make Gideon's byproducts look like a gentle spring rain by comparison." He made a noise. "Ungh. Food gets broken down by my essence, and when it gets disturbed in the process, it creates—"

"Yeah, I don't need to know about this, either," Hendricks said, wishing he'd saved kicking the door off its hinge for now, or that his ears were still ringing like hell. Instead he just wandered out the front door right about the moment that Arch and Alison were coming up, three kids in tow. They looked almost like a family, except Arch had a bearing about him, all stiff-necked and shit, that made him look like he'd never been around a kid in his life. "Well, that's a hell of a thing."

"How you doing, Hendricks?" Alison called from down the sidewalk. She was carrying one of the kids, a hell of a lot smaller than Jacob from last night, lucky for her back, he suspected.

"Well, I'm not as burdened as you," he said. "I'd worry more about Arch and how that stick up his—uhhhh," he caught himself before he said "up his ass," in front of the kids, "his, you know, is going to end up broken." The kids were all looking at him, and he felt mightily uncomfortable. "And stuff," he finished lamely, not even sure why he was saying it.

Alison rolled her eyes, making her way up the walk past the sheriff's car on the lawn. The baby in her arms pointed at it as they went past, googoo-ing out something as they went by. "Arch," Alison said, stopping next to Hendricks, "take these kids to Brenda, will you?"

"They're out back," Hendricks said. "Might want to go around that way." He pointed to indicate the way that was free of broken glass, past the police cruiser sitting like a pink flamingo in the middle of the lawn.

Arch's eyes got big as the sun. "Uhhhh ..." He plainly didn't intend to argue with his wife, so he dutifully stuck out his hands and received the baby, which he clutched awkwardly to his chest. "Okay." He looked down at the other two, who seemed a little red in the face to Hendricks. "Come on, then." They followed after him, though one of them lingered behind, casting looks at Alison as Arch took them around the house.

When Arch had disappeared, Hendricks looked back in the door. Erin and Duncan were gone, probably to check with the survivors in the rear. He glanced at Alison, wondering what was going on with her, but she was just staring at the cruiser in front of them like it was holding a deep secret of the universe or something.

"You all right?" Hendricks asked, not really sure what else he could say.

Alison blinked a few times, like she was coming back to herself, and then refocused on him. The corner of her mouth twitched, and she pushed long blond hairs out of her eyes. "Tell me a joke," she said, dead serious.

"Uhm." Hendricks just stared at her, trying to figure out if she was pulling one on him right now, asking for this out of the blue. "What?"

"Just tell me a joke," she said, toneless. "I know you got some."

"Any joke in particular?" Hendricks asked.

"Anything," she said.

"Well," he said, put right on the spot and watching his memory for every joke he'd ever heard just recede into the sunset like early morning clouds evaporated under the break of day, "I, uhh ... well, I just thought of one, but it's pretty tasteless and crass."

"So tell it," she said, with the air of patient expectation.

"Okay," he said, reddening a little as he started, "this guy decides to go bear hunting, so he heads back in the woods and sits there, next to a tree, waiting, until a bear comes wandering through. He raises his rifle, takes a shot, and when the smoke clears—"

"What is this, black powder season?" Alison asked, making a face.

"It's just a joke, follow along," Hendricks said. "When he goes to check, he can't find the bear. Suddenly he feels a tap on his shoulder, and turns around to find the bear right there, pissed as hell. And the bear says—"

"Oh, it's one of these type of jokes, with talking bears."

"Yeah, it's like the cartoons of our youth," Hendricks said. "This would go a lot easier if you weren't constantly interrupting—"

"Fine, go on."

"So the bear says, 'I'm so fucking sick of you hunters shooting at me. I'm going to teach you a lesson. Either blow me right now, or I'm gonna maul you so hard that when you piss it's gonna spray out like one of those lawn sprinklers with the rings—"

"How does a bear know about lawn sprinklers?"

"Did you want a joke or not?"

"... Okay. Proceed."

"So what can the hunter do? He gets down on his knees and does as told, then leaves afterwards—"

"Doesn't even get breakfast. What a disgrace."

"—and he goes and buys a more expensive gun, with better optics, and he goes back to the woods to the same spot the next week. And he sits there for a little while, and sure enough, here comes the bear again. So he raises his gun and he shoots, and when the smoke clears or whatever, he goes looking and there's no carcass. He feels this tap on his shoulder—"

"Oh, boy."

"—and the bear is just staring down at him again, pissed as hell. 'You know what to do,' he says, and points down. The hunter looks at the bear's claws and he knows there's no way he'd get the gun up in time. So he drops and makes it happen again—"

"I bet he was spitting out hairs for a week."

Hendricks stopped and made a disgusted face before going on. "Anyway, he goes and buys an even more expensive gun, top-flight optics, and he's fucking ready for revenge. So he goes out to the woods again, same spot, and he's sitting there, and sure as shit, here comes the bear again. So he steadies the gun and aims so carefully, not even taking a breath, and he fires, and when he goes to check where he thinks the corpse has fallen, there's nothing. And then there's a tap on his shoulder, and he hears a voice—'You're not in this for the hunting, are you?'"

Hendricks finished and waited, watching Alison's face to see what she thought. She was a hard read sometimes, but she had a real thoughtful look on her face, and finally she spoke. "I thought you said this was a crass and tasteless joke."

Hendricks blinked. "Uh ... most people would say so."

"Really?" She didn't look impressed. "I'd say it's got a very distinctive flavor." She smiled impishly. "Kinda salty and chalky—"

"Gross," Hendricks said, closing his eyes as he laughed a little.

"Oh," she said, with a taunting air, "he can give it but he can't take it, folks ... except up the ass."

"The hell?" Hendricks stared at her. "Were you in the Corps at some point? Because you talk like a Marine, and I like it."

She just kinda laughed that off. "Thanks. That wasn't bad."

"Hey, I'm good for a few things," Hendricks said, and they fell into silence for a second. "Thank you, by the way."

She cocked her head as she looked at him. "For what?"

He stared hard at the shot-up police cruiser in front of them. "For not treating me different since ... for not acting like I'm broken glass or a bomb about to go off."

"Yeah," she said, looking down. "Well. I get the feeling we all get lic—err, hit sometimes in this demon hunting business."

"I've taken my fair share before I got here, it's true," Hendricks said. "But since I got here ... it's been worse. Worse than any other hotspot."

"Part of that might have to do with the company you keep," she said, and it sounded just a little like she was poking at him on that.

"Well, I don't intend to get rid of y'all," Hendricks said, "so—"

"I was talking about that red-headed harlot you're still palling around with," Alison said, turning her head to give him a knowing look. "She's been showing up at your motel, hasn't she?"

Hendricks just froze. It wasn't like he'd done anything wrong, but he had a feeling like she'd caught him with his pants down. "Nothing's happened."

"Something will," Alison said, looking away from him. "It'll happen sooner or later, you just watch. She's setting you up for it."

"I can't even—" Hendricks looked back to make sure no one was lurking inside the house and lowered his voice. "I can't even sleep at night, Alison." He stared right at her, and she didn't dare to look back. "Ain't nothing happening."

"It will," she said, full of self-assurance and still refusing to make eye contact. She started off around the house, and he didn't follow. "I just hope when it does, nothing comes out of it worse than a case of syphilis."

Lauren was on her way out to the site of the attack to make a house call, with Reeve next to her in the car, when her phone buzzed hard in the pocket of her scrubs. "What fresh hell is this?" she asked, tossing out her favorite Dorothy Parker quote as she went to answer it and stopped as soon as she saw the number.

"What?" Reeve asked. The man was all slumped against the side of her car, and the Advil she'd given him hadn't taken hold quite yet. Not that any OTC medication was going to do much, but even if she'd written a script for him, it wasn't like he'd had a chance to stop by a pharmacy and get it filled yet, anyway.

"Work is calling," she said, frowning at the caller ID. "Probably my boss." She cast Reeve a look that was designed to prick him with a little guilty. "Likely pissed that I evaporated right before my shift was supposed to start."

"Oh, well, just explain to him your town has been flooded with demons and I'm sure he'll back right the hell off," Reeve said, clearly trying to beat her at her irony game, the fucker.

"In all seriousness, how am I supposed to deal with this?" she wondered, mostly to herself, as she sent the call to voicemail.

Reeve grunted as the car hit a bump, and then lapsed into a silence that she interpreted as him actually trying to come up with an answer for her. "Maybe you should ask Arch," he finally said, and she couldn't tell if he was resentful or just being shitty, "I think he came up with a few gallons of bullshit when he was in your situation."

"Why does that not surprise me about the pious and holy one?" Lauren rolled her eyes.

"Because you're predisposed to dislike him," Reeve said with certainty. "Why is that, exactly?"

Lauren just grunted in a similar manner to Reeve's noise when he hit the bump. "Doesn't matter."

"Probably not to Arch, no," Reeve said, "but it's clearly a bee in your bonnet. You might think about letting it out at some point, if only for the novelty of it stinging someone else besides you."

"I'll take that under advisement as I'm doing more unpaid work while my boss probably reams me a new asshole via voicemail," Lauren said.

"That's the spirit," Reeve said, once more playing the sarcastic asshole to placid perfection. "Charity work is good for the soul, anyway."

"It's not so good for the wallet or the résumé, though, especially since you can't add it to your résumé. 'Worked as a doctor in a demon-riddled hot zone.' Yeah. You don't see that much."

"So you'd be saying you have unique experience. Seems like a selling point to me."

She rolled her eyes again, but she doubted the asshole noticed. Home or career, that was what this came down to. Why was it she'd suddenly been driven to pick the former, again?

*

"So it has come to this," Brian said quietly, staring at the phone and the radio in front of him like they were his mortal nemesis. They weren't, not really. His mortal nemesis was actually the Marvel movies/TV shows/corporate synergy product. But the radio/phone combo was running a close second at the moment, just barely edging out Wall Street and the Koch Brothers.

"I'm so glad you've finally found a job," said his mother, a master of the backhanded compliment. "I was worried after you came back from Brown, figured it was like you crawling back with your tail between your legs, an admission of defeat. But you persevered, biding your time, smoking your ganja down in the basement—"

"Mom," Brian said with a horrified look. Mrs. Reeve, the sheriff's wife, was standing right there, barely containing herself from laughing. "Oh, hah hah, I smoke marijuana and I'm unemployed, so obviously I'm ripe for lots of little shots, because this is the South, where intelligence and drug use are worse than being an actual member of the Knights of the Ku Klux Klan."

"I said I was proud of you," his mother said lightly. "Which I wouldn't be saying if you had joined the KKK, I assure you. Though I doubt they'd have you. Probably figure you for a snitch."

"This is just …" He put his face in his hands, hanging over the radio and phone. "This is not how I pictured my life turning out."

"I don't think anyone who's been fighting these demons imagined this was how their life was going to turn out, my darling boy," his mother said, pulling a chortle out of Mrs. Reeve. "I suppose I could be wrong, it might be that Erin Harris was just waiting for the day she could become a demon fighter—"

"That's not what I—" He slumped. "Would you just ... maybe leave me alone for a few minutes?"

"I can take over for you if you want, Brian," Mrs. Reeve said, surprisingly gently over the air of amusement.

Brian didn't look up from the task before him: watching a radio and phone and waiting for one or the other or both to make noise at him. "No, I've got this. Why don't you ... go get donuts for the team or something and just ... leave me to this for a while."

"We could get some lunch for everybody," his mother said, clearly already moving on to being solicitous. She'd scored her points on him and his ego already, anyway. Her work was done, and he felt appropriately shamed for his lack of humility.

"That sounds like a real good idea," Mrs. Reeve said as they gathered their purses and made their way to the door. Brian listened to them go without looking up from the desk.

When he heard the door close, he said, "Now maybe that fucking possession demon will get his ass over here and end me." And a little piece of him actually wished it would happen.

*

Alison watched the kids playing in the backyard with a more detached eye than she had before. She wasn't in charge anymore, thank God, and that was just fine by her. She'd done what she'd needed to, and was perfectly content to pass off the responsibility to someone else, at least in this regard.

But she kinda figured it might be different if the kids had been her own instead of someone else's.

Listening to the two older kids trying to do handstands and cartwheels and failing, laughing all the while, was like a potent reminder that when adults took spills like that, they didn't usually do it with as much grace. In this, she was thinking of Hendricks. Her conversation with the cowboy had left a bitter taste in her, a worry she'd pushed to the stove's back burner for a while. Him, by himself, being all self-destructive following what Kitty Elizabeth had done to him, that was worry enough.

Him plus that cunt Starling? That felt like a formula for disaster. Like mixing chlorine bleach and ammonia in a toilet and expecting not to die horribly.

She didn't mention a peep of this to those around her, though. Because although her dad, Duncan and Erin were here, so were Taylor and Brenda Matthews, and she didn't need that thought to get spread through the entirety of Midian, metastasizing like cancer, out of control and garbled like the message in a game of telephone.

That bounty hunter Lonsdale was lurking out on the far end of the yard. Alison saw him and furrowed her brow. "What's he doing here?" she asked, giving no fucks if her wonders about a British demon hunter spread from here to Timbuktu.

"He said he wanted to help me," her father said in his smooth voice, "but he hobbled his way after me slower than an old lady, and he disappeared on me when I came up to the storm the back door of this house."

She stared out at Lonsdale, who was wandering around the side of the garage of the house across the back yard from them. He looked like he was sniffing the ground or something, peering down at the grass. "That's peculiar, isn't it?"

"It is indeed," Arch said, getting into the conversation. "Maybe we ought to go have a conversation with him."

Alison chewed on that for a second. "Maybe I ought to get my rifle first."

*

Arch had collected Hendricks with the intent to talk a thing or two over with Lonsdale, but when they actually got over to him, any questions he might have asked went poof like smoke before he got a word out.

"I think this demon is splitting off pieces into other bodies," Lonsdale announced, surprisingly clear for once. He was squinting against the daylight, and Arch wondered if he was just used to more cloud cover in England.

"Well, it seems that's what he does, Mart," Hendricks said, making it sound like Lonsdale was stupid in the process. Arch didn't necessarily approve of making people feel bad, but Hendricks was a different sort of communicator than he was.

"Fair enough, fair enough," Lonsdale said, coming away from the side of the garage. "I think he stole these peoples' car." He landed a hand on the side of the garage. "Door's open, no vehicle inside."

Arch looked at the house. He wasn't real sure who it belonged to, but that wouldn't be a hard thing to find out. He keyed his mic. "Dispatch, this is fifteen."

It took a minute, and then Brian's voice came crackling back. "Uhh ... I guess I'm dispatch. What do you want?"

Arch waited a second. "I need to know about who owns a certain house."

There was another pause. "Lemme ... okay, I got Google up on my phone. Fire away." The sound of Brian whistling on the other end filled the air.

Hendricks spoke up. "Does the idiot not realize he needs to let go of the button in order to let you speak?"

"He's a tit," Lonsdale opined, causing Arch to frown at him. "I didn't even use rhyming slang on that, you don't know what a tit is?"

"I know what a tit is," Hendricks said. "They're real fun to—"

"Oh, sorry!" Brian crackled back. "Okay, I'm letting go of the button now."

"The address is 916 Worth Street," Arch said, and he settled in to wait.

The answer took a minute. "I have the Calhoun County Property Tax search record here ... man, I'm surprised they put this online ... owner is Michael Fordham."

Arch turned that name over in his head. "I don't know who that is."

"Yeah, I've never heard of him, either," Brian came back. "I guess I could Google him, too ..."

"You know we have tools to search for property owners without having to resort to Google like a civilian," Reeve's voice broke into the conversation. He sounded a little funny to Arch, and when he turned around, there was Reeve, across the lawn at the back door to the house with Dr. Darlington, who was tending to people. Reeve was talking a little breathless, like he was still hurting.

"Yeah, my on-the-job training for this position kinda sucked,"

Brian said. "I'm trying to narrow the results for Michael Fordham."

"Don't bother," Reeve said. "Michael Fordham is in a nursing home. His granddaughter lives in the house now. Her name is Clarissa, I think."

"Where does she work?" Arch asked, looking at the sheriff across the sixty or so yards of empty lawn that separated him. He looked tiny, and he was slumping a little.

"I don't believe she had a job," Reeve said. "I think she was on disability for some reason after the factory she worked at downsized her."

Arch exchanged a look with Hendricks, who didn't look worried, per se, but he didn't look happy, either. "If she was home and this demon came a callin'," Hendricks said, confirming Arch's suspicion about his mood, "she might just be part of our problem now."

*

Chester and the others pulled up to the farm in the country, the sounds of nature all around them as the car's motor faded to silence. He stepped out of the vehicle and just listened for a moment. William had been right; this was so much different than Queens, and certainly a worthwhile place to seek a change.

A light breeze whipped around him as he stared up at the older farmhouse. It was fading in the sun, dark crimson paint turned rust-colored by time and weather. Chester had no opinion about the aesthetics of the look; his attention was centered on how it would fit for their needs. It had taken almost twenty minutes to get from town to here, which Chester considered a reasonable margin of distance to keep them away from the law that would be hunting them. In addition, the farmhouse was owned by a very distant relation of their newest acquisition, and thus it was unlikely that the sheriff, Reeve, and his allies would manage to track them down here.

Chester took a deep breath of the air around him and nodded to their newest body, who was under the control of Thurston. Thurston nodded the woman's head and headed toward the door. Thurston had almost fifty of their fellows within the body, which would make it eminently possible to quietly subdue any resistance within the house.

Yes, this was the next move, Chester thought as he heard

Thurston knock upon the door. Chester took a deep breath of the cool, crisp, country air as the door opened, and a greeting was given and then cut off halfway through as Thurston merely touched the newest member of their team, the latest prize in their war. That was the beauty of what they could do, really; turn any person, no matter how old or young, into a fighter for their cause.

William would have liked this place, Chester thought, as he marched up onto the porch once he was assured that the house was theirs. But even he would not have liked what was happening now, Chester knew, the things that would be done in his name. It was a shame that it had come to this, but it had, and Chester's resolve to finish the thing left him without a doubt about what had to be done next.

5.

The search of the nearby houses had been a deeply unsatisfying bit of business for Reeve. He'd knocked on doors with the rest of them, and when he did find people home, a good portion of them viewed him with absolute suspicion, eyes narrowed like they were waiting for him to kick down the door. That may have been normal in the city, but here in Midian he'd always enjoyed the full cooperation of the citizenry, and seeing just how many people slammed their doors after talking to him with only the thinnest veneer of civility was disheartening, to say the least.

As if that wasn't bad enough, somewhere along the way, that idiot Brit demon hunter, somehow more annoying than Cowboy Hendricks, had started following him around like he was a brand new puppy put in Reeve's charge. "Why don't you go on back to the house and wait there?" Reeve asked, gesturing toward down the street toward the front lawn where his old car was still parked, driven by Erin up onto the lawn.

"I'll just follow at a distance," Lonsdale said in a heavy accent. At least he didn't throw in any of that nonsense slang. "I won't be any Barney at all." There it was, goddammit.

Reeve just kept his rage on a chain. Letting it go on this bastard wasn't going to do any good anyway. He keyed his mic and spoke into it. "Dispatch, this is One, over."

It took a second for the response to come back, Brian Longholt's voice breaking over the air. "Yep, what's up?"

Reeve just shut his eyes and sighed for a second before keying the mic. "I think we're done here, unless anyone else wants to keep knocking on doors and talking to people who don't want to talk to us."

Arch's voice crackled through. "The response today does seem a lot frostier than usual."

"Goddamn Pike," Reeve said, not bothering to filter his assessment of the situation. "He's turning the town against us."

"Uh, Sheriff?" Erin broke in. "What are we supposed to do with Evelyn's kids?"

Reeve thought about it for a second. "Leave 'em with Brenda, unless someone wants to take them back to the station while we're in the middle of planning a damned war."

"Uh …" Erin paused, and Reeve could hear muted conversation. "Okay, Brenda says that's fine, she'll get ahold of Evelyn's husband if we haven't already."

Reeve cursed, keeping his finger off the mic button. When he pushed it again, he was keeping his rage bottled up inside, but only barely. "Dispatch usually handles that."

"Oh, uh, yeah, I don't know how to do that," Brian's voice came back, not even the least bit apologetic.

Reeve closed his eyes against the mid-afternoon sun and counted to five before answering back. "You seemed pretty handy with that Google thing a little bit ago. Why don't you try it again? Or maybe just have Erin, who's on scene, ask Brenda for Evelyn's husband's cell phone number?" Wasn't Brian Longholt supposed to be some kind of brilliant kid? Didn't he go to one of those fancy schools? This was not exactly contradicting Reeve's assumption that people who went to those schools lost connection with reality and common sense.

"Oh, uh, yeah, good idea," Brian said. "Erin—"

"I'm getting it," Erin came back, cool but not harsh.

"Great. Thanks."

Reeve sighed again, then again, then just took a breath in and held it, trying to let the stress bleed out. He turned around to start heading for the house so he could get the fuck outta here and back to the station, but Lonsdale was just standing there, big grin on his face. "What the fuck are you smirking at?" Reeve asked.

"It's not healthy to hold that all in, you know," Lonsdale said, and the fucker looked like he was having the time of his life.

Reeve suppressed the urge to find a septic lagoon to drown the man in and let his feet carry him up the road. "Healthier than letting it all out right now."

*

Chester stared off the back porch and out into the empty, rolling fields behind him. The hill territory of Tennessee offered such a lovely vista for him as he stared over the sun-drenched hills. A chilly wind blew over him, prickling at his flesh.

The plan was simple, and the approval was near universal within him. Only a day ago, they had been fiercely divided, and William's faction had all their ire. Coming to this place had clearly been the single greatest failure they had ever undertaken, and the condemnation would have been universal—if William and his fellows were still with them.

Instead, within them, there was no argument, only rage. William and his followers were eulogized, their failings forgotten for the time being, and their virtues celebrated over and over in thousands of voices. Chester knew of no other time when the whole of them had been so in uniform agreement. True, they were fewer now with William's brethren gone, but he had never even heard such universal accord even in his own corner of their little world.

"You all know what to do," Chester said. He had six good bodies before him, and they had "loaded up," taking over six hundred souls among them. They had a simple task ahead of them, to propagate and spread, to insinuate themselves where needed. There was a plan, and while its aims were fixed, the methods employed would be loose and subject to change for best possible results. "Does everyone know the phone number for this house?"

"Yes," came the chorus, nods following. Chester could see their faces, but they were all meaningless to him. He could not see the faces beneath at the moment, just the human flesh atop them. He did not want to know who lay beneath, not truly, because if he did, he might hesitate at a crucial juncture.

"Then go forth," Chester said, harkening back to a passage he had long remembered, "and spread into the swine of this town, and prepare ... to leave our mark upon them."

*

Hendricks headed into the old brick station with slow reluctance, like his will was forcing him to drag along inside even though the greater part of him didn't want to be here. He could think of better places to be, had a jonesing to get back to the Sinbad and shower for a spell, trying to let the hot water wash away his memory. He had trouble with feeling clean nowadays. No matter how hard he scrubbed, no matter how often he'd shaved, he still felt—

"You gonna put some get up and go in your step or do we need to fetch you some more coffee?" Reeve asked as he came around Hendricks on the left side. Hendricks watched him go past, the sheriff sending a sour look back at him and getting cool neutrality in response. Lonsdale followed along in his wake, and Hendricks had an inkling where some of that irritation was coming from.

"By all means, go first," Hendricks said, exaggerating with a hand wave to indicate he should pass on by. He stopped and let both Reeve and Lonsdale enter the station, the sheriff clearly in a great blazing hurry by the force with which he opened the door. It stirred a little wind, probably from the air conditioner, which felt cold as fuck, like someone had piled blocks of ice in the station house. Hadn't it been boiling hot earlier, that dry furnace air pouring out of the ducts during their meeting? Reeve just barged on in like he didn't feel it, and Lonsdale trailed along like a toady, which was funny. Just this morning he'd had his own toadies, and now he was one.

Hendricks counted out ten seconds, peering through the entry and mentally counting up who was inside, waiting. It looked like a full house, and there was food spread all along the counter. He could see boxes of fried chicken, and now that he thought about it, he'd probably caught a whiff of it when Reeve had opened the door. Lauren Darlington was hovering near the side items portion of the impromptu buffet, like she was trying to decide if anything was worth the calories. She didn't even have a plate in her hand, unlike Arch, who was loading up on mashed potatoes, and Alison, who was following behind with a slightly smaller load on her own plate.

Hendricks stared in at the lot of them. This wasn't what he'd had in mind when he'd dropped off that trucker's running board into Calhoun County a couple months back. This was just another hotspot at the time, and making pals with the locals hadn't been his plan, ever. He'd been pointed in this direction just like he'd been pointed everywhere else the last few years, and he trusted the lady who held his fate in her hands well enough to know that when she said something was there and gave a good shooing toward it, there was something there and he ought to get to it.

But none of the other hotspots had been like this. They'd all been demon kills, plain and simple, where he was the hunter and the demons were the hunted. They fought back, sure, but they didn't have grand plans, they didn't go in for revenge, and they damned sure didn't mix up with demon hunters. They ran like chickenshits most of the time, or stood and fought and died and it was over. They were dumb, they were easily frightened, and you could go get drunk in a bar after a good fight without worrying eight charlagarn were going to come crashing through your motel room door afterward to fuck up your night.

"What's so goddamned different about this town?" Hendricks mumbled to himself. His eyes flitted again to Arch, and he wondered if he might be the answer to the question. *Archibald Stan is the man who will bring about the end of the world.* The words went charging through his head again, ping-ponging around a few times before they stopped.

"I keep asking myself that same question," Duncan said. Hendricks looked over his shoulder; the OOC had snuck up on him so quietly that he hadn't even realized the demon was there. "Because it's not playing out like other hotspots."

"No," Hendricks agreed, feeling a little stiff next to Duncan, who joined him at the window next to the door, looking in like the outsiders they were. "It's really not."

"So why do you think it has something to do with Arch?" Duncan asked, and Hendricks must have blanched a little, because Duncan tapped his own head. "You're as clear as the sky today, at least right now. A lot louder than everyone else in there, with their mingled relief and barely contained worry about this possession demon."

"If you guys wiped out possession demons, why would one come here, and right now, no less?" Hendricks folded his arms. "That's weird, right?"

"It's weird that one's still walking the earth at all," Duncan said, shifting slightly on his feet. "It's truly bizarre that one would have survived all this time only to come here right now, yes. But hotspots are bizarre, so …"

"Do you even know what kind it is?" Hendricks asked.

"No," Duncan asked, and here he seemed vaguely uncomfortable again. "I don't sense runes on them, but when I try and get a read on him—or her, I guess, not that it matters—it's muddled, like a picture taken of a person running, where it blurs, you know?"

"So you know jack and shit about them, that's what you're saying."

"In so many words." Duncan folded his arms. "Nice deflection, by the way." When Hendricks looked at him, the OOC looked back. "About Arch, I mean."

"Arch prays, fucks his wife and fights demons," Hendricks said. "There's nothing else about him to discuss."

"We could talk about how for some reason you seem to think he's going to end the world," Duncan said. He turned and looked right at Hendricks. "Lemme tell you something about doomsday prophecies, speaking as someone who's heard one a week for the last few hundred years—they're all crap."

"Really?" Hendricks asked, feeling like he had his back up, ready to defend the position he was in. "You charged in pretty quick with us that time Starling said letting that carnie blow his load was going to lead to the world ending."

"Yeah," Duncan said, "but not for the reason you're thinking. The first part of what she said was that Midian would fall. Then she linked that to the rest of the world descending into the apocalypse or something, I don't really recall, mostly because I don't believe in it enough to care. She had me at the first part of it, Midian falling." He shifted, moving his arms to hang by his side. "Towns disappearing off the map is bad business. Bad enough for Home Office to want to stop it. You can mewl all day about the Rog'tausch supposedly being tied to the end of the world, but the end of Midian and a demon smashing his way through is more than enough to get an OOC off the bench and fighting."

"I'd probably take that better if it was coming from a place of real compassion," Hendricks said, "instead of you just wanting to make sure demons are kept secret."

"Full on demon-human wars are no picnic for either side," Duncan said. "Don't get me wrong, I like your chances—you bugs have overrun the globe, come up with technology beyond bronze-age swords, and blown up your population by billions since last we scrapped, but don't kid yourself into thinking it'd be a painless little fight in which you roll over the evil demons by dinnertime." He cast a wary look at Hendricks. "Demons can use guns and bombs and tanks and WMDs, and they would. An all-out fight between our peoples would leave scars on this world that would never heal." He waved a hand vaguely. "A possession demon is small potatoes compared to some of the other things on our 'side.'"

"Doesn't feel small," Hendricks said. "Maybe I'm just paranoid after watching it walk two mothers away from their babies and getting another to draft her teen to fight in a gun battle, but this is the sort of shit that makes my brain jump a little. How do we even know where it is? How do we know it doesn't have one of the people in there in its thrall?" He pointed to the station house.

Duncan frowned. "I could probably read that, if it was the case."

Hendricks snorted. "I love the certainty."

*

Lauren was eyeing the fried chicken, considering whether it was worth the effort later to burn it off. She didn't have the quickest metabolism in the world, and often watched Molly consume delicious and terrible delicacies with considerable envy, knowing her teenage daughter would show little to no sign of her sinful delight. Meanwhile, Lauren was still trying to get rid of that donut hole she'd eaten three years ago, the one that clung bitterly to that spot on her inner thigh, with cat claws, refusing to let go.

"Oh, that's good," Arch Stan said, licking some mashed potatoes off his finger. She glared at him and he didn't even notice. He looked fit enough that he probably didn't suffer from having to worry overmuch about what he ate, either.

"Yeah, y'all dig in," Reeve said over in the corner, standing next to his wife. He was holding himself like he'd broken his ribs, favoring that side, clearly. "Then let's settle it on down and talk for a bit."

"I feel like we've had this meeting before," Brian Longholt said, still sour as a Lemonhead, from his place behind the dispatch desk. He had a laptop computer set up in front of him, and Amazon's "Thank you for your order!" screen was emblazoned across it. "Maybe just a few hours ago."

"Well, the situation has changed, obviously," Reeve said, plainly strained from more than just pain. "Believe me, I don't like having meetings for the sake of meetings any more than the rest of you do."

"Should we wait for Casey and Father Nguyen?" Bill Longholt asked in that soft yet solemn voice of his as Hendricks and Duncan came in from outside, both stoically silent and clearly chewing on something between the two of them. Probably not chicken, Lauren figured.

"No." Reeve shook his head. "Getting this crew together for a meeting is starting to feel like convening a session of Congress, and we ain't even added any of the potential new people in yet, like Barney Jones or Mike McInness."

"Don't forget Melina Cherry," Erin said with a gleam in her eyes. Lauren watched the point ding Reeve like he'd taken a poke to the broken rib, and his expression grew jaded. "She's just aching to help."

That rubbed Lauren the wrong way. "We should be happy for any help we can get at this point," she said and watched Deputy Harris bristle a little at her returned poke. "I don't care where it comes from."

"I agree with the doctor," Arch said, making Lauren wish she'd not said a damned thing. "The way things are going, and based on what we saw knocking on doors, there ain't a real friendly air in Midian toward us at the moment."

"Yeah, well, anyway," Reeve said, sallying on past all that argument, "I don't know where Casey is, and Father Nguyen is consecrating something, I think, so—"

"He's consecrating something for Casey, I think," Duncan said.

That drew a moment of silence as Reeve frowned. "What the hell would Casey get consecrated? And who's paying for it?"

"Not I," Bill said, not without a little jading of his own. "Casey Meacham is a man of a little bit of means of his own, presumably he would pay on his own account."

Reeve just shook it off. "I guess I have a hard time imagining Casey swinging any sort of weapon, that's all."

*

"Are you sure about this?" Father Nguyen stared at the object in his hands, absolutely sure that no priest in any parish had ever consecrated one of these before. He stared down at it, turning it over a few times. "I mean … it's a …"

"Tomahawk," Casey said with a little more pride than Nguyen thought was due. It had a long wooden handle and a steel head that showed signs of long wear. Nguyen didn't want to know what it had been used for, but the handle was short enough that he suspected it probably wasn't for hand-to-hand combat of any kind. "You know, like the Ind—errr," Casey blushed like he'd got caught doing something terrible. "That the Native Americans used," he finished, plainly pleased with himself at changing his vernacular at the last second.

Father Nguyen just shook his head. "All right. This is going to take a while, though …"

"It's all right," Casey said, shrugging his shoulders. "I got a Fleshlight and some magazines out in the truck. I'll just hang out for a bit."

Nguyen shrugged and carried the tomahawk off toward the altar. There wasn't much point in inquiring about what Casey was talking about. Nguyen didn't know, but he was equally sure after hearing part of the man's confession earlier that he didn't want to know. "Ignorance really is bliss," Nguyen concluded, leaving the strange taxidermist to his wait.

*

"So now we have a real threat at hand," Reeve said, feeling like he was calling to order his third meeting in less than twenty-four hours. "Duncan, what can you tell us about these possession demons?" The smell of the food was getting to him, and he planned to dig in once they settled things out in some manner. The thought of that thing grabbing people up was worrying him, though, so he fought the hunger back.

"There are several types," Duncan said, just launching straightaway into it. "We can't rule out any of them at this point."

"I hope you have more than that," Reeve said, frowning when the OOC paused.

"A little more," Duncan said with a shrug. "So, the way possession types work is—well, it's a broad category. There are some that just do flat-out mind control, like hijacking your body and turning you into a piece of their hive-mind. There are others that split their essence, inhabiting multiple hosts at the same time. Again, bottom line is that this is a hive-mind type situation, one overarching intelligence putting its will into others and acting in a coordinated fashion—"

"That's not what we saw at the first encounter this morning," Arch said, his plate full and yet untouched. Clearly the deputy was into this shit in a way that Reeve wasn't. He eyed the man as Arch went on. "Remember? The demon that was in Lonsdale over there," he gestured at the demon hunter, who was standing irritably close to Reeve, about ten feet away, "called the other one Chester when he got stabbed, and Chester called him Bill or William or something."

"Yeah, yeah," Lonsdale said, snapping his fingers in front of him. "There were like a thousand screaming voices in my head. There was one that was loudest, true, but it was almost like being in a crowd in there, too much to fathom all at once, like trying eat a bite but ending up with a whole week's worth of meals shoved in your gullet at once."

"Oh," Duncan said.

"'Oh'?" Hendricks was first to perk up at that. He was just standing there like a big black void in his coat and hat. "That's all you have to say?"

"Multiple voices with a 'speaker' to talk for them," Duncan said, blinking a few times. "Yeah ... that's probably what we call a Legion."

"Like ... the French foreign one?" Dr. Darlington asked.

"Not exactly," Duncan said. "Multiple essences without a shell of their own, so they're forced to inhabit human or other demon bodies."

"When you say 'multiple,' you mean how many exactly?" Reeve asked. "Because if it's like ten, we gotta be well on the way to wiping them out—"

Duncan took a minute to speak again, and everyone waited with bated breath for his answer. "Impossible to say exactly, but ... no. Not ten. More like ... thousands. Or ... hundreds of thousands. Or—"

"Please, Jesus, don't say millions," Alison said quietly into the stunned silence.

Duncan stopped. "Could be. I don't know."

"How the fuck do your people lose track of millions of essences?" Erin Harris asked, nonplussed and channeling the question Reeve himself might have asked if he'd had a little better grip on how the demon world operated. "I mean, you said you OOCs wiped these things out, but now you're saying that this—this—"

"Legion," Arch said solemnly, crackling across everyone. "*My name is Legion: for we are many.*"

"That sounds awfully ominous," Lonsdale opined.

"It's from the Bible," Arch said.

"That explains it, then," Hendricks said dourly.

"You lost track of millions of essences," Erin said accusingly. Reeve was just watching, hoping something useful would come out of this. "How?"

"Because we've got a lot more than 'millions' to keep track of," Duncan said simply, "and it's not as though there was a census in the early days. We weren't as organized as the Roman Empire, and it's not like we could just tell everyone to go back to their hometown for a counting."

"So we're up against potentially millions of these things," Reeve said, trying to wrap his head around this whole concept, which had landed in his lap like one of his grandbabies with a sour diaper.

"Potentially," Duncan said without much in the realm of feeling. "Probably less, but hundreds of thousands wouldn't be out of line for one of these 'colonies'—"

"Should we even ask what they're doing here?" Hendricks asked. "Do you have any clue, now that we've narrowed it down?"

"Other than getting pissed that you apparently vaped part of their colony?" Duncan shrugged. "I don't know. They've clearly been hiding and off our radar for a long time since they escaped the purge of their kind. These 'Legions' were like a society crammed into a human body. Every one of them took on different characteristics, just like if you went to any different nation or sometimes even different towns on earth, you'd find differing cultures, upbringings, values. Whatever this particular group has going on, I think it's safe to say that if they vowed revenge, it's because they're stinging from the loss of their people that were bunked in Lonsdale." He pointed at the demon hunter. "And odds are good they've all been together for a really long time, like … thousands of years, so the bonds of affection are likely to be pretty tight."

"So now they're super pissed at us," Reeve said, feeling a little more heated, "because they feel like we struck down some of their own."

"Yep," Duncan said.

"Well, they can join the fucking club." Reeve crossed his arms, his own fury burning hard inside. "Because that's how I've felt for weeks."

"They are a fucking club," Lauren muttered. "A country unto themselves, with borders of flesh."

"How are they going to come at us?" Arch asked, and he put his plate down without a bite taken.

Duncan started to open his mouth to speak, but the doorbell jangled and stopped him.

"Well, isn't this a cozy little gathering of picnickers," came the voice of the man at the door. His hair was slicked back, his suit jacket was pressed and in perfect order, and he was almost smiling, a thin layer of satisfaction plastered across his tanned face.

"County Administrator Pike," Reeve said, as the tension in his belly ratcheted from a 9.5 on a scale of 1 to 10 all the way up to 327 in a hot second. "I wish I could say it was nice to see you again … but it's really not."

6.

"I'm mighty thirsty," County Administrator Pike pronounced with a smart aleck smile that Arch took personal offense to. "Where do y'all keep the Kool-Aid you've been drinking?"

Alison landed a hand on Arch's forearm that suggested to him to keep his mouth buttoned up. It wasn't his first instinct, but he followed her guidance and let his eyes bounce on over to Sheriff Reeve, who was over in the corner. The man's face had gone red; plainly he was just as affronted by the jibe as Arch was.

"It's right over there next to the ignorance antidote," Reeve said, motioning toward the buffet of food spread across the front counter. "Take a big ol' dose of that first, because Lord knows you need it."

"Oh, my," Pike said, still smirking, walking his lanky frame on into the station, apparently undeterred by the hostility leveled in his direction. An uneasy pall had fallen over everyone in the room save for him and Reeve, and Arch had a feeling that this was a contest best settled by the two of them. "Well, if ignorance of your mythical demons is supposed to be some sort of insult, I reckon I'll be okay with keeping my so-called ignorance … though I call it a connection to reality, one which I can only assume your Kool-Aid causes people to lose."

"Who the fuck is this tosser?" Lonsdale piped up.

Pike looked right at Lonsdale. "I'm gonna guess by your accent you're not an eligible voter."

"Voting for what?" Lonsdale asked, clearly puzzled and out of his depth.

"Do y'all even vote for people over in England?" Pike asked, and Arch had a feeling he was ribbing Lonsdale, "or is it all the Queen over there?"

195

"I wouldn't worry about England just now," Reeve said. "Seems we got bigger problems right here in Midian than who's got a queen."

"We do indeed," Pike said, and something about the way he was conducting himself gave Arch the willies, like the man was holding something back, ready to deliver unpleasantness but savoring his moment first.

Reeve apparently picked up on it, too. "I don't suppose you stopped in to offer your support this time, did you?"

"I did not," Pike said, stepping up to the counter and sticking his nose over the nearest box of chicken. He leaned over and took a long whiff. "Mmmm. That smells mighty good. I doubt it's as good as that Hot Chicken they got up in Nashville, but ..." He reached right on down into the box and pulled out a drumstick, sticking it right into his mouth and taking a bite. "Oh, yeah, that's good. But, like I thought ..." He tossed it right back in the box and then smeared his greasy fingers on the counter, then looked up in challenge to see if anyone said anything to it.

"You can't fucking do that," Erin said, taking the bait. Arch almost flinched, and not at her use of profanity. Reeve was standing back, burning, but taking it pretty steadfastly in Arch's opinion.

"Oh, but I can," Pike said, and finally he got down to business, reaching into his jacket's front pocket and pulling out a folded piece of paper. He wagged it in front of him, greasy fingers leaving their mark on the page. "Anyone want to see why?"

"If you think the mere threat of a recall election is going to stop me doing my job to the best of my ability—" Reeve started.

Pike shut him down fast by slamming the paper down on the counter. "I'm not threatening anymore. I got the signatures and they're being certified right now." He grinned. "But until then ... I have this. Do you know what this is?"

"Looks pretty messy," Brian spoke up, "so probably your degree from Hamburger U." Everyone in the room looked at him. "Just a guess," he added, making Arch feel the first bit of affection for his brother-in-law in a long time, "I mean, it could be a certificate of completion for the second grade."

"That's a sick burn there, Ivy League," Pike said, not put off one bit by Brian's insult and turning one around on him so fast it tipped Arch to the fact that for some strange reason, Pike knew who was on

Reeve's crew. "You know all about burning 'em, though, don't you?"

That one tripped Arch's trigger, and he threw a look at Hendricks, who was still standing not too far from Pike, his arms folded in front of him but the alarm bells ringing all over his face when Arch caught his gaze. The cowboy stepped back from the counter and his hand fell to his coat, surreptitiously going for his sword.

"Hey, Mr. Pike," Alison said, letting go of Arch's arm and striding up to the counter. Arch got a quick chill, because he realized she'd caught Hendricks's motion and was spurred to some action because of it, "anyone ever told you that you are the very definition of a cocksucking Yankee asshole?"

Pike's eyebrows launched right up his forehead as Alison parked herself squarely across the counter from him. "I don't believe anyone's had the gall to say it to my face before, no, so I guess you're the 'Winner Winner Chicken Dinner' in that particular contest. I'm not surprised that you'd be one in this group to have the biggest pair of—"

Alison made a quick motion and Pike blanched, pulling away from her like he'd been struck, backing from the counter with a look of pain and anger. "What the hell are you playing at?" He held up a hand and scarlet blood ran down the side, toward his wrist, moving fast toward the sleeve of his suit.

"Oh, I'm sorry, I thought we were poking at each other here," Alison said, and she moved her coat aside enough that Arch could see her return her consecrated knife to its place on her belt. "Figured maybe you'd want to take it into the physical realm instead of just doing it verbally."

"Nice," Pike said, putting the bloody wound, only a little larger than a pinprick up to his mouth and sucking on it for a second. He looked over to Lauren Darlington. "I seem to have been assaulted, Doc. Any recommendations for me? Since I doubt law enforcement is going to do a damned thing about it."

"I wouldn't put that in your mouth if I were you," Dr. Darlington said coolly.

"Because of bacterial colonies and all that?" Pike asked, removing the side of the hand from his mouth.

"No, because the sheer volume of shit that comes out of your politician's mouth suggests to me that a three-dollar hooker's gullet would be cleaner than yours," Dr. Darlington finished. "Actually, any of her orifices would be."

"And here I thought you and I understood each other," Pike said, his smile fading to coldness.

"I feel like I've got a pretty good understanding of you at this point," Lauren said. "By the way, you've lost my vote."

"That's all right," Pike said, opening the piece of paper he'd been brandishing for the last little while and tossing it onto the counter, a few more grease stains marring its surface. Arch could still see the black typeface all over the inside of the paper, though. "You've all just lost your clubhouse." He brightened back to a grin. "That's a temporary restraining order from Judge Matheson removing Sheriff Reeve from office until the recall election can be held next Tuesday." His smirk grew wider. "All of y'all in here just lost your deputizations so ... you got ten minutes to get the fuck out before I have you all arrested for trespassing."

*

Braeden Tarley was ready to put Abi to bed even though it was only afternoon. She'd missed her nap and it was obvious as all hell that she had, such was her behavior at the moment. She was alternating between that manic state of joy and the powerful crash that came after it, the sobbing fits where she would throw herself on the floor because some tiny little thing went wrong, most of it related to Daddy and how much attention he was paying to her at the moment.

Braeden, for his part, was ready to sleep himself, but unfortunately that just wasn't in the cards. Abi let out a shriek of joy as she put a puzzle piece where it belonged in one of her wooden cutout puzzles as he sat on the couch, watching her with one eye while he flipped through the local news station with the other. It wasn't exactly local; it was based out of Chattanooga, and they were on about some shit going down at a plant there, something Braeden didn't give two fucks about at the moment.

"This is so damned stupid," he muttered under his breath, then caught himself. Sometimes he swore in front of Abi, but he tried not to make a habit of it.

"We're not supposed to say stupid, Daddy," Abi said, looking up from her puzzle.

Braeden just frowned at that. "Sweetheart, some people are stupid, and it doesn't do us any favors to be shying away from that."

Abi made a face. "But Miss Cweek says we're not supposed to say that."

"Well, maybe Miss Creek is stupid," Braeden said, feeling his blood boil again at the thought of that woman just walking away and leaving his baby alone like that.

"That's not nice, Daddy."

Braeden bit his tongue, because it was the only way to keep from going on a tirade that would probably teach Abi a new word if he let his real feelings out. He'd already had to break her of using the f-word, which had taken some doing. It had sounded cute the first time he heard it pop out of her mouth. She'd been playing with a Mickey Mouse tool set and mimed hitting her thumb with a hammer. "Fuck!" she'd shouted, in a pretty good imitation of Braeden himself. That had worn thin mighty fast, though.

He flipped the channel and found Dr. Phil getting all up in someone's junk, confronting them about something or other, and he clicked past without wanting to even see what it was about. He had enough problems of his own without worrying about somebody else's shit. Paramount on his mind was who was going to watch Abi when he worked tomorrow.

"Daddy," Abi said, causing him to look over at her on the floor again. She was lying flat on her belly, resting on her elbows and looking up at him with those big eyes.

"Yes, darlin'?"

"Do you think Miss Cweek is okay?"

There he went struggling with that diatribe again. "I hope so," he said instead, though he didn't really give a shit about whether Miss Creek lived or died at this point. He felt like she'd crossed him, and because of that she was dead to him.

"I hope so, too," Abi said, going back to her puzzle. It was only six shapes, but she was laboring with it. All it'd take would be another minor little setback and she'd burst into tears again. He was tempted to put her to bed, but if he did, he knew by long experience that she'd wake up at the ass crack of dawn, ready to go, and it'd screw up her schedule for days. This was the crap they didn't tell you about having kids. "I hope I get to see her again tomorrow."

"I wouldn't hold your breath on that one, sweetie."

Abi's little dimples poked in as she frowned again. "What does that mean, holding your breath?"

Braeden sighed. He knew he wasn't the most patient with answering questions, and one tended to lead to another like rolling down a hill. "Don't worry about it, darlin'," he said instead, and for now, she just went right back to her puzzle, thank God, though he was sure it wouldn't last.

*

"I am eagerly waiting your wiseass response to this one," Pike said, dangling the temporary restraining order in front of all of them. Alison was still standing up near the counter, and she was sorely tempted to pull her knife and draw a little more blood, but she held it tightly to her and looked back to Reeve instead, to see where he was going to lead in all this.

Reeve was looking pretty implacable to her eyes, but he finally spoke up. "Well, I ain't gonna argue with the law, if that's how it is." He looked around at the watch. "Come on, then, let's go ahead and pack up. Seems we're not welcome here anymore."

"Oh, that sounds so sad," Pike said, really rubbing it in. Alison was sorry she hadn't voted in the last election now, because it would have been nice to go back in time and punch the ballot for the other guy now. At least she hadn't voted for this dick, though.

"You're making a big mistake," Arch said, and Alison looked back to see him all looming and stony-faced. She knew her husband well enough to be able to tell he was closer to blowing up on this than Reeve was.

"Well, ain't this just Holborn Viaduct," Lonsdale said.

"Apparently I'm not with the law anymore, so you can just shove that slang right up your ass and talk normal," Reeve said, not missing a beat. He worked his way up to the counter at last, apparently no longer content to shoot back and forth with Pike from across the room. "Should I ask who the acting sheriff is, now that I've been deposed?"

"Indeed you may ask," Pike said smugly.

"Who's the new sheriff?" Reeve asked quietly, apparently not feeling the need to go big with his feelings at the moment.

"I believe you know Ed Fries," Pike said. "He's a longtime law enforcement professional, and he's next in line for the job, in terms of seniority." He shot a spiteful look at Arch and Erin in turn. "I sincerely doubt either of y'all's services are going to be needed for the time being, so ... just consider yourself suspended without pay for ... well, whatever. Being crazy as hell, something like that."

"You're going to regret this," Arch said.

"Don't go threatening me," Pike said, pulling his lanky ass up tall, like he could compete with Arch in any way, "or you'll never work for this department again."

"I wouldn't want to work for a department that turns a blind eye to evil when it rears its ugly head," Arch fired back.

"Then why are you working for this one?" Pike asked. "I mean, really ... crime goes through the roof and you and your boss blame demons." Pike's face twisted with stark amusement. "Demons. Not criminals, which are your job to catch, but demons ... which are not. Your job performance is so poor that you have to invent boogeymen to explain your incompetence." He shrugged. "Which is more evil? Failing? Or lying about it in order to cover your own ass?"

"You cannot believe all this is the work of simple criminals," Reeve said, much calmer than she figured he would be.

"I do, actually," Pike said lightly. "Why wouldn't I? It's a lot shorter leap to that than uncontrollable surge of ghostly activity or whatever. Anyhow ... the timer is ticking for y'all, unless you want to try and force a confrontation here." He put both elbows on the counter. "Don't get me wrong, I think you'd win, since I'm unarmed and at your mercy, but ... I also think that'd probably just add grist to the mill of people saying you ain't fit to do the job of keeping the law in Calhoun County."

That landed with a crack, and Reeve didn't pause to answer it. "Come on, y'all," the sheriff said, "let's get our things and go. We got enough trouble already without adding to it."

There was a loose shuffle as everybody sort of came back to their senses. Alison looked backward and saw Mrs. Reeve just burning in the corner, showing a lot more fire than her husband was at the moment. Alison caught her mother doing a little burning too, and she knew exactly how both of them felt.

"I'll need your badges." Pike stuck out his hand. "And your car keys. Anything else that belongs to the department. Ed'll be along in a little bit and I wouldn't want to have to send him out to arrest any of y'all for theft of county property. We're in bad enough shape as it is without wasting time on that."

That caused a moment of silence, and then Arch was the first to bring up a jangling set of keys and toss something right at Pike. It hit him lightly on the chest and then clacked onto the counter. "It appears that Mrs. Stan is not the only one of a mind to assault me today," Pike said with no small amount of amusement.

"That's not assault," Arch said as he stepped up to the counter with enough mustard that Pike jumped back automatically by reflex. His smug smile vanished on seeing Arch bear down on him, and even when his brain caught up with his body's instinct to figure out he'd just been fucked with, the smile didn't come back. Arch just smiled, and Alison didn't bother to hold back one of her own; her man had played it real well. "You heard the sheriff," Arch said, still using Reeve's title in spite of everything Pike had just said. "We got other places to be." That got the watch moving again.

*

Brian figured that being ousted from the dispatcher chair only a few short hours after the first "Oh, shit" moment of sitting down in it would come as a relief. He couldn't have been more wrong. Instead it had come with an "Oh, shit" of its own, except this time it was down to the giant angst bomb of watching their headquarters and all their resources just evaporate with one piece of paper that heralded the end of all things.

"Fuck," Brian swore under his breath as he took himself and not a hell of a lot else out of the front door, sandwiched between his mother and father. Such was his distress that he didn't even feel self-conscious about walking with his mom and dad like this, something he hadn't felt comfortable doing since before he was a teenager.

"Language," his mother said.

"Goddamn fucking shit," he replied. "We just lost our HQ, in case you didn't notice, and the big cheese of Calhoun County just set himself foursquare against everything we're trying to do here." A few of the others had streamed out, like Hendricks and Duncan and Dr. Darlington. Most of the rest were still cleaning shit up. He'd seen Erin and Arch go to clean out their desks. Reeve was probably doing the same, though he'd taken everything so stoically it wouldn't have surprised Brian to hear a gunshot ring out from the building following by the news that he'd either shot himself or Pike.

"I wouldn't worry yourself too much," Bill said, looking at his son with his typical muted personality.

"Because you have a plan?" Brian ran both hands through his hair.

"Because you'll get an ulcer," his father replied.

"That's not helpful in the slightest," Brian said. "I just ordered our new radios, but even with Prime, they're not going to be here for a couple days."

"We've made do before," Bill said, acting like it was all no big deal.

"You were also operating out of shithole farmhouse in the sticks," Brian said, unleashing his aggravation with the new status quo through biting sarcasm. It was what he had to work with. "We're not going to go back to that, are we?" His hands were sweating and he was wiping them in his hair. "How are we supposed to carry around holy swords and knives without the sanction of the law?"

His father blinked. "I don't expect I'll be following the law on that directive."

"Great," Brian said, "so we're going to give Pike in there a reason to arrest us all. As though he's not going to be looking for an excuse."

"What about this new sheriff?" Hendricks asked with a frown.

"Ed Fries," Bill said, casting a look over his shoulder back into the station. "He's a good man for the most part, but his intellectual horse ain't gonna be winning any races, if you catch my meaning."

"So, he's a dumbass," Duncan said. "That's probably better than having a real smart, on-his-game type guy in office. Easier to work around."

"Does it not worry any of you that we've got work around him at all?" Brian asked. Clearly these people were not getting it.

Hendricks looked at him with his usual helping of devil-may-care that just cemented his place in Brian's mind as a complete dullard, bereft of a brain of his own. "Some of us have already gone against the law in this town, so I guess we're used to it now."

"Some of us haven't," Lauren Darlington said with acerbic

perfection, "and aren't looking forward to it. I didn't get into this so I could develop that criminal record I've so neatly avoided thus far in my life. I'm trying to save my town here, not create a rap sheet that would build my street cred in NECX."

"You might just get both here," Hendricks said with that infuriating smile of his.

Brian had finally had enough of the smug cowboy, and he was pretty well through taking the man's shit just because he could talk tough and fight demons. "Well, lucky us," he said. "That may just be the most exciting news of the day to a lowlife drifter like you, but for those of us who have a future, it's not great news."

Hendricks just stared at him for a long few seconds during which Brian wondered if the cowboy was going to cross over to him and punch him one real good or worse. He didn't look away from Brian, and Brian didn't dare look away, even if he felt like he was in the crosshairs of a predator.

Hendricks looked away first, though, turning and walking off. "Call me if we manage to get our shit together," he said, and headed for his car.

"And if we don't?" Bill asked.

Hendricks just disappeared into his SUV and fired it up, pulling out of the parking lot past them a few seconds later without ever answering.

"If we don't," Duncan said cheerfully, with maybe the most emotion Brian had ever heard from him, "I think this town is gonna be proper fucked or 'Holborn Viaduct', as our new friend would say." And then he headed off to his own car, leaving the rest of them standing there with not a lot to do.

*

"I'm following the demon hunter with the cowboy hat," Marthe said over the phone, the sound of a car on the highway rattling in the background.

"Excellent," Chester said, then hung up, still staring out over the afternoon fields behind their new hideout. They were green and gorgeous, so different from the sprawling, decaying buildings of Queens. William would have loved this, too.

LEGION

*

Hendricks found her waiting when he got back to the motel, because of course she was. "I hope you're not gonna tell me about some shit storm blowing toward Midian," he said by way of greeting. The stale air smelled like no one had been in or out of the motel room all day, which they probably hadn't; housekeeping in the Sinbad sucked.

Starling cocked her head at him from where she lurked in the shadows near the sink. "No. There is no world-ending threat hurtling this way besides the inevitable one, and it slouches toward Midian."

Something about that prickled his mind. "If you say so," he said and started to strip down. If the phone rang, he planned to ignore it. He tossed his coat aside, running hands over his t-shirt afterward. It felt fine, and he gave it a sniff. Still clean enough, probably, though it did have some grass stains. Not nearly as many as the drover coat, though, but those would wipe off easily enough. The knees of his jeans were looking pretty green, too; he'd have to change those out.

His eyes flicked up and looked at her, still lingering there in the bathroom. "Don't you have a job to get to?" he asked.

The curtains were drawn, just a little bit of light peeking through the cracks, barely enough to give the room any light at all. "No," Starling said simply, and he wondered if she really didn't have anywhere else to be, or if the Starling persona was royally dicking with the other one, the one that worked as a hooker in Ms. Cherry's brothel. Hendricks had met them both, and they were worlds apart in terms of personality, though he wouldn't have claimed to know the hooker—Lucia—well enough to say whether he liked her any better than the cipher that was Starling.

"You just gonna wait outside my bathroom again while I shower?" Hendricks asked. Alison's earlier warning was annoyingly present in his head, ringing out as he said it. It irked him a little, this dance he was doing with her. She was a looker, no denying that, but there wasn't an ounce of heat between them.

On the other hand, it had been a while for him. Not nearly as long as his last drought, but ever since that bitch Kitty had made him hers, he'd been too revulsed to take his own piece in hand. It was all building up, but he was ignoring it as fast as he could, figuring it'd all work out at some point.

Starling didn't answer at first, like she had to give it all due consideration first. "Is that where you want me?"

Hendricks felt a little swell of disgust that had nothing to do with the girl in front of him and everything to do with the way he was feeling about himself at present. "Well, I damned sure don't want you in there with me," he said, turning that prickly, angry feeling outward as he went past her, even though he wasn't quite sure what he said was true. Hell, Hendricks didn't know what he wanted, other than to feel normal again. He shut the door behind him and locked it, even though he was under no illusions that it would stop her if she meant to get in.

*

"This is a fine kettle of fish," Arch said as he stowed a box of stuff that he'd left behind at his desk in the back of Bill's car. He'd taken the Explorer to work this morning, of course, leaving Alison's car behind at his in-laws' house, and now they found themselves without a car because County Administrator Pike had swooped in and shown himself to be a fool. Arch was still burning from what the man had said, though at least his wife had been clever enough to give them all the peace of mind that they were dealing with a straight-up jerk of the human variety rather than a demon. That was something, he reckoned.

"Tell me about it," Reeve said from across the parking lot, stowing his own box of stuff. Arch had caught glimpses of him packing in his office while he'd gone about his own labors; he felt sorry for Reeve because the man had far, far more room to spread out and bring in his own things than Arch had, and he'd taken full advantage. Reeve had two rifles he'd pulled out of the gun cabinet in his office slung over his shoulder, personal ones that he'd brought in and never bothered to take home—until now. Pike had watched him suspiciously, and he'd indignantly told the bastard they were his. Silently, Arch had applauded this display of fire from Reeve, especially since he'd taken so much garbage from Pike with more dignity than it deserved.

"So what do we do now?" Brian asked. He looked like he'd been chewing his fingernails nervously, or somesuch. Didn't seem much comfortable, that was Arch's impression of his brother-in-law at the moment. Not that he'd ever exactly been the calm and cheerful type, but even Brian wasn't normally quite this full of nerves. Maybe he really had quit smoking pot.

"We'll get together a little later," Reeve said, slamming the trunk of his wife's car with some misplaced gusto that Arch suspected would have been better directed at County Administrator Pike's nose. "I don't know about the rest of y'all, but … I need a short break to let some things settle before I start clamoring to make my next move."

"Except that Legion demon is out there right now, and who knows what he's up to?" Brian held his hands up. "Anyone? Are we supposed to just … sit back and let him wreak havoc or whatever?"

"If you know where he's at," Reeve said, and under the afternoon sun the man just looked tired and haggard, "I'm all for some action in that direction. But you heard Duncan: this guy could come at us from anywhere." He frowned, his face looking pinched. "Where is Duncan, anyway?"

"Left in a huff just after Hendricks," Lauren Darlington said. She looked slightly less concerned than Brian. She might have been more concerned, for all Arch knew, but was hiding it better. "This isn't the end, is it?"

"I'm not done," Reeve said, heading for the driver's door of Donna's car. She was still hanging back; Arch got the feeling she wasn't real comfortable around large numbers of people she didn't know well. Reeve parked it next to the door, the car between his body and the rest of them, his hand resting on the roof of the sedan. "But I do feel like I've gotten my ass good and kicked this last day or so, and I need a hot meal and some cave time to think over a next move. Let's talk after supper, all right?" He didn't wait for an answer, just got in the car and started it, and Donna got in the passenger side without looking back at any of them. He pulled out and gave 'em all a wave, but the tension was evident in his eyes.

"Shit, this thing is over, isn't it?" Brian said, causing Arch to roll his eyes. For a smart guy, his brother-in-law was awfully dumb sometimes.

*

"I'm following the man named Reeve," Clara said, and then hung up the phone on Chester. No words were needed, really, other than what she'd relayed. The fields were so green, and this was the third such call he'd gotten. Besides Marthe following the cowboy, there was also Jack who was after the man in the t-shirt who had left just after the cowboy. Chester had not seen him, but Jack had given a full description, and he suspected it was the OOC who had been on the front porch of the house earlier, the one that had helped kill Bentley and Mary.

His people were in place, doing as they were supposed to. Meanwhile, Chester sat here, staring out over the countryside while sitting in a rocking chair. "This was as it was meant to be," he said to no one, because William was not there to hear him.

*

"Nothing is over," Alison said to her brother, lacking patience and warmth and anything approaching gentleness. She'd been putting up with Brian's crap for way, way too long to feel like she needed to spare the rod when it came to slapping his happy ass with the truth. "We just took a hit and we're coming back off the ropes, okay?"

Brian made that sour face that she recalled from when they were kids. In a lot of ways, her brother had never really grown up. He was still the damned baby. "You pick a boxing-related metaphor to explain this to me? To me? Do you even know me?"

"Sometimes I wish I didn't," she sighed, keeping from rolling her eyes only because her mother was present and she'd inevitably tut tut her disapproval of Alison's tone and behavior. She was always overprotective of Brian that way, and it pissed Alison off to no end.

"Alison," her mother said, and there it was, just minus the tut tut. "Your brother's just worried is all."

"We all are," Arch said, trying to get right in the middle of it to make peace. Alison glared at him. He thought she overreacted to Brian, but he hadn't had to grow up in the same house as the little prick. It was easy to be magnanimous when you hadn't been putting up with someone's shit for twenty years.

"Yeah, well, I'm sick of his griping, whining ass," Alison said, just blowing it all out in one. She could feel the hard squeeze of anger pulling her down, and it was an unusually aggravating thing. "Like we ain't got enough to worry about. This is just like it was when we were out at the farmhouse. I'm concussed, Hendricks is taken by Kitty Elizabeth, and he's gotta show up and be a prick about demons not existing so he can catch Daddy in a lie." She wheeled on Brian. "What are you even doing here?"

Brian paled immediately. "I'm—I —"

"You hate this town," Alison said, just unloading on him, "you don't like the people, you don't even belong here—"

"Ali, that's enough," her father said with quiet disappointment.

"I don't think it is," she said, not taking her eyes off Brian, whom she'd locked onto like a hawk swooping down on a field mouse. "What is it you're after here? Because there ain't no glory, obviously. And whatever reasons you had for peacefully sitting around getting high have clearly evaporated. So now you're—what—gonna play like you're a fighter? Brian, you been running from every fight that doesn't involve strongly worded snark since you were four. You can sling fire with a sentence like no one else but put a sword in your hand and you just wilt back like someone's breathing it at you." Her anger was suddenly spent, and she felt exhausted. "What are you even doing here?"

He tried to answer, she saw, but his mouth moved and moved and he couldn't get a single word out. He didn't know. He didn't have a damned clue. Alison sighed. "Yeah. I kinda figured it was like that." She eyed the car, her mom's Lincoln Navigator that they'd all be riding in since Arch's Explorer had just been repossessed by the sheriff's office under the new management. "Dammit," she muttered to herself, seeing her parents and Arch all looking deeply uncomfortable but apparently unsure what they should say to her or Brian. This was going to be a damnably awkward ride home.

*

Amanda Guthrie had been waiting for this. She was pacing the beige-yellow hotel hallway again, smooth, thin carpet underneath her feet, staring at the pattern of blue broken by gawdawful ugly tan starbursts woven into it at intervals of every few inches. She'd walked it a hundred times before she'd finally figured out what those little tan monstrosities were, and now that she'd walked it a hundred more she was starting to feel like the starbursts were morphing into something else. The OOC had to be coming back soon, didn't he? He couldn't wander about town all day, could he?

Of course he could.

She'd smiled tightly at the two other guests she'd encountered in her walk, but they'd kept their heads down and ignored her. One of them was a demon, she'd caught that much, the other a human who was likely in town for a funeral, which was the only business booming in Midian at present. She had a suspicion that the wiser among them were starting to leave, which was a smart move. Rats fled sinking ships for a reason, after all, and it wasn't because the thought of a swim appealed to them.

She was hanging out in the room with the icemaker and the vending machines again, just lurking, listening for the elevator. The quiet hum of the icemaker was a pleasant enough sound, like fluorescent lights turned up to twelve. It alternated on and off every little while, and the sound of ice being dumped, crackling, into the machine was a pleasant distraction every once in a while from her thoughts. She thought about the new ice hitting the old ice, mixing, becoming a heterogeneous mass of water turned solid. She thought about water a lot; it was something she pondered when she had spare time. Which she'd had a lot of recently.

The ice crashed down into the machine and just beneath that, she heard the faint ring of the elevator. It caused her to stiffen in place, all senses crashing to alertness, the yellow-beige walls of the hotel snapping back into stark clarity and the starburst patterns in the carpeting coming back into clear focus. She didn't have irises or lenses in her eyes to adjust, but still somehow she could lose focus. That was cause for more pondering, actually.

She eased up to the door, listening carefully. The gears and the cables in the elevator shaft were squeaking as the box came to a halt, and now she could hear the doors sliding open. She paused at the door, her dark hand a hard contrast against the white trim of the frame, and if she'd had breath, she would have waited with it bated.

This was the time.

She heard footsteps against the hard carpet, thumping along, someone in a great damned big hurry. The movement was not subtle; it was the steps of someone in a rush, wanting to get down the hall, eager to retreat from the world, to turtle inside their room, maybe even hide in the bed and pull up the covers.

Interesting. That's what Amanda Guthrie thought.

She knew it was the OOC by his footsteps, could tell it was him by the urgency, by the lack of the sound of breaths being taken. He was sure he was alone in this hallway, too, which meant he was reaching out with his senses, even though he was going with a full head of steam toward his room. Something had happened, that much seemed obvious, and she would have bet anything it had something to do with the sound of gunshots she'd picked up earlier.

But none of that mattered now. He was almost to her, and the moment was at hand. He was moving at demon speed, assured of his own safety, certain that he was alone.

It was going to be worth it just to yank that certainty away for a second.

She timed it perfectly, jumping out as he passed. She smacked into him and he was knocked solidly off course. He almost went through the wall but caught himself just in time, perfectly expert, getting hold of his balance before he tumbled through drywall and wood into some empty room, and his head snapped up to look right at her. There was a burning in those eyes, and she knew she'd caught him completely off guard, scared the shit out of him—if OOCs had done much in the way of shitting—and he was left staring, the reflex to strike back about to take hold.

"Duncan," Amanda said, backing off and smirking at him. He was scanning her hard right now, had to be, trying to figure out how he'd gotten blindsided. He didn't show much in the way of emotion, but she'd known him long enough to know that his self-preservation instincts, the ones ingrained so deep in even demons, were flaring hard right now. His bland face was all hard lines, his eyes aglare at Amanda, but they softened slightly at her relaxed posture, her sudden backward movement.

"Who are you?" Duncan asked, and he had the baton out, in his hand, undeployed. He was giving her the benefit of a doubt, but only a tiny little bit. The question was playing across his essence, probably, trying to punch through Amanda's shell and get to the answer, to figure out just who the hell she was, because if he just vaped her, the answers would be lost to the wind.

"St. Louis," Amanda said, smiling enigmatically, "1904. You go on a hot air balloon for the first time, and it shows you a view of this old world that you can't even believe. Two years later you stand at the edge of the Grand Canyon, and you shed a little tear; a piece of your essence worms its way out of your eye and evaporates in the air like a human crying out salt water."

"How do you know about that?" Duncan asked, his grip on the baton not loosening, not even a little.

"Ponca City, Oklahoma, 1933," Amanda went on, locking eyes with him, seeing flickers of what was going on inside the shell. "You see the Dust Bowl with your own eyes, and you start to feel bad for the humans. It opens the door to empathy, and suddenly you're wondering what the hell you're doing here on this planet."

"I know what I'm doing here," Duncan said, and his hand shook, the baton gripped in his fingers, one of them hovering over the switch that would trip the spring and open the telescoping baton with a THUNK! "My question is ... who are you? And what are you doing here?"

"Bosnia, 1993," Amanda went on, and if her eye could have twinkled, it would have. "A herd of entwastle falls upon a group of refugees, ripping them to shreds before you can thin the herd and send it running."

Duncan bristled harder at that. "So ... you've been talking to Lerner." He opened the baton, THUNK. "I guess now I know who you are."

Amanda eyed the baton without concern. She figured she had another thirty seconds or so before he decided to come at her with it. "You're threatening someone from Home Office? Ballsy, Duncan. Ballsy."

"Funny how quiet Home Office has been lately," Duncan said, practically seething. "Why, I haven't heard from you at all."

"We've been busy," Amanda said, and the baton wavered slightly. "But I'm not from Home Office. I've just ... been there recently."

Duncan's eyes flickered. "Is that so?"

"That's so." Amanda met his gaze hard in return, and she let down a little of the shield built into her new shell. It was fancy, this year's model, and a hell of a lot better than the last one she'd had. She just had to do a little motion, and Duncan would be able to see ...

Duncan staggered, his baton dropping to his side, then falling out of his fingers and clattering to the ground. "It's ... you're ..."

Amanda just smiled at him. She'd had to lead the horse to water and let him drink at his own pace, and it had been worth it just for this moment. "That's right." Her driver's license might have said Amanda Guthrie, but that was a lie, just as much of one as the last one she'd held, the one before, for the other shell—the one that had said her name was Lerner. "I'm back, baby."

*

Why the hell am I here? Brian wondered as the car rolled along, turning a curve gently. His dad was at the wheel, and whenever his mother was in the car, Bill drove like an old lady. Hell, he drove like even more of an old lady than his mother did, which meant that in Brian's eyes, it would have been better if his mother had been driving. It was almost like his dad's protective instincts were going overtime, over the top, and Brian didn't like it.

And here he was, squeezed into the back seat, Arch on one window, him on the other, and Alison in the middle, like she hadn't just embarrassed the hell out of him in front of everybody, ripping him to pieces in the parking lot of the sheriff's office. The only good news was that Dr. Darlington had already left, because if she hadn't, Brian would have been twice as embarrassed. He had a little crush on the doctor; there was no point in denying it. Equally apparent to him was the fact that the doctor didn't reciprocate, and that was perfectly well and good and all, but he was still only slightly less mortified that she hadn't been present while he'd been dressed down. It felt a little like being a child again and stripped naked in front of strangers for changing. There was a burning shame that stuck in his throat and made him want to cry just a little.

The worst part of it was how hard she'd hit him right in the feels. It wasn't like he was oblivious to the truths she'd blown into his face like an opened can of whoopass. He knew how much he stuck out in Midian, he wasn't oblivious to the fact that he didn't really have any friends here; it was obvious to him that of this entire watch, he was the odd, odd, odd man out. And that took into account the demon, the pervert, and the guy who went everywhere dressed for the world's most emo cattle drive.

It was even more obvious to him that maybe running to New York and finding work in a publishing house as a junior editor or assistant or someone who did coffee runs would be a hell of a lot safer than someone doing the same here in Midian.

That was a frightening thought. Someone walking through the back streets of the biggest city in the US might have better survival odds than someone in Midian if things kept getting worse, as had been suggested that they would.

Brian sighed and his breath fogged the window. It reminded him of being a kid again, as though just being stuck in the back seat next to his sister wasn't enough to do that. If that wasn't bad enough, and her ripping a piece out of his ass while being such a vicious witch wasn't, he also had to deal with the fact that she was all up in his space. It wasn't her fault, even he knew that; Arch was a big guy and the middle seat wasn't exactly huge, but still, in spite of the fact that he could feel that she was contorting her body not to touch him, she still felt alarmingly close. Close enough that he could hear her breathe over the sound of the road, and it irritated him.

She hadn't always been like this, though. She clearly had some anger built up, the way she'd blown off at him like Old Faithful. She was often snappish, but he usually did something to prompt it, because ... well, because he could.

Going after his soft spots, though? That sucked. That made him feel like a loser, cast doubt on the tiny shreds of certainty that he'd started to pull together. Like being handed a behind-the-desk job hadn't been bad enough for his self-esteem.

Why was he here? Talk about a question he'd pondered in the course of his philosophy degree. He figured he'd beaten that one to death, and the fact was, even after all that, he felt no closer to an answer as they pulled into the driveway than he had earlier, sitting at the desk, looking at what he thought was his new normal.

*

Lauren hadn't figured on waiting around in the parking lot. Why would she? Reeve had left, the Stans and the Longholts were plainly of a mind to take off, and hanging around to try and talk some sense into County Administrator Pike seemed like a losing effort. She'd talked to him only a few weeks earlier and he'd been all kind and decent, going on about pulling together, uniting the community, not making people feel like they were alone in all this, and now here he was ripping Sheriff Reeve out of his job like he was pulling a weed out of a garden. She had her suspicions about the man, but at least Mrs. Stan had proven he was no demon. That made him either truly misguided or a real prick. Either way, she was feeling pretty burned about it at the moment.

Plus, the thought of these possession demons running around Midian kidnapping people? That was a troubling thought, to say the least. Lauren hadn't exactly wrapped her mind around it yet. She'd just gotten acclimated to the idea that yes, there were demons, and yes, they were from hell, and yes, they were in town and killing people. She'd seen them, she'd fought them, she'd burned a few alive and vaporized some more, and that was enough to get her brain twisting around the concept.

But the idea that one could just … jump into your body? Take it over like you were a suit and it was putting you on? That was scary stuff to her, the kind of thing she didn't care to dwell on. That was like going from one plus one straight to multivariable calculus. She considered a couple possibilities for how one of those things might work and then tried to discard the thought for fear she'd have a blow out of paranoia. The fact that they'd already taken Evelyn Creek and disappeared was concerning. That they'd vowed some kind of vengeance on Sheriff Reeve and Arch Stan was even more worrisome.

But that wasn't her immediate problem; the loss of their new headquarters was a more immediate concern, and it wasn't hers to bear alone, she reflected as she pulled into her driveway. Her mother's car was waiting under the carport, and she parked next to it, feeling some of the tension bleed out as she put the vehicle in park. A shower, some food, some time talking to Molly—that's what she needed right now. Time to process, to make sense of things. Later, she'd meet up with the others and they'd figure out the next move.

She just hoped nothing bad happened to any of them in the meantime. Because having a possession demon after you? Well, she thought as she slammed the door after her, stepping out into the cool, early evening air, the smell of fall all around her, that didn't sound like any fun at all.

"We've followed a dark-haired woman to her house," said Mera, her host's husky voice crackling over the phone. "This body does not know her, but seems to think she's a doctor."

"Doctor Lauren Darlington," Chester said, nodding as he looked out over the field before him. The sun was drifting down toward the edge of the horizon, hiding behind the trees in the west. "Penelope saw her leaving the sheriff's department as you went after her. She appears to be part of their group, so ..." He didn't need to finish the thought, and Mera hung up without further comment.

Chester felt the cool prickle of the wind as it picked up. They had people on Deputy Stan and the family that he was with, the Longholts, as well as on the OOC, Duncan. He had dispatched additional reinforcements for that one, figuring he would be a tricky fellow.

Chester felt as though he had these peoples' fates in the palm of his hand; only a squeeze would see them delivered unto pain. The sheriff was under their watchful eye, as was the cowboy demon hunter. Their little watch was practically waiting to be slaughtered, but Chester was not of a mind to slaughter them, no, not yet. At least, not all of them. The OOC, certainly, he would need to be eliminated. But the others? They had possibilities, weaknesses, people they cared about as he had cared about William. Well, perhaps not that deeply, but close enough, for their kind, and now he would make them feel it—a lesser version of what he had felt. Shallow creatures that they were, they couldn't feel exactly what he felt, of course, but he could make them feel something.

Living for as long as he had, Chester had a complexity and depth to his emotions that he knew humans could not fathom. He had lived among them, known them, even respected them. They had reasons for feeling the ways that they did, reasons for doing the things that they did. Knowing them as he had come to, he had respected them, respected life, and expected that respect to be returned.

But he had forgotten that these humans did not know what he and his brethren did. They were not united in their beliefs, did not share everything between themselves, did not have the common vision and values that he and his people shared. They were fractious and alone, and their lack of unity had caused them to act foolishly, to strike out at William.

He had wondered in the moments since it happened, he and the others, if only the humans had been more like him and his brethren, if only they understood among themselves, communicated, shared, felt the openness of connection the way he and his did, if things would have been different. He did not wonder for long, though, for he knew without a doubt it was true. If the humans had been more like him, none of this would have happened. They would not have backed William into a corner so foolishly, they would not have accosted him—those demon hunters first and the police second, not that there was a difference between them, really, was there? They were all humans, all fractious, all foolish, all isolated and dangerous.

If only they'd been like him, like his people, this would not have happened. Their division was their weakness; it created a terminal lack of understanding, and because of that ... they knew pain. And Chester would heap more upon them, these people, these guilty, guilty people, for that was the only appropriate response. He had pain to share in abundance, for now that he had felt it at their hands, he and his brethren had no desire at all to keep it to themselves any longer.

*

Lauren was barely in the door when Molly caught her in a big hug, the kind that she remembered from when her daughter was knee-high to a cricket, toddling over to tackle her when she got home from med school. Those had been the best hugs, the ones where a spontaneous and joyful outburst of "MOMMY!" had been followed by a hard squeeze around the neck, and lovely coiling of warm arms and weight as she'd picked her daughter up and hugged her right back.

It had felt like a long time since those days of happy greetings, but Molly came at her today, and she was caught a little off guard. This wasn't the hug of a two-year-old squeezing with all her heart, though, but the hug of a teenager who was either genuinely happy to see her mother or else wanted something. Lauren was pretty sure it was the former, but if a request for an iPhone or something popped out in the next sixty seconds, she wouldn't have been shocked.

"I was worried," Molly said, hugging her tight. Lauren hugged her in return, not quite as tight, but enough. Molly was still a pretty thin girl, with tiny shoulders. She could have benefited from eighties shoulderpads if those had still been in vogue, but slender was okay anyway, so Lauren supposed it didn't really matter.

"I'm fine," Lauren said, and Molly broke off, eyes all brimming with worry.

"I heard shooting," Molly said, hands still resting on Lauren's shoulders. Her daughter was tall, now, almost as tall as Lauren was. When did that happen? "I figured maybe you were involved."

"Only at the end," Lauren said, "after it was done. And no one got badly hurt, so ..."

"Whew," Molly said, undisguised relief flooding her voice. "I feel like we dodged a bullet again."

"Several," Lauren said. "Or shrugged a few off, at least." That one got Molly frowning, so she explained. "Demons just sort of ... well, bullets don't hurt them much."

"Oh." Molly steadied herself, letting go of Lauren. "So ... are you in for the night?"

"I blew off work, if that's what you mean. Got a meeting later," Lauren said, heading on through into the kitchen, where her mother was standing before the stove, looking like she was about to get to making some dinner but had paused to listen to Lauren. She was peering at her as she came around the corner, just staring at her all serious, clearly eavesdropping while she was out of sight of the door. "Administrator Pike got a judge to issue an order taking Sheriff Reeve out of his job. We got kicked out of the station."

Her mother's reaction was barely insulated horror, wrinkled hands popping up to cover her mouth. "Good Lord!"

Molly's was a little baser. "Holy shit." Lauren gave her a look of horror all her own. "Errr ... dang?" Molly corrected.

"I know," Lauren said, not really breaking off the dirty look aimed at her daughter. "It came as a blindside to us, too."

"I wonder if Pike's a demon?" Molly asked, like she was starting to warm up. Whenever she got this look on her face, frenzied discussion and a shit-ton of questions followed.

"Nope," Lauren said, causing her mother's penciled-in eyebrows to rise, "Alison Stan poked him with a holy blade."

"Well, that's rude," Vera said.

"That's clever," Molly said.

"It was a little bit of both," Lauren said, "but it worked. Now we can be assured that he's probably just operating from a deep-seated sense of denial."

Molly frowned. "You don't think it's something more sinister?"

Lauren's lips puckered into a frown of her own. "I guess it could be, but ... if he was really trying to be dark and evil or something, I think he'd be doing something a lot worse than trying to remove the sheriff from his job. I mean, a true villain would just kill the shit out of—"

"And you wonder why she talks like that," Vera muttered.

"—whoever was in the way of their evil, right?" Lauren shrugged. "Yeah. I think he's in denial, because if he really wanted to tear things up," she gave her mom a pointed glance, "he could do a lot worse than use the court to order the sheriff out of his job."

"I guess," Molly said, but she didn't sound totally convinced. "I suppose true evil would come off a lot more ... uh, evil."

"Exactly," Lauren said, starting toward the stairs. "And you would recognize him by his villainous theme song. There'd be deep, foreboding music anytime he entered the room, y'know?" She sniffed the air as she heard her mother start to pre-heat the stove. "How long until dinner?"

"Half an hour," Vera called back.

"I'm gonna get a shower," Lauren said, making her way up the stairs.

The doorbell dinged when she was about halfway up, and she heard Molly scamper on the wood floor. "I got it!" Molly shouted, and Lauren just yawned. The call of the warm shower and its pulsating head was a lot more powerful than her sense of curiosity about who was at the door.

*

Reeve came into his house a step behind his wife, entering the dim, wood-paneled dining room and smelling the smell of home, which brought him next to no comfort. He'd been silent on the drive home because he hadn't had much of anything to say, dammit. Having his job ripped right out from under him by that goddamned Yankee had been bad enough, but turning in the keys to his office, his car, cleaning out his desk—hell, all that had been nut-kick frosting on the castration cake. He'd just considered himself fortunate that prick Pike hadn't demanded he rip off his khaki uniform as property of the sheriff's department, because that would have just about exposed his newly impotent penis to the damned cold.

Donna turned to look back at him, the same concern in her eyes that he'd been ignoring whole way home. She couldn't help but worry, because that was her way, but he didn't love that part of her. It was a nuisance, because while his temptation would be to take all these shitty feelings that were burning him up inside like a lit cigarette in dry brush, she would damned sure want to talk about them, every one, leaf by crackling leaf, until he'd want to take a blowtorch to the pile himself just to get it over with.

"Nick ..." she said gently, and he could feel where this was going before it even made the turn.

"I don't want to talk about it," he said, and it came out a fair sight less kindly than he'd intended. He just about bit her head off over it, really, and he knew that, and while on a normal day it would have made him feel shitty, this damned sure wasn't a normal day. He looked down at the khaki uniform and it lit the blaze even harder in him.

He'd spent his whole adult life serving this department, this town, this county, and now they thought he was a liar and a fool. Of all the kicks to the nuts, that might have been the fucking absolute worst. He stared down and felt a wave of revulsion pass over him, a sick to his stomach feeling that was entirely directed outward and not inward. He'd been attacked, insulted, derided, mocked and now his reputation among the people he'd spent his life protecting was in tatters.

"I need to go change," Reeve said, just about spitting it out, disgusted at himself, at the people of Calhoun County, and mostly at the damned uniform at the moment. If he could have, he would have burned the thing right now and been done with it. Hell, maybe he would, as a giant fuck you to County Administrator Pike and that goddamned traitor Ed Fries. Not like Fries's fat ass would fit into it anyway.

Fuck it all, that was how he felt, and he stalked off toward the bedroom to change. The sound of a doorbell dinging in the distance only penetrated his consciousness enough to nettle. "Whoever it is, tell them to go fuck themselves," he shot over his shoulder at Donna. As mad as he was, that was as civil as he could manage to be. He'd apologize later, after he'd gotten off these goddamned khakis.

*

The awkwardness had stayed with them on the entire car trip, but Alison didn't care. She felt sick to her stomach, and it didn't have a damned thing to do with her brother and what she'd said. She wasn't sorry for tipping over his little emotional applecart, because he deserved it and worse, as far as she was concerned. She might normally have been a little more merciful, but Alison was not feeling anything other than irritation at present. Irritation and nausea, and riding in the back seat, stuck between her brother and her husband on the windy roads toward home, hadn't helped.

When she came in the door, held open for her by Arch, bless his heart, quiet as a mouse, it smelled like nobody had been cooking for a day, and she was still hungry as hell. Ravenous didn't even describe it, like carrying around kids had burned all the calories she had and more, and she just needed to rummage the pantry and start opening cans to dump them down her throat. She had the weirdest craving, too, like mixing canned ravioli with pickles was a great culinary decision that everyone had been overlooking all these years—

"Oh, shit." She stopped dead in her tracks, and Arch just about tripped over her as he shut the door and came in. Her mom and dad and Brian were all ahead of her, wandering quietly off to do whatever they were aiming to do, plainly wanting to get clear of her in case she was about to go off again, ticking time bomb that she was.

"What?" Arch mumbled quietly as he came up beside her in the mud room. He was talking low enough that no one else could hear him, even if they hadn't been working hard to get the fuck away from her at present.

"Let's ... go to our room," Alison said numbly, suddenly aware in a way she hadn't been before, and worried and sick all at once. It was the nausea and the crankiness and the sudden delirious hunger mingled with weird cravings that had finally tripped the trigger for her ... but ... she couldn't be, could she?

Arch frowned at her. "Uhm ... right now?" He had that clumsy suggestiveness to his tone, like he thought she wanted ... but she didn't, not now. He never was that good at reading her.

"We need to talk," she said, clarifying, as her head ran through it, jumping like an Olympic gymnast along through a routine, through questions. She hadn't been on birth control since ... well, over two months now. She just hadn't thought of it because she'd intentionally gotten off it, and when everything had happened with the demons and their sudden exodus out of town, she just hadn't considered ...

Well, shit. She was pregnant. Probably. Almost certainly. She knew her body well enough to know that something was amiss, and she was way, way too young for menopause.

"What about?" Arch asked, loosening a little and sounded disappointed all at once. "The meeting later? Because—"

"No, not about the watch," she said, brushing him off with a frown that probably came off a lot more irritable than she meant it to. "It's about ..." she looked into his eyes. They were dark brown and lovely, the eyes of the man she'd fallen in love with.

Maybe the same eyes their baby would have.

"I think I'm ..." She actually felt a little bubble of excitement make its way over the nervousness. Was this really happening? After all their efforts had failed, had they just sort of stumbled into ... well, not stumbled, because they'd been screwing like rabbits since this war had started, but ... had they really just wandered into it naturally after all that hard work at the beginning had failed?

Arch looked at her with a steadily deepening frown. "You're ... what?"

"I'm—" The doorbell sounded, and Alison nearly swore out loud. What the hell did it take to get a moment of peace around here?

*

Hendricks was drying off and he heard something thump outside his door, like a faint knocking in the distance. He was all resolved to ignore it, but it came again, persistent and annoying, like Starling had taken it upon herself to thump his headboard while he was showering, knocking her hooker head against it with a client between her legs. That was a strange visual for him, but it was the one that came to mind, and he found it distasteful. It didn't come with just the image, either, he got a strange whiff of sex when it came, but wrong somehow, different; it wasn't just sweat and pussy, it was more sulfuric, nauseating, like it was forcing itself up his nose unasked. He almost dropped the towel and shoved his wrist up to his nose in order to make it stop.

He paused, took a breath through his mouth, and it was gone, fresh steam and soap smell returned, though he still felt like he could visualize that scene happening just outside. It triggered a weird feeling in him, the thought of the red-headed hooker who could change into a fiery angel in a heartbeat taking some dude in his bed. He knew that wasn't happening—or was pretty sure it wasn't happening, anyway—out in his room, but the image persisted like a vision that wouldn't leave him alone. He could practically see her sweating, freckled shoulders in front of him, some dude just giving it to her. Now she was face down, burying her moans in the pillow, and Hendricks felt sick. He was sweating again, and not from the heat of the shower.

He also had a precipitous rise in the front of his towel, and that somehow made his stomach churn even harder, revulsion running through him hard, like that time he'd kicked down a door in Ramadi and found an old lady three days dead. The flies had been everywhere, the stink had been rancid, and he'd just about dropped the barrel of his M-16 and chucked on the dusty floor.

He put a hand on the edge of the toilet to steady himself, and that thumping noise came again. He pictured Starling's red head bumping against the headboard as some unknown John put it to her from behind, her moans reminding him of—

—of—

He dropped to his knees and vomited, barely getting the toilet lid up before his stomach emptied itself. He retched, then retched again, but got control of himself before he spewed. It was all about control, wasn't it, and he'd never felt this out of control in his life; not when he'd washed up dead, not when Renee was taken from him, not ever. He'd had the benefit of being unconscious while that happened, at least, after the ass-kicking, he hadn't been awake and alert and forced to—

Now he couldn't hold it in anymore; he vomited hard. It was like someone took his stomach and turned it inside out with violent force, and yellow bile sprayed out and splattered the porcelain. It came in three successive waves, his choking, acid-tinged upchuck, and by the time he was done it was dripping out of his nose. He stared at it, tears rolling down his face from the violence of the experience or maybe something else, heart beating in his ears, and then he heard—

The door burst open and she was there, staring down at him, his towel discarded in the middle of his sickness. He felt heat rush to his cheeks at the violation, unexpected and unwelcome, Starling standing there fully clothed and looking down on him in some kind of judgment. He opened his mouth to speak, bile-filled drool still dripping off his chin, but she beat him to it.

"They are coming," she said. A hand hammered on the door to his hotel room, and Hendricks stiffened, still leaned over the toilet, naked as the day he was born, a cold chill running over him that had nothing to do with his nudity or the sickness he'd just felt.

*

"So you're back," Duncan said, staring at "Amanda Guthrie" like she'd evaporate without so much as a holy implement to touch her skin. It wasn't a reasonable fear, but then, nothing that was happening in Midian, Tennessee, was exactly reasonable, was it? She knew Duncan well enough to know the questions that were surely rolling around in his essence at the moment, and they were some juicy ones.

"I'm back," Amanda announced. "Minus the name, of course."

"They renamed you." Duncan nodded idly. It wasn't a big deal; Lerner hadn't been his name before, just as Duncan's name wasn't actually Duncan.

"You gotta admit," she said, indicating her new female form, "the old one didn't quite fit anymore."

"I heard they were going a little more diverse with the new shells." Duncan eyed her. "Still, it's a little weird to see it done this way."

She looked down at her hand; it was true, seeing the dark tone there where before her shell had been white as a cloud was requiring some adjustment. "I don't think it's the skin color that's tripping you up."

"It's not," Duncan agreed.

"It's the fact you can't read me," Amanda said with a dickish smile.

She could still pull that off, though she'd looked in the mirror while she'd done it, and it definitely was not the same as the Lerner shell.

"That's disconcerting, yes," Duncan said, "but not that unusual in this town. Not lately, anyway—"

"Fucking Spellman," Amanda said, feeling that old anger come right back. "You still haven't ripped that screen to fucking pieces?"

"It's not an easy thing to pull off," Duncan said.

"Yeah, well," Amanda said, getting up off the bed, "that's practically my mission in life at this point, ripping that bastard to tiny pieces of shell and sulfur."

Duncan stared at him. "Is it? Is that why they sent you back?" There was a deeper question there, and Amanda had been wondering how long it would take him to bring it up.

Amanda gave him the sly smile, slightly less dickish. "Maybe."

Duncan didn't like that, plainly. "You got sent back from the pits. That doesn't happen, remember?"

"I remember," she said.

"But you got sent back."

"Obviously."

The suspicion just dripped off Duncan. "I haven't heard from Home Office in months."

"So you said." Amanda just stared back at him. "And?"

Duncan opened his mouth to reply, but the hotel door exploded off its hinges at that very moment, and it spared Amanda the trouble of trotting out a very well-practiced lie. She forgot all about it for a little while after that, too, because the two of them were fighting for their damned lives about five seconds later.

*

Hendricks barely had time to haul himself off the cheap linoleum before Starling darted out the bathroom door, vanishing around the corner. He listened, strangely frozen in his naked state, wondering exactly who "they" were and how bad this was going to be. He fumbled for the sword he'd left between the shower and the toilet, neatly slicing his finger as he strayed a little too close to the blade below the guard. He cursed and grabbed the hilt, bringing it up, too worried about what was about to go down to try and squeeze his junk into his jeans instead of leaving it flapping in the damned breeze. He didn't even bother to wipe the vomit off his mouth, he just came around the corner with his sword up, just in time to see Starling jab someone with a finger hard, in the shoulder, sending them rolling back out the door.

He heard them hit the ground with an "Oof!" as the air rushed out of their lungs. They just sat there for a second, on their back, then a head came up and he recognized Lonsdale, blinking and looking stupid, some lady lying next to him that Hendricks had never seen. Lonsdale stared in through the door at Hendricks, utter puzzlement on his face. "Fucking 'ell, Lafayette. What am I doing outside your room? And where are your bloody pants, Brov'ner?"

Hendricks sagged against the doorframe, looking to Starling, who stood between him and the Brit. "What the hell is going on here?" he asked, and then it clicked. "Legion." And the panic he felt on his knees by the toilet a few minutes earlier suddenly seemed like a long-ago worry, like being scared of a little yippy dog until the angry, bloodthirsty wolf showed up.

*

Lauren was undressed and showering, and it was fucking heaven. She hadn't checked her voicemail from her boss yet, because she was presently in the real-life version of LA LA LA-ing at the top of her lungs against reality's attempts to intrude in on her, but she was sure it was going to be a doozy. The hot water helped keep her mind off it, though, making her quite glad that she'd been able to find this short little span of time for herself. Showers were her nirvana, her place where she could just relax and be herself, without any demands on her as a mother or doctor or daughter or demon fighter. She'd left her cell phone in her room and was quite content to leave the world outside the bathroom door.

The warm water ran over her skin, scalding hot, just like she liked it. Her arms were already red from the warmth of the spray, a perfect exfoliation by heat. Her skin always tended toward oily instead of dry anyway, so the loss of moisture from boiling herself wasn't a big deal to her. She'd put her hair back before she got in, intending to keep it dry so she didn't have to deal with it when she got out, but that resolution lasted about thirty seconds and then she said fuck it and just let the water dribble down through her hair, all warm and wonderful. She'd just do a ponytail, who fucking cared.

The sound of the water against the porcelain tub was a steady, soothing sound, and she got lost in the rhythm. She closed her eyes and just listened, warm wetness just rolling down her skin from forehead to neck, from shoulders to shins, the smell of the hot water like bliss.

A click from beyond the curtain made her open her eyes, blinking the water out between her lashes. She had locked the door, hadn't she? Immediate discomfort leaped upon her, and she said, "Umm, occupied."

The door clicked shut again, and she closed her eyes once more. Probably just Molly, not thinking, barging in to pee. Her daughter had a powerful ability to get so distracted she barely noticed the world around her. Usually it manifested while she was reading, but Lauren wouldn't put it past her to have it extend to just walking around, especially now that Molly's head was constantly in the clouds about demons. Or, maybe more like in the ground about demons? Where was hell, anyway?

Chilly air drifted down from above the shower curtain, causing Lauren to shiver. Jesus, that was something, just a sudden draft out of nowhere. She shuddered again, the cool air causing her flesh to immediately prickle and pop into goose bumps. "Fuck." She put a hand on the knob, ready to turn it to an even hotter temperature to overcome the sudden chill. Someone must have turned on the air conditioner or something—

The shower curtain rattled as it was pulled back suddenly, the sound and rush of unexpected light as it moved scaring the hell out of Lauren; if she hadn't already been standing in a stream of warm water she would have sworn she'd peed herself first at the fright, and then again at what was waiting beyond the curtain.

Molly was standing there, staring right at her.

But she wasn't alone.

There was another woman standing there, Yvette Something-or-other, a lady Lauren barely knew, who lived somewhere out of town. And between her and Molly stood her mother. Vera looked about scared half-shitless, her glasses askew on her nose.

That was what Lauren saw in the first second after the curtain was pulled back; conscious only of the three of them, of her own nudity and shock, it took her a second more to realize the real horror of the situation, which was—

Oh, God.

—that Molly had a very serious, very angry look on her face ... and she was holding a knife to Vera's neck, a little trickle of crimson blood already working its way down her throat. The terror was stark and obvious on her mother's face, and whatever warmth Lauren had felt a moment earlier vanished just as surely as if someone had turned the shower knob all the way to cold.

*

Reeve had barely stripped off his uniform in disgust when it hit him that he was doing this, really doing this, something he never would have imagined. He could have seen himself losing re-election at some point in the future. Hell, he'd thought it could happen, had pondered it only a week or two ago, before he found out about demons for the first time. Since then he hadn't had much time to give it a think, but he'd considered the possibility that maybe he'd run again, after this was over, and lose. He'd thought just yesterday that maybe he'd fail to win the recall election that Pike was going to mount. He hadn't spent a ton of time dwelling on that, but he'd at least given it a little consideration in the sleeplessness of last night.

But it hadn't even been a mote of possibility that he'd get dragged out of office this very day by the goddamned wolves of Calhoun County politics.

He held his uniform shirt in his hands, staring down at the khakis. His rib ached faintly, but he ignored it. He sniffed and smelled something a little pungent, but ignored that, too. He'd put this uniform on when he was a hell of a lot younger man, with good intentions. He'd wanted to protect this county against whatever came its way, wanted to help people, dammit.

Now he was holding it with loathing, looking at it like it was a disease-soaked blanket hurled at him. This uniform was something he'd given his all to, especially lately. If there was anything more he could have done, especially since he'd had his eyes forcefully opened, he didn't know what it was.

"I've done all I can," Reeve murmured to himself. There wasn't much reassurance there, maybe a speck's worth at most. He sniffed again, and that smell …

God, what the hell was that?

He blinked and stared at the shiny badge pinned beneath the breast as it caught the light. It gleamed, all but the part where the word "Sheriff" was carved into the metal in a dark line of exposed copper that made the metal look a little black. Putting on this badge, the one that dropped the word "Deputy" from it, had been the proudest moment of his professional life.

Now, that pride was ripped off like his uniform, burned like—

Jesus, the smell in here. He wrinkled his nose and looked around; he'd pulled the bedroom door to, closing it from the hallway to the rest of the house, but something was wafting its way in, like someone was cleaning a lawnmower engine out there. "Donna?" he called. "Do you smell something?" He waited a second for an answer but got nothing. "I hope to hell that's not dinner," he said under his breath.

He looked back down at the uniform, pants puddled beneath him, his belt with the gun and sword on it poking out of the tent of fabric. Reeve held the shirt's slightly rough cloth between his fingers, and let it fall out of his hand. To him, it was like letting go of the past. He was done being sheriff, at least for now, it looked like. Sure, he could go try and get a lawyer to fight for him, to sue the fuck outta the county on his behalf, but why? Unless something major changed, he was going to lose the recall election. Seeing that show of hands in the meeting hall last night had convinced him of that much. He was just about out of persuasion, too; this far down his rope, he was more likely to start telling people who doubted him to fuck themselves instead of trying to gently show them how wrong they were. It irritated him most that now he finally understood why Arch had done what he'd done when he'd run; most people just couldn't wrap their damned heads around demons. It was just too much—

"Goddamn," he said, nose wrinkling again. It near took his breath away, this time, and Reeve stuck his hairy wrist right up under his nose, trying to block it. He couldn't ignore it anymore to marinate in his own anger, and whatever unhappy introspection he might have wanted to do, he could do it after he figured out what the fuck was stinking up the house like someone had dragged a gas pump in here and just let it loose—

He opened the door to find Donna standing there, staring at him with dead, burning eyes, wet like she'd been out in the rain. Fumes hit Reeve square in the nose, taking his breath away, and he knew in an instant that she was—goddamn, she was fucking drenched in it, a trail behind her, dark, wet carpeting stretching down the hall—in gasoline, and an old cigarette lighter was perched between her fingers, thumb ready to strike it up.

*

Brian had answered the door without really thinking about it. If he had been thinking about it, if he hadn't had his head completely and totally in his self-pitying and self-involved situation, stewing in his own juices, he might not have opened the door. But he did, and when the autumn breeze came creeping in through the open door, Mrs. Lester's hand did, too, and touched him lightly on the back of his before he could realize that her eyes were way, way different than he could ever remember seeing the older lady look at him before.

There was hate in those eyes, he realized a little belatedly, as she touched him. It wasn't a gentle touch, either, it was like her fingernails dug into the back of his hand as she did it, like she sunk them in good, aiming to draw blood, even though he didn't see her do anything like that. It wasn't the only thing he felt as the breeze slunk past him, chilling him. Those were just the little things he noticed, the preambles to a larger, longer hell that followed a second later.

Brian's vision blurred, knives jabbed into his temples, but he didn't react at all, at least not physically. Everything got fuzzy for a second, signal interruption working its way through his brain, and the pain in his hand became a distant memory. The feeling of cold air finding its way through his clothes stayed, though, and maybe got worse; it was hard to tell through the knives in his brain.

You belong to us.

Brian couldn't think of a good response to that. It wasn't like a polite overture, something simple like, *Hey, you wanna go grab some dinner?* Or *Hey, you want to go back to my place and fuck?* No, it wasn't pleasant, it wasn't nice, it was a scream in the ear in a quiet night, a punch to the groin that you didn't see coming, and two-by-four to the back of the head that made a cracking noise that had nothing to do with the board.

You belong to us.

Brian didn't want to belong to anyone. All he wanted was to leave town and never come back. He didn't want anyone telling him how it was going to be. That was the shitter about living at home, really; his dad and mom got to boss him around a little. He didn't like it, and he didn't tolerate much of it, because in a contest of wills, he wasn't going to—

You belong to us.

That fucking Lonsdale, what did he say? Like a chorus of harpies? That sounded about right, and he heard it, right in his brain, like a bunch of needles being dragged along vinyl. The voices were scratchy and hard, unyielding and angry, God, so fucking angry that it made that girl he'd accidentally called by the wrong name during sex that one time look fucking happy as a clam by comparison.

Brian closed the door on Mrs. Lester. She was already walking away anyhow, wandering off down the walk to a waiting car when he heard the click of the lock. Brian was left alone—

Not alone.

—in the entryway to the house, staring around at the long hallway in front of him.

His dad peeked his head out at the far end of the hall, cell phone up to his ear, hand covering the microphone, but inadequately. "Who was it?"

Oh, Jesus, Bill—Dad—you have to—

"Ding dong and ditch," he said—well, it came out in his voice, but he didn't say it—

"Hmm," his dad said, shrugging and disappearing around the corner. No worries about that, then. "Yes ... yeah, I need your help on that ..." His voice trailed quietly as he went, speaking to whoever was on the phone.

Brian walked down the hall, the world curiously dark around him. It wasn't nearly night yet, but the world had taken on the tinge of shadow, like darkness was bleeding in around the edges. Brian walked crisply, slowly, taking it all in, running fingers down the wall. He saw trace amounts of finger oil being left behind, and thought about how his mom used to yell at him about that when he was a kid. "Keep your hands off the wall!" she'd shout. Yeah, like—

Holy shit holy shit oh God! Holy fucking fuck somebody—

Brian walked out into the living room where his dad was waiting, just hanging up the phone and saying something in a hushed voice to his mom. They both looked up as he came in, stopped talking as if they'd been caught discussing him; well, him or Alison as regarded him—

SHIT! NO! MOM! DAD! JESUS CHRIST—

"What are you talking about in here?" Brian asked, and it sounded just—just a little sarcastic, just perfectly on point to hit the tone he might have taken in the same circumstances, if he hadn't just had his balls ripped off in a public setting by his sister—

ALISON! ARCH! FUCK, SOMEBODY! ANYBODY!

His father was only a few feet away now, and Brian stopped where he was standing, waiting for the answer. "Well," his dad said, and Brian could tell he was thinking fast—

DAD! MOM! GET OUT OF HERE! Fuck fuck fuck—

Brian moved a couple steps closer, waiting to hear the answer. A goofy, shit-eating grin was plastered all over his face, he could feel it, and it was too wide, too smarmy, too—

NO! Don't do this! You don't have to do this!

Brian blinked as his father started to open his mouth to answer. Before he could Brian reached out, hand blurring with speed, and went right for the pistol he knew his dad was carrying under his jacket. He yanked it out before his father could even react, turned it upward with a flick of the wrist, and pulled the trigger. The muzzle flash blinded him for a second, but when it faded he saw the blood, everywhere, running down his dad's shirt and jacket, covering him, and somewhere within Brian Longholt a silent scream died trying to make its way out of his mouth.

7.

Amanda Guthrie had vaped more than her fair share of demons, but she hadn't done it in her current form. That didn't much matter, because the shell wrapped around her essence was just a shell; one with a few cool new perks and a different look, but not one so radically different from the old Lerner one that she was unprepared for a fight using it. She was up to her ass in fucking demons right now, though, and it was bringing back memories.

Duncan was across the room, swinging for the fences with his baton. His frustration was showing like the cracks in the hotel room walls, more and more obvious as they continued to appear. Sometime real soon, in fact, the demons-in-human-bodies that they were fighting might even realize that Duncan was upset, Guthrie figured. She'd dealt with him for a long time, after all, and no one could read Duncan like she could.

She wasn't without her own frustrations at the moment. She bashed one of their attackers in the skull, breaking skin, and watched the black fire rip an essence out of that body while the human being that wore that skin took control again. It was a sad thing to watch, that dazed look in a person's eye when they realize they've been out of it for a while, that slow dawning of understanding when they blinked away the sleepy feeling and saw that they were in a hotel room with a bunch of people moving faster than anything they'd seen before ...

Except every time Amanda had seen that happen so far, that sweet moment of victory only lasted about two seconds and another one of these demon fuckers would swoop back in and touch the poor bastard, and that light of awareness would get snuffed out hard, and they'd jump right back into the fight.

It was getting to the point where Amanda was seriously considering just killing the damned humans to stop this repetitive cycle. Who the fuck wanted to keep knocking the same face around constantly?

"I think we should—" she started to say.

"No," Duncan cut her off. The bastard. He still had it. "There has to be an end to these things."

Amanda gave him a stinkeye for a quarter-second between swings. "Legions. Fuck. I knew Home Office had a good reason for wiping these out."

Duncan didn't respond, at least not immediately. "Yep," he finally said, taciturn as ever.

It was good to be back. Even with this shit to deal with.

*

Reeve was stuck staring, dumbstruck, at Donna posed just outside his door, lighter in hand, reeking and covered head to feet in gasoline. She was just soaked, like she'd gone for a midnight swim in a gasoline watering hole and not bothered to take a stitch off first. Reeve just stared at her, slack-jawed, disbelieving, before it clicked in his head what he was dealing with. "Legion," he said, barely whispering it.

"It is our name, for we are—" The voice came out of her mouth but it wasn't hers, it was that of a grating, angry man. The eyes that had once looked at him with such love held nothing but hate, in a way that he'd never seen from these eyes before. They'd had arguments in their years of marriage, sure, but even when Donna had been pissed off and spitting fire, she'd never looked at him like she was looking at him now.

Her hand came up, the cigarette lighter clenched between the fingers, poised to strike the flint and push the button.

"Wait!" Reeve shouted, voice bellowing out in fear and echoing through the quiet house. "Don't—"

"We pleaded with you," came the angry man's voice from between her lips again. "Told you we were no threat. That we didn't want violence. And still you—"

"Your compatriot apparently didn't feel the same about violence," Reeve said, mind frantically racing to try and defuse this situation.

These bastards had him over a barrel, now, it was plain, and he needed to get right to the root, get them talked off the ledge before something real bad happened here. "And I'm real sorry about how that played out—"

"Your apologies are meaningless," the voice rose, even more furious. "Your words are empty."

"I mean it, sincerely," Reeve said, digging deep and hard, ripping his pride out without even thinking about it. Apologize to a demon? He wouldn't have thought so this morning, but then, a lot had changed since then. "I am sorry. People do funny things when you threaten them and their loved ones." He gestured out with a single hand to indicate Donna. "We had no choice, and I'm—"

"Stop apologizing!" the voice screamed, and Donna's face contorted with anger, gasoline dripping out of her grey hair, dark and soaked in the petroleum.

"I don't know what else I can do for you," Reeve said, voice shaking. "Tell me what you want. We can—"

"What we want?" The voice paused, and the dead eyes stared at him.

"Everybody wants something," Reeve said, keeping his hands as neutrally placed as he could, not daring to go for a weapon. If he went for anything, it was over, because that demon in Donna's skin could flick that lighter faster than he could draw a sword and nick her arm. "What do you want?" He licked his lips, tentative. If he could just get them to tell him what they wanted, it'd be something. They could find some common ground, start working toward a solution that didn't involve—

"We want …" the voice came again, long and dragging, pauses between some of the words, "… we want you …" the eyes lit up with a sort of furious glee, "… to suffer."

Donna's hand flicked the switch and with a whooshing sound, she ignited, like a piece of tinder thrown on a fire, and Reeve screamed as the burst of sudden heat hit him in the face with all the force of a punch.

*

"Molly," Lauren said, straight to pleading, the shower still washing over her, warm enough to defray some of the cold chills that were covering her from neck to feet and everywhere in between, "what are you ...?" She asked even though she knew the answer, even though she was sure that her daughter was possessed and standing before her with a knife to her mother's neck because of a demon, a goddamned demon that had invaded her home and bathroom and was about to—

Oh, Lord.

"Lauren ..." her mother said with a shaking voice. Her eyes were brimming with tears that came from absolute fear, from being manhandled by her granddaughter, who suddenly had far, far too much strength for her small frame. Lauren looked at her mother, just a quick glance, enough to see the fear there, to note the bright drip of red under the knife's blade, working its way down her neck to her old blouse's flowery collar. There was a dark spot there where it had started to pool, slowly spreading down the cloth.

"It's okay, Mom," Lauren said, almost positive that it wasn't. She was standing naked in her own bathroom, shower pouring down over her, goose bumps running over every square inch of her skin that could pimple up. She dropped a hand to her bare thigh and felt them there, then ran it up to cover her across her chest, trying to reclaim a little bit of her dignity in this moment, almost unconsciously. "I ..."

"It will not be okay," Molly said in a high voice that was nothing like her own. "You should be honest with her."

"I ..." Lauren swallowed heavily. "I ... why are you doing this?"

Molly's eyes bored into her. "You took some of ours."

Lauren blinked, droplets of water falling like tears out of her eyelashes. The simple statement hit her in the face. If the watch had taken some of "theirs," some of the demons' own, then the logical conclusion to that was that the demons—

"Please don't," Lauren said, shaking her head, her wet, water-soaked hair forming a natural ponytail as it all banded together in thick strands off the back of her head. "Please don't—"

She didn't get any more out before Molly's hand ripped in a quick motion horizontally. It was done in a second, just a jerk of the hand—

Blood sprayed across Lauren's face and head and chest and down her front like there was another showerhead in front of her, and she closed her eyes in surprise at the sudden, unexpected violence of the motion, like someone throwing a punch at your face in order to make you flinch.

She was surprised at the sudden darkness as her eyes went closed, the afterimage of her mother's fear just frozen there. Her rational mind watched it all again in the second after it happened, and she diagnosed it—tearing of the carotid artery and the jugular vein, the throat—

Good God.

—heavy tissue damage, there was the airway, cut clear to the—

Mom.

—almost the spine, the throat opened to—

Jesus.

Lauren opened her eyes less than a second later and her mother just hung there before her, the world tinged with sudden red where before it had been pale blues and whites of the quiet, serene, country-style bathroom with its china-white porcelain and deep blue accents. There was blood on the walls, blood on the white tile, already diluted blood on her hands and arms, extended before her like she'd tried to feel her way through a dark room.

Molly was completely drenched in scarlet, a smile of dark satisfaction turning up one corner of her mouth.

"Did you like that?" Molly asked with that wicked satisfaction. There was a coldness there that was unfamiliar to her, and she was as familiar with Molly as she'd ever been with any human being, really, even more than any of her lovers who'd known her body inside and out. Her daughter had grown within her for the better part of a year, and she'd wiped her nose, pulled her toes, brushed her hair, taken her everywhere ...

Lauren just stared at her mother, whose jaw was twitching open and shut very slightly, the muscle and nerves so damaged only inches below that she was finding it near impossible to get any motion going. Lauren stared at her clinically, trying to hold back the familiarity that would only result in crippling fear and nausea. Vera, her mom, the one who had done for her all the things she'd done for Molly, stared back at her with undisguised terror, mute and unable to give voice to it.

Then Yvette and Molly let go of her shoulders as one, and her mother sagged to her knees, out of control. She landed hard on the edge of the tub, the shower sprinkling down on her as Lauren took an inadvertent step back and nearly slipped. Her mother's hair fell under the shower's spray and went dark from wetness in a second. Washed-out crimson liquid flooded down into the tub, carried by the shower's watery spray, and swirled toward the drain like a still frame from *Psycho*. Lauren watched it happen, watched it go as her mother's legs twitched, her body hanging half in and half out of the tub, her blouse speckled dark with water spots in the back.

The horror hit Lauren all at once, her clinical detachment shattered as it hit her that—*MOM, oh, God, MOM*—her mother was bleeding to death right in front of her. She dropped down in a second, all thought of propriety and decency and all the things her mother would bitch about when she went out wearing a halter top and a short skirt thrown to the four winds, washed down the drain like her mother's own lifeblood.

"Mom!" the word burst out of Lauren's lips as she knelt hard in the porcelain tub, her mother hanging limply beside her. Lauren fumbled to try and grab her at the neck, to frantically stop the exodus of blood, to stem it at least until she could get to—*there's no trauma center within forty-five minutes of here*—a hospital, to surgery—*there's no chance*—anything to buck the odds against—*the blood loss is too severe, it has to be nearing a half gallon by now, surely, maybe more*—death, to slow the rushing tide.

Anything, Lauren prayed, though she wasn't sure who she was praying to.

She stared her mother in the eye, because she could only see the right one from where she was kneeling. It was fixed on her for about a second, and then it lost her, wandering down to the red-stained porcelain as the blood dribbled steadily out, washed down by the relentless flow of the shower. Vera's mouth moved, but it was like a fish gasping one last time, and then she lost consciousness—*she's fucking dead, Jesus, she's dead for all intents and purposes, you have no way to replace that blood volume, DOCTOR*—for the last time, Lauren somehow knew.

Lauren just stared into her mother's unfocused eye, and wondered if she'd had enough blood left in her brain before she'd passed out to know what she was looking at. "Did she see me?" Lauren asked, faintly, her training at its end, all thought of what she could do, this treatment or that treatment giving way to the fact that she was naked.

In her bathtub.

Demons had just possessed her daughter to slit her mother's throat.

And her mom had just died.

"Did you enjoy that?" the voice came again, from Molly's mouth but not in Molly's voice or tone or inflection. Lauren didn't answer, because she had no answer to give, and strong, impossibly strong, arms grabbed her under the armpits and wrenched her, flailing, over and away from her dead mother as they dragged her, dripping with blood and water, out of the tub.

*

Brian couldn't believe what his eyes had just seen, what his voice had just said, what his finger had just done, and he had control over none of it, not one little bit. He was still screaming from seeing a gunshot blast a hole in his father's head, opening up the top of his skull and painting the white kitchen ceiling with blood and brain matter and—*oh, God, Jesus*—a little piece of what looked like skull that was just laying there on the counter.

Brian held the gun in his hand as his father tipped over backward and hit the ground, dribble of blood already rolling out the side of his mouth. Bill Longholt wasn't a small guy, and Brian hadn't inherited his father's size, but he'd held him hard in place while he'd fired the gun up through the bottom of his jaw and out through the top of his head. He'd just held him there, a grin fixed on his lips, a scream held back in his head, while he blew his father's brains out.

Jesus.

"BRIAN!" His mother screamed, blown right past panic to horror and shock, eyes pinwheeling around from his fallen father to him and back again, throwing in a blink here and there for good measure and—

Oh God oh God oh God—

Something slammed into Brian from behind, clipping him in the knee with stabbing force and agonizing pain set in, screaming pain, like someone had—

Stabbed me—

The chorus of harpies was gone in an instant, replaced with screaming pain in his knee as Brian's leg buckled. A whirling burst of black fire whiffed in the back of his throat and he was suddenly overcome with the smell of wretched sulfur as he hit the ground on all fours, landing atop his father's legs, hacking and coughing.

"Jesus, Brian," Alison's soft voice came from behind him. He blinked like he'd smoked five bowls and didn't have a drop of Clear Eyes handy, looking back at her and then down at his handiwork.

"Dad," he whispered softly, staring at his father's face, the soft drip of blood running down his cheek nothing compared the steadily growing pool oozing out the crown of his head and the slow flush of scarlet washing out of the gunshot wound below his jaw, the intensity of the gush fading with each flagging beat of his father's heart.

*

Hendricks was in his car the second he got his jeans on, not even bothering to try and pull a shirt on. Starling was next to him in the passenger seat, silent, her fingers playing over the soft cloth of the rental car. Lonsdale was in the back, moaning and groaning like he had a headache—again, the motherfucker. The air was blowing full blast on cold, the heater not yet fired up as he thumped hard out of the Sinbad parking lot and floored it onto the highway, trying to remember how exactly to get to Arch's in-laws' house.

"Fuck fuck fuck," Hendricks said, shaking his head, watching the road with fearful expectation. They'd fucking come for him, that fucking Legion, and if it hadn't been for Starling and her patented ability to extract his dick from the teeth and jaws of hellish death, he'd have found himself probably in a pickle. Or with a pickle up his ass. Something like that.

"I can't believe I've been possessed twice in one fucking day," Lonsdale moaned in the back.

Hendricks shot him a furiously nasty look. "This is all your goddamned fault, Lonsdale."

Lonsdale was suddenly innocent as a churchboy. "Me? How is being possessed by a demon my fault?"

"Because you, you fucking lousy sorry fuck—" Hendricks grabbed an empty pop can and threw it right into Lonsdale's face with all the hate that was bursting out of his heart at the moment, "just had to go and fuck with demons that hadn't even fucking done anything, you lousy piece of shit—" He threw an old water bottle, only a quarter full, right at Lonsdale's nose and it hit its target, eliciting a sharp, "Oww!" from the bastard.

"I weren't doing nuffing that we demon hunters aren't supposed to be doing," Lonsdale said, resentful eyes peeking from behind his hand, which was perched over his nose to prevent any further attacks, clearly. "Killing demons is our thing, innit?"

"Killing your cunt ass through anal penetration with my sword is about to become my thing, you motherfucker," Hendricks said, swerving as he put his eyes back on the road and found he'd drifted hard into the other lane. "So help me, if these fucking demons have done any damage, I'm going to kill you myself. Turn your skin into jerky for the local vreetackatharouns." He looked at Starling. "How bad is this?"

She stared straight ahead into the windshield, ignoring his diatribe, pondering his words. "Bad."

Hendricks clenched the wheel tighter and squealed tires in a tight turn. "Goddammit."

*

Reeve could feel the heat, like a summer's day, even though summer had long gone. The smell of gasoline burning was distinctive, too, and he had his hands up in front of his face to ward it off. It was instinct, blind instinct; when an explosion went off in front of you, even one so mild and lacking in concussive force as someone lighting up gasoline, the instinct was the shy away from the heat. And shy away Reeve did, for at least a few seconds.

His next instinct was panic, to freak the fuck out, trying to figure exactly what he should do. He'd seen some crazy shit, especially lately, but his own wife lighting herself on fire while possessed by a demon? That was beyond him, beyond anything he'd seen. The only close contender was that poor homeless bastard who had burned up on the square a couple months ago, and Reeve hadn't given a great deal of thought to that because—well, because it was one of a hundred bodies he was dealing with.

Donna stood in the middle of the flame, the fire burning hard around her, and he realized at last that she seemed to be totally fine in there, just standing with the inferno burning up around her, smoke pouring up to the ceiling and giving the room a scent like chem-fired barbecue. He reached out to touch her and pulled his hand back in a heartbeat, remembering all too well how that damned Rog'tausch had burned him on the arm.

He stared at Donna in the middle of the flames, looking back at him as the flames spread down the gasoline trail, lighting their house as it crept along. Reeve was dumbstruck; he didn't know what to do, just stared at his wife's face peering at him from the middle of the raging fire. She took a step toward him and he took a step back instinctively, not wanting to be burned again.

"Do you see it now?" that angry voice came again.

"I see fire," Reeve said, the words popping out before he could give them thought.

She strolled across the room, leaving flaming footprints in her wake. He gave way for her, and she ran a hand across the top of the dresser, over the doily that laced the top of it, and set that aflame as well, starting a fire among the pictures of kids and grandkids that decorated the top of the piece. The flames ran down the sides of the wooden dresser in seconds and soon it was being consumed as well, more fuel for what the demon was doing to his home.

"Jesus," Reeve breathed, and Donna stamped a foot down in his discarded Sheriff's uniform, setting it a-kindlin' as well. He might have wanted to burn the damned thing, but not like this. She stared down into the burning cloth as it caught, and Reeve realized he didn't have his sword on his belt because he wasn't wearing his pants and that they were right there, next to his shirt—

"Shit," he muttered, and she swooped down and drew his own sword. He stared at her, wondering why she'd ignored the pistol on the belt, and then she answered that for him a second later.

"Fuck you," she said in that hellacious voice, and turned the sword around, stabbing herself right through the heart before Reeve could so much as open his damned mouth.

*

Amanda wasn't enjoying this fight anymore, and she'd had about enough of this fucking Legion's shit and crap tactics, and was ready to start splitting skulls. She said as much to Duncan, and he replied, "Please don't."

"Fuck these fleshbags," Amanda replied, cracking one of them upside the head with a baton hard enough to start a good gusher of blood down the back of the lady's scalp. She looked like she might ordinarily have been pretty frail, with her crepe-like skin and thick, old-lady glasses and grey hair. "You getting soft on me?"

"Not as soft as you were when you vaped," Duncan said, and Amanda could tell he was fishing.

"Still don't trust me entirely?" Amanda asked, driving a baton into another one of the Legion's drones at the belly. He didn't break skin there, unfortunately. Hendricks might have had the right idea, using a sword, that cowboy fuck. "Even after reading my essence?"

"I'd be interested to know what you did to get out of the pits," Duncan said, throwing a punch that cracked a demon-possessed human's head around. It didn't stop the real face of the demon from showing through, though, and two more jumped on Duncan right after he spoke. *Stupid*, Amanda thought. This whole approach was just stupid.

"Not much," Amanda said, tossing an elbow of her own. She was through fucking around with these pricks, no matter what Duncan said. Innocents got hurt in life, that was just a fact. She whipped a baton around with enough force to split a skull, and when the blow landed, she did. A line of blood splattered the hotel room's wall and the human dropped, black fire surging through the eyes and gaping mouth as the guy hit his knees. Amanda kicked him right in his flapped-open jaw and sent him crunching backward into a wall. "They came to me, told me I was going back."

Duncan was under a mountain of opposition, but Amanda heard the reply even through four or five bodies piled on him. "That doesn't make any sense."

Amanda leapt across the room, capping her damned head on the ceiling and ripping a five-foot gash across the popcorn white as she came back down. Her hair was trailing little pieces of the ceiling behind her, but she drove her baton hard into the back of a human's exposed neck, busting skin and breaking the spine. She tossed the limp body, demon still vaping inside, off Duncan and smashed another one in the side of the head with a similar lack of mercy. This one was a woman, probably in her thirties, blond, and that was all she noticed before she added her to the "don't give a fuck" pile and threw her, unresisting, through the nearest wall. She was probably dead, and either way, she was out of the room and thus out of reach of another possession attempt.

"Stop fucking doing that!" Duncan shouted from beneath the last few demons he was fighting to get out from under. "You're killing these people!"

"That's the point," Amanda said, but she hit the next one coming at her squarely in the nose with a little less force and just shoved her, nose broken and bleeding, blackness vaping out of her eyes, through the hole in the wall like she'd done to the last one. This one would probably get up again, though. Maybe need a little cosmetic surgery, but she'd live. "I'm sick of punching the same faces over and over and getting nowhere."

"There can't be that many of them left!" Duncan shouted, way more emotionally exposed than when Amanda had left this planet. That couldn't be good; Duncan was already soft. Loosening up further was probably a terrible, terrible sign that things were going awry here and that Duncan was opening himself up to the fleshbags.

"There's enough to kill us," Amanda said, suddenly missing the Boston accent that she hadn't even noticed she'd had in the Lerner form. Now she spoke in very highly educated tones, lacking any local inflection. "You should treat this deadly seriously."

"I'm not sure I do anymore." Duncan threw a human body across the room, it snapping at him as it arced over the bed. "Not since they're apparently just letting people out of the pits these days, just turning them loose all willy-nilly—"

"You willing to bet your eternity on that?" Amanda hit him with that one, because she didn't want to have this discussion yet. Not nearly yet. Maybe never, if she could have swung it, but she knew Duncan too well to think he'd let this go for very long.

"I'm not willing to kill these people for it," Duncan said, and he drew the damned line. Amanda didn't like to hear it, but there it was, and it was a bad sign from where she was sitting. They'd seen hundreds and thousands of humans die since they'd partnered up. That was the laws of nature, and it was no use getting too sentimental about it. You didn't see humans weep giant tears over the passage of flies.

"I am," Amanda said, and rammed her baton through the ear canal of some poor bastard who looked about twenty. His whole life was probably in front of him, or it had been until Amanda rammed six inches of steel into his brain, then pulled it out, watching the black horror of a demon returning to its origin, and a human's life fleeing right out of there in tandem.

Duncan hardened up right then, she could feel it. "So that's how it is, huh?"

"That's how it is," Amanda said, drawing a line of her own. "My instructions were clear." She watched Duncan make a face, a real subtle one. That little thing she'd thrown out was just bait, for later, to try and keep him going in the wrong direction. She'd need him to, at least for a while, because if Duncan got his head out of his ass and started focusing on what was really going on here instead of what the humans were concerned about … well … that was why Amanda was here, after all.

*

Lauren was dragged, naked and screaming, out onto the lawn, and while she wanted to believe she didn't make it easy on Molly or Yvette, that other lady, she was pretty sure her resistance didn't make one hell of a lot of difference either way. She ached and burned, cuts on her knees and forearms from trying to fight and claw and scratch and grab onto furniture and doors giving her nothing but a little more blood to show for it. She was sticky with the stuff already, most of it her mother's, and now she'd just piled on a half-dozen aggravating little wounds, each oozing their own marks of protest at her rough treatment, trailing down her naked flesh and catching there in globs.

Now she was palms down in the dirt, her chest hitting the front lawn and shocks of pain running up through her body like a twin tit punch. Her knees were crying in protest, too, but it was lost in the chorus of a thousand agonies and buried under the trauma of watching her mother get her throat slit right in front of her eyes.

Lauren pushed herself up onto all fours, her hand finding a twig that resisted her, buried in the grass like a dagger. Dirt clung to her body like a thousand tiny pebbles, the grains glued to her skin. She pushed herself up, desperation and fear crackling through her, her wet hair still hanging over her shoulders. Little droplets of water fell past her nose, disappearing into the dirty, thin grass that made up the lawn.

A hard rubber sole kicked her right in the butt cheek with alarming force, driving her forward into the ground again. She jerked her head at the last second but still ended up facedown in the sod, unable to prop herself up with her flagging arms. She hurt, from the kick, from the impact of her landing face-first, the emotional bruise of watching her mother slaughtered like an animal in front of her eyes by her own daughter ... it all just hurt.

It made Lauren just want to lie there. What else was she supposed to do? She'd fought as hard as she could against those two demons on her way out of the house and it had done not a damned thing. They hadn't dragged her anywhere near a weapon she could use to do anything, and now she was naked, in the middle of the front lawn, and if there was anything else she could do to fight them, she was dogged if she could see it.

She thought about playing dead, the dirt and grass against her cheek, just leaving it there. She could lie here for a good long while. She was still in pain, but moving was worse, wasn't it? When they brought someone into the ER suffering from trauma, it wasn't like she advised them to get up and run around, after all. Moving was stupid. Fighting back was just going to get her hurt even worse than she already was. She was bleeding from enough places already. There was no hope of actual, effective resistance that would do a damned thing.

It was time to just lie there, she decided. That was the right course.

A little drop of water snaked its way down her temple and stopped when it touched dirt. She could feel it float there as the dry ground started to absorb it, leaving her feeling like there was a crust on her skin, a residual sign that she'd either cried a tear or dripped blood or water. A little mark of what had happened to her just now, a sign of her surrender.

"Get up," the voice came back to her again, and strong arms clawed at her armpits, fingernails digging into the bare skin and hauled her to her knees. Hadn't they just kicked her into the dirt? She went limp and made them hold her up. Fuck them. If they wanted to drag her around, she was through giving them any help doing it, or fighting them. She'd just lie there like a jellyfish, like she was dead.

Because inside ... she felt like she kind of was.

"Up, up," the harsh voice came again, blaring out of Molly's mouth like a bad dub of a foreign film. They held her there, and

Lauren just let her head loll limply forward, fixing her eyes on the lawn. Why did it even matter if she was up? Who gave a shit whether she was—

"What the hell is going on out here?" Lauren's eyes snapped up to see Albert Daniel looking in barely contained horror at the spectacle happening on her lawn, reflection of light hitting his glasses. "Molly, Yvette ... what are y'all doing to her?"

Lauren looked right at Albert, and she felt no glimmer of hope. He was older, after all, and the likelihood that he had any kind of a holy weapon on him was about as likely as her growing clothes to cover her nakedness. The sheen of dirt clinging to her skin wasn't going to do it. He wasn't a bad guy, though she'd never liked him. He'd gawked at her once when she went for a run in a sports bra, and that had set tongues to wagging. He was exactly what she hated about Midian, actually, and yet somehow, looking at him now, she couldn't help but hope he would just shut up and get away and save himself from this horror show that she'd gotten dragged into.

She opened her mouth to say some version of that, but it wasn't in time. Not nearly.

Yvette reached under her sweater and drew a pistol, taking cool aim faster than Lauren could properly tell what she was doing. She pointed it right at Albert's head, and BANG, there was another spray of red not unlike what she'd seen when Molly cut her mother's throat. Albert dropped like she had when she'd gotten kicked in the ass, just folded and fell, facedown, planting on the concrete sidewalk so Lauren could see the gaping hole in the back of his head where the bullet had kicked its way out.

Lauren wanted to scream, wanted to cry, wanted to shout for divine intervention, but something in her just clammed up harder. She sagged to her knees as the demons let her go, and she just stared at that gaping hole in Albert's head, like it was a black hole that would suck her right up into it, away from this fucking hell that was eating Midian alive.

"All right," Molly said, in that voice again, that voice of horror and awfulness, that voice she'd spoken in before she ran a dagger hard against Vera's neck. Lauren didn't dare look up at her, she was concentrating on Molly's shoes. They were white and spotted with red everywhere, like she'd painted in them, or like they'd come polka dotted. "Eyes up here," Molly said, and Lauren didn't look. She didn't dare.

"I said fucking look at me!" The voice screamed out of Molly's mouth, and Lauren couldn't avoid it anymore. Coercion was coming. She'd be compelled to look at some point, through force, just like they'd ripped her out of the shower and out of her house, torn away her last shreds of safety and exposed her to the world. They'd torn everything away from her—well, everything except one, that last thing—

Lauren raised her head, almost certain she knew what she'd see. She was not disappointed, either; Yvette was standing there, knife in hand, and she had it poised over Molly's heart. And when Lauren looked up, both of the demons grinned down at her with their real faces, because they knew—they had to—that there was nothing she could do to stop them from killing her daughter right in front of her.

*

Reeve didn't even finish screaming before she stabbed herself. He barely heard it, a kind of high-pitched, girlish "NOOOO!" at the top of his lungs before he saw a spark of blackness through the flames, the sign of a demon being sucked back to hell riding the thunder.

Donna's hands jerked once, and the impermeable, invincible flesh that had shown strong through the burning fire instantly lost its strange luster. Her skin started to char and blacken immediately; her clothing had long ago burned off to reveal the body he had seen naked in front of him more times than he could count.

There was another sound, too, beyond that of the pop and hiss of flames. It was another scream, deep and powerful, pain and agony that cut off after a long few seconds as Donna jerked spasmodically in front of him, the fire consuming her flesh.

Reeve's body came back to him, back to his senses, the smell of burning flesh now added to the rest of the fiery stink that was flooding his sinuses and threatening to gag him. He launched forward and tackled her, slamming her to the ground, the words, "Stop, drop and roll," thundering back to him from more yearly safety visits to the local schools than he could count. He hit the ground and bounced off her, smacking his back into the doorframe as he tried to do the "roll" part of the thing. It didn't go so well, penned in as they were by the wooden frame, and the heat rose around him as Reeve hit full panic.

He'd been in fights, he'd been in scrapes, he'd taken on a few demons of late, but watching his wife burst into flames and then stab herself in the heart had been something so sick and demented he wondered what sort of torturous bastard had come up with this plan. He knew the answer was a demon, but it was just so far beyond the pale that when he hit the doorframe for the third time trying to roll Donna to snuff the flames, his brain just snapped into default self-preservation and he tried to push her away. She was limp and unresisting, and that meant something he didn't even want to think about. Not now, not ever.

Reeve tried to fight back to his feet, tried to figure out the next move. The damned house was starting to burn around him, which was a special kind of alarming, and Donna was just out and burning next to him, like she'd just gone to sleep at his side and they'd woken up with everything on fire. He hoped he'd snap out of it, find out this whole thing was just a shitty nightmare, the mack-daddy worst of them all, but when the fire licked at him, burning him, he knew this shit was all too real.

"Dammit," Reeve whispered. His head locked onto a new plan—get Donna out of here somehow, because he couldn't put out the fire on her while everything else was burning. He went to her feet and grabbed her ankles; they were so charred, her socks burned crispy so that the cotton flaked off in ashy pieces like it had never been there, revealing scorched skin underneath.

He ignored that and grabbed a solid hold and started pulling, dragging her back into the bathroom, away from the hallway that was fully engulfed. He lifted his head up enough to realize that black smoke was pooling at the ceiling, and that was dangerous. This was fire department shit, not his deal, but he had to get her out of here before it was too late. Something was scraping the floor hard, resisting his attempts to pull her along and he finally realized it was that goddamned sword of his, stuck through the middle of her chest. The blade was ripping up the finish on the wood floor, he realized dimly. He looked up and saw the dresser burning, the lifetime of family pictures being eaten up by ravenous fire and realized that the scratch to the floor was the least of his problems, so he gently tugged the sword out of her chest with one hand and kept dragging her across the bedroom floor with the other, displacing the rug between the bed and the vanity as he did so. It was on fire anyway.

He stopped when he got to the window on the back bedroom wall. He needed to break it, needed to create an exit, and—no, wait. He needed to put her out now that he was clear of most of the fire. He looked down at the rug he'd caught her on and had his answer. He grabbed the edges and beat them against her, trying to snuff the flames that were already dying anyway. They must have been running low on fuel, the gasoline mostly burned off by this point. He had them out in a few seconds, coughing and hacking like his lungs were turning black all the while.

Reeve tried not to look at her, at the blackened skin like a catfish left in the oven for too long, and he focused on his next problem, brain chugging along faithfully, pinging to one thing at a time. Now he needed to get her out the window. Which meant first, he needed to get the window open.

That was simple enough; he hit the latches and ripped it up, the window squealing as he lifted it so hard that glass broke. He ran the sword around the sill, clearing the fragments and shards, then stuck his head out the window and took deep, hungry breaths. He hadn't even realized how bad his coughing had gotten, with deep, racking spasms as his lungs sought fresh air.

Taking a deep breath, he tossed the sword out the window and ducked back inside. Distantly, he heard the rattle of the blade against the pavers out back and ignored it as he reached down and grabbed Donna under her arms. The smell of meat cooking over an open fire held a strange appeal, reminded him of his camping days, and he felt sick as he realized that was his wife that he smelled. He ignored the feeling of slippery flesh tearing as he lifted her, utterly obsessed with just getting her outside. That was all he could do, get her out and follow after her. Everything else could be worked on from there, one thing at a time until they fixed it all. He'd get her out, then get her to the hospital, then get the doctors working on her, maybe find Dr. Darlington first, come to think of it, get her on the problem ...

Donna wasn't a small woman. He'd carried her over the threshold on their wedding night, but it hadn't been the easiest thing he'd ever done, and he didn't remember trying to repeat the feat since that time.

He was doing it here, though, lifting and pulling dead weight, trying to lever her up over the window ledge. He was coughing again uncontrollably, and it was affecting his ability to do anything, to exert himself. He shoved his head out the window for a second and took deep, cleansing breaths again. He lifted, trying to pull her up and out, and he got her up a couple feet with some serious effort. He felt like he was lifting a car or a boulder, and she wasn't helping, goddammit, she needed to help …

He got her up over the frame and she tumbled out, hitting the ground with a thump he barely heard. She was there and then suddenly she was gone, dropping out of sight over the sill and leaving him stunned for a beat, almost clueless what to do. Then Reeve threw himself up over as well, rolling over the sill and coming down harder than he expected.

He landed on the ground and rolled down the short slope to where Donna lay, a few shards of broken glass falling down behind him. He coughed hard, trying to expel the smoke from his lungs, hacking loudly for what felt like long minutes of agonized spasms throughout his entire upper body. He forced his eyes open, got up on an elbow and started to think about the next problem, which was—

"Jesus," Reeve said. "Oh, Jesus, no."

In the burning room, Reeve hadn't seen Donna, not really. He'd looked around her but not at her with anything more than a glance that slid off, that gave him enough information to do what he needed to do but nothing else, like his vision was zoomed in on one thing and one thing only, like staring through a telescope.

Now that his lungs were full of clean air again, the smell of burnt meat still hung in his nose, the faint light of fading day still closing out above him, he got a real good look at her under the flickering of the lights behind the house, still burning bright in the waning day.

Donna was burned from top to bottom. Her steel hair was blackened and even entirely gone in some places, and her skin looked like it was wet, puckered like a running sore. Her clothing was scorched and burnt into the skin in some places, and when he looked at her chest …

"Holy fucking shit."

Her chest didn't move up and down; she took no breath as he sat there, watching, waiting, hoping, the panic doing nothing but rising with every moment she lay there—still as death.

"Goddammit!" Hendricks shouted, slamming a hand into the steering wheel as he hung up the cell phone Lonsdale had handed him. He'd memorized Arch's number in case of emergency, but otherwise he just used 911 if he needed to get hold of anyone lately. It had worked pretty well, except for that time he'd had to go through the damned call center Reeve had hired to take the emergency calls at night.

"They got murder on their hive minds," Lonsdale said from the back seat. "These things. The demons."

"I fucking knew who you were talking about, Lonsdale," Hendricks said. He was already driving close to ninety, and even Starling was holding on at this point. "Sonofabitch." He was racking his brain. "Who all were they after?"

Lonsdale's answer was way too damned slow in arriving, and even when it did, it wasn't anywhere close to what Hendricks wanted to hear. "Everyone," the Brit said simply. "They're mad as hell at you lot."

"Sonofa ..." Hendricks took a corner, slowing to sixty to do it and busting the mirror off someone's pickup as he cut it a little too close. He was still at zero fucks given though, since the rental wasn't his and he had better things to worry about than the cherry state of someone's superdiesel dually. Without directory assistance to get him to so much as Duncan's hotel room, without any other numbers committed to memory—

Wait.

Hendricks did know one other number by heart, but it wasn't one he'd called lately. It was one he'd put in his mind early in his stay here and it just stuck, kinda like terrible commercial jingles, way past their use. He glanced at the phone for a second and took out someone's mailbox, then just decided to go for it and dialed the number in a hell of a hurry. He thrust it against his ear as he ran off onto the shoulder at sixty and waited, the ringing sound like a fucking countdown of doom.

"Hello?" Erin Harris answered, kinda curious, like she was wondering who the hell was calling her from a strange number.

"Erin, it's Hendricks," he said, it all coming out in a rush. "This Legion motherfucker—he's going after everyone. He just sent two people to kick down my hotel room and one of them was Lonsdale and he's after—"

"What the fuck, Hendricks?" Erin asked, and he could practically see her squinching her face up at him even over the phone. "What the hell—"

"The possession demon, Erin!" Hendricks shouted. "He's in play! He's coming after us. Arch isn't answering and I don't know anyone else's number."

There was a pause that felt like forever but was probably only two seconds. When she spoke again, her voice was small. "What do we do?"

"You gotta get to somebody," Hendricks said, just off the top of his head. "We gotta—gotta fight these fuckers off. They tried to just bust down my door, but, I mean, if they came at everybody else the same way—"

"They didn't," Lonsdale said, the dreadful voice of knowledge from the back seat. Ever since the bastard had started to come out of his post-possession delirium, he'd just been one fucking helpful nugget after another. "They were—they were going to come at them through people they knew, people they knew and loved. Your whole—what is it, a watch or somefing—?"

"Oh, fuck," Hendricks said. "Did you hear—?"

"I heard," Erin said. "I'll call Reeve and start—I'll get my car and see what I can—fuck, Jesus—" She hung up on him without any further word on the matter.

"Son of a motherfucking fuck," Hendricks said, because he couldn't come up with something that fit any better than that.

"This does seem dire," Starling said.

"Dire?" Hendricks jerked his head around. "*Dire?* Are you fucking—?"

He blinked; she was gone, the passenger seat empty beside him, her red hair that had been glinting in the glow of the sunset only a moment earlier completely gone, and the blinding light of sundown was now staring him right in the face ... just like the fact that the entire watch had just gotten bushwhacked, and Hendricks had no fucking idea how everyone could possibly survive this one.

*

"Daddy!" Alison dropped to her knees, shoving Brian away. She heard him squeal in pain and didn't care, her empathy for her brother gone like a cloud on a windy day even though she knew he'd been possessed by a demon when he'd done what he'd done. She'd seen it in his eyes in the second after Arch jabbed him through the leg, had known it by what he'd done. Brian was a shit, a fucking asshole, a know-it-all, but a guy who would grab a gun off her daddy's belt and cap him with it? Entirely ruefully, she had to admit a nasty truth— Brian couldn't have shot that straight even at point blank range.

She pushed him away and let her left hand hang there for a second, not really sure what to do. The right hand was holding her up, palm hard against the tile floor, imprinted in a puddle of sticky blood. She stared down at her father, whose face was—it just looked— wrong. There was a gaping wound pumping blood slower and slower out the bottom of his jaw, and the puddle of red spreading above his head looked a little like a halo radiating out from his skull, like he was joining the angels in one of those religious icons of old.

Alison just froze that left hand there, thinking maybe it'd be smart not to shake the man. He'd been damaged, maybe fatally, by that shot, and trying to jar him out of the state he was in seemed like a feat of dumbfuckery right up there with lighting firecrackers out of your ass. Her hand wavered, just a second as she tried to figure out what to do, and then her fingers just shot right over to that hole in his jaw. She stuck her fingers inside and tried to staunch that flow of blood. It washed out around her, though, at a little slower rate.

"Fuck, fuck, fuck," she said solidly as she sat there, like a little girl with her finger in a dam. She'd taken first aid classes once, hadn't she? Had there been some part she'd forgotten where they dealt with someone bleeding out like a dying animal in a slaughterhouse? Because she couldn't recall that at all, if it had been in there. It had mostly been shit like "disinfect the wound before you apply the Band Aid," and "fourteen compressions, two breaths," when it came to CPR.

The CPR thing jolted her, and she realized that if her daddy kept bleeding like he was, he was liable to need CPR, and soon, to keep his heart beating or else he'd ...

"Addy," Arch said from behind her, "call 911. Tell the lady in the call center we need an ambulance." The words bounced around until they stuck to Alison's momma, and she took off to do as ordered with a feeble nod of her head that Alison saw in her peripheral vision as she watched blood continue to wash around her fingers out of her daddy's neck. Arch had never called her mother "Addy" before that she could recall.

"Brian," Arch said, and she only turned her head slightly to see the conversation between the two of them. Arch had his sword at his side, at the ready, ready for anything, maybe, and Brian just looked dazed and in pain. "Who did this to you?"

Brian was grimacing hard, but he blinked and looked at Arch. "The doorbell," he said, voice a scratchy whisper. "When I answered it, it was …"

Arch tore off around the corner and Alison heard him fling the door open in the distance. She was staring at her own completely ineffectual handiwork but she was listening hard for him, trying to figure out what she was supposed to do here. Fourteen compressions, two breaths. That came back again. Her daddy was bleeding out his skull and neck, and she was going to have to do this soon, this nasty thing, this pushing on the chest and breathing into lips like angel kisses.

A gunshot cracked out and Alison flinched. Another rang out, then another, and the sound of something spanging against metal and brick made her want to hug the floor out of survival instinct. She wavered for a second, wanting to go grab her rifle, do something she was good at for a spell, but she hung where she was, trying to put pressure on her daddy's wound. "Brian," she snapped in lieu of going off to look for Arch, hoping he was still fine since she hadn't heard him cry out, "get over here!"

Brian winced and half-crawled over to her, dragging his injured leg behind him. Arch hadn't been unmerciful in how he'd done the job wounding her brother, but he hadn't been kind, either. He'd caught Brian right behind the kneecap on a hard charge, and there was a decent amount of blood seeping out of there, enough that he'd need some stitches and more, maybe. He dragged along and Alison grabbed his hand as he came close, taking him by the finger and pushing it in where she'd just pulled hers out of her daddy's jaw. "Stay there," she ordered.

She crawled along to the top of her daddy's head and looked in where the bullet had come out. It wasn't as big as she would have thought it'd be; she'd been firing a fifty cal for so long she was starting to dream about the massive holes she was leaving in targets and in demons, but the handgun her brother had used to do the job had been a nine millimeter, and it didn't even have hollow points in it; they'd switched to full metal jacket rounds a week ago because they just did a little better punching a demon in the face.

"Hello? 911?" Her mother spoke behind her, tentative, frightened. "My husband has been shot. I need—I need an ambulance. Y-yes, that's our—that's our address ..."

Blood was dribbling out of the dark wound, but it wasn't coming out wildly in spurts like she would have feared it. It was a steady flow, a dribble, and it was covering the tile.

Her father's breathing started to get shallow, and now Alison knew he had to be running kind of low on oxygen. This was where she came in, where she was going to have to do the only thing she knew how.

She ignored the fact that Arch hadn't come back yet, just waited until her father stopped breathing, and then she started doing CPR, just like she remembered, while Brian watched along in pain and her mother talked into the phone somewhere behind her.

*

When they were done with the fight, Duncan was left staring at Amanda over what was practically a mountain of human bodies. The resentment was festering between them as if the corpses had already started to putrefy. They hadn't, of course, but they might as well have by the way they smelled. She'd even left some of them alive, for fuck's sake.

"I can't believe you just did that," Duncan said, as he vaped the last demons right out of a middle-aged man.

"I can't believe I held off as long as I did before I started," Amanda replied, securing her baton and ignoring the slick of red gleaming on the point. "This is stupid. These people ... if we don't do what I just did, how long do you think they're going to survive after they kill us and move on? Because I haven't been dealing with this particular Legion like you have been, apparently, but to me it's looking like a kamikaze mission all the way." She folded her arms in front of her and hit Duncan with a hard look. The Amanda Guthrie shell had an amazing Resting Bitch Face. The Lerner shell had been a little smirky, comparatively. Resting asshole face, she supposed.

"That doesn't matter." Duncan's voice rose, his essence swelling inside him. "They could have lived if we had just taken the cautious approach and dispensed with the demons one at a time, and—"

"Oh, blah blah," Amanda said, rolling her eyes and walking away, mostly for effect. "You're sitting here whining so loud you can't even connect the dots on what this was." She paused and looked back over her shoulder, waiting for Duncan to pick up what she was laying down. "Can you?"

If Duncan hadn't been in a shell, if he'd had actual cheeks with actual blood in him, the poor bastard would have paled. "Ambush," he said weakly.

"Yep," Amanda said, flashing him a smile that was probably only fifty percent as smug as the old one. "So ... what are you going to do about it?"

*

Arch wasn't fond of getting shot at, and he couldn't rightly recall ever having a demon do it to him, at least not until now. But he'd just been fired on by a demon, sure enough, not that he'd seen the eyes to be certain of it. He'd thrown himself down just inside the hallway and listened to the bullets hit the front of the house, hoping everyone inside was far enough toward the back of the dwelling to avoid what was coming at the front.

When he raised back up to peer out the front door, Arch saw the street. It looked empty enough, the tall-ways mail-slot part of it he could see, but then, he hadn't but barely seen the demon's car before they'd opened up on him. He wondered how they knew he was trouble, how they were sure he wasn't possessed, but he answered that one for himself pretty quick. If he'd been possessed, they could have shot him all day long without worry.

He belly-crawled a little at a time back to the front door, trying to catch a glimpse of the car that had opened fire on him. He stopped when he saw the front bumper and tire, because it had taken him a good ten or twenty seconds just to get in this position. There were sounds behind him, people talking, Addison maybe, on the phone. Arch tried to direct his listening skills out the front door, though, attempting to concentrate for footsteps.

He didn't hear them.

What he did hear was the sound of something like squealing tires in the distance. An engine revved, pretty far off, but then got steadily closer, rumbling like it was coming toward them. He stared out the front door, holding still, just listening to that car get closer and closer, until finally he heard another squeal of tires—

The bumper he'd been watching lurched forward as someone slammed into the back of the car and sent it smashing forward. It spun out from the force of the impact as the brakes tried to hold and failed to gain any traction as the back end of the car was ripped from the ground and twirled like someone had pulled the e-brake on a hard turn. Arch watched the sedan come to rest, ninety degrees off the axis of where it had started, and he was on his feet and out the door before it had come to a full stop.

He saw Mrs. Lester sitting behind the wheel, staggered, bobbing around in the front seat like one of those punching bags that dropped to the floor after a hard hit and sprang right back up. She was shaking her head, wave of grey hair half in her eyes, as Arch came straight down and up to the driver's side window, sword in hand. He poked down hard through the shattered window, stepping in the little pebbles of safety glass as he caught her right in the shoulder.

The effect was immediate, the expulsion of the demon obvious in Mrs. Lester's eyes, the yellow glare returned back to normal steely blue, even a little dull, just a second later. She had an old rifle lying next to her on the seat, but she kept her hands well away from it as they came up to her wrinkled face and covered her eyes. "Unghhh ..." she said, and then she looked up and blinked at Arch, staring up at him like she was looking directly at the sun.

The sun was going down, and it was off to his side, and all there was where he was standing was him, him and a whole sick feeling in his stomach as he came to a few realizations about what had just happened inside the house.

What was still happening inside the house.

"Arch!" Hendricks came out of the shattered SUV that had caused the crash, shirtless and bleeding in a few places. The cowboy wasn't even wearing his hat, and to say he looked distressed was like saying Arch looked like he was a little disturbed. "We're getting fucking bushwhacked, man."

Arch didn't know how he could fit what he was feeling into words without bleeding out some emotion all over Hendricks. He'd seen the damage to his father-in-law, and he knew it was bad. You didn't gush blood out of a brain injury and have it turn out all kittens and rainbows. "I know," was all he said, and Hendricks, no prize to start with, suddenly looked a whole lot worse. Arch figured it might have been something he said.

*

"Please don't," was all that Lauren could get out of herself. It was like she'd been run under one of those steamrollers, smashed flat of emotion and feeling and hope, and looking at her daughter grinning at her with a knife poised under her sternum was just barely enough to try and squeeze another drop of blood out of her. There just wasn't much left to give when you'd been all wrung out.

"Do you know what your people have done to us?" Molly asked in that hateful voice. "You've declared war."

"I'm sorry," Lauren said. She had nothing else for it. She had nothing else, period. Her naked body was lying exposed in the chill air of autumn on her own front lawn. Her house, the only place she felt secure, had just been violated in the most disgusting, terrible way, and her mother's throat had been slit in front of her. She knew that no matter how much she begged for Molly's life, this was not going to have a happy resolution.

Demons were evil, heartless, soulless things. She'd seen them treat people like meals, like bumps in the road, like impediments and animals ... but she'd never seen anything like this.

"Sorry doesn't fix the damage you've done," Molly said.

"I ... I didn't do anything," Lauren said feebly. It would have sounded feeble even if it hadn't been a clumsy denial of guilt. "I wasn't there when anything happened, I never even met you before—"

"This is all your community's doing," Molly said.

"We don't ... have much of a community right now," Lauren said.

"Your watch, then, as you call it." Molly leered down at her. "You all share the guilt. The blame."

"Blame me all you want," Lauren said, trying to muster up courage, feeling, anything. She came up onto her knees, and clasped her dirt-covered hands together, the individual grains of sand and grit covering her like she'd been frolicking on a beach. "But ... please ... my daughter had nothing to do with—"

"Your little community needs to pay," Molly said, and her eyes were bright yellow, like a cat's, and full of just as much disdain as the most calculating one she'd ever seen. "Where one must suffer, all must suffer. Your crime ... was considerable. More than murder. And so the punishment must be correspondingly larger. Pain in measures beyond those you might consider reasonable." Her eyes narrowed harshly, the glee gone. "And now you will—"

Yvette stiffened behind Molly, and her eyes flared black. She opened her mouth to scream and Lauren could see the writhing blackness that told her a demon was being sucked back to hell from within her body. Molly saw it too, and hissed like a snake, recoiling from Yvette.

Yvette toppled over, falling past Molly, something strange sticking out of her back. Lauren blinked at it as Molly stumbled away, still hissing in the dusk air, the sound permeating the quiet neighborhood.

"That's right!" Casey Meacham shouted, charging up with Father Nguyen a few steps behind. He was wearing a flannel shirt with the sleeves cut off, and he stooped a second to tug that something out of Yvette's back. Lauren blinked at it as he brought it up, and realized it was a tomahawk, probably only as long as her forearm, but with an axe head and a point at the rear of it. He'd apparently thrown it at Yvette from behind and the pointy end had stuck in her back. A small wound showed through her shirt, probably no bigger than a scratch. "Someone call for the cavalry?"

"Casey," Lauren said, still on her knees, "my daughter, please—"

Casey snapped his head around, looking right at Molly. He reared back his hand with the tomahawk to throw it, but Molly hissed in a demon voice and shouted, "This isn't over—Mother!" But she said it so furiously that Lauren didn't recognize it as her voice. It sounded like it was booming down from on high, or on low. Real low.

Molly gave her the devil's own look again and leapt into the air.

She landed on the roof of the house, hissed once, loud enough that the sound filled the whole street, and then leapt off behind the house in a jump big enough to clear the row behind them.

Lauren watched her go and she felt ... cold. She shuddered in her nakedness, on her knees, feeling completely broken, hair still dripping cold on her shoulders. The sound of silence followed that last angry hiss, broken only by Yvette's moans of pain as she came back to herself a few feet away.

"Goddamn, Lauren," Casey said, meandering up, "you are starkers, girl." She heard him rustling about, and then felt soft cloth on her shoulders, something that smelled funny, like it had been treated with chemicals. Like a taxidermist would have, maybe. She looked down and saw that he'd put his sleeveless flannel over her shoulders and was trying to thread her limp arms through the sleeve holes. "Maybe we should go inside?" he asked as he started to button it up the front.

Lauren shook her head, unable to make a noise. The front door was open, and once upon a time it might have looked inviting. Not anymore. If she could avoid it, she'd never go inside that house again. She stared up, up to the roof as Casey buttoned her up, and wondered where Molly had gone, and if she'd be back ever.

*

"Sheriff Reeve!" The voice burst across his ears, jarring him out of the little reverie he'd been indulging himself in. Reeve was a man of action most of the time, but he hadn't taken any action for a spell here, he'd just sat beside his wife's body and stared off into the purpling sky, not really cognizant of a damned thing except that Donna's burnt hand was starting to get cold next to him.

He blinked and looked up as Erin's face darted before him. Her eyes were wide with worry, which felt a little funny to him. Donna was already dead, after all, and he plainly wasn't, so what the hell was there to be worried about? She shook him by the shoulder and he looked down at her hand in mild surprise. "Erin, I'm right here, you ain't got to shake me."

She stared at him in numb disbelief, her mouth slightly open before she spoke. "Reeve ... Nick ... your house is burning down behind you." Her voice sounded a little husky. He guessed she was taking it bad, kinda like him.

Reeve blinked and turned his head to look. Sure as shit, it was burning, all right, flames coming out of the windows. It was fully involved, now, the flames reaching out to kiss the heavens from the roof, rolling high into the air above him. He hadn't even realized he'd dragged Donna a good fifty or so feet away, out into the yard, which had been pointless, since she was dead. "How about that," was all he said.

"Sir," Erin said, voice still a little rough, like she was trying to hold back her feelings, "we—we got attacked, sir. Hendricks called to tell me that his door got kicked down. He thinks this possession demon went after the rest of the watch, too."

That was a hard pinch to Reeve's nipples. "Damn," he whispered, feeling a little stir of something. He'd been in a real fine mire of apathy for the last little bit here, but the thought of Arch having shit like this done to him was a quick slap to the face, a goosing with a cold hand on a warm night. He started to get to his feet, bones cracking and popping as he did so. He hadn't been seated in the most comfortable of positions, after all, and he'd been sitting there for quite a spell, it seemed. "We got any word from any of them yet?"

"I don't—" Erin froze, and her phone was buzzing. She swiped it up and held it to her ear. "Hello?" She was listening intently, the shade of a nearby willow tree catching her with shadowed impressions of its branches to darken her face. "Jesus. Is he—? Fuck. And everybody else? Good God. Okay. Watch your back." She hung up, the hand with the phone in it going limp as she let it drop to her side, swallowing hard before she spoke to him. "Bill Longholt caught a bullet to the head. Demons possessed Brian and made him do it. Arch stabbed it out of him, but he's hurt."

Reeve felt strangely tense, leaning in to listen to this bit of news. "Is Bill dead?"

"They're working on him, I guess an ambulance is on the way, maybe, but it don't sound good," Erin said. "Hendricks said a demon possessed Brian and shot at the house some when Arch went out after them. Also got that jackass Lonsdale and tried to make him bust down Hendricks's door, but Starling stopped that from happening."

Reeve didn't know too much about this Starling character, but she seemed awfully convenient a lot of the time. "We should …" He was still having trouble getting thoughts together. "We should check on Dr. Darlington and Duncan—"

"I sent Casey and Father Nguyen over to Lauren's," Erin said. When Reeve frowned at her, she elaborated. "I guess they were together at the time, doing something."

"That's a strange pair," Reeve mused, "like peanut butter and guitar strings." He felt a cold chill creeping up his back as he remembered what was waiting just behind him. "Did …" He tried to compose himself. "We haven't heard anything from those two yet, I take it?"

Erin's phone buzzed a second later, before she could answer him, and she picked it up. "It's Casey." She pressed the accept button. "Hello? Yeah—Jesus!" She cringed. "I mean—sorry, Father. Yes. Okay. Well … we need to find a place to meet, because—yeah, uhm, the sheriff's house is …" She looked over Reeve's shoulder and he glanced behind him by force of habit.

The roof beams had fallen in and he hadn't even noticed it. The roar of the blaze was loud as hell. The house was coming down, no doubt about it. He'd lived here his whole adult life. He and Donna had bought it right when they started out, and they'd been here their entire marriage. They'd raised their kids here, had all their—

"Jesus," Reeve whispered, and looked down at the body behind him. It really was just a body at this point, because there was nothing left of Donna in there. "Jesus … they took … they took everything …"

"Yeah, we need to find another place," Erin said. "Hm? St. Brigid's? If that's all right with you, Father. Yeah. Okay, I'll get him—get him moving here."

Reeve looked across the ruin of his house, his life. It was so goddamned unfair. He'd known about demons for all of a week now, and they'd just—the wind had whipped the fire across his yard, and it was singeing the picket fence behind the house—they'd taken everything. Donna's car was under the carport and it was burning, the roof collapsed over it, the grill blazing flames.

All their memories.

All their treasures.

His whole life.

He looked down at Donna, and he didn't recognize her anymore. He'd known her since they were practically kids, had seen her when she was young and her body was all curves and pale, smooth skin, and he knew her now, with a few extra pounds and more wrinkles than he could count, and they'd changed together. He still thought she was beautiful, and he would have recognized her thirty years from now, if things had stayed on the course they were on.

But they hadn't. And now she lay a few feet away from him, scorched and burned, and if he hadn't been there to see it happen, he wouldn't have had the first clue it was her.

These demons … they'd taken everything from him.

"I'm sorry," he whispered to Donna, even though she wasn't here anymore, not really. It was so damned unfair that this had happened to them, to their house, to their town. What the hell had they ever done to deserve this, aside from try to do their best to live good lives? To be good friends and neighbors?

"We should go," Erin said, putting a hand on his shoulder. "Nick … I don't know if Fries is going to come round here for this, but … the fire department has got to be on their way by now." That was probably true, Reeve realized dimly. The Midian fire department was all volunteer, and it took them a while to get to the station and get the trucks moving when there was a fire. "If Ed comes a calling … I don't know what he's gonna do when he finds your house burning down and Donna like … like this."

Reeve blinked at her. "Are you saying …?"

Erin swallowed heavily. "I'm saying he might come after you for murder, because I'm guessing you and Donna were the only ones in the house when this happened, and whatever the truth is, it probably sounds about twelve kinds of nuts."

Reeve stared past her shoulder, off into space behind her. Donna had drenched herself in gas, lit herself on fire and then stabbed herself in the heart with his holy blade. A holy blade which he could not afford to have taken away right now, since they were in the middle of a flood of shit and it was one of a very, very few paddles available to them. "There's no easy explanation for what happened here, no." He rubbed a hand over his bald head and it came back blackened with soot. He wondered if that came from being in the house during the fire or from handling Donna.

"We should go," Erin said gently. "We should get out of here Father Nguyen offered us his church as a meeting place. I need to tell the others, but … we should go."

Reeve listened intently, trying to hear anything over the crackling flames of his life burning down behind them. He heard nothing. No sirens that said help was coming. No shouts and cries of neighbors filling buckets and coming to his aid with their garden hoses. "We should go," he agreed, and he followed Erin out to the street. He looked back a few times, to say his goodbye to what remained of Donna, but when he looked back to the street again, he saw only a few people even out of their houses watching. Most were still hiding their faces behind panes of glass, watching the chaos that was consuming Midian from behind their thin veil of safety. He wanted to tell them that it was all an illusion, that this would be happening to them all too soon, these people who'd been his friends and neighbors, and who had abandoned him at the first sign of trouble.

He wanted to say all of this, but no one came up to him as he walked to the car. They all watched from their yards or from behind their windows, safe in their own minds, and so he kept these thoughts to himself as Erin started the car and drove him away from his life, his home, his friends and his neighbors, pretty sure that all he had left now was a real keen desire to beat the living shit out of a demon or fifty.

*

"This is fucked up," Hendricks said as the paramedics loaded Bill Longholt up onto a stretcher. Their careful movements were underpinned with a damned frantic energy, that edge of panic undergirding their desire to not do harm as they were transporting him. The fact that he was still alive was kind of a miracle, not that Hendricks believed in those things. He'd seen the hole in the man's head and it was just gaping, a neat swath of brain blown clear out by his own son, of all people. That was like the jizz icing on the fucked cake, and Hendricks felt a little sick even thinking about it.

"At least you haven't had fucking demons in your brain twice today," Lonsdale said, still lurking next to him. Wherever he went, Lonsdale stayed within about two feet of him. Hendricks had a suspicion the dumb bastard was still leery after getting possessed this most recent time. That was probably a smart move, at least for Lonsdale, but if it kept up he was going to have to ask Lonsdale to shake his dick for him when next he pissed, because the bastard would be better positioned to do it than he would.

Hendricks was standing with his arms folded at the accident site. He'd trashed Kitty Elizabeth's rental SUV when he'd crashed it into the car that held the demon shooting at Arch and now he was pretending he'd never seen the thing before in his life. He suspected there wasn't going to be a hell of a lot to come out of that, because the sole remaining Calhoun County Sheriff's Deputy/Acting Sheriff was bound to be worrying about things other than a rental car smashed on the street outside a shooting. Hell, the fat bastard hadn't even shown up to this one yet. Law and order in Midian was pretty close to the breakdown point, Hendricks figured, which might have been good in this case, because Brian was bound to get his ass thrown in jail otherwise.

Hendricks cast a look over at Arch, who was holding Alison in his arms as they watched her dad getting loaded into the back of the ambulance. She'd asked to go with them, but the paramedics had warned her off. Probably with pretty good reason; Hendricks had a suspicion Bill wasn't going to survive the ride to Chattanooga or wherever they were taking him. Arch had called for Dr. Darlington a few times but she hadn't answered her phone. Hendricks had a bad feeling about that, but when he'd talked to Erin she'd said she was sending someone else to look into it. He didn't want to call back and check in, not yet, because … well … it was Erin. She'd call if she needed him.

Alison had a sick look on her face, standing perched between her momma and Arch. The paramedics slammed the ambulance doors and the driver ran around the side and got in. The siren sounded and the ambulance did a quick U-turn to get the hell out of there, and it almost sideswiped a town car on the way up the street as it burned out toward the hospital.

"I need to go after them," Alison said as Arch patted her on the shoulder.

"I'll go with—" Arch started.

"No," Alison said, and put her arm around her mother, guiding her smoothly away. "Arch ..." She had a hard look on her face as she glanced back at him. "You got work to do."

The meaning of that was unmistakable, and Arch took it. "Yes'm," he said, nodding once at his wife as she and her mother headed up the driveway. "You need help getting Brian in the car?" When she looked blankly back at him, he said, "Because of his knee? Get him some help for it, maybe, while you're there?"

Alison stopped, frowning, her bare feet making a scuffing noise on the driveway. "I hadn't even thought about it."

Arch had a pained look on his face. Hendricks knew Arch had done the damage to Brian himself, and suspected he felt a little guilty. A lot more guilty than Alison would have felt at the moment if she'd done it, Hendricks was sure. That woman was closed down like a liquor store on Sunday, and seemed to be carrying a chip on her shoulder the size of Ayres Rock.

"Yeah, we should ..." Alison started, but then shrugged and drifted off, heading toward the car. Hendricks was tempted to tell her to get some shoes while she was at it, wandering around with jeans and a shirt and no shoes might be cause for the emergency room to deny her service, but it was an emergency room, not a grocery store, right? They wouldn't turn away the shoeless, especially given what she'd gone through today with her daddy being shot, would they?

That town car that almost hit the ambulance came screeching to a stop a few feet away and Lonsdale nearly jumped out of his fucking skin. Hendricks gave him a wary eye, half expecting the Brit to grab hold of him for dear life, and then glanced over at Duncan's car to see that Duncan, in fact, was not driving. There was a black lady at the helm instead, someone he'd never seen before.

Duncan got out of the passenger side and Hendricks gave him a look. The OOC didn't look too pleased, and that took some doing since Duncan was a fucking stoic son of a bitch if ever there was one. "You all right?" Hendricks asked.

"Peachy and keen, in equal measure," Duncan said, but he sounded super pissed. Hendricks looked at the black lady as she got out of the car. She was tall and pretty, her skin tone fairly dark, with some really sculpted cheekbones. She was wearing yoga pants and a tank top and looked athletic. Her hair was straight and came to about halfway down her neck. It was kind of a bob look, carefully styled. He had a hard time pegging her age, but figured she was at least older than him. He couldn't help checking her out, either, as she came around the hood, because she looked pretty damned in shape and hell, it had been a while since he'd gotten off. It was like a rising toxicity in his blood, even at this moment, and he felt stupid for staring but did it anyway.

"Who's your friend?" Hendricks asked, looking right at the lady. She looked right back at him and then smiled. It wasn't a great look for her, it felt all wrong somehow.

"I'm so disappointed that you don't remember me," the lady said as Duncan rolled his eyes hard, his lip twitching slightly. "How could you ever forget me, Lafayette Hendricks? I may just cry." The way she said it all, he was left with zero doubt she was totally fucking with him, but he was no closer to knowing who she was.

Arch was standing there staring as Alison pulled out of the driveway, her mother and brother in the car. She peeled out, not even a backward glance at the little confab on the lawn, and that distracted them all for a second or two. Arch seemed to come out of it first. "So who are you?" he asked the woman.

"And you too, Archibald Stan?" She just grinned at them. It was fucking unsettling.

"It's Lerner," Duncan said, stealing the thunder. Hendricks was kind of relieved, because he was already getting annoyed.

"Yeah, I can't figure out why I couldn't recognize you," Hendricks said. "When you went to hell, you were a tall, pasty white guy, now you're a pretty damned fine black lady. Makes perfect sense."

"I identify as Amanda Guthrie now," New Lerner said, coming around the town car. "Clearly I've transitioned."

Hendricks shut his mouth before he could put a foot in it up to the knee. Lonsdale apparently did not possess the same self-restraint. "So before this one was a white bloke and now 'e's a black bird? This bloody world's gone mad off its axis, I tell you."

"Yeah, I'll be woman of the year anytime now," she said, stepping up the curb onto the lawn and kicking a piece of bumper out of her way. It flew like a soccer ball across the lawn and came to rest about a half foot before tearing up a flowerbed. "Looks like I came back just in time, though."

Hendricks frowned at her, then gave Duncan a glance. "I thought you said he wasn't coming back."

"She, now," New Lerner said. What was the name again? Amanda Guthrie?

"Fine, she," Hendricks said. "I thought she wasn't coming back."

"I'm totally fucking with you, cowboy," Guthrie said, with that unsettling grin. "I don't give a shit what you assign to me, I'm as much a woman now as I was before, which is to say—not at all, except for the pieces." She waved vaguely toward the Y of her yoga pants. "Which I also don't give a shit about."

"Right, well," Arch said, clearly uncomfortable. "Did you get attacked by this possession demon, too?"

"We had a few visitors, yeah," Duncan said tightly. Was it Hendricks's imagination or did he look like someone had given his balls a few solid twists? "Fought 'em off, fortunately." He puckered his lips. "We might not be able to go back to our hotel, though."

Hendricks frowned. "What happened?"

Duncan gave Guthrie a sidelong look. "There were casualties. Dead, I should say, and some that will need a hospital."

"Good heavens," Arch said, stirring, his arms still crossed in front of him. "Did you call an ambulance?"

"I did," Duncan said pointedly and then nodded at the car wreck in front of them. "I expect they're busy at the moment, though."

Hendricks just shook his head. That was another point in the favor of his argument that emergency services in Midian were about to break down, but he didn't want to bring that up at the moment. It was a pretty downer argument. He turned to say something to Arch, and noticed something for the first time in the distance. "What's that?" He pointed at a pillar of black smoke on the horizon.

Arch turned to look. "I don't know. Looks like a big fire, though."

"I figured before I left that this place was going to go straight to hell," Guthrie said. "I actually thought it would get there a little faster, but it seems to be well on its way now."

"I'm starting to think coming here was a bad idea," Lonsdale said.

"We regrouping?" Arch asked Hendricks, who shrugged. "You gonna call about it?"

"You don't have a phone?" Hendricks asked. "Because I'm using Lonsdale's, and I'm beginning to worry that the stink of loser is going to rub off if I keep touching this thing."

"Fuck off, Hendricks," Lonsdale said.

Arch just sighed and drew his own phone off his belt. The man was still wearing his uniform. Shit must have gone down before he'd had a chance to change. He dialed up a number and waited. "Hmmm," he said after a minute. "No answer from Reeve." The big man frowned, and then turned to look at the black cloud in the distance. "I suppose it could just be coincidence, but Sheriff Reeve lives in that direction, I think."

Hendricks raised an eyebrow. "Uhh ... are we believing in coincidences at the moment? Because when a coordinated demon attack goes off, I don't believe in random black clouds of smoke on the horizon."

Arch hesitated only a moment. "Lemme call Erin." He dialed and put the phone up to his ear and got an answer a few seconds later. "Hey." Hendricks tried to listen in, inching closer to Arch, but the big man turned away and stuck a finger in his other ear, maybe to hear better. "You're kiddin' me," Arch said, which was his version of, "Are you shitting me?"

"That sounds bad," Duncan opined.

"I'll put an Archer on it being the sheriff's house that burned down," Lonsdale said.

"You fucking ghoul," Duncan said.

"That's a dick move," Hendricks said, "considering you were following him so close a couple hours ago that if he stopped too fast you would have been able to give him a visual colonoscopy, no camera necessary."

"I'll take that action," Guthrie said. Yeah. That was Lerner, all right.

"Dang," Arch said, muted. He turned around and looked at Hendricks. "It was Reeve's house." Guthrie made a face at losing the bet. "Donna's dead," Arch went on, looking pained as he said it.

"Fuck, they did bushwhack us," Hendricks whispered.

"I guess they did something to the doctor, too," Arch said stiffly. "Meacham and Father Nguyen are over there now. They said Darlington's a wreck. It sounds bad."

"You wanna take odds on how long until this town slides into a perfect hellscape?" Guthrie asked Lonsdale. "I'll give you two to one on anything outside of a fortnight."

"Nobody says fortnight anymore," Lonsdale said, peering at Guthrie suspiciously. "You're a bit of an anachronism, aren't you?"

"He's an OOC, Lonsdale," Hendricks said, and watched the Brit jump back. "Given how hard this possession demon has hit us, I got a suspicion this fight ain't over. That was a hell of an opening gambit."

"This is a nasty fight, that's for sure," Duncan agreed. "Whoever's running this show, it sounds like they've come out of retirement or hiding like a bear out of hibernation."

"What the hell did you people do?" Guthrie asked, frowning. It was a very un-Lerner-like expression, and once again Hendricks felt disturbed looking at her. Even more disturbing, he traced her curves with his eyes before he jerked them back up to look at her face. "We had possession demons all wiped out, and here you go unleashing one." She shook her head. "I told you this was a special kind of hotspot when we came here. You guys have been fighting hard to keep it out of the fire, but what's going on here … there's no holding back this tide. Not with the kind of things that have been coming out of the woodwork here."

"You weren't even here for the Rog'tausch," Hendricks added coolly as Arch hung up the phone in the background.

"I heard about it," Guthrie said, equally coolly. "Something like the Rog'tausch being reassembled tends to produce a shockwave or two, even in the demon world." Duncan just frowned at his partner. Ex-partner? Hendricks sensed some tension he hadn't seen from them before. "I take it you took care of those fucking bicyclists?"

"Oh, yeah," Hendricks said. "We got 'em."

"Good," Guthrie said, nodding with a certain satisfaction. "I fucking hated bicyclists before, but now … I see some motherfucker ride by on one of those and I'm at the wheel, BAM! They're done. Human, demon, I don't even give a shit."

"We're regrouping at Father Nguyen's church," Arch said, re-entering the conversation. "ASAP."

"I'm driving," Duncan said, snatching the keys out of Guthrie's hands with a frown.

"Pussy," Guthrie said with a taunting smile. "You're a real humanitarian, Duncan."

"I'll catch a ride with you, Arch," Hendricks said, hurrying to catch up with the man as he strode up the driveway to where Alison's car was parked.

"Hey, wait up!" Lonsdale called, now attached to his ass like a tick. Hendricks just rolled his eyes. Now Lonsdale was on him so close he'd fall in if Hendricks stopped too fast.

*

"Lauren, we gotta go," Casey said softly. Lauren was sitting on the lawn, ass in the grass, the blades faintly tickling her undercarriage. She gave not one shit about that, though, because she had way too much on her mind to even process everything going on. "We're meeting at the church."

"Which church?" Lauren asked, mind weirdly blank. It felt impossible to think, to plan, to string more than a random thought or two together before her head jumped to something else. The song "Get Me to the Church on Time" tinkled a few stray bars through her head and then disappeared like dust in the wind.

"My church," Father Nguyen said from behind her. He and Casey were both at a shoulder, like Casey was the devil on one and Nguyen was the angel on the other. Casey had saved Molly, though, at least for a minute, tomahawking Yvette before she could gut—

Lauren's brain jumped the track again, and she felt the faint tickle of a blade of grass against her bare butt cheek. She reached down to scratch the itch, not even caring. There was sand everywhere, all over her, and her hair was still drying in the steadily worsening chill night. "I don't think you need me for that," she said.

Casey put a hand on her shoulder, pushing the soft, smelly flannel against her skin. Her shoulder had dried a while ago, the cloth picking up the moisture and locking it in so she still felt damp. The cutoff flannel covered her down to her backside, not that she cared. She suspected her eyes were puffy as hell, probably red as Brian Longholt's had been up until recently. She glanced in through her open front door, and then looked away suddenly. Albert Daniel was still lying on the grass, splayed off the sidewalk. Yvette was gone, probably run off in panic once she got her head on straight. Lauren should have run, too, after what she'd seen but she seemed to have lost the ability to move.

"Lauren, you ought to come with us," Casey said. "We can't just leave you here."

"Why don't I go get you some clothes from inside?" Father Nguyen wheedled. He was so nice, so very nice.

"You can if you want," she said. She didn't want to go inside. He started forward, and she called after him, "I'd stay out of the bathroom if I were you."

Nguyen looked back at her quizzically, then walked up the front steps and into the house. She stared after him for a second and then looked away from the gaping front door, staring at the begonias in the front flowerbed, the trellis that stretched up to the second floor. She took in the whole house, the place where she'd been raised, and it left her cold.

This wasn't home.

Not anymore.

"GOOD HEAVENS!" Father Nguyen came scooting out the front door a moment later, crossing himself fervently, some clothes in his hand. He looked like he'd seen the Holy Ghost, or maybe the opposite, and he was motoring fast enough that even Lauren's broken mind found some amusement in seeing it. He came to her side and stuck out his hand. A pair of pants was clutched in it, as well as a jacket and some socks.

She just stared at them blankly. "Shoes?" she asked, wondering why she even bothered. She lacked the energy and motivation to even get dressed at this point.

"I ... I don't want to go back in there," Nguyen said, shaking his head. He looked sick to his stomach.

"What?" Casey asked, getting to his feet. "What is it? What'd you see?"

"There's ... my heavens, it's ..." Nguyen stammered.

"My mother," Lauren said, dimly aware she'd spoken but surprised at the cogent sound of the content. "My mother is in the bathroom, dead. Molly—the demon in Molly—slit her throat right in front of me." She sounded flat, uncaring, like she'd just observed a surgery and was speaking clinically about the results. She held up her hands and showed them, the faint traces of dried blood still crusted here and there on her palms.

"Is that where all the blood came from?" Casey asked, sounding like he was musing it over. "I was wondering, because those cuts all up and down you didn't look like enough to cover ye." He said "ye" instead of "you." He stood up, seeming to steel himself. "I'll get you some shoes." And he headed for the front door, casting a look back. "You need anything else?"

Lauren just shook her head. She stared at the socks Nguyen had thrown at her, along with a pair of panties and jeans. "A shirt," she said, and when he looked back, she tugged on the cut-off flannel. "No offense."

"None taken," Casey said with a shrug, and she realized he was wearing a stained wife beater that hugged his skinny body. "I'll get you a bra, too."

"Oh, uh, yes," Nguyen muttered, "I forgot that for, uh, some reason."

"Lack of experience," Casey said with a grin and disappeared inside.

"Uhm, Dr. Darlington," Nguyen said, and she looked up at him to find his face filled with discomfort. "We should ... you should start getting dressed."

"Right," Lauren said, taking hold of the socks. She took hold of one of her feet and gently brushed the sand away. It reminded her of how she'd brush the sand off of Molly when she was a little girl on the playground. Lauren would stroke her fingers through those dark locks, finding granules hidden all in there, and—

She sobbed, unexpectedly, frozen halfway through brushing off her foot. There was still blood half-dried on her ankle from one of her cuts, and her hands were shaking now.

"Oh, God," she whispered. "Molly ..."

Father Nguyen, perhaps wisely, said nothing, as she put her socks on one by one, ignoring the dirty, gritty feeling. Then Lauren got to her feet on her own, on wobbly legs, and started to dress herself so that she could go find out what the hell she should do next.

*

The sun had set and Chester felt a small burst of elation coupled with bitterness. The elation sprang from the returns, or at least the few who had returned. Some expected, some unexpectedly, but most bearing at least some good news. He stared at his growing convocation, standing in the near darkness on the porch of their newly seized headquarters, and Chester smiled.

"This is both a sad and glorious day," he said and saw a chorus of nods. He nodded to one of the new returns, Melba, who had taken over the body of the doctor's daughter. "We've struck some blows that they will feel." He looked at Carisse, who had been responsible for the attack on the sheriff. That man deserved a healthy amount of pain for his part in all this. "And we are not done yet."

"What should we do next?" Melba asked, through that teenager's mouth. She had reported the clearest victory. Chester suspected others had gouged some wounds in these people, too, but he hadn't heard back from Ygritte, who'd attacked the house with Deputy Stan or heard a peep from Winston, who had inhabited the sheriff's wife, though that was always intended to be something of a suicide mission. He'd seen the pillar of smoke and it hinted that things had gone well for them there. The sounds of distant sirens, they had been music to his ears.

Chester had been thinking about the answer to that question as the sun had fallen below the horizon. In planning things, the start of things, he'd been so very focused on the most responsible parties. Reeve and Stan, and the cowboy, Hendricks. He'd branched out a little to include others who had been part of their little group, but as the sun had set and the cold grew hard and settled on his bones, he'd had a little revelation that chilled him.

Chester had tried to respect the humans, to live among them, to see the good in them. He'd watched them live their disconnected lives, pitied them for their lack of community even as they attempted congress in their small way. He'd believed that they were doing their best, but now … all he could think about was how loathsome and pathetic they really were. In that regard, he felt William's view had been right.

And if their failure of community was responsible for what he had suffered, what William had suffered … then didn't it make sense for their whole community to pay for their sins?

"Next …" Chester said, smiling faintly, "… we're going to broaden things a bit." He held out a hand, and they formed a little chain, exchanging essences, knowledge, and a plan. And along with all that, he felt the warmth of knowing spread among them as well, the sweet satisfaction of feeling that revenge, bitter, nasty, and wonderful, was soon to be at hand.

Braeden Tarley felt like even though this day had landed squarely in the middle of a diarrhea-filled shitter, at least it was closing out on a reasonable note. He was sitting on the edge of Abi's bed, about ready to fall asleep himself after dealing with a busy four-year-old all afternoon, fighting to keep those eyes open, doing his damnedest to try and figure out what kind of bedtime story he ought to tell.

"How about something with a gunfight?" he asked, only about half-serious and knowing how that was going to play.

Abi gave him a frown, clearly taking it way more seriously than he had. "No, Daddy. I want a princess story."

Braeden didn't make a disappointed sigh, but not because he didn't want to. Abi was very picky about her princess stories. He'd told the Disney ones about a thousand times, and while she never seemed to get tired of them, he did. She also tended to call bullshit when he got too cheesy or too close to something she didn't want to hear about. "Okay," he said and started racking his brain to try and come up with something new-ish, something that would make her smile instead of frown. She'd done a fair amount of frowning today already, still worried about Miss Evelyn.

"Once upon a time," Braeden said, mind racing, "there was a princess ..." This prompted the anticipatory smile from his daughter, something just shy of a full-beam smile. "... And this princess lived in the magical land of, uh ... Tenzee," he said, speeding up Tennessee so he thought it would be unrecognizable.

"Where's Tenzee, Daddy?"

"Not too far from here," he said, trying to shoot right on past that question before she could dig too deep on it. "This princess had lived in Tenzee her whole life, and her name was, uhm ... Missoula." That was a city in Montana, but Abi didn't know that, right? It was a name he and her mother had considered for her and discarded because Abilene was better anyway.

"Princess Missoula was a very pretty princess," Braeden said, looking at how dark his fingernails looked, the thin shaft of light extending from the hallway light into Abi's room. He could still see the grease and oil that had worked their way around the edges. He'd let her paint his fingernails a couple times and that tended to hide the grease some, though they inevitably looked like even worse a few days later, after he'd worked on engines for a spell. "And her problem," because all these princesses had problems, Braeden had figured out, "was that she was so very pretty, and so very smart, that none of the princes of other kingdoms wanted to talk to her because they were all scared that she was smarter and prettier than they were." Braeden was laughing madly at this on the inside, because to him it was a game of just making up shit as he went along, and he had no fucking idea how he was going to square this circle he'd just drawn around himself.

Abi frowned, critical mind clearly whirring into action. "Princes can't be pretty, Daddy. Only princesses."

"You tell that to a pissed-off drag queen," he muttered under his breath, "see how it goes." He thought quickly and said, "So anyhow, Princess Missoula couldn't find any prince in all the land who wasn't too, uhhhh … intimidated to uhm, be okay with how smart and pretty she was. Her daddy brought in prince after prince to try and impress her, but she always seemed to send the poor bastards scurrying away because she was just too, uhh … smart or pretty."

He felt a little twinge inside as he told the story, because it hit him suddenly that this wasn't exactly made up out of whole cloth. It was pretty much the story of Abi's mom, because she'd been the prom queen, all gorgeous and smart, and she'd tried to date a few guys who were in her social status, and it turned out they were real assholes about that kind of thing. Not that Braeden considered himself an intellectual giant, but hell if it bothered him that Abi's mom had been so smart. That was lucky, he figured, especially as he got old enough to realize exactly how little he knew. It was nice to have someone tell him, in a gentle way, when he was being a dumbass. Sometimes he even missed that as much as he missed everything else about her.

"So, what did Princess Missoula do, Daddy?" Abi asked. She had that look that told him her critic hat might have been put away for a spell, because she was leaning off the pillow, waiting to see what came next.

"She, uh," Braeden kind of hiccupped, a little emotion coming out as his voice cracked, "she decided that maybe a prince wasn't the best idea for her, since they were all a bunch of, uh, tools."

Abi frowned. "Like the kind in your shop?"

"No, not …" Braeden blushed a little. "They were jerks," he said, steering around the word 'asshole,' even though it was a lot more appropriate for the use he had in mind, though not the audience. "Anyhow, Princess Missoula decided to look among the commoners for someone who would love her as she was, and she found a, uhm ... a baker, yeah ... who, while not as smart or pretty as she was, would love her as much as she deserved."

"And did he become king?" Abi asked, bouncing a little. That was usually the sign she was really into the story, but not a great one for his efforts to calm her down.

"Sure," Braeden said, "someday. After the old king died, I guess."

"Why did he die?"

"Uhhhm," Braeden said, but in his head he was saying, Oh, shit. "He just ... got old, you know. That happens."

Abi slowed her bounce, rocking just slightly back and forth. "How does it happen, Daddy?"

"Dying?" Braeden felt his stomach tighten. They'd had this conversation before, and every time they did he was left with the feeling that Abi just couldn't quite get her head wrapped around death as a concept. He didn't blame her, because he didn't think he got it, and he had twenty years on her. "Well, it ... it happens quick, see."

Abi sat on her bed, fiddling with her covers, and he was draped across it below her feet. She stared down for a second, then looked up at him. "Is it scary?"

Braeden felt about dumbfounded. "Is it ... no, baby. It's not ... not bad." The lie felt toxic. Her mother hadn't had an easy death, had she? He'd gotten the details and they made him sick. But Abi was four and the thought of her hearing any of this nauseated him worse than reading about how it happened or from hearing some paramedic tell the story without knowing he was in the bar. It was a long, involved tale about a woman in a car accident who had been pinned inside and couldn't be easily cut out. By the end, Braeden was mainlining tequila and listening intently, feeling like he was gonna need the whole bottle and every other single one behind the bar just to cope.

"What does it feel like?" Abi asked. Now she was shyly testing him.

"It doesn't hurt." He jumped right to that lie, figuring it was the one she was most worried about. That was what kids worried about, right? Whether shots or a skinned knee, it was the pain that scared them, that backed them off whatever they were doing. "It ... happens real quick and easy, like ... like going to sleep."

She puckered those little lips. "Sometimes I don't go to sleep very easy. You told me so. You said—"

"I know," Braeden said, nodding. "I know, sometimes it ain't easy to get to sleep—"

"I never sleep," Abi said resolutely. "I never have, not once. I just stay in my bed all night until you come get me in the morning."

Braeden made a face of his own. "Baby ... that just ain't true."

"Yes, it is."

"No, it ain't."

"Yes, huh."

"Okay," he said, a little too tired to labor through the point. "Well ... for those of us who do sleep and aren't tiny baby vampires ... it's like that."

"So ..." she said, hesitant, "... it's not bad?"

"No," he said, shaking his head.

"So it wasn't bad for Mommy?"

That innocent little question hammered him like a punch to the nose in a barfight. He tried to smile, to brush off that feeling, but it wasn't easy. "No," he said, that lie burning his throat, "it wasn't ... bad ... for Mommy." He pushed off the bed, pulling himself up to sitting, ready to get the hell out of here and out of this conversation.

"Daddy?"

"What, baby girl?" He felt trapped in place again by those doe eyes, even though he wanted to leave.

"Are you going to die someday?" So innocent. And a little worried, he thought.

"Not for a very long time," Braeden said, trying to come up with a smile. He figured he probably looked like a politician, grinning for a newspaper picture, or like Pike had this afternoon when he was trying to sway Braeden's vote on this recall. What a goddamned mess. "Good night, sweetheart." He kissed her on that soft, smooth cheek.

He got up and almost made it to the door. "Daddy?"

"Time to sleep, baby," he said. She could ask him questions all night. Or at least, she'd certainly never seemed to run out of them before, even if she needed a short break to fiddle with her sheets or count her little toes or something. "You can ask me ... whatever else ... in the morning, okay?"

"Okay, Daddy." She gave a sleepy little sigh and closed her eyes, smiling wide—way too wide for the subject matter they'd just talked over—and obviously pretending hard to be trying to sleep, since she apparently didn't sleep at all, ever.

Braeden got out of the room and into the hall, turning off the main light and letting the night-light take over, casting its weak orange glow into Abi's room. She had one of her own in there, a Cinderella night-light that cast characters and scenes onto the ceiling. Between the two of them, she seemed to feel safe and could see to get up to go pee in the middle of the night if she needed to.

When he was back in the living room he took a deep breath. Sitting there on the couch next to him was her princess Halloween costume, and he picked it up and tossed it carefully to the back of the chair just across from him so he could stretch out on the couch without accidentally putting his feet on it or tearing the seams or something. He lay down, snatching up the remote and finding ESPN. "Am I gonna die someday?" he said to himself, finding some strange amusement in that question. He'd thought himself youthfully immortal for a good long while, arrogant enough to think he could do dumbass things and not have any consequences from them. Race a car? No problem? Ride his bike without a helmet? He'd never gotten so much as a scratch.

That changed when Abi came, to some extent, and even more when Jennifer died. Now that feeling of immortality was good and faded, and Braeden didn't feel like chancing the odds anymore. He didn't even ride a motorcycle these days. Too dangerous for him now that he had someone relying on him. "Hopefully not anytime soon," he answered her question, and then he started dwelling on his other answers to her, about how death actually happened. He figured he'd fall asleep real soon, but for some reason it did not come easily tonight. Not easily at all.

8.

"Seems like we got caught with our pants around our ankles," Hendricks pronounced. They were all sitting around St. Whoever-the-fuck's, Father Nguyen's church, which he didn't catch the name of for either lack of caring or maybe because of the urgency of their meeting, "and these bastards bent us into a pretzel and fucked us so hard we'll never shit straight again."

Arch just stood there next to the pew, shaking his head. "You do have a way of describing things, don't you?"

"It's colorful," Hendricks said.

"It's profane and disrespectful," Arch replied. Sometimes he got all mother hen, and Hendricks had no time for that shit. "Especially here."

"Yeah, I doubt your God's ever seen anything like that before," Hendricks cracked. "I probably just taught him a couple new words, too."

"Maybe we should get back on track here," Erin said, pronouncing a little of her own displeasure in the way she was looking heat at Hendricks. That wasn't surprising to him; Erin had been pissy to him for a little while now, and he still didn't care. She was sounding a little rough, though, like this whole thing had gotten to her, was making her weepy or something. Or maybe she'd just taken in a little too much smoke at Reeve's house fire.

"What track are we getting on?" Lonsdale said, prompted by absolutely no one and paid heed to by absolutely no one. Hendricks didn't backhand him, though not because he didn't want to. The little shit might prove useful at some point maybe, and with as many hits as they'd taken, help was getting to be a fleeting thing.

"Sheriff?" Arch honed in on Reeve, who was sitting quietly in a pew, just listening along. "You got anything to add here?"

Reeve looked like hell, like shit, like a thousand other awful things Hendricks couldn't quite imagine. Hendricks had taken genuine pleasure in giving the man a bitch of a time at the meeting this morning, and now he couldn't imagine saying squat to him. His undershirt had probably started the day white, but it was stained black now. The sheriff's face looked like he'd jumped into a coal bin for a swim, with lines marking where sweat droplets had rolled down the only thing breaking the tragic mask. He wasn't wearing pants, and his boxers were in shit shape, too. He reeked of fire, enough that Hendricks was suddenly hungry for barbecue, but the knowledge that the man had lost his wife in this blaze ... that was taking away any ire Hendricks had for him. Now he just felt sorry for the poor bastard. He'd lost his job, his wife, and his house all in one shot-to-the-nuts-with-a-cannon day. Hendricks could sympathize with at least one of those things. "I don't think I'm going to be of much use in making any plans at the moment," Reeve said, bringing a hand up and smudging the hell out of his brow. "Y'all might want to go ahead and leave me out of it for now."

That brought on an uncomfortable silence broken by, naturally, Guthrie-Lerner. "This is the shit that happens when I leave town for a few weeks."

"This is the shit that happens when you come back to town," Duncan snapped before Hendricks could launch a reply of his own.

"Wait, who is this?" Erin asked. She'd eyed the tall black lady when they came in, but had clearly had a few other things on her mind, trailing in the wake of Reeve like she was gonna have to catch him if he fell down. And he'd looked like he might have at any moment.

"It's Lerner," Hendricks said, depriving Guthrie of the opportunity to be a huge dick.

Guthrie's face fell. "You never change, Hendricks; you're a constant thorn in my side."

Erin gave Hendricks what felt like a very mild look of thanks before shifting attention back to Guthrie. "So ... you're a woman now?"

Guthrie just grinned wider, and Hendricks would have sworn he saw a little of Lerner leak out. "I'm also African-American now, in case you missed it, sweetcheeks."

"Oddly enough, that didn't escape my notice, no," Erin said roughly, though she was flushing mightily. Hendricks could sympathize with that, too, because it was treading close to the racism line that tended to make every white person he'd ever met uncomfortable. Except that one big-time racist he'd met. That guy didn't give any fucks.

"How's Dr. Darlington?" Reeve asked, surprising Hendricks at his ability to still string words together. "And Bill?"

"Bill's on his way to the hospital still, I expect," Arch said. He stopped short of saying something else, which Hendricks predicted was along the lines of, "Assuming he's still alive."

"Alison, Brian, and Addy are on the way, too," Hendricks said, heading toward helpful and away from actively causing chaos and dickery. He felt like Guthrie would probably take up his slack in that department. "They have to be getting close by now, don't they?"

"Probably," Arch said. The man was tense. He was always tense, but now it was even more obvious to Hendricks. "I doubt we'll hear from them for a while, seeing as they'll be getting Brian some help, too, when they get there."

"And the doctor?" Reeve asked again. His eyes were a little clearer now, though it was obvious by the redness that tears had probably been shed, and Hendricks wouldn't have considered the man human if they'd all come from the fire and smoke.

"Father Nguyen and Casey are bringing her here right now," Erin said, the strain just cracking her voice. "I guess ... I guess they got her mother, and Molly's ... well, she's ..."

"Possessed," Arch finished for her. "Molly's possessed by these things."

"Well, goddamn," Reeve said mildly, more like he was amazed than angry. "They really did hit us right where we lived, didn't they." There was no accusation there, just a statement of fact.

"They damned sure did," Hendricks said, feeling the malice take hard hold. "And I'm wondering when we're going to hit back."

"I'd be inclined to agree," Arch said. "Clearly they snaked their way around us, following us back to our homes from the station, watching and figuring out how best to hit us right where it hurt. It stands to reason that they're probably not finished yet." He looked around. "Right?"

"I don't ... I don't know what these things are doing," Erin said, sounding almost helpless, "but ... how else could they possibly hit us? I mean, they came in like a damned hammer last time. Not one of us is even home at this point because—I mean they nailed us right there, and ..."

Hendricks picked up a little something funny, like someone tickled long nails right across the back of his head as he started to tune Erin out. She was starting to go on, talking about future plans and how vulnerable they were, and something bothered him about that ...

Why hadn't these bastards hit Erin? She'd left the station at the same time as the rest of them, hadn't she? They'd come at him, Arch and the Longholts, Reeve, Duncan ... everyone who'd left the station, they'd picked off, even that shithead Lonsdale.

But not Erin?

Hendricks frowned, watching her talk. She was amping up her delivery, kind of launching into a speech. Her voice still had that funny twinge to it. Then there was the fact that speechifying wasn't really her thing, especially lately, when she'd been surly and downcast. He looked over at Duncan, who was staring straight at her, arms folded in front of him, no sign of anything on his face, just nodding along as he listened.

He'd pick up on it if Erin was possessed ... wouldn't he?

Hendricks just stood there, trying to figure out how to handle his little inkling suspicion. It wasn't exactly a fun thing to be pondering, and it wasn't like he and Erin didn't have enough shit between them right now without adding to it. He was trying not to be a dick, dammit, and yet here was this, this nasty, lingering suspicion just hanging right over his head like a black cloud. Why would this Legion go hard after every single other person in the watch but just let Erin skate? That defied all logic, and meandered right into nuttytown.

Duncan looked up, catching a glimpse of Hendricks or reading his soul or something. Either way, he stared right at Hendricks, and Hendricks stared right back. Hendricks stood just behind Erin, where she was in the aisle, and tried to signal with his eyes while he had Duncan's attention. The OOC had read things off his mind before, hadn't he? He darted his eyes toward Erin three times in quick succession, and finally, Duncan nodded once.

Hendricks took an easy half-step toward her. He couldn't be sure, after all, but damn. If she was possessed by one of these demons, he didn't want to tip her off. For fuck's sake, it was actually a pretty brilliant idea, just seeding one of their own people with a demon and slipping them right into their midst. After an ass-kicking like they'd just gotten, who would even be thinking about that? Hendricks hadn't even really been hit and he was numb with shock. If they'd pulled off what they'd intended, Arch's whole family of in-laws would probably have ended up dead and Hendricks himself would have kicked the bucket—again. Duncan, too, probably.

No one would have given a fuck at that point if Erin was a plant.

He listened hard to her voice as he took another easy step closer to her. Duncan was concentrating hard on her now, and took a slow, easing step sideways and forward, clearly trying not to clue her in. He was pretty casual about it, Hendricks would give the OOC that. Or as casual as he could be while wearing a red t-shirt with the Sriracha logo on it.

Hendricks let his hand drift toward his sword. Starling would know what to do in this moment. She always did, charging in like the damned cavalry. Of course whether she would share that info was an open question.

"We can't let them take us down like this," Erin said, her voice cracking again. He listened, and heard a scratchiness that didn't sound like congestion. That was weird. "We have to find a way to fight back."

"I couldn't agree more," Duncan said, nodding fervently and stepping up so he was only a few feet away. His footsteps echoed in the church, crisp and clear in the momentary silence after Erin's long speech.

Hendricks started to draw his sword, slowly, less than an inch at a time. This was going to be tricky, trying not to clue her in. If she was a demon, she'd have super hearing, probably, which meant that as soon as she knew what he was up to … He could smell the damp, lightly chlorinated scent of the baptismal font over in the middle of the entry. If he could drag her over there, dousing her would be a painless way to expel the demon, wouldn't it? He discarded that idea as bad, because it required him, a human, to drag a demon. Hopelessly optimistic wasn't even the right word for that. It was more like suicidal, like thinking he could tame a tiger and drag it around by putting it in a headlock.

No, there was only one thing for it, he thought as he pulled the sword slowly, so slowly, out of the scabbard. He had to do this just right. A little poke in the back and she'd be all good. Just a little—

His boot scuffed slightly as he started to take another step, and Erin's head snapped around, her eyes finding him immediately. She didn't seem surprised or scared, just pissed off when she took in the sight of him with his sword half-drawn, caught in the act. He probably couldn't have looked more guilty if she'd caught him with his pants around his ankles and his prick in his hands.

"Fuck," Duncan said mildly, and then shit went real sideways.

Erin lashed out, spinning as she came at him. It wasn't much consolation to know he'd been right when the back of her hand came flying at him with the speed of a Ferrari. He had a little bit of room to maneuver, which was just about all that saved him. He dodged just out of her arm's sweep, but she caught him along the cheek with a lone finger. It should have felt like a simple flick against the skin but it was like a knife wound instead, like someone had jabbed him in the face with a stick they'd just used to stir the fire. Blood ran down his face and he hurried to draw his sword before she could get any closer, sweeping it out of the scabbard and forcing her to retreat out of the range of the blade. As she did, she yelped, and a trickle of blood ran down her cheek in the exact spot where she'd hit Hendricks.

"Well, well, well," Guthrie said, deploying her baton with a CHUNK! "Looks like we got a party crasher. And not a very bright one, either, seeing as she has apparently forgotten the rules in these holy places."

Erin's face had changed, the cheekbones going high and pointed, her eyes going dark, her teeth extending like she'd been bitten by Tom Cruise or something. The blood dripped down her face and she touched it lightly, smearing it along the new lines of the demon's face. "I am but a watcher," she said, her voice a little higher and a touch angrier than it had been when she'd been imitating Erin's. "Watching you all spin in circles, chasing your own tails." There was malignant glee there, an angry defiance coupled with the flush of success. This demon knew how much her pals had hurt them, and here she was, reveling in it. That burned Hendricks. It burned him a lot.

"So you people do have rules," Arch mused, his own sword drawn. "And about churches, no less."

"Later, holy man," Guthrie said, still holding up the baton. "We have bigger problems to deal with at the moment."

"You will all of you feel the pain of suffering," Erin said. "You will feel the pain of vengeance."

A gunshot rang out and Erin staggered a step, bobbing forward as she was struck from behind. She half-turned to look, and Reeve was there, holding a gun, a small one. It looked like a back-up pistol at best, the kind of thing you'd tuck away and hope never to use. "We've felt it," Reeve said, looking hard at her. "We all felt it, some more than others. But you … you're gonna feel the pain of getting your ass wiped out like a bunch of cockroaches." His face twisted, angry and hateful. "You're a bunch of plague rats, and you've had your goddamned day." He pulled the trigger again, and Erin staggered from a shot to the face. "We are gonna wipe your ass out, you mark my words on that."

Erin stood there only a second, and then leapt up into the air, soaring through the gap between Reeve and Guthrie, who had been circling around to try and catch her unawares. Erin smashed through the stained-glass window that ran the whole side of the church and was gone in a second, disappearing out into the night.

The church doors burst open and in came Father Nguyen, running, Casey Meacham leading Lauren Darlington a half-dozen paces behind. "What happened?" Nguyen asked breathlessly. "I heard gunfire."

"Our villain snuck a demon into Erin," Hendricks said before anyone else could respond. He stared at the darkness through the enormous hole in the stained-glass.

"Who?" Nguyen asked.

"Deputy Harris," Duncan answered for him. "She tried to … well, she gave Hendricks a good poking."

"I remember when it used to be the other way around," Guthrie cracked.

Hendricks hand went straight to his cheek. They were right, she'd gotten him, little more than a good scratch as she grazed him. But he'd seen that wound visited right back on her. "Why didn't that expel the demon?" he asked. "That—whatever it was—"

"Holy effect," Guthrie answered, swerving in front of Duncan to respond first, the fucking know-it-all. "Stung her possessor like hell. It's the least a church can do to a demon. With the appropriate blessings, they can turn up the juice and really make these places intolerable for our kind."

"And I'm going to have to do exactly that," Nguyen said, almost sadly. "I was hoping to avoid it, but I think creating a sanctorum in St. Brigid's is now at the top of my list of things to do." He looked at the broken window, and sniffed slightly, probably detecting the aroma of gunshots, Hendricks figured.

"What do we do about Erin?" Hendricks asked, figuring he'd have to be the one to bring it up. "She's demon possessed, so—"

"So is Molly," Dr. Darlington said as she came up the aisle, Casey Meacham at her side. "They ... they took my ..." Her lip quivered. "They took her."

"They're trying to take everything," Reeve said and none of his earlier dottiness was present anywhere on the man. Seeing his deputy turn on them seemed to have snapped him out of whatever half-ass catatonic state he was in. "They will damned sure do it if we just keep sitting back and letting them."

"How do we find them, though?" Arch asked. "They could be anyone. Anywhere. They could be next door, or ten miles out in the county. We go house to house, they can pretend they're not even demons, the way they work." He gestured toward the middle of the aisle. "We had one standing right here and no one even figured it out until—" He glanced at Hendricks. "How'd you know?"

"Because they didn't attack her, apparently," Hendricks said. "It was kind of a stupid mistake, and I doubt they'll make it again."

"They know us," Arch said. "They know our families because they're taking our friends and neighbors. They can guess our weaknesses because they're sucking up all the knowledge they need from those people to guess what matters most to us."

"They killed my mom," Dr. Darlington said, almost ghostly. "They stole my daughter."

"They killed my wife," Reeve said, still resolute. He was clutching that pistol in his hand so hard Hendricks worried it might go off, because he couldn't see whether the sheriff had his finger near the trigger.

"The law is likely to blame you for that, by the way," Duncan said, drawing every eye. "Think about it. They could possess your new sheriff and act like he's going to arrest you on suspicion of killing your own family members. As soon as you comply, he has you in the back of a police car, unarmed, and they could just parade through every single person you've ever known and murder them right in front of your eyes while you're cuffed and in a cage. Just add suffering and they get everything they want."

"Don't trust anybody," Arch whispered.

"I never do," Guthrie said. Hendricks believed her.

"I wouldn't go that far," Hendricks said, and lifted his hand up, holding it steady in front of him. With a touch, blade to the back of his wrist, he opened a cut no more than a centimeter wide. "I trust the blood to tell the truth."

Arch stared at him, eyes smoky, then nodded. "The truth is in the blood." And he did the same, running his sword blade along the back of his hand just a touch. Dark liquid welled up, then dripped onto the tile floor.

"Blood will out," Reeve said, and took his own blade and did the same.

"Hell, yeah," Casey Meacham said, pulling out a tomahawk and poking himself with the hard, pointed back edge. "Oops." He dug it in a couple centimeters, and the blood came oozing out a lot faster than it had for any of the others.

"Uhhh," Father Nguyen said, "would everyone please stop bleeding in my church?" He chucked a thumb behind him. "You could just drink holy water, or dip a foot in the baptismal font."

"Probably shouldn't do the former after the latter, though," Hendricks said, "just for sanitary reasons."

Nguyen shook his head, then fumbled in his pocket, pulling out a little glass bottle. With care, he pulled the stopper and dumped a little in his hand, then smeared it down his own face. "See?" He turned around and flicked a little in Dr. Darlington's face, and she blinked as the water hit her.

"I'll have a shot of that, luv," Lonsdale said, weaseling his way forward. "Not cuts for this lad, please."

Guthrie whipped her baton around and smacked him across the hand. "Too late."

"Anthony Blunt!" Lonsdale stuck the back of his hand in his

mouth. "That fucking hurts!"

"Yeah, but you're not a demon," Guthrie said with a shrug. She looked around. "I trust no one wants us to crack open our shells and prove we're not possessed?"

"I'm leaning toward not minding if you did," Duncan said, and Hendricks could just feel the tension.

"You don't count," Guthrie shot right back.

"So that's all of us," Hendricks said. "And ... we're down quite a few people here."

"Yep," Arch said, nodding solemnly. "We've got some who are going to be out for a bit."

"And others who aren't coming back at all," Reeve said, and goddamn, did he almost make Hendricks want to cry. He just looked so damned sad.

"We've got no plan," Duncan said, "and I can't track them."

"Obviously," Guthrie said, "or Home Office wouldn't have let these douches slip under the radar for all these years."

"So ... what do we do?" Darlington asked, as vulnerable as Hendricks could recall ever seeing her.

"We gotta hunt 'em," Casey Meacham said, stepping into the center of the little circle, his hand dripping blood out of his self-inflicted wound. "We gotta get out there like bloodhounds and sniff around," he took series of sniffing breaths through his nose, flaring his nostrils comically wide, "put our noses to the ground." He started to bend over, but then dipped and came right back up. "Shit. I'm feeling a little lightheaded."

"You're bleeding a lot, you idiot," Darlington said, seeming to come out of her torpor slightly. "Let me stitch you up," she said a little grudgingly.

"Even if we wanted to hunt these things like he says," Reeve asked, "where would we start?"

Hendricks got the idea at the same time as Arch, apparently, because the big man's eyes lit up, and he spoke first. "With bait."

*

Brian didn't say much on the car ride to the hospital. What was there to say? Demons had possessed his body and used it against his will to shoot his own father in the head. Now his dad was racing ahead of them in an ambulance, probably dead by now, and he was stuck bleeding over the back seat of his sister's car in silence, unable to walk without help, and with the sick worry of not knowing, for sure, whether he'd committed patricide.

It wasn't enough that he just had to dwell on that, either. Sometimes being smart was a curse, and this was one of those times, because he'd had all manner of probabilities and possibilities run through his head along the ride, and he didn't feel comfortable discussing a single one of them with his sister and mother, neither of whom were speaking and neither of whom did he dare speak to right now.

Because while a demon might have been controlling his actions, he couldn't shake the feeling that his own family were thinking that Brian had shot his own father. That maybe he could have fought the demon back, somehow, himself.

He hadn't told them yet that it wasn't just one demon, it was at least five, and that while one of them steered him, the other four forced him back, kept him under control, assaulted him in his own mind. He was pretty sure none of that mattered, anyway, because it didn't change the irrefutable fact: his father had been shot in the head, and he had been the one to pull the trigger.

He was pretty sure the cops would see it that way, too. Maybe not with Reeve in charge, since he now knew what was what, but Brian doubted the new sheriff in town would just let an easy, open and shut murder case sail by without closing that sucker right on his face. They'd have everything they needed—witnesses who had no alternative story, fingerprints and DNA evidence all over the gun, and no alibi at all. What would he even say? *I was in the room, with the gun in my hand, the blood on my clothes, sure, but I didn't do it! For realsies!* Even with his own tendency to try and look for every alternative explanation, Brian himself would have convicted his own ass if he were on the jury.

And even if by some miracle he was acquitted ... he still had the image burned into his brain of shooting his own father in the head. It was like he could see it happening in slow motion when he closed his eyes: the gun rising up to just under his father's jaw, the crack of shot being fired, the shock and betrayal on his father's face ...

Brian felt the sick feeling in the pit of his stomach from all the uncertainty and it was almost as bad as the screaming pain from his knee.

He was clutching his leg but it didn't help. Squeezing it some seemed to, but it wasn't bleeding too hard, just a steady trickle. Arch could have done a lot worse than what he'd done, and it didn't seem like he'd hit any major veins or arteries, but it was still a slow trickle that hadn't stopped in nearly an hour. Some preliminary scabbing might have been happening near the edges of the wound, but the center was pretty much still wide, no matter how much he tried to press the sides together to speed things along.

And maybe saddest of all, Brian kept thinking he'd probably have to get a tetanus shot since he'd been cut on metal. That was always a tetanus shot, right?

ARGHHHHH! Why did his brain keep bringing this stupid thing up? Who gave a fuck if he needed a tetanus shot? He wasn't a kid anymore, why would his head get stuck in this groove, this rut, this continuous, stupid string of thought, like it had nothing better to fixate on? His father could be dead, and this, THIS was what was on his mind?

He rubbed a bloody hand across his forehead as he lay across the back seat of his mother's Lincoln. Surprisingly Alison was driving, or perhaps unsurprisingly. They were slowing, now, taking another turn onto a surface road. They'd been off the freeway for a while, so they had to be getting close to the hospital. Soon, they'd know for sure. And that would be good, to know for sure. Because the wait was killing Brian.

*

Lauren took her time, took it easy, working on Casey's hand by first irrigating the wound, then readying butterfly bandages. Stitches might have been better in this situation, with the blood still welling out of the fairly deep wound, but it was arguable, and she didn't trust her hands not to shake.

The church was quiet, with Reeve sitting near the entry and Father Nguyen murmuring some sort of chant as he paced around the walls of the church, speaking in Latin. The priest had leaped right to work as soon as things had been settled, and he'd been moving ever since.

"You got to get me back up and in the fight," Casey said, almost mewling. She looked right into his eyes and saw some bravado there, the machismo of a man who maybe hadn't lost anything personally important to him yet. She felt a pang of guilt for criticizing him so harshly in her mind, but it was hard for her not to weigh out the scale with what she'd lost and make comparisons to those around her. Reeve was the only one who would probably understand, and he was just sitting quietly with gun and sword guarding the entry to the church, in case any of these demons brought trouble back before Father Nguyen had put his protections in place.

"I don't think they're coming right now," Lauren said, washing away some of the blood. She had rubbing alcohol and a first aid kit, which wasn't a lot to work with, but her medical training had already taken over and she was doing this without even thinking. Which was fortunate, because she wasn't sure she was too able to think clearly at the moment, either. "I think Hendricks and Arch were right."

"I ought to have gone with them," Casey said, aw-shucks-ing, "them and those demon fellers. They could have used my fierce moves." He made to raise the tomahawk with his other hand and moved his hand a little, cringing when the pain hit him. "Ow."

"Maybe we'll need your help here," she said, giving him a resentful look as she moved his hand back into place and continued her work.

"Maybe," Casey said. "Just maybe."

They lapsed into what felt like, to her, a comfortable silence. Apparently Casey didn't feel the same, because he broke it less than a minute later. "What was your daughter's name?"

Lauren felt suddenly cold. "Molly." She'd stopped cleaning his hand without realizing it and nudged herself back to work. "Her name *is* Molly. She's still alive."

"Sorry, I didn't mean it like that," Casey said. "I should have thrown the tomahawk at her, I guess, but Yvette was right in the way and I worried I couldn't hit her. Hell, I barely got Yvette." He lifted the tomahawk up, but more carefully this time. "Throwing this thing is not nearly as easy I thought it would be when I picked it out."

"Why not pick a crossbow instead?" Lauren asked, not really thinking about it.

"You know, I gave that a ponderin'," Casey said, "but I decided that having Father Nguyen consecrate arrows was too much work, because, I mean, you gotta have a decent number to start with, say twenty—and that's like two hundred and fifty hours of consecrating right there. And you lose a few to shafts breaking or maybe the heads themselves getting dull, and pretty soon you gotta build up your stockpile again ... but with the tomahawk, you just get it done once and forever more you just—" He brought it up and mimed throwing it, but the weapon slipped and smacked, blade-first, into the wooden ridge that made up the pew back.

Lauren flinched as it chipped wood and sent a splinter bouncing off her jacket. It didn't hit her hard at all; she didn't even feel it through the clothing, but she blanched nonetheless.

"What are you doing?" Nguyen cried from somewhere across the church.

"Sorry!" Casey called over to him. "Accident! Won't happen again." He grabbed the tomahawk by the handle and started to pull it out, but failed the first time. "Shit. That sumbitch is wedged."

"Be careful," Lauren said, "I don't want to have to fix up any other wounds." She could feel her ire rising a little, the first feeling she'd really had since ...

... since ...

"God," she whispered, lowering her head and laying the first butterfly bandage. They had taken Molly, and here she sat, bandaging an idiot who was now threatening to damage himself again. "I need to get out of here."

"That's not a great idea, Doc," Casey said. "What if they try and get you? If we're gonna spring this ambush thing, we ought to have only one piece of bait dangling in the water." He straightened up. "You gotta stay here with us where we can protect youuuuuuuuuuuuu—eeeeeeeeeeeek!" He moaned in pain as she applied a little extra pressure while bandaging him.

"I don't need you to protect me, Casey," she said, now that he was groaning softly. "I need my water gun so that when the time comes that we go face to face with these demons again, I'm ready ... and not stuck in a position to be dragged around by these bastards." She gave him the look to shut him up and it worked, probably because he hadn't seen it from her before. But she knew that she'd wallowed long enough, and that was that. No more sitting catatonic while the demons had Molly.

They might have taken her mother before she could so much as open her mouth about it, but she'd be damned if she let them just walk away with her daughter without fighting someone to the fucking death.

*

Duncan was driving through the Tennessee night in the demon town car, doing about seventy on the freeway and probably squeezing a little more out of the old girl. Amanda Guthrie, AKA black lady Lerner, was in the passenger seat, Arch was behind her, and Hendricks was behind Duncan, and it was the tensest fucking ride Hendricks had ever been on, bar none. And that included the times they rode into Ramadi to kick down doors and face certain death.

The silence was pretty fucking oppressive, even for a stoic like Hendricks who would rather have plucked every single one of his ball hairs one by one rather than talk feelings with a bunch of guys—and Guthrie/Lerner, who he still kindasorta perceived as a guy, new look and all assertions to the contrary. Still, somebody needed to say something.

"You two don't seem like you're ready to kiss and make up," Hendricks said, drawing a startled head-turn from Arch, who frowned pretty deeply at him, presumably for intruding into his private thinking time with something as bound to stir the shit pot as this.

"What did I tell you?" Guthrie said, turning to Duncan. "Less than fifteen minutes."

"You never said shit to me." Duncan kept his hands on the wheel, the dark shadowed trees blurring by on either side of them.

"I thought it real loud and figured you'd pick up on it," Guthrie said.

"Doesn't work that way anymore, remember?" Duncan's tension was obvious, even if he'd been a normal person. For him, it was fucking over-the-top.

"Oh, right," Guthrie said casually. "I forget you can't read my very essence anymore. You must feel terribly deprived of my killer wit."

"Well, you've certainly proven the 'killer' part," Duncan said.

"What is going on here?" Arch asked, clueless.

Hendricks should have figured the big man had his head up his ass, but this was pretty deep, even for Arch. "They're in a tiff," Hendricks said.

"Really?" Arch was still frowning.

"We're not in a tiff," Guthrie said, "but seriously, shut up while Mommy and Daddy are talking, kids, or I'll pull this fucking car over and start administering spankings."

"She's not the same," Duncan said, turning his head to talk back to Hendricks and Arch. "That's what's wrong."

"No shit she's not the same," Hendricks said, cocking an eyebrow. "Because she's a she. And black."

"That shit is all irrelevant," Duncan said, taking a hand off the wheel to wave it at him, "that's just a fucking shell. It could be deep purple and with nine hundred and twelve different sets of genitals and I wouldn't care. It's what's inside that changed, not the surface bullcrap."

"Oh, come on," Guthrie said. "I'm still me. Still a sarcastic asshole—"

"That much seems true," Arch said under his breath.

"I can tell you missed me, even if Duncan didn't." Guthrie said, turning around and giving him a wink. "Don't even try and deny it."

"I missed you," Duncan said, "but I missed *you*. Not this new you, but old you—"

"Screw you, chew you, frou-frou you," Hendricks said, getting everybody in the car to look at him again. "Sorry, I'm just ... trying to make the word 'you' make sense again after all those repeated uses."

"Nobody stays the same forever, Duncan, not even you," Guthrie said, cooling rapidly. "I still remember when you were newly hatched, a true believer—"

"Wait, you hatch?" Arch asked. "Like ... birds? Or lizards?"

"—and now look at you," Guthrie sneered. "There's probably a reason Home Office isn't sending you orders. Would you even take them anymore?"

"Does this mean Lerner—" Arch started.

"Guthrie," she said, turning her head around to look at him. "You have to call me Amanda Guthrie now. It's the rules."

"—isn't on our side?" Arch finished, bravely soldiering on over Guthrie. "And ... is Amanda Guthrie your real name?"

"Sweetcheeks," Guthrie said, "I wouldn't tell you my real name if you had that sword half a millimeter from my shell and speaking it aloud would blow up your head. You don't give out names in the demon world. Not real ones, anyway."

"I think it's safe to say that her loyalties are compromised, yes," Duncan said.

"What the fuck are we riding in the car with her for, then?" Hendricks asked, grabbing for the hilt of his sword. "Why not just—"

"Don't." Duncan shook his head. "Don't say what you're thinking about saying. Threatening an OOC is grounds for immediate extermination. Kinda like threatening a royal."

"And we all know how well you enforced that one," Hendricks muttered, still keeping his hand on the sword hilt. He saw Arch mirroring his movement in the seat next to him, but he said nothing.

"Yeah, that one sounded real tough, that pickle Kitty Elizabeth put you in," Guthrie opined. "Sit back and let her assemble the Rog'tausch, break cowboy into tiny, beef-jerky size pieces, or go against the edicts of royalty."

"In fairness, we didn't know she was assembling the Rog'tausch until later," Arch said.

"Yeah, well, that's because you're all idiots," Guthrie said casually. "Anyway. Tough call. Good work. Lovely resolution, what with her now having to masturbate and torture with only one hand. Happy endings all the way around." He glanced back at Hendricks. "Maybe not for you, but everyone else … so happy."

"What happened to you?" Duncan said under his breath.

"I fought for your pet cause and burned in hell for it," Guthrie said, putting a little heat on it at the end then loosening right back up. "Next question?"

"Why are you coming with us?" Arch asked, into the silence that was broken only by the sound of the highway.

"Because there's a Legion on the loose," Guthrie said, "and I think we all know how Home Office feels about those. There are gonna be some really red faces over this, I'm telling you, and not just because demon skin tends to be more crimson than humans, either." She readjusted herself in her seat. "Time to nip this problem right in the bud before word gets out."

"So you're a company m—err, woman … now," Arch said. "That the gist?"

"That's more than the gist," Guthrie said, turning back and smiling sweetly. "That's the whole enchilada, ballgame and all else. Don't forget it, either."

"Or what?" Hendricks didn't like it when people made demands. It tended to be the fastest way to piss him off.

Guthrie just shrugged, no big deal. "We're all a little too old for cheap threats, aren't we?"

"Nah," Hendricks said, "sometimes it's good to just get one out there, especially if it's the real deal. That'd make it not cheap."

Guthrie just nodded. "Fine, then. Don't forget it, or the weight of demon law will grind your fucking bones into dust." She smiled. "That sound about right?"

*

Alison hadn't even helped Brian into the emergency room when they'd gotten to the hospital. She'd let some orderlies know when they pulled up, and they'd come for him with a wheelchair, helped him out of the car and her mother had gone with him. Alison had held her tongue, gotten back behind the wheel and waited until they'd pulled him out, moaning quietly, and taken him away, before she dared look after him. Then she parked the car.

She couldn't help but resent him. He may not have been in charge of his own body when it happened, but her baby brother had pulled her dad's gun and shot him, with his own damned hands. Demon in the driver's seat? Yeah, she could buy that. But it still didn't stop her from being pissed beyond belief and making him the target, at least for now, until she found a better one.

Besides, it was better this way. Brian needed to be on the sidelines for a while, and this was just the ticket for that. He was sensitive and in pain, and the combination of the two of those things should keep him reeling, make him turtle up. That'd push him off the board, which was exactly where he needed to be with this Legion on the loose, trying to put them all in coffins.

Alison covered the ground between the parking lot and the Red Cedar Emergency Room without even realizing she was doing it. She had dim flashes of following the glowing ER lights, of feeling the faint buzz of her cell phone ringing and ignoring it, of passing through the automatic open doors with a whoosh, and even of asking about her dad at the front desk and being told to go to the fourth floor.

The elevator ride she remembered, if only for its clacking and disquieting hum. Red Cedar had been built somewhere around the turn of the 20th century, and its brick exterior was of that old style, the kind that inevitably carried a historical look to it. Alison liked that, normally, but she preferred it on buildings she could appreciate with a clear mind, and not ones she had to enter and navigate while wondering if her father was dead.

When she came out on the fourth floor, the lady at the desk directed her to a waiting room. The whole place smelled sterile, like someone had just come through and mopped with a strong disinfectant, Pinesol on steroids with a limeade twist. She found herself sitting in an uncomfortably stiff chair a few minutes later without much recollection about how she got there, her arm having already developed a checkmark pattern from the cloth against her skin.

"Have you heard anything yet?" Her mother came in soundlessly, not that Alison would have noticed in any case. She tried to recall the drive here from Midian, but that was all a blur of sunset fading into night.

Alison stared at her, then shifted to look at the TV, which was playing a rerun of *Friends* with the sound off. Subtitles played across the bottom. "No, I haven't heard a thing," she said.

"They're working on Brian now," Addy said, pouring herself into the chair beside Alison. "They say he's going to be just fine, but he's going to be walking with a limp for a little while. Maybe longer." She was tense, high-strung, felt like a spring crammed into a confined space. Maybe like a gun spring, ready to burst out the moment it had a chance. Yeah, Alison liked that comparison. It felt right to her, not only about her mother but for herself as well.

"Ali?" her mother asked, causing Alison to turn her head and look, almost as if commanded. "That's good, isn't it?"

Alison stared at her blankly. "What is?"

"About your brother." Her mom was getting mad now, reddening in the face. "That he's going to be fine."

"Magnificent news, yes," Alison said, but she suspected she sold it about as well as a nun running a side business as a pimp.

"Alison," her mother said stiffly, "this was not your brother's fault."

"He answered the door," Alison said dully, perfectly happy to deliver that one with all the surly snottiness she was feeling toward Brian at the moment.

"But he didn't do any of those things after that. Surely you must realize—"

"I realize my father had a giant hole in his head because Brian didn't so much as think before opening the door," Alison said, keeping her voice down. "That's what I realize. If Daddy makes it through all this okay, we can talk about forgiveness."

"You would have done the same thing in his shoes," Addy said. She was judging Alison, and Alison could tell. "You don't just stop answering the door."

"In this town?" Alison asked. "Right now? Yeah, yeah, I just might make that a rule I followed, not answering the door."

"But it's not this town, is it?" Addy said, lowering her voice and placing her hands in her lap, concentrating on them. Alison noticed the myriad wrinkles across her mother's skin. "It's Midian that's in hell. It's home. And it's hard to shake off the sense of home, of safety, of being able to answer the door at midnight if someone comes calling, without being afraid they're gonna murder you."

"I expect it'll be a lot easier to shake that feeling off after today," Alison said.

"Good grief," her mother said and rummaged through her purse, coming out with a tissue that she applied to her eyes, which were damp. "Good grief, yes, after today … I expect that's so."

*

Arch might not have ever been happier to get out of a moving vehicle than he was when the town car pulled up to Red Cedar. The tension between Duncan and Guthrie had been palpable the last half hour of the ride, after Hendricks had provoked their little confrontation. Arch might have figured demons would have a better way of feuding than bitter silences and angry looks, but no, apparently not, because they both sat in silence and Duncan kept sending dirty looks toward Guthrie, who seemed pretty well indifferent.

Arch stepped out into the night, the overhead lamps lighting the parking lot and filling the air with a quiet hum. The early autumn air was maddening, just cool enough to cause Arch's skin to tingle after a moment's exposure. He started to stalk toward the door, but a raised voice held him up.

"Hey," Hendricks said, rushing after him, "hold on." Arch waited, and the cowboy came alongside a moment later, hat bobbing. "You can't go into a hospital like that."

Arch looked down. He was still wearing his uniform. "Why not?"

"Because you've got a sword on your belt," Hendricks said, nodding his way down. "They tend to take that shit pretty seriously, hence the drover coat." He spread his arms wide.

"Well, shucks," Arch said, looking down at his sword's hilt. "What am I supposed to do with it?" He'd be danged if he was going to just leave it in the car. Their plan suggested they would need them, after all.

"I'll carry it for you, under my coat," Hendricks said, waving him over. "That way we'll have it on hand and it won't draw as much suspicion."

"There's nowhere you won't look suspicious in that thing," Duncan said helpfully from where he and Guthrie were lurking a few feet away.

Arch ignored them and started to unfasten his belt so he could take the scabbard off. Guthrie made a catcall noise. "Just kidding," she said, when he paused in unbuckling. "You know, I thought maybe I'd be more interested in the male form now that I've got a girl shell, but I still just don't give a fuck about you peoples' soft and squishy parts."

"Our parts aren't soft and squishy," Hendricks said. "They're hard and—"

"I was talking about your brain, numbnuts," Guthrie fired back before Hendricks even finished. "Not your throbbing micropenis, which I'm sure is nature's way of overcompensating for your breathtaking desire to leap into idiotic action without so much as a single forethought."

Hendricks took Arch's sword sourly, still staring sullenly at Guthrie. "You don't know me, OOC."

"Sure I do," Guthrie piped up. "We got to see footage of Kitty

Elizabeth's party down in the pits. It was kind of like showing a starving man one of those gourmet cooking shows. Admittedly, they cut away after the part where you charged into a room that was supposed to have eight or so demon guards in it, along with royalty, but not before we got to watch you get clocked from behind by Kitty's butler and then pulped a little by her." Guthrie didn't smirk. "So ... how does demon royalty taste, exactly? I'm guessing you found out, and I'm guessing the answer was 'sulfuric.'"

Hendricks paled under the parking lot lamps. "Congrats. You got to see me at one of the lowest points of my life, and now you get to deliver commentary on it. Kudos to you, OOC."

"It's all right, kid," Guthrie said, wheeling away from him, "whatever she did to you, I assure you that after our little watch break, they did ten times worse to us." She almost sounded like less of a dick there.

"What's the plan?" Duncan asked, a little more muted than before as Arch started back toward the hospital entry. He checked to make sure Hendricks was following behind, and he was, but he was lagging a bit.

"You two on perimeter, if you can stand being around each other," Arch said, nodding at Duncan and Guthrie.

"We can stand each other a lot better than the cowboy can probably stand me at the moment," Guthrie said. "If shit goes down out here, we're not likely to have time to call you on the phone, so better just be listening for a scream."

"Are we likely to hear a scream from inside?" Arch asked.

"You'll hear it if we do it," Duncan said, exchanging a look with Guthrie, who nodded. "We can make ourselves heard in a crunch."

"All right, then," Arch said, and headed through the emergency room doors, Hendricks a few steps behind, holding his coat close against him like he was warding off the cold night.

*

Reeve was sitting in front of the door, waiting in case this Legion decided to pay another, stronger visit to St. Brigid's. Part of him hoped they would, because he had a debt to repay to those fuckers, and there was a sharp pain in his belly that made him want to get right to settling that account. It had been all quiet so far, though, and so he'd just been stuck sitting in front of the door, stewing in his juices, listening to the baptismal font built into the floor make its burbling noises.

Father Nguyen came by again, on his umpteenth lap around the church. He was chanting and had some kind of incense burner on a long brass chain. He was saying something in a language Reeve had no clue about, and he shrugged it off as Nguyen continued to walk past, eyes nearly closed, speaking softly. Somewhere across the church, Lonsdale cleared his throat loudly enough to annoy Reeve, not that it would take much from that asshole.

"I'm sorry about Donna." Lauren Darlington's voice came from behind him, prompting Reeve to take his eyes off the doors for the first time in an hour and look back to the dark-haired doctor. She came up behind him and stopped a few steps off, her arms folded, her face as tired as he'd ever seen it. She was wearing some pretty mismatched clothes, and there was dried blood in specks all over her. Part of him wanted to do the sheriff thing and investigate the obvious crime, but he knew damned well he wasn't sheriff anymore, and he knew who was responsible for the crime and what had happened. She lingered at his shoulder, quiet, but only for a few seconds. "We got hit the hardest."

"Ayup," Reeve said. What was there to disagree with? "I'm sorry about your mother, and Molly. She was a good girl."

"Is," Darlington said in a near-whisper.

"Of course," Reeve said. "I'm sorry."

"They still got her." Darlington eased around him and pulled out a metal folding chair with a cloth padded seat. She sat down, and it squealed against the tile floor of the church. "Your kids all moved away, didn't they?"

That had been a particularly unpleasant fact for Reeve for a long time, like a piece of chicken bone stuck in your throat. Now, suddenly, with Midian all gone to hell, he felt lucky his kids had moved away. "Yeah, they did. Still come to visit on holidays, though I think I'll wave 'em off this year if hell hasn't left by Thanksgiving."

"Why do you think they hit us the hardest?" Darlington asked, her face china white, her dark hair hanging in stringy ringlets. He'd never seen the doctor this taken apart, not just in terms of how she looked but how he suspected she was doing inside. "You and me, I mean. We lost more than—"

"We don't know if Bill Longholt is gonna live," Reeve said. "That'd be a ... a sizable blow to that family if he dies, especially if Ed decides to go after Brian for his murder once this all settles out."

"You really think he will?"

"I would, if I were him," Reeve said. He left out the part where he suspected Ed would be coming after both of them as well. Well, maybe not the doctor. Ed always did have a soft spot for a pretty lady. Reeve frowned at her. Well, they'd get her cleaned up before she talked to Fries, and everything would be just fine for her, at least. Maybe.

"Still," she said, "they didn't go after Hendricks or Arch like that. Just us."

"They mighta gone harder after Arch if Brian hadn't gotten taken out pretty quick," Reeve said. "Mighta had Alison kill herself in front of him, since that sounds like something they enjoy." It was a gruesome thing, what these bastards did. He kept seeing Donna, over and over, on fire, her eyes aglow with demon hate up until they slid that sword right into her and made her human again. It killed that demon in the process, and they knew it was coming, but they hated him so much that they did it anyway, the ultimate act of spite. "And Hendricks ... hell, he ain't got much else to lose, I suppose." Reeve straightened a little. "Maybe Erin, come to it, though they been strained lately." He shook his head. "No, I think they intended to hit the whole watch that hard. They maybe only just succeeded so well with us."

"What's the difference?" The doctor stretched, uncomfortably, straightening her back in the chair. "I mean, really, when it comes down to it. They might have tried with all of us, but you and I ended up getting it the worst."

"Yeah," Reeve said, "but the difference is ... the next time? They probably won't back off it until they hurt the rest of them just as bad." He looked right at Darlington and saw the horror in her eyes as that one sank in.

*

"Arch!" Alison's mother bounded up from where she was sitting in the waiting room, practically running across the space between them to hug Arch hard around the neck. Alison watched with detached disinterest, feeling a vague relief that her husband was present and that still-nagging feeling that he was too late because they still hadn't heard anything, and no news, in this case, was awful news.

"Ma'am," Arch said, Hendricks trailing a little behind him, coat all buttoned up and snugged, lurking behind like the world's most conspicuous shadow. He looked suspicious as hell, like he was all set to open his coat to reveal himself wearing nothing beneath. She had a vision of him waggling his penis at some poor, unsuspecting old lady, and it almost caused her to giggle.

Alison picked herself up, the cloth pattern of the chair just about etched into her arm at this point, and made her way slowly over to Arch. He looked at her tentatively, like she might break, and she gave him a big hug as her mother made way, thank the Lord. "Hey, Arch," she said, burying her head into her husband's shoulder.

"Hey, honey," Arch said, quiet and reassuring, perfect timbre and warmth, like he almost always was with her. "How you doing?"

"I'm okay," she said, and she knew he got what she was saying with that: *I'm as okay as I can possibly be given the shit going on.*

She held him there tight for a few seconds longer than necessary, then broke. "What's the word?" She kept her tone level, but she needed to know why he was here, because she wasn't expecting to see him, and certainly not with Hendricks following behind.

"The word is that these demons are madder than a nest of ticked-off hornets," Arch said with his usual gift for cleanly phrased understatement. "We think they're going to try and hit y'all here."

Alison frowned. "Really?"

"Can you think of a better place to strike?" Hendricks asked, easing up next to her mother, who gave him a frowning once over. "St. Brigid's is all locked down by now, the father is doing something to it to keep the demons out."

"But this isn't in the hotspot," Addy said, like she was repeating the rules for proper etiquette.

"This demon doesn't seem to give a fuck," Hendricks said in his usual crass way. It didn't bother her at all, but Arch cringed. "He wants to put a spike in all our asses, and he's doing a mighty fine job so far."

"We came down here to protect you," Arch said, a little more reassuring.

"And to use you as bait," Hendricks said, causing Arch to twitch.

"Might want to check on Brian, then, Hendricks," Alison said, looking past Arch to tell him.

Hendricks didn't look enthused and said so. "I can think of some things I'd rather do, like put my junk in an electrical socket."

"There's one right over there," she pointed to the corner, "and it looks like all you need to do is just spring your coat open and you'll be all set."

He looked down at himself. "What are you saying?" He asked it a second before he caught it for himself.

"That you look like a pervert about to expose yourself," Alison said, "so why don't you go do that to Brian, who will surely appreciate it more than any of the rest of us?"

Hendricks gave her the smirk. "All right, then," and started to saunter off.

"I'm going to go with him," Addy said, rubbing a hand over Alison's arm. She was all covered in blood, and when her mom's hand came away, it was tinged with crusty red at the tips of her fingers. Addy looked down at it in disgust, her faint smile disappearing quickly as she realized it belonged to either her husband or her son. She meandered off after Hendricks, still staring at her fingers.

"You want to sit?" Arch asked, gesturing to the chairs where he'd found her when he came in.

"I've been sitting for hours," Alison said, "but … yeah, weirdly enough. I do." They wandered over and sat down, both of them walking like old people.

"Lerner's back," Arch said, which was a jarring piece of news that had Alison sit up and take interest.

"Is he?"

"Doesn't look the same, in that he's a young black lady now," Arch said, "but indeed, Lerner has rejoined us—in a way."

"In what way would that be?"

"In a different form and with a slightly different disposition." Arch was bullshitting her and she knew it.

"Something's wrong with him that you're not saying."

"He's different, that's all." Arch hesitated, then it came out. "A mite more hostile. It appears going through hell might have changed him slightly."

"If he came back a black lady, I'd say it did, yeah."

"Personality is different, too. He was always a bit of a peckerwood who liked to cause a ruckus, but now *she's* flat out cold. Duncan suggested she was excessively brutal to the possessed when they got attacked."

"You could have been a touch more brutal when Daddy got attacked and I would have been fine with it," Alison said, surly as she thought about her brother. "I don't reckon I can fault Lerner for that without tarring myself at the same time."

"I suppose," Arch said and got quiet again. "Erin got possessed. Dr. Darlington's daughter, too. This demon has 'em both now, and he killed Donna Reeve and Darlington's momma."

"Shit," Alison said quietly.

"I was thinking something along those lines myself."

She leaned across the arm of the chair to rest her head on his shoulder. It was awkward and a little painful and worth it for the small measure of comfort it gave her. "So the demons are gonna come here?"

"Stands to reason, since they're all-fired mad at us. Duncan and New Lerner are outside."

Alison wrinkled her nose as she frowned. "They had no cause to be mad with Erin or Darlington, or even Duncan. None of them were there when we killed that possession demon."

"Seems they're mad at the watch as a whole entity, then," Arch said, explaining it away.

Something about that didn't sit right with Alison, either. "Blaming us all and killing the ones we love … and not holding it to just the ones directly responsible." She shook her head. That was crazy, and she couldn't quite get her head around it. But it was demons, so she really didn't have to. She felt reassuringly for the holy knife on her belt under her coat nonetheless, though, and gave it a reassuring touch as she laid there with her head on Arch's shoulder and hoped she'd hear something soon that was not just the beat of her husband's heart.

*

"Goddamn," Brian said after Hendricks had run through it all for him. He didn't feel any better knowing he'd not been the only one snookered, not at all, strangely. "They donkey punched us good, didn't they?"

"What's a donkey punch?" Addy asked.

"Yeah, they slipped it in the backdoor hard without even a courtesy finger first," Hendricks agreed. The cowboy was a profane motherfucker, and really, that was just about the only thing Brian liked about him. "But now we know their game."

"Uh, their game?" Brian asked. His leg was bandaged like crazy and he was resting in a bed behind a curtain in the ER at Red Cedar, waiting for them to admit him. "Their game appears to be bowling, and we're the tenpins."

"Yeah, and once you know that, you can start dodging the ball and knocking it into the gutter," Hendricks said. "And I don't know about you, but I want to knock their fucking balls in the gutter."

"Oh, goodness," Addy said with a noise of distaste.

Brian gave that a thought. "Yeah, maybe. Seems weird that they came after me and shot my dad, though, doesn't it? I mean, he was only at your second showdown with them, right at the end. And none of this Legion got out alive with a look at him, did they?"

"They're coming at the whole watch," Hendricks said. Brian cringed. He hated calling it 'the watch.' It was so melodramatic, and it reminded him of Christopher Walken's speech from *Pulp Fiction*. "They took our hits personally and responded in kind. Not that hard to understand if you've got a little bit of a head for vengeance." Brian caught the implication, dripping with scorn, that apparently he was too soft to understand wanting revenge.

"Yeah, I get reciprocity," Brian said, "but ... this is like ... widespread. You'd think this demon would have gone a little tighter focused with his anger. Do more damage that way, right? Like, a, uhh ..."

"A rifle versus a shotgun?" Hendricks asked, arms folded, unimpressed.

"Yeah, like that." Brian gave a little ground on that one, hoping the cowboy would take his point.

"Demons are demons," Hendricks said, "and they're usually not the smartest."

"This isn't just one demon, though." Brian gnawed at his lip. They'd given him painkillers, and the knee was down to a dull ache now with the occasional sharp pain when he moved it. He'd be on crutches for a while, but it wasn't hellacious right now. "This is a whole society of demons, all in one body. That would suggest there'd be some intelligences in there, even if the median was—"

"Yeah, well, anyway," Hendricks said and turned away from him, heading for the curtain that marked off Brian's little space in the ER. "I'll check on you again in a little while." He pushed aside the curtain without much in the way of grace and was gone.

Brian stared after him for a second then just let his head sag back on his pillow. "Nobody listened to me before," he said to his mother, "and I suspect it's only going to be worse now."

"Well, darling," his mother said, "maybe it's the way you go about it."

Brian had heard that so many times that it surprised him how much it stung. Even through the painkillers, he felt tears threaten to spring up in his eyes. "Why don't you go check on Dad?" He tried to look strong for her. "Let me know ... how it goes."

She smiled faintly at him and gave his hand a squeeze, then left him there among the tangled, cheap sheets, carefully pulling the curtain closed behind him. Brian just sat there alone, under the bright fluorescent lights, thinking about what had happened today, and wondering if there was any way at all he'd be able to fix it ... or at least do something, anything to make him hate himself less than everybody else did.

9.

"Daddy Daddy Daddy!" The guided missile that was Abilene Tarley came soaring into his bed at a little after six, thumping hard right on his belly and just barely missing Braeden's groin. He made an involuntarily "oof!" sound as he was ripped out of a pleasant dream involving a pretty girl who was much, much older than the one that had just cannonballed him into wakefulness.

"Ohhhhh," Braeden moaned, turning sideways to hide his mammoth erection as his daughter wiggled across his chest. The dream had been oh-so-pleasant, too, and seemed to be heading somewhere that Braeden hadn't been in entirely too long. Abi's little bombing was letting the air out of that balloon, though, and quickly, he hoped, because it was uncomfortably awkward for her to be snaking her way across his chest right now. "Yes, my dear?"

"Do you know what day it is, Daddy?" She smiled a ten-thousand watt smile at him. How could she be this happy this early in the morning?

"I'm guessing it ain't Daddy's sleep-in day," Braeden said, brushing his hair out of his eyes.

"Nope!" Abi said, "it's Halloween!"

Braeden blinked, his eyes sticking open. That was right. It was Halloween. He felt a little tingle of fear, and he answered her slowly. "It surely is."

"Yay!" She chirped, bouncing lightly on his steadily increasing belly. "I can't wait to get candy!"

She tended to talk at a high volume, even indoors, loud enough now that Braeden cringed, still feeling like he was suffering from sleep desiring to take his body over again. Still, her stream of thought raised in him more than a little concern. "Baby girl ..." he started, trying to figure out how best to inform his daughter that there was no way in hell he wanted her out trick or treating tonight. This town was in the shit heap, after all. What was to stop whoever was causing this crap to come roaring in on kids trick or treating?

"Am I going to get to see Miss Evelyn today?" Abi asked, switching tracks quicker than his sleep-addled brain could keep up. She looked so damned earnest, her lower lip pooched out a little. "I want to show her my princess dress."

Braeden opened his mouth and closed it, afraid of letting out a toxic cloud of morning breath. Abi had commented on that once or twice, not so politely. "Uhh ..." Braeden said when he opened up again, "... well ... you're probably coming to work with me today."

"I get to sit in the office with Tracy and Mr. Haskins!" She stiffened in excitement, apparently all thought of Miss Evelyn forgotten in favor of something better. "Yippeeeeeee!" And she bounced on him again, roiling his belly.

Braeden just lay back and let her knock the air out of him a couple times. It seemed a fair exchange for what he was going to have to do later, when he'd be forced to tell her there wasn't going to be any trick or treating tonight. Between this and Evelyn Creek going nuts, Braeden had to admit it was not shaping up to be Abi's best week.

*

Sun was streaming through the stained glass, right through the broken window, and Father Nguyen was still orbiting the church slowly, chanting under his breath as Reeve listened, the fatigue settling in on him like his bones turned to lead inside him. He could hear Casey's soft snores somewhere behind him, and Dr. Darlington was passed out on a pew a couple rows away. Lonsdale was still twitching up near the altar, the demon hunter apparently having had enough of demons for the near future.

Reeve could sympathize with that. He'd certainly had enough demons to last him a lifetime or twelve, too.

The front door hadn't opened all night, and they'd heard not one word from the team at the hospital. Reeve had his doubts about the Legion attacking there, though he'd had to concede when Arch and

Hendricks floated the plan, that that was as good a target as any, especially if Father Nguyen went and made St. Brigid's impregnable to their fucking devil faces.

Reeve sniffed. The smell of his own smoky undershirt and boxers wafting up through the donation clothes Nguyen had provided him to cover his near-nakedness mingled with the incense Father Nguyen was shaking as he walked, and it combined to make a smell that wasn't unlike the sandalwood shit that Donna used to burn to make the house smell better.

Oh, Donna.

Reeve sat there in the chair, the pad on the seat long ago having lost its battle to keep his ass from touching the metal beneath. Sure, there was still cloth between them, but that pad had fought valiantly to hold him an inch up and failed completely. His tailbone was just about directly on the metal, and it hurt. His legs ached, and his ass was numb. His thoughts were chugging slowly, too, reminding him of one of those motion-activated sprinklers that would spritz like crazy when a duck walked in front of it. In his case it was like he was sleeping when the thoughts weren't spritzing out in quick sprays, then settling back to nothing but congealed brain drippings.

He was trying not to think of Donna but was failing. He couldn't even help it, his cheeks were sticky and had that dried-out feeling. He hadn't made a sound, but sure enough, for about the second time in his adult life, he'd wept, big ol' tears running down his face as he sat watching the door for trouble. He'd zoned out for long stretches, and then come back to it, alternating between trying desperately to hold it all in and all that feeling just bursting out and dripping down his face.

"You should sleep like the others," Father Nguyen said, the chain on the incense burner squeaking as he stepped in front of Reeve. This had to be his thousandth orbit of the church. He'd been going tirelessly since last night, whenever it was that they'd all gotten back together here.

"Don't want to leave the door unguarded," Reeve said with an inescapable yawn. He reached a hand up to cover his mouth and smelled nothing but the scent of fire. He jerked his hand away quickly, but not quickly enough.

"The church is now a sanctorum," Nguyen said with a yawn of his own that he didn't even bother to cover. He was busy holding the incense burner in one hand and a book in the other in any case. "They couldn't do anything here if they wanted to now."

"You'll forgive me the irony if I don't put my entire faith in that," Reeve said dryly. He was surprised he could be that clever at this moment. He figured any sense or wit had left him a long-ass time ago, somewhere in the night, or maybe during the fire that took everything else.

"There are other people we could call," Nguyen said, "to watch the door." He looked at Reeve carefully, like he was aware that his attention was flagging due to fatigue. "Mr. McInness, Chauncey Watson, Ms. Cherry—why, even Pastor Jones from the Methodist Church."

"I like how you put the Methodist after the madam in your list."

Nguyen smiled faintly. "There's help if we but ask."

Reeve didn't smile. "I feel like we'd be dragging these people into a fight they don't deserve to be dragged into." He straightened up in his chair, adjusting in the seat so a different part of his ass could go numb. "There's being in a fight, and then there's …" He just shook his head. "I don't know what you'd call this. A massacre, maybe."

"I can't begin to imagine what you're going through," Nguyen said, "and I doubt my words or prayers would bring you much comfort at this point. But … what's going on in this town affects us all. Ms. Cherry, Pastor Jones—"

"Seriously, hookers before Protestants? That's really how you see the world?"

"—Mr. McInness, and Mr. Watson … they live here. They're part of the town, the only part that believes you, it would seem." Nguyen smiled, adjusting his collar. "Believes us. This is a community, and has been for as long as I've been here, which admittedly is less time than the rest of you. Being part of a greater whole means that … sometimes you have to put aside pride or fear and ask for help when you can't do it alone."

"I guess I hope we can do this alone," Reeve said. "This one thing, dealing with this Legion. I hope we can deal with it on our own, because … I mean, these other demons, they've come to destroy the town, and invade and pillage and wreck … but they've never made it personal, as I understand it. Not that cow thing, not the guy who wanted to flood the town, not the Ferris wheel guy or the Rog'tausch.

They just wrecked shit—errr, stuff. This Legion, though ..." Reeve sighed, shaking his head. "He just wants to hit us right where it hurts. Hit us all where it hurts. Pulling in other people right now? Feels like we'd be pulling them into this blood feud with us. And all they'd get is theirs shed."

"Perhaps you're seeing it wrong," Nguyen said pensively, his eyes moving slowly over the church. "Sometimes ... people who care want to get involved in your problems. They want to help. And at the very least, they might wish to be forewarned in case this ... this thing broadens the scope of its attacks. Innocent townspeople are already being caught in the middle."

"You might be on to something there," Reeve said, rubbing his eyes and adjusting in his seat again. "On the other hand, it wouldn't be too hard for that Legion bastard—errr ..." He blushed, looking at Nguyen apologetically, "... to take what Erin knows about the people who supported us at the meeting the other night and just preemptively possess them."

"You're facing demons, sheriff," Nguyen said, putting a hand on his shoulder. It was small, but strong, and he shook Reeve gently. "And not only demons, but demons who specifically take over bodies. They are uniquely positioned to sow distrust, to divide us from one another. And yet if we fail to trust, it is entirely possible that divide us they will, destroy us, and then ... what happens to Midian when the next threat comes along? Because as you say, it seems personal with this Legion, rather than them just destroying the town as a means to an end. But with us out of the way ...?" The priest shrugged his small shoulders. "Who else will stand between the town and the next threat? Because I'm guessing Mr. Pike won't."

"Maybe that's why we should keep Barney Jones and the rest of them in reserve," Reeve said. He knew there was wisdom in what Father Nguyen was saying, but it was like the priest was his corner man, telling him to lean into the next punch coming his way. Maybe that was the way to do it, to try and score a hit, but he'd be damned if he could get over the sense of a man who'd taken one of those punches before and had it floor him." He bowed his head. "I'll think on it."

"You do that," Nguyen said, standing up, his incense burner rattling as he lifted it. "I'm going to go sleep for a while if it's all right with you."

"Yeah, I'm tired but I'm not ready to lay down, if you know what I mean." Reeve glanced back at Dr. Darlington, eyes closed, her pretty face frowning in her sleep. There were no sweet dreams going on there. "I'll keep watch on the door."

"Sleep if you need to," Nguyen said, dragging away, the man's energy clearly spent walking the last however many hours. "This place is safe now."

"I'm not sure anywhere is safe from this motherfucker," Reeve said, but he said it so quiet he knew the priest couldn't hear him. He felt guilty about swearing in the church anyway, though.

*

Amanda Guthrie was still not used to the name but didn't give it a lot of worry. She had other things to worry about, after all, what with Duncan avoiding the hell out of her as they paced around the perimeter of the Red Cedar hospital, trying to look incognito while they were prowling. Security hadn't come out to ask them shit yet, not that it would matter if they did. Duncan and Guthrie both had badges that would leave them with the strong impression that they were federal agents on a case, which would clear the road enough for their purposes. The fact that no one had asked and they'd been out here wandering for hours suggested to Guthrie that security here was not much of a thing.

She caught a glimpse of Duncan as she came around a corner, the sunlight gleaming off the hospital walls. They were kind of a whitish, rocky brick of the old school, and the place had a distinctly gothic feel to Guthrie, like an old train station or city hall. She'd been inside, briefly, and it was all modern in there, like they'd done a renovation at some point, but the exterior still looked like an old hospital ripped right out of Victorian England or something.

The sun was shining down on Guthrie's shell, clearly trying to cut down on the morning's natural chill. She was keeping her eyes peeled basically for people who looked like they were keeping their eyes peeled for her. It wasn't as though she could detect these Legion fucks, after all, so her method of detection was limited to the visual, watching out for people who weren't walking around like most humans, heads so far up their asses they were experiencing partial digestion of the face.

So far, it was mostly people blissfully unaware of anything outside of their own existence or their cell phone screens.

She had seen Duncan, though, just before he turned another corner. He gave her a look back first, like he had the last few times she caught sight of him. Then he burned off again, hurrying to keep away. He'd never been much of a conversationalist to begin with, it seemed their recent tension was making him even less willing to listen to Guthrie's occasional lecture. It wasn't exactly fine with her, but after spending a few months in fire, she could imagine a lot worse fates.

She walked past the hospital dumpsters again, catching a faint whiff of what was waiting in there. She ignored it. She could do that, because her senses, while much better than a human's or even her last shell's, did not interpret the smell of garbage with an automatic revulsion reflex. Nor did she feel said reflex on much of anything, really. Even less than before, when she'd been Lerner. It would probably come in handy.

She came around another corner and there went Duncan, around the next, hoofing it to stay well ahead of her and any conversation they might have. That was probably for the best, too, though he didn't know it. Guthrie didn't want to explain everything to him. Not yet, anyway.

*

Hendricks woke up in a chair to hear Alison let out a choked sob. He blinked the sleepy crust out of his eyes and saw her standing in front of a doctor, she and her mother and Arch all lined up in a row, having a hushed conversation. He focused in on them and held his quiet, not wanting to intrude on this family moment, but pretty damned curious about what was going on with Bill.

"We really just need to wait for him to wake up now before we can make a full prognosis," the doctor said. It was a woman in her forties, easily, still wearing a mint green surgical cap. She had glasses on, and her mask was hanging off of one ear like she'd just gotten out of the operating room and couldn't be bothered to take it off. She had to have changed some, though, didn't she? Because she wasn't wearing a plastic surgical gown, just scrubs.

"But he's still alive?" Addy Longholt asked, her hands hovering around her mouth like she wanted to bite her fingernails. Hendricks had seen her fingernails and doubted they'd been within a mile of her mouth since she grew to adulthood. She looked like she was ready to stick one in now and have a good chew, though.

"He's alive," the doctor said, "and he's stable. But I have to warn you …" she got grim, "… the amount of brain tissue that was lost in the gunshot … there's almost certain to be impairment to his cognitive functions in some way or another." Her mouth turned into a thin line as she paused before dropping the big bomb. "He may never be the same again."

Hendricks could tell from where he was sitting that Arch was getting it all and processing it a lot more impartially than Alison or Addy, but he was also keeping his mouth shut and letting them work to it. The big man was just wearing a frown.

"Never be the same again how?" Alison asked. She was a smart cookie, and she was clearly still thinking, even after the incredible lack of sleep and all else. "Will he ever walk again?"

"It's impossible to say right now." The doctor just gave them a half shrug. "We'll know more when he wakes up."

"Will he be able to talk?" Alison asked, plunging on ahead. "Will he—"

"We just don't know for sure," the doctor said, and Hendricks thought he smelled bullshit couched in polite terms. They had to know where the bullet went through, didn't they? Wouldn't that tell them what Bill would be able to do when he woke up? "We'll need to assess when he's awake." The lady doctor started to withdraw, Hendricks could see her desire to pull away, to keep from fielding any more questions she wasn't ready to answer. "Hopefully we'll find out more later today."

"Thank you, Doctor," Arch said, closing the conversation for her and putting a hand on his wife's shoulder, presumably to keep her from following the lady down the hall and bombarding her with questions until she vanished behind those big double doors in the distance. Hendricks watched her retreat. It was a thing of elegance, he decided, dignified and practiced, like she'd done it a bunch of times before and would be prepared if someone followed her like a puppy.

"It's gonna be all right," Arch said, taking his wife into his arms.

Alison looked stunned more than anything, Hendricks decided, her eyes off in the distance as she came around in Arch's embrace. She looked right at him and he didn't close his eyes quite fast enough.

"You hear all that?" she asked quietly when they made eye contact. She didn't sound accusatory, but Hendricks cringed inside anyway.

"Most of it," Hendricks said, feeling like he'd gotten caught beating off.

"She seem like she was lying to you?" Alison asked.

"Being cautious, more like," Hendricks said, as Arch raised an eyebrow. "I get the feeling she doesn't want to get your hopes up or crush them, just wants to let things take their course and see how your dad's doing when he wakes up."

That seemed to satisfy her, and Arch let out a breath of relief. Hendricks could read that sudden comfort in the thought that maybe his wife wouldn't be crawling the walls, overthinking everything. He remembered that feeling vaguely from being married himself.

"No word from Duncan or L—Guthrie?" Alison asked, pulling off Arch slowly.

"I've heard the same thing you have," Hendricks said, yawning. "Maybe less." He looked around the small waiting area. "I suppose I could go look for them, see if I can get an update."

"Or we could just call them," Arch said, relentlessly practical and clearly an enemy of exercise.

"I should go check on Brian," Addy said, her face softening. "He's due to be released sometime later today, figure he'll want to come up here."

"Great," Alison said with a complete lack of enthusiasm.

"Don't be like that," Addy said, gathering her soft sweater about her shoulders. "He didn't have anything to do with this and you know it, Ali." She turned and headed for the elevators.

Alison stuck out of her tongue after her mother in a fine display of five-year-old maturity. Hendricks snorted loudly, but Addy Longholt did not hear before she disappeared around the corner. "That's great," he said, in all sincerity. "Prize winning wit, there."

"Sometimes there just ain't nothing else to say." Alison rested her hands on her hips, frowning. "Why hasn't this Legion made their move on us yet? We're sitting ducks here."

"Hmm," Hendricks said. "Might be they're capturing fresh

manpower. Last attack could have left them thin."

"Or maybe they went after the church after all," Alison said. She had a fierce gaze, showing no sign of fatigue. Hendricks did not feel the same.

"I suppose I could go check on the rest of the crew back at St. Brigid's," Hendricks said, yawning again.

"Or just call them," Arch said again, like he was ready to throw his hands up in the air.

"That's what I meant," Hendricks said with a good-natured grin. "I'm not driving all the way back to the middle of nowhere right now." He held up a hand to stifle another yawn. "I'd be a road hazard."

"As opposed to the ordinary kind you are the rest of the time," Alison said. She didn't smile this time, though, as Hendricks took Arch's proffered cell phone and made to head outside, away from the signs that proclaimed, "NO CELL PHONES," presumably because they made the waiting area an inhospitable environment or some such. Hendricks just didn't understand that; it felt to him like if you were waiting for bad news, listening to some obnoxious jackass having a conversation in public might be a good distraction ... But then again, it wasn't like anything would have distracted him when he'd had one of these tragedies himself.

*

Braeden Tarley was not having the best of days. He was up to knuckles in grease again, and he'd had to wash his hands so many times already this morning that the Zep TKO dispenser was running low. Seemed like every five minutes Abi had some urgent need for him in the office. He didn't let her step a single toe into the shop for safety reasons, so naturally he was obliged every single time she had an urgent "Daddy, I need you!" moment, to stop, wash his hands, dry them off, come inside, and try to ignore that his skin was raw and white with dryness even though that was typically a winter problem, not an autumn one.

"Daddy!" Abi called again, pretty singsong. She was getting used to making that her clarion call, and Tracy wasn't doing much to stop her. Tracy was a shit babysitter, and if Braeden hadn't been paying her ten bucks an hour already, he might have cut her pay. There was definitely not going to be a raise this year, especially if he couldn't get some engines serviced and fixed. He'd almost have wanted Haskins or Tucker to take over, but Tucker had the day off and Haskins had run to Chattanooga for parts. Which was a shame, because Abi loved both of them to pieces.

"Baby doll," Braeden called, glancing back to make sure she was hovering at the entry to the garage and hadn't crossed that line out of the office. If she had, he'd be obliged to shoo her back, forcing him to halt his work again and putting him even further behind. "Daddy's gotta work, sweetie."

"But Daddy," she said, and by her tone he knew that whatever she had for him, it was clearly the most important thing in the universe right this minute, "I need to tell you something."

Braeden had heard this particular song before. The last thing she'd needed to tell him was a pretty long-winded explanation about how she'd drawn a caterpillar while Tracy watched and answered the phones, nodding along with insufficient enthusiasm. This Braeden couldn't fault her for; there was only so long he could handle these moments of inane babble before he tuned out, too, no matter how hard he pinched himself trying to pay attention. "I'm sure you do," Braeden said, "but it's gonna have to wait an hour until lunch." He worked the wrench, then realized he had lost focus and was turning it the wrong way. "Goddammit," he said under his breath, barely keeping it from sailing out at full volume.

"But Daddyyyyy!" The sound of a four year-old with utter disbelief echoed in the garage. He glanced back again to make sure she hadn't crossed into the garage. "That's so long!" She had her little mouth slightly open and was playing with one of her pigtails that he'd styled for her before they left the house. He'd packed them both lunches, peanut butter and jelly for her, bologna and mayo and mustard for him, with some chips and dill pickle slices. She liked to take a bite of the pickle and then wrinkle her nose up at the sour taste. "That's forever."

"It's actually an hour," Braeden said, going literal on her. He didn't hold out a lot of hope it would persuade her, but then, her attention was flagging harder by the minute. He suspected she'd about run out of things to do in the office, and he was starting to lose faith in

Tracy's watchful eye, damn her. It wasn't like the phone was ringing off the hook or they had scads of paperwork that needed doing.

Abi stomped away, and Braeden chortled to himself very quietly at the sound. Hell had no fury like the pouting of a four-year-old. He couldn't even help himself sometimes, because she looked so darned cute when she got mad. She was the miniature version of Jennifer.

"Well, hello there," came a drawling voice from just outside the garage door. Braeden looked around the truck to see County Administrator Pike smiling, silhouetted in the bright sunlight from outside.

"Got another petition for me to sign?" Braeden asked, peering into the sunny day.

"Nah, no petition this time," Pike said, grinning as he stepped into the garage. "Some good news, though. We got enough signatures to start the recall process, and I got a judge to issue a temporary restraining order that pulled Sheriff Reeve right out of office until the election decides things." He sidled on up, walking along the side of the red diesel truck that Braeden was working on. "I reckon it's not gonna be pretty, but for now Ed Fries is sheriff, and he's working real hard on restoring order, getting things back to normal. Which is the reason I came here to talk with you."

"Oh, yeah?" Braeden stopped and set aside his wrench.

"I expect you've probably noticed it's Halloween." Pike ran a hand along the dusty cab of the truck, pulling it up to look at his palm. He didn't evince any sign of distaste at the fact he'd been dirtied, just a quick shrug as he brushed it off on his jeans.

"That hasn't escaped my notice, no." Braeden waited for him to come around to the point. The fact Reeve had actually been yanked out of office didn't make Braeden feel any safer, strangely. He figured he'd have been ecstatic about it, but he was definitely muted. If it paved the way for this crime wave to end, though, he was all for it.

"I know people are pretty tentative right now," Pike said, his grin fading away like it had never been there. "Hell, I don't blame 'em. But if we're gonna start rebuilding Midian, making people feel safe again, we need to come together. Really draw a line against the darkness. So …" He pulled out a piece of paper from his back pocket, smudging it with his dirty hand. "I'm circulating these around, trying to drum up support of a different kind than I was yesterday. Yesterday was about pulling out the infection. This is about stitching up the wound and letting the healing begin."

Braeden peered at the page in Pike's hand. He couldn't see it terribly well until the Administrator took another few steps closer, and then he saw emblazoned across the top, "Midian Halloween Party—Bring your kids to a safe trick or treat experience!" It had a little pumpkin graphic right in the middle of the flyer. "The hell?" Braeden muttered.

"I figured trick or treat this year couldn't run like it has in years past," Pike said, now starting to smile a little more, sort of warmly. "People are scared. The idea of putting their kids at risk is a bridge too far for most of us. But let's face, all this shit that's happened, it's all been in the shadows. Well, I figure we put this front and center, hold it out on the town square, make sure all our adults are there, the new sheriff's gonna be there, we all turn out in force. Make a stand. Show up as a community, shine our light kinda thing."

Braeden stared at the paper, feeling a little churning in his stomach. Pike was right; all the bad shit happening in Midian seemed to be going on in the shadows, in the quiet. People getting run over in the streets while no one else was around, people getting murdered in their homes in the dead of the night when no one heard it. Hell, even that mess where the east side of town got torn up, no one seemed to have seen exactly what was happening.

"In a time like this," Pike said, real quiet and solemn, "our kids need to feel ... comforted ... by the routine little things we take for granted, you know? We all know what's been going on, and hell, most of us adults are scared. It's natural for that to trickle right on down, until everyone from young to old is petrified. But these people doing this shit to Midian ... they're just hiding. They ain't got the balls to come out and show their faces, which is why Reeve could say it was demons, or boogeymen, or the monster under the bed, because no one could argue it. But if we all show up, and we do this, and we make our stand and link arms, give our kids a sense of feeling safe, of the normal routine of life going on again ..." He shrugged. "Well, I reckon it might be a good turning point, a chance to unite us all again on the same goal—bringing Midian back from the scary-ass brink."

Braeden looked around. The thought of doing something as touchy feely as this might not have appealed to the younger him, but damn if it didn't sound good to the man who dreaded telling Abi that trick or treating wasn't going to happen. Everything Pike said was true, and if they could get fifty or a hundred people all together in the town square to hold hands and sing "Kumbayah," well, that wasn't exactly Braeden's scene, but he'd do it if it meant Abi could get a little candy and he could feel a little normal in his hometown again.

"So, whaddya say?" Pike asked, his Yankee accent bleeding through. He was back to grinning, but it wasn't a cocky sort of grin, more like one trying to corral Braeden into making the right choice.

"Hell, we'll be there," Braeden said. "With bells on." And a .38 snubby he kept in the top of his closet, too, but he didn't need to share that part, even if it made him feel a hell of a lot better. This was Tennessee, after all, and he doubted he'd be the only parent to show up armed to this shindig.

"Damned good," Pike said, nodding his head. "I think we'll have a real good turnout for this." He sauntered over to the toolbox where Braeden had set his wrench, opened a drawer, sliding the flyer in and then shutting it so it wouldn't blow away in a breeze. "We'll look forward to seeing you then. What's your daughter coming dressed as?"

"She's a princess," Braeden said, and he couldn't help but smile a little, too. Now he wouldn't have to watch Abi's face fall, or deal with the tantrum from missing trick or treating. And he could feel good about it in the process. That was all win to him.

"Aren't they all?" Pike asked with a wide grin, as he started to head for the exit. "We'll see you tonight."

*

Lauren woke up staring at the wooden beams of a church, her back aching, and for a moment she wondered where she was, and then where Molly was. The answers to both questions came back to her a second later and she wished they hadn't. The old smell of the church had settled over her, the stink of hymnal and Bible pages with their oniony thin paper a poor substitute for the scent of baking biscuits as her mother cooked breakfast.

Then she remembered what happened to her mother, and the appeal of breakfast in any form fled just as quickly.

Lauren sat up, got the head rush from doing it too fast, and held her skull as she steeped in the shit that had happened in the last twenty-four hours. How the hell could everything have gone bad so quickly?

She heard quiet voices behind her and turned her head, trying her best to ignore her cobbled-together clothing. There was bright sunlight streaming in from the stained glass windows, including the broken one, but it looked to her like the sun itself was way, way overhead by now, and it was chilly enough in the church that she shivered, and probably not from her memories.

She looked toward the narthex to see Father Nguyen standing there, looking a little disheveled, Sheriff Reeve sprawled out on a folding chair, his neck cricked back and his mouth open, gentle snores coming out of his mouth every few seconds. It wasn't loud, more of a quiet gurgling that told her he was alive even though he was in a position that seemed utterly impossible for sleeping. He was also wearing the most ridiculous attire, old man clothes with corduroys and a cross-striped shirt. The only thing missing was suspenders to complete the getup.

"Finally, the princess awakens," came that hard British accent as the demon hunter, Lonsdale, sat down in the pew in front of her.

"God, I hope you're calling yourself the princess and not me," Lauren said, massaging her neck. Just looking at Reeve made hers hurt all the worse.

Lonsdale's eyebrows soared and he made an O with his mouth in amusement. "Feisty, too, aren't you?"

She gave him the stupid look so she didn't have to say anything. It felt better than mincing words with this moron. "You're bored, aren't you?"

"Well, everything seems a bit of comedown after having your brain possessed by demons twice in one day," Lonsdale said.

Lauren stared at him for only a beat before turning back around to look at Father Nguyen. He was talking to someone it took her a second to recognize, but when she did, Lauren came to her feet and found herself carried over to the front door, watching the conversation happening in the narthex with rapidly growing astonishment.

"I'll just sit here alone, then," Lonsdale called after her. "Maybe find something to entertain myself with. Do some drawing on the back of these offertory envelopes, perhaps."

Lauren didn't respond. She passed Reeve and brushed him, stirring the sheriff out of sleep with a gasp and a groan as he apparently realized he was in pain. The folding chair squeaked under him as he readjusted himself, his moan and that of the metal reaching some sort of harmony. "What the …?"

She nudged him and pointed at the conversation going on not ten feet away, not daring to speak yet. She was still a little stunned at what she was seeing.

Melina Cherry was talking quietly with Father Nguyen, their heads close together, the priest listening to something she was saying just above a whisper, and nodding along as she spoke.

"Well, this explains why he favors her above Protestants," Reeve said, getting out of his chair. His entire body sounded like it was crackling as he did it, popping with enough volume that Lauren looked at him in involuntary alarm even though she knew full well that it was just air leaving his joints. "Sorry," he said.

"Oh, hello," Father Nguyen said, either tipped off they were watching by the loudness of their conversation or Reeve's joints, she couldn't be sure which. "Melina here was just telling me the scuttlebutt around town."

"Never would have figured you for the gossiping type," Lauren said.

Nguyen reddened slightly. "I hear all manner of things in the confessional, but this is, perhaps, a bit different." He indicated the madam with a wave of his hand. "In this case, Melina came to tell me about what's being said around town regarding the sheriff's house burning down and your, uh …" He looked right at Lauren. "Well, the incident at your home."

Lauren's stomach did the plunge from the top of the Empire State Building, no elevator. Of course they were gossiping about it in Midian. Why wouldn't they be? "What are they saying?"

Melina Cherry apparently decided to speak for herself. "Well, the sheriff," she directed a muted smile toward Reeve, "is probably under investigation, but who can say? The deputy in charge now—"

"Ed Fries," Reeve said, interjecting that without much in the way of feeling.

Melina Cherry rolled her eyes and made a scornful noise. "A preposterous man. Everyone seems to think you are under investigation for the murder of your wife and for your house burning down."

Reeve looked about half-stunned, in Lauren's estimation, like maybe he'd seen this coming but couldn't fully dodge or digest it. "That about figures," was all he said, and he looked chalky white.

"No one seems to know what happened at your house," Melina Cherry said, and it surprised Lauren how much discretion the madam spoke with. It probably shouldn't have, since on a daily basis she dealt with matters Lauren wouldn't have felt comfortable broaching even in the context of a doctor/patient relationship. "Other than that Albert Daniel was shot on your lawn, and your neighbors tell some ... very confusing stories. At least they're confusing to those who don't believe in demons as an explanation."

"Well," Reeve said, still looking pretty grey, "demons are the only explanation that makes sense. Wish everyone else would just get on that page already."

"You can't blame them for not coming around so quickly," Melina Cherry said with an impressive amount of dignity. She was wearing a coat that wouldn't have looked out of place on any soccer mom in town, though her jeans were kinda tight and she was wearing some fabulous open-toed shoes that caught Lauren's eye for a second before she snapped back to the reality at hand. "You ask them to change their view of all reality in less than a week, darling. The thought of demons makes people feel ... out of control of their lives. Everyone's live are out of their control to a certain extent, but the illusion is what makes it bearable. You ask them to give all that illusion up, and of course they fight to keep it, like having a tug of war over sheets." She smiled, but there was a hollow look in her eyes that slipped out for a second. Lauren caught it and wondered if anyone else did.

"I don't blame 'em, but it's not doing us any favors having people think we're responsible for this shit," Reeve said, and he sounded like he'd been woken squarely in the middle of the nap, even though a minute ago he'd been a lot more energetic. "And now we're probably being thought of as murderers."

"The new sheriff has said nothing so far," Ms. Cherry said with a shrug. "No one has talked to him or seen him, so for all I know, he hasn't even visited the crime scenes. He could be fishing on the Caledonia for all we know."

"Doubtful," Reeve said, and when everyone looked right at him he said, "Ed's not much of a fisherman, really. But ... I need to talk to him."

Lauren gave him the same look she gave Lonsdale a few minutes earlier. "Are you nuts? What if he wants you to come in for 'questioning'?" She made air quotes to show what she thought of that idea.

"I need to at least try to square things with him." Reeve was still wearing his fatigue on his sleeve, but at least his color was getting a little better. "He's the law in this town now."

"He could be possessed by the Legion," Nguyen said.

"Yeah," Reeve said. "But if he's not ..."

"Then you'll just be going to jail where you'll be a sitting duck for the Legion to possess you and then turn you against us," Lauren said, and then she flashed a suspicious look at Melina Cherry. "Say ..."

Nguyen cleared his throat. "I checked her myself. With holy water."

"He sprinkled it on my face," Ms. Cherry said, looking sly. "It was much more pleasant that what usually gets—"

"Sorry I brought it up," Lauren said, and Ms. Cherry flashed her a smile coupled with a quick waggle of her eyebrows. "So ..." She turned back to Reeve.

"I need to at least talk to Ed," Reeve said. "Face to face, man to man. He's not a totally unreasonable guy, but he's probably ... not drinking the Kool-Aid, as they keep saying about us."

"I suspect I know where he'll be later," Ms. Cherry said, pulling a piece of paper out of her pocket and unfolding it. It crinkled as she did, and Lauren stared as she opened it to reveal some pumpkin clip art surrounded by words and text, a pretty typical flyer of the sort used to advertise just about everything. Ms. Cherry held it up. "See? The law will be in Midian tonight for certain, according to this."

"Well, that's good to know," Reeve said, taking it gingerly as he frowned at it.

Lauren stared at it as well. "A Halloween event? What the hell?"

"Like Duncan said, it'll be fine," Reeve said, staring down at the paper in his fingertips. "These demons don't want to shit in their sandbox, after all. They like conducting their business in the shadows a little too much to ring the dinner bell on this one." He blew air out from between his pale lips. "And this just might be the chance I need to talk to Ed, face to face." A ringtone trilled and Reeve looked down impatiently, pulling his phone out and then answered. "Hello?" He looked pretty serious as he listened for a second before replying to the question Lauren was sure she was wearing all over her face. "It's Hendricks."

*

Hendricks had the cell phone pressed to his ear. He still wasn't used to these things, feeling like the crabby old man who was telling kids to get the fuck off his lawn every time he looked at the little device and felt the scorn bubble up. To him it felt like a leash, a chain to keep him hooked to. He'd had one when he was younger, of course, but coming back after Iraq, he hadn't wanted the tie, preferring to just use a hotel phone when he needed to do a consulting call.

Was the cell phone supposed to be this hot? Didn't the batteries blow up on these things sometimes? These thoughts were all rolling through his head as he listened to Reeve say, "It's Hendricks," to someone in the background, like he couldn't fucking hear the man.

"Yeah, it's Hendricks," Hendricks agreed, subtly jabbing the sheriff and feeling a little bad for it afterward. "Listen … I just wanted to check in again."

"Mother hen," Reeve said. The sound was a lot better than Hendricks remembered from his old flip phone, which was the last one he'd had before giving up on that particular branch of modern technology. And most others, actually. "We're all still here. Ms. Cherry from, uh … well, maybe you haven't met her …"

"Oh, I've met her," Hendricks said quickly. "Real striking lady. Dark hair, beautiful eyes, rack like she's defying all attempts of gravity to bring her down, curves like the roads around Mount Horeb, and an ass that means she can probably charge whatever she wants for anal. Stone fucking cougar, and hotter than a stovetop left on high all day."

Reeve was silent for a long moment, then his voice crackled, kinda tinny. "So I guess you've met, then."

Someone let out a snort in the background, and Hendricks heard, faintly, a woman saying, "So sweet, darling."

"So, you, uh, put me on speakerphone," Hendricks said, blushing a little. "A heads up, maybe, next time?"

"Or you could just keep your observations on other people's asses to yourself," Reeve said a little stiffly, reminding Hendricks of every boss he'd ever hated. "Anyway, Ms. Cherry stopped by to give us the word on what's going on after ... yesterday."

Hendricks perked up to that one. "Oh, yeah? What's the word on the street about what happened to Bill?"

There was a pause, and Ms. Cherry's European accent came through a moment later. "I haven't heard much about that. Just the basics, that he was taken away in an ambulance. No one's talked to the family, so I suppose the rumor mill doesn't have as much to go on as it does for Sheriff Reeve or Dr. Darlington."

"Hrm," Hendricks said. "I guess that's something."

"Yeah," Reeve said sourly, "they can count their blessings that no one thinks Arch or Brian or Alison is a murderer. So that's good. How's Bill?"

"He still hasn't woken up yet," Hendricks said. This was the second time he'd checked in with Reeve, the first being earlier that morning. He'd been alternating between sitting and sleeping in the waiting room, which had seen decent amount of traffic throughout the day. Arch, Alison and Addy had been allowed into Bill's room, but Hendricks had stayed out, checking with Duncan every now and again and Brian even less frequently. He'd avoided the hell out of Guthrie, though.

"Is that good or bad?" Reeve asked.

Hendricks didn't know how to answer that one, and counted himself fortunate when Dr. Darlington did for him. "Probably not good," she said, her voice a little scratchy. "The longer it takes, the worse it generally is, unless they're keeping him in a medical coma."

"I don't think so," Hendricks said. "I think they want him to wake up so they can kinda see where he's at, cognit—err ... cognately? Cogn—errm ..."

"Cognitively," Dr. Darlington said. "Yeah. I don't know. I'm not a neurologist, but my guess is if he doesn't wake up in the next day or so, and they're not medically inducing a coma, it's going to be a really, really bad sign."

"The hits just keep coming," Reeve said with a sigh.

"Yeah, sounds like it's grim all fucking over," Hendricks said, and heard Father Nguyen make a clucking noise of disapproval.

"At least there's still Halloween," Ms. Cherry said, a little lightly.

Hendricks furrowed his brow. "Beg pardon?" *What the fuck?* was what he almost said.

"Pike's trying to reinvigorate confidence in the community or something by having a trick-or-treat in the town square," Reeve said, rolling right on through it with only mild disapproval. "Frankly, I can think of worse ideas."

Hendricks just shrugged. "I guess." It was a fair point; demons who preyed on people looked for weak and isolated ones, or families they could overpower in a blitz attack. They damned sure didn't go charging into town events looking for trouble, because that was fucking suicide, even for demons. People got pretty particular about their kids, after all. "So ... basically nothing else to report, then?"

"Not much has changed, no," Reeve said. "We're just turtled up here. Might stick our heads out later for a peek around."

"Make sure you look out the window first," Hendricks said, and Reeve grunted in reply. "I'll call you in a couple hours, or earlier if the Legion makes their play here."

"All right then," Reeve said, and the beeps from the sound of hang-up rang in Hendricks's ears as he headed back into the hospital doors, leaving the cool, crisp fall day behind him.

It had been damned beautiful, he'd give it that. Warm, even, thanks to a strong showing by the sun and an absence of clouds. It wasn't anything like the Halloweens he was used to in Wisconsin, that was for sure. There were plenty of those nights where he remembered his mom heating up apple cider on the stove so that he'd have it ready when he came in from trick or treating with his dad. Here, they might need that after the sun went down for a while, but it wasn't anything like Amery, Wisconsin.

He got in the elevator and rode it up to the second floor, waited 'til he heard the ding and stepped out past a couple nurses in pink scrubs. He wasn't too proud to take a look, though one of them had blonde hair so close to platinum that it made him shudder and take a step away from her. Putting that out of his mind, hand shaking a little unintentionally, he headed down the hall and knocked, that hand still shaking as it rattled at the door. "Room service," he said in a falsetto, his voice cracking a little unintentionally as he tried to hit the high pitch.

"Hey," Brian Longholt called, sounding about as weary as the egghead looked when Hendricks came in. He didn't seem to have taken this whole experience well. Not that there was an easy way to take being possessed by a demon and shooting your father in the head, Hendricks supposed.

"How are you feeling?" Hendricks asked, mostly perfunctory so he could tell Addy when she asked. If he saw her before she came down here; she was developing a pattern of orbiting back and forth between Brian's room and Bill's.

"Like shit," Brian said and plainly felt it. "And they're taking for goddamned-ever to discharge me."

Hendricks held on to the joke stemming off the phrase "discharge me," because it was a pretty nasty one involving Brian's dad. If his dad hadn't been in critical condition, Hendricks would have sprung it for certain. But even he would have found the timing tasteless on this one. Instead he sighed, wistful at the loss of a chance to poke at this self-important prick. "Yeah, hospitals are like that," he said instead.

"Any word from upstairs?" Brian asked, getting serious again.

"Nothing's changed," Hendricks said, "at least not as of fifteen minutes ago when I saw Arch."

"Hm," Brian said, going back to glum. Not that he'd had a lot of hope pop out, but Hendricks had seen a little just now. "Anything else going on?" There it was, fainter this time.

"Just talked to Reeve," Hendricks said matter-of-factly. "He and Darlington might be seeing some trouble with the law over what happened. Sounds like you're in the clear, though."

"Yay," Brian said without enthusiasm. "How'd he hear that?"

"Ms. Cherry stopped by St. Brigid's," Hendricks said, smirking slightly. He couldn't help himself.

"Wow," Brian said mildly.

"I know," Hendricks said. He found the image of a madam in a church pretty damned hilarious, too.

Brian got all serious and pensive for a few seconds, then he came out with something that burned Hendricks's ass, of course, because the pencilneck couldn't keep from doing that for more than thirty seconds. "My town is so fucked up. All small towns are, really, but mine, in particular, seems to be the worst for that kind of ... I don't know, hate or something."

Hendricks rolled his eyes. "There's a hooker in a church, man. Just take it in the humorous spirit and move on, don't use it as a chance to kick the ball toward the goal on your 'Midian sucks' agenda, okay? For fuck's sake, if you hate the place, don't fight demons for it, all right?" He stared Brian down, and the dumbass meekly looked away. Hendricks suspected he might not have done that a couple days ago, but now here he was, folding without a look at his cards.

Now Hendricks felt bad again. How many people was he going to pistol whip while they were down, anyway? He sighed lightly, feeling the vitriol flow out of him. "You know what else they're doing?" He asked, his version of a peace offering.

Brian took hold of it real tentatively. "What?"

"Some Halloween trick-or-treat thing on the square," Hendricks said, almost chuckling. "Sounds like a real hold-hands-and-sing type circle jerk."

"Huh," Brian said, frowning. "Isn't that ... I mean, I know we talked about it and Duncan was all, 'Halloween is safe', but ... is that smart?"

Hendricks shrugged. "It's probably fine. Demons go after the basket of eggs no one is watching. The people hiding in their houses are probably in more peril than the ones going to this display of chutzpah. The last cop in Midian is probably gonna be there, after all, and if not, you've still got a bunch of young twenty- and thirty-something parents, some of whom are bound to be armed."

"I guess," Brian said, clearly expressing his skepticism. "I just don't get it, though. Why not just hide until it's over? Or leave?"

"What's the point of living if you hide in your house all the time?" Hendricks asked with a shrug. "And keep in mind, I just asked you roughly the same question, yet here you are."

"It's not the first time I've been asked," Brian said, shifting uncomfortably in his bed.

"Oh?" Hendricks tried to sound interested, but probably failed. "What was your answer last time?"

Brian looked like he was thinking pretty hard about it. "I don't know," he finally conceded. "After everything that's happened now ... I feel like I'm less sure of what I'm doing than ever before."

Chester had found the farm and its sprawling view of hills reassuring when first he'd arrived. But a day of lingering about had left him cold on the whole concept. In truth, it was the same problem as he'd had before; in spite of their triumphs, William was still gone, and Chester was still alone at the top of a dwindling mass of angry essences. They'd lost quite a few now, and of course countless others were spread around the new bodies.

As a result, the voices within Chester's body felt more muted, quiet and lonely than he could ever recall. The discussion had been tabled, all controversy and argument set aside for the time being. They were of one mind, one purpose, and the recent victories over this watch had left them galvanized, their losses serving as a bitter, ash-tasting reminder that they were in a war, and for all the casualties they'd taken, the pain they'd dealt in return was sizable.

Not nearly enough, though. Not for the loss of William.

Not yet.

Chester stood upon the back porch, watching the day's light fading away bit by bit, sinking below the horizon. He could see Mount Horeb in the distance, its heights shaded by the coming sunset. It was beautiful, really, the sort of thing William would have loved.

But William would never see it, and to Chester, that was like a gloom that would never end, like a night had fallen upon him of which there would be no dawn.

"The time draws near," Melba said from her new body, the one named Molly Darlington. Melba always had a taste for the overdramatic.

"We're almost ready," Kelly said, having taken control of the deputy called Erin Harris. "We have ... so many at hand, ready to do this thing."

Chester nodded solemnly. He tried to remember when this all had begun, this inescapable cycle toward destiny, and kept coming back to the cave, to the day when he and William had surged out of the broken vase and taken control of this body for the first time. He hadn't wanted to come out, not at all, and even now, a part of him and his brethren clung to that idea. But William had forced the issue, had forced the move to Tennessee, and he had the majority on his side and so they had come.

But as Chester stared out across the green fields, he thought back to that moment when the first demon hunter had confronted them in the cave, right after they'd come out. "Let it be merciful," he'd said. He'd felt bad for these people, had felt empathy for them, in their pitiful desperation, their disconnection from each other.

He didn't feel bad anymore.

Now he was going to make them feel bad. Now he was going to make them suffer the way he'd suffered. Their disconnection mattered not at all to him, for he saw that they were bound—primitively, to be certain, but there was a tenuous web between each of them to the others.

And soon they would feel it, this community. Pain, grief, rage—all the things he felt, he would spread from his flock to theirs. And then they would see how it felt. All of them.

*

Brian lay in his hospital bed after Hendricks had left, twirling the rough sheets between his fingers. Hospital linens weren't exactly his mother's Egyptian cotton, and he noticed the difference, though he didn't have anyone to remark to about it. He suspected there would be an even more dramatic difference between hospital linens and prison linens, and he hoped to hell Hendricks was right and that he never had the chance to confirm that suspicion firsthand.

The guilt was racking him, and the pain in his leg wasn't enough to keep it at bay. Not that he wanted to keep his guilt at bay, but his mind was busy going in a lot of different directions. Without weed to help, he felt pretty much like he was caught in a spinning rip current, just going around and around. Then again, if the weed had been the wrong kind, it probably just would have hit him with the paranoia, and that wouldn't have helped at all.

"What the hell do I even do?" Brian asked himself. Why did he get involved in this? Why did he get in the back of his dad's truck in the first place, setting this whole stupid fucking chain of events into play? Boredom? Immature desire to be an asshole to his parents? Smug superiority?

"Yeah, a superior intellect is really taking me far," Brian muttered, half-tempted to click the button to turn the TV on. His painkillers were fading and TV was almost the next best thing. After giving it a moment's thought, he passed. He didn't deserve to have his pain killed, anyway.

"Why did you ever think you could help?" Brian said to himself again, whispering. There were the rocks and shoals of self-pity that he'd been smashing himself up on all day. What fun.

Maybe he'd been a dilettante coming into this, just looking for something to cut the boredom while he was in Midian.

Maybe it had been better than trying to convince himself that he was an unseen diamond, glittering in the quiet dark here.

Maybe it had just been a convenient distraction to take his eyes off his own flaws. Whatever the case ...

"Nowhere to run," Brian said, into the quiet hospital room, the sound of machines beeping out in the corridor, the hum of the lights. "Nowhere to hide from ..." He didn't say it out loud, but he was thinking it: *From what a worthless shit you are.*

He hadn't been able to do one damned thing to help this watch. Not one. The ad thing? Probably wasn't even him. Even if it was, he'd shot his own father when possessed by a demon, which subtracted his gain back to zero sum. He was lower than low; he was a skidmark on the underpants of humanity. He couldn't wield a sword, and he'd never shot a gun effectively until demons had seized his body and put it under their command. Now he was just sitting here, waiting for demons to come and do God-knew-what to—

Brian frowned, his scalp tingling. This Legion ... there was something wrong with the planning. They were a bunch of souls stacked into a body like a colony ship. They'd lost one of their own ... like a second ship getting blown up, and now the ones that were left were spreading all over the watch like a virus, and his own people were just trying to weather the storm.

Except this virus ... this storm ... it was a collective intelligence. Like Midian itself poured into a human body. Something about that got in Brian's head and spun a couple times. A collective ... a group ... an angry, angry group ... making war on the watch, specifically ...

"No, they're not," Brian said, still tingling. "They hit Dr. Darlington and she ..." Well, she was part of the watch, but not part of the watch that fucked with this Legion, at least not at first. So ... she was collateral damage? A message?

No ... she was part of the community of the watch, made war upon by the community of Legion ... and they weren't like the other demons that he'd seen, heard about, fought. They were on a suicide mission, a lot of them. They didn't even fucking care, did they?

But ... if they were willing to widen their war once, what if ...

"Oh, my God," Brian said, and his scalped stopped tingling and his whole body went cold as a frightening possibility came full bore into his mind, and he gave it chilling voice. "Halloween."

10.

Brian had no phone on him, his broken in the struggle after his father had been shot, and so he tried to leave his bed. He rested almost no weight on his leg and it folded underneath him, drawing screams of pain out of him as his voice echoed in the private room. The door was open, but he heard nothing outside, and after a few minutes of trying to get himself under control, he started crawling.

Searing agony came from the area behind his kneecap, pain beyond pain, wrapped in anguish. Brian gritted his teeth like he'd never done before. He was usually a creampuff in the face of pain, but there was something about the terror-inducing nature of his revelation that had him in a cold sweat before he'd even tried to get out of bed.

"You don't ... go after ... fucking kids," he said under his breath as he slow-crawled, using his good leg to push himself along.

His chest ached from the exertion after only a few feet, his pectorals burning. He was taking hard breaths, and realized that his cardio fitness was awful, especially as related to his upper body. He had his wounded knee crooked at an angle to try and keep it from getting hurt while he dragged himself along the smooth, white speckled tile floor. It smelled of disinfectant and rubber soles, or maybe that was just the rubberized trim.

He made it to the door on determination alone, and then stopped, gasping, his head peeking out into an empty hallway. Why couldn't he have had this revelation while Hendricks was with him? He could have told the cowboy, the cowboy could have spread the word, and they could have launched an immediate defense that would save the day.

Because in this case ... they had to save the day. That was what heroes did.

He took deep, sucking breaths, and looked in either direction. He needed help, dammit, but the hallway was empty. What was happening here? A brief spell of panic shook him and he held his breath. Was the Legion attacking the hospital now?

Brian tuned his ears, listening hard, and the normal, ordinary sounds of a quiet hospital reached him instantly. Somewhere in the distance a respirator was making that mechanical sucking sound as it breathed for some poor soul. The soft hum of the overhead lights was quietly buzzing, and in the distance he could hear a couple hushed voices talking in one of the rooms.

He was a half-second away from bellowing out loud when he spotted his salvation just ten feet from his very own door. It was like a gleaming, shiny, personal savior, or at least the closest thing to it Brian had ever believed in. Taking a last breath, he started his crawl again, heading right for it, knowing that this was going to be the thing that would help them win the day … because losing simply wasn't an option.

*

Braeden's day at work had gotten a little better after Pike's news. Abi had calmed down and even fallen asleep for a little while in a supply closet where they'd made her a little bed with blankets. She'd gone in crabby and come out two hours later all buzzing with new energy and a considerably better attitude. Braeden never ceased to be amazed at that transformation, because it was sincerely one of the coolest miracles a parent could hope for. Peace and quiet for a couple hours, and then, afterward, a happier, slightly more obedient kid. Because Abi still didn't exactly listen to every command.

Now she was buzzing around the house, because it was almost time to leave for the Halloween on the square. The longer he thought about it, the more Braeden had come around to the idea. Going out was perfect, especially since he only had designs on doing it for an hour or so and then they'd be on their way home.

"I want to eat all my candy tonight," Abi informed him, dancing around in her blue and purplish princess dress. Braeden couldn't remember if she was supposed to be Elsa from Frozen or Cinderella, he'd just picked the costume she wanted at Wal-Mart and rolled with it. It was a lot better option than the goddamned sexy nurse or witch costumes that seemed to be the only options for the older girls. While he might have embraced the results that lack of choice produced in his youth, now he looked at it with a wary eye and no small amount of concern.

"Two pieces," Braeden said, calling out as he headed back into his closet. He heard Abi bump around out in the living room and listened. She was jumping on the sofa cushions. Normally, he did not care for that, but he wasn't gonna call her out on it right now because he could hear her and knew she wasn't anywhere near him—which was what he needed.

"Ten pieces!" she shouted back, and he heard another couple bounces on the cushion. It always seemed to turn into a negotiation with her lately, and as much as he was bent around her little finger, these were the moments where they had friction.

"I said two," he called back, snaking a hand up into the top of his closet. He lifted an old comforter and moved it aside, feeling around carefully. He bumped his rifle and then his shotgun before he laid his hand on an old Lemon Squeezer .38 revolver. His daddy had given it to him before he'd moved to Montana, and he'd kept it in the top of his closet, unloaded. He felt around a little more and grabbed up the box of shells. "And I mean two."

The bouncing didn't cease, but it slowed for a second. "Five?" Abi countered.

"Still two," Braeden said, opening the cylinder and hurriedly starting to load it. He didn't keep the pistol loaded, but he did have rounds in the shotgun. He figured that was his best bet if someone broke in.

He almost had it done when she called out, more tentatively. "Three?"

"And we're still on two, but I'm leaning toward one," Braeden said as he clicked the cylinder shut. He looked over at the shelving to his side and opened one of the drawers. He had an old holster on top and put the .38 in it, then it stuck right behind his kidney on his belt. He pulled an old flannel off a hanger and put it on as he slid the comforter back down in the top of the closet.

"Okay, two," Abi said, scaring the shit out of him as she appeared at the door of his closet. He hadn't even noticed the couch had stopped squeaking, and he spun around to see her standing there, in her princess dress, hands nervously behind her. "Whatcha doing?"

"Dressing warmly," Braeden said, finishing up the last few buttons. "You have to wear your thick coat tonight in case it gets cold."

She made the pouty face, and it was adorable. "But Daddy, my princess dress." She made a sweeping gesture, up and down her, like that explained everything. "No one will be able to see it under my jacket."

Braeden gave her a wary eye. "Well, we're gonna bring it, then, in case you get cold. You carry your pumpkin for candy and I'll carry the coat, all right?"

She beamed. "Okay!" And then she flounced out of the room, apparently glad to have won something this round.

Braeden just sighed, and started toward the door to grab his coat. And they said these years were the easiest with girls. He was not looking forward to the teenage ones.

*

Alison felt like her eyelids were in a perpetual war with her, her tugging them up and gravity fighting to bring them back down, down to their natural state. Coffee hadn't helped, going to the bathroom and splashing water on her face hadn't helped, though it had left her with a wet sleeve and smeared makeup that she'd just cleaned off in resignation. Even pinching herself hadn't helped, and so she was just starting to settle into the idea that a nap could be in order when she got the bright idea to take a walk.

She and Arch and her mother were all arrayed around her daddy's room, the breathing machine hissing softly every few seconds, the beeping of his heartbeat monitor making a strange composition when those two doodads were combined together in concert. She found it strangely soothing, but then, in her current state of fatigue, she might have found a heavy metal symphony at full volume in her ear to be soothing.

Alison got up on unsteady feet. The soles of her feet ached like she'd just worked a double at Rogerson's. She would have given just about anything to have a soak in a warm bath, maybe drift off and drag herself to bed when she snapped awake again, but instead she started for the door and Arch sat up, looking a little dazed himself.

"Where you going?" he asked, brusque from fatigue, all his normal politeness sapped.

"Walk," she said, not even bothering to put the word into motion by adding the "—ing," to it.

"I'll come with you," he said and got up, much slower than usual. He stretched, soaring up nearly to the ceiling with those long arms of his. He adjusted himself left and right, doing a quick twist of his hips, then he followed her out.

Alison wasn't sure she would have noticed him there if she wasn't finding herself bumping into him every few steps. Whether it was her that was dazed and tired and unable to walk straight or him or some combo of both of them, it was happening, and as she shot him a faint smile, she got one in return that was just about as weak.

They made it down the hall and into the waiting area before they stopped, Alison's attention dropping on a painting of a beach, with its tall green grass and beach sand looking mighty inviting. She could just about see herself there with Arch, laying out a blanket and sitting down for a picnic lunch. She could hear the sound of children playing in the distance, and waves lapping at the seaside.

The reality sure did suck balls compared to the fantasy, she conceded as Hendricks unfolded himself from the waiting area chair and gave a good stretch of his own.

"What's going on?" Arch asked, drawling.

"Nothing much," Hendricks said. He breathed a little at Alison and she caught a whiff of halitosis like the cowboy had chowed down on an onion before speaking, or maybe just eaten straight out of the trash. She snorted as an incredibly inappropriate thought occurred to her, something about asking him if he'd just gone down on a demon, but her brain caught up with her mouth just in time to remind her that, yes, that actually had happened and it wasn't fucking funny, stupid brain, so she clamped her jaws shut as her cheeks burned with embarrassment at her near-idiotic lapse. "How are y'all doing?" Hendricks asked, dropping into that slight Southern accent he seemed to have picked up.

"Still waiting," Arch answered after probably waiting five seconds to see if she was going to answer. She wasn't; she was still trying to keep the lid on that other thought, the one that had almost resulted in her swallowing her foot well up to her knee. "Any word from back home?"

"Not a lot going on," Hendricks said, blinking a couple times. "The church is still safe, and I guess Pike's answer to the town's problems is to throw a party, so ..." He shrugged. "Clearly this man is a leadership guru. I would say demon, but obviously Alison proved that wasn't the case."

"Obviously," Alison said, finally feeling in control of herself, her giggles and her embarrassment enough to speak. "I assume by the lack of screams and dying around us that the Legion isn't assaulting the hospital right now."

"I guess not," Hendricks said with a long yawn. "Unless they're doing it vewy, vewy quietwy."

"It's not even wabbit season," Alison said. "And—"

There was a clamor from near the elevator bank around the corner, and a slight shriek, followed by a woman saying, "Sir, you're bleeding!"

"Get out of my way!" That was Brian's voice, and then she heard the squeak of something against the tile floors, and grunting, and a few seconds later Brian came around the corner in a wheelchair, red in the face and—sure enough—leaving a little trail of blood behind him from his knee, which looked like it had been reopened. "Jesus, thank God I found you."

"Doubt he had much to do with it, since you knew where we were," Hendricks said wryly. Arch frowned at him, and Hendricks turned around explicitly for the purpose of seeing his reaction, Alison could tell. The cowboy was always doing that shit to get Arch's goat. It mostly worked, that was why he kept doing it.

Brian went on, ignoring the hell out of both of them. "You have to get back—back to—" He had to stop and take a breath, panting from exertion. "The Halloween thing, the party, it's—"

"Dude," Hendricks said, looking a little distant, "I told you, it'll be fine."

"It's not fucking fine!" Brian shouted, and Alison noticed that the lady who'd seen him bleeding at the elevators was a nurse, and she was lingering at the corner, watching them all with concern bordering on alarm. "The Legion—they're gonna go for it." He took a panting breath and stopped for a minute.

"That's suicide," Hendricks said calmly. "There's gonna be—hell, a ton of adults there, probably. No demon would walk into—"

"No normal, petty, random-ass demon would," Brian interrupted, fighting for every breath. "And that's the point. It's motive—it's motive and ca—" He took a heaving breath. "These things, the Legion—they're not like other demons—"

"I'm calling psych," the nurse at the corner said, starting to move.

"He's fine," Alison said, trying to sound reassuring, though she wasn't sure the nurse was wrong.

"—they're not like anyone else," Brian went on, babbling, trying to get ten feet of thoughts out a one inch hole. "They don't care if they live or die, they've proven that. And they don't want the same things that other demons want, they just want—they want to hurt *us*."

"Okay," Arch said, clearly skeptical. "That's great and all, but they already did that."

"Yeah," Hendricks said, "they proved they can hurt us with your dad and Mrs. Reeve and—"

"And Dr. Darlington's mom," Brian said, huffing. "Which should strike you all as odd, because Darlington had *nothing* to do with the attack on Legion. She wasn't there, she didn't—"

"Yeah, but," Hendricks said, now dropping to a small smirk, clearly enjoying that he had to explain the fact of things to the overexcited college boy, "she's with us, and they saw that. They know that, so—"

"No." Brian shook his head so fast Alison wondered if he'd keel over from rattling his brain too hard. "She's part of our *community*, don't you see?" He looked at all three of them, and Alison got a sick feeling. Arch and Hendricks were looking at him blankly; they didn't get it. "It's all about community to them, because they're a town or a city or a nation in a single body. And they think we hurt them, except they're seeing this as us versus them in terms of a whole community instead of *mano a mano*, the way we would—"

"Jesus Christ," Alison muttered, her skin prickling all up and down her.

"They're going for the Halloween event," Brian finished, sagging back in his chair. "That's why they haven't attacked us at the hospital. Because they think they're attacking *us* at Halloween, except their definition of *us* is a hell of lot broader than we've been considering because we're thinking of it our way, not theirs."

"Holy shit." Hendricks's face went ashen, sick as shit. He'd got there, finally, and Alison could feel it because she was right there, too.

"Mother of Mercy," Arch said, milder but just as sick. "We gotta get back to Midian *now*—"

"I gotta call Reeve—" Hendricks said, talking at the same time.

"Duncan and Lerner Two—" Alison started, lunging forward.

She almost made it around the corner to the elevator, charging past the nurse, but stopped before colliding with the lady, who had panic in her eyes. "He needs that knee taken care of," Alison said, getting all up in that nurse's face, her eyes wide like a semi's hubcaps. "And so help me, if you Nurse Ratched him before I get back, I will tear your ass to pieces." She shot a look back at Brian. "Thanks, little brother."

"Just hurry," Brian said, face pale, clearly spent. "You have to … to save the day …" And he slumped against the back of the wheelchair as Alison headed around the corner toward the elevator, Hendricks and Arch right behind her.

*

Guthrie had almost caught Duncan on the last lap. Walking around the hospital all day was clearly wearing on him. She wanted to feel a little triumph about that, but it had been a long one, and her essence was being squished by the stupid bra that they'd given her when she appeared on earth. These things were fucking torture, and she was not happy about wearing one, at all, especially for long days. Short days, not terrible. Long days, it was like the old days of corsets that they had to use a winch to tighten, and Guthrie hated it.

"These are the times I miss being a guy," she said under her breath. Well, and when it came time to urinate, which she tried to avoid assiduously now. What a drag.

She came around the corner at the back of the hospital, where the parking lot was, and almost stopped in her tracks. The hospital was laid mostly in a rectangle, with the front and back being the long sides and the entrances being in the middle of them. Whoever had designed the place had embraced the symmetry. The portico out back looked like it had been added sometime after the hospital's construction, and they'd put a parking garage across the street on one of the sides, with a walkover bridge to keep the street clear of pedestrians. Guthrie had thought about vaulting over it on one of her infinite laps, just to cut the boredom, but decided against it in the name of keeping a low profile.

Now, she was watching a clear confab of Duncan, Arch, Alison and Hendricks having a meeting of some sort under the exit portico, and inconspicuous wasn't a word in those idiots' vocabulary. Not with head dunce in that long black coat standing there, in the middle of the damned portico, waving his hands around like—

Aw, shit.

Guthrie kicked it up to a run, human-style. Not fast enough to draw attention because of its blurriness with inhuman speed, but enough of one that she felt it through these heeled shoes after a day of walking in the damned things. Oh, the shit these people put women through …

She could hear them as she drew closer, Duncan locked into place as Hendricks spoke, the words drifting over to Guthrie as she hurried toward them. "… and he thinks this Legion is going to regard the whole town as part of our, uh, community or tribe or whatever and so this Halloween deal is fair game."

Duncan's back was to Guthrie, and he didn't have muscles to tense, but she could tell he was taking it all onboard like a cannonball to the face for a normal person. "That sounds … pretty logical," Duncan said as lamely as he said almost everything else.

"He seems pretty certain about it," Alison Stan said, practically quivering in her too-tight jeans. Guthrie didn't envy her those.

"It's a convincing argument," Duncan said, and he looked almost … paralyzed. "Legions think differently than we do. It might just be that they view this as a war between tribes, and collateral damage is … well, it's just damage."

"What's all the fuss about, kids?" Guthrie asked as she slowed to join them. They were all standing there, looking tense and about half-useless, like they were gonna break and run any second. "Something about this All Hallow's Eve got you riled?"

"They think," Duncan said, "that this Legion's gonna attack a town event in the square in Midian. Make a slaughter of it."

That one raised Guthrie's eyebrows; it was the sort of thing that even an OOC feared. "This hotspot ain't hot enough to absorb that one without blinking yet," Guthrie said, stock still in her version of stunned. They couldn't be right about this. Home Office had given guidance, but the guidance was to keep things simmering for the time being, not let them get to a boil—and this was beyond boil. This was like nuking all the water.

Duncan shot him a filthy look that was in actuality barely a raise of the eyebrow and a twinge of the lips. "Also, lots of people are going to die."

"As an Officer of the Pact, that concerns me," Guthrie said coolly. "So ... we just gonna stand here and jaw, or ...?" She motioned toward the car.

"Let's go," Hendricks said and lurched into motion just behind Alison, who looked about ready to charge into a battle. Her face was all twisted up with emotion, most of it leaning toward hatred. Guthrie fell in with them, hurrying to get to the car first so she could drive.

Only a couple days back on the job and things were already turning to shit. What was it about this place that—

Oh, right. She knew that. She shuddered and quickened her pace as she sped to the car.

*

Reeve was just about to head to the town square on his own when the phone rang. It was actually Erin's, fortuitously left behind when she fled through the window. He was still standing in the narthex of St. Brigid's when it went off, a long, trilling ring that was probably disrespectful given the environs he was in, but he was all about extraordinary times requiring extraordinary measures, and he hadn't wanted to miss an important call, so he'd ditched the vibrate and turned the ringer on full blast.

"Hello?" he asked. He noticed it was Arch's number but anticipated Hendricks again.

"Reeve!" Hendricks practically shouted in his ear, "Halloween!"

Reeve just blinked for a second, Dr. Darlington furrowing her brow as she looked at him. She could probably hear it without the speakerphone, but he pulled it away from his ear and hit the button anyway, just to be sure. "I know it's Halloween, dumbass," he said. "I'm not that out of it—"

"The Legion is going to attack Halloween!" This time, Hendricks bellowed it, and Reeve was glad he didn't have the phone near his ear.

"I thought Duncan said—" Lauren started.

"*Normal* demons aren't going to attack Halloween," Hendricks said. "The Legion is."

Reeve didn't think he quite heard that, either time. "Excuse me?"

"They're giving no damns about collateral damage," Hendricks said, "so they're gonna hit Halloween and we have to stop them. We're like …" He stopped, and there was a muttering in the background, "… forty or fifty minutes away, but who knows when this thing is gonna start?"

"Halloween?" Ms. Cherry piped up. "It's starting right now." She held up a lovely platinum wristwatch with diamond accents.

"Holy shit," Reeve said, and he almost dropped the phone. "We gotta go. Now."

*

The town square wasn't the busiest Braeden had ever seen it, but it wasn't bad, either, especially considering what Midian had been through lately. The sun was dipping closer to the horizon, and the streets leading up to the square were alive with laughter and kids, moving around in groups with adults close at hand. Even teenagers were prowling the streets in groups, apparently a little afraid of what was going on, in spite of the fact most of them thought they were invincible. At least, that's what Braeden had thought when he was their age.

"Ooh," Abi said from the back, peering out the window from her car seat. She was in a forward facing now, and turning that sucker around so she could see while he was driving had been the happiest day of his parenting life. She'd gone from hating car rides to loving them in a minute, and now he could take her just about anywhere, and if she was tired enough, she'd just conk right out in the car.

Braeden pulled up and parallel parked, thumping the curb as he pulled in. He hated parallel parking, which was the second reason he seldom came to the square, the first being the almost total lack of anything to do here. He managed to find his spot on a side road about a block away, and he'd mostly gotten her between the lines, the nose of his truck sticking out just slightly beyond the perimeters—but good enough. He killed the ignition and got out. Three more cars passed him looking for spots as he made his way around to get Abi out on the curb side, and the more people he saw, the better he started to feel about this little excursion. If there was strength in numbers, Midian was putting on a grand ol' show of strength.

He saw a careful knot of parents go by with six kids between four adults, their worried eyes not dissimilar from his own. One of the mothers looked like a nervous wreck, but one of the dads was smiling wide, and the kids were all on his side of thinking. One of them was dancing about, turning around and walking backward to yell something to one of her little friends, all excited to be out and dressed in a faerie costume complete with aluminum foil-wrapped wings. Braeden saw cheeks red from the chill wind, and smiles all around.

He couldn't help but put one of his own on as he opened the back door and clicked the red button on Abi's five-point harness. The weight of his revolver pulling on his belt was reassuring, telling him that even if, for some reason, things got bad, he'd have things under control. "Come on, baby doll," Braeden said, unclicking the chest straps as Abi wormed her way out and ignored his hand, his little princess stepping down from her carriage all on her own.

*

Arch was beyond tense in the back seat of the car, Alison squeezed between him and Hendricks, Duncan in front of him in the passenger seat and Guthrie at the wheel. Even she seemed worried about what was going on, and Arch didn't think that came too naturally given the personality change she'd acquired with her new body. He had his hand firmly planted on the Plastileather door, wanting to be somewhere that he could open the darned thing and get out, start planting his sword in demons, doing some good.

But they were still burning up Interstate 75 toward Midian, and Arch felt like he was late for the world's most important party.

"How bad could this get?" Hendricks seemed to echo Arch's nervousness without a channel for action, and he looked across his wife to see the cowboy chewing a fingernail idly.

"A host of angry demons cutting loose in a square filled with people?" Guthrie said, answering before anyone else—like Duncan—could. "Gee, I dunno. How much do you like blood and carnage? Because if you're an aficionado, it could be a grand ol' time."

"Did you come back with a menstrual cycle?" Alison sniped. "Because it seems like you might be experiencing a little PMS."

Hendricks chortled, but Arch held in his feelings, which bordered on mild dismay. At least she kept it clean.

"I came back to a town that's going straight into the shitter," Guthrie said, steering the town car around a truck at about 85. She didn't bother to signal, Arch noticed, and it caused him to quiver a little, thinking about the ticket he'd have written if he'd been in a position to. "No bleeding or cramping necessary to make me testy. It's days like this that make me long for sweet, eternal torment."

That was a sobering thought, at least for Arch. It didn't seem to do much for Hendricks, though. "What did they have you doing?" the cowboy asked with a twinkle in his eye. "Cleaning out Rosie O'Donnell's toilet?"

Guthrie didn't miss a beat. "More like being sodomized by a cleg'ham'rrvar every hour of the day for six weeks." She looked back, and nothing about her expression suggested that she was joking. "They're worse than they sound, by the way. And what they shoot out makes our old pal Gideon look like he's been drinking pineapple juice all the live-long day."

Hendricks's eyebrows were up, his cowboy hat seemingly like it was angled to slide off the back of his head. He didn't gulp, but Arch expected it was only because he was holding it in. "Oh," was all he said, and that was enough to throw them all back into a tense silence as they sped along toward home, hoping like heck it wasn't too late.

*

Lauren watched the fading day with a nervousness bordering on nausea. Her stomach was doing its own version of calisthenics, jumping around like some sort of crazy, possessed bean. It wasn't just the town being at stake, after all, that had her nerves on full alert. It was that maybe, just maybe, somewhere in this crazy plot by the

Legion crew to make a disaster happen at the Halloween event, Molly would be there, and involved.

They were rolling down side streets, Melina Cherry at the wheel of a beautiful white Land Rover. If she hadn't been about to shit bricks, Lauren might have admired the vehicle, because it was totally pimped out, which she considered appropriate given who its owner was. The madam wasn't sparing the horses, either, but Lauren had other things to worry about besides traffic laws; most of the people of Midian did, too, though she doubted they knew it yet.

"This is going to be a clusterfuck if it starts before we get there," Reeve said, in the passenger seat. Casey Meacham and Father Nguyen were in the back with Lauren, and Lonsdale was sitting in the hatchback area. Lauren had seen him clutching at his sword, the demon hunter plainly anxious for some action. Meacham had his tomahawk in his non-bandaged hand, but at least he was keeping it still. Father Nguyen had loaded up a couple pistol squirt guns with holy water and had put one of the brass crosses that stood on a wooden stave in the back of the Rover. What he was planning to do with that, Lauren had no idea, but he also had a Bible laid across his lap, and he looked nervous.

"Depending on how many of your people they've possessed, us being there might not have much of an effect on the outcome of said clusterfuck," Lonsdale offered from the back.

They were about six blocks from the square and Lauren could see the traffic increasing a little. There was a reasonable amount of street parking around here, but it was starting to fill up. There were also people walking down the sidewalks, something she couldn't recall seeing towards sundown, at least not lately.

"You think your boy Fries is going to be there?" Casey asked, leaning forward with his bloody, bandaged hand to ask Reeve the question. Lauren adjusted herself as she stared at it; she really should have changed it before they came, but there wasn't time.

"I don't give a damn," Reeve said. "But if he comes after me, you all know what to do. I'll see if I can distract him by running."

"You think you can outrun him?" Casey looked at him questioningly.

Reeve looked back at him, clearly annoyed at the question. "Ed weighs about three bills, maybe even three-fifty. Yeah, I reckon I can outrun him, even on my old knees."

"Let's hope it doesn't come to that," Ms. Cherry said nervously, plunging them forward into the heart of town, "because if these 'legions' are as bad as you say, we're likely to need your help to stop them."

*

Abi was in seventh heaven, holding Braeden's hand with one of hers and carrying her lime green plastic trick-or-treating pumpkin with the other. She had a big ol' grin on and had yielded to putting on her jacket as soon as she got out of the truck, which Braeden considered real lucky, because he didn't want to carry it. It wasn't a purse, but holding onto a hot pink puffy coat wasn't really his jam.

They were walking toward the square, and the air was alive. None of the fear that had settled on Midian was present here except in the lowered voices of some of the parents. The kids could feel the energy, and it was electric. There were Queen Elsas everywhere, skull masks, every stripe of Avenger that Braeden could imagine, even some blocky head that looked like someone had just taken a perfect cube, colored in a funny digital pattern and stuck it on a five-year-old's gourd. He almost laughed at that, getting caught up in the moment. Abi sure did.

A gust of cold wind tore down the street and caused the growing crowd to actually "Ooh!" as it came through. It was a brisk breath of fall, like an ice gust out of the north, and Braeden had a daydream about heating up some hot chocolate or maybe some apple cider later tonight, sitting with Abi on the couch after this was over and talking about how exciting it all was. Those were the fun parts of parenting. Not the occasional screaming matches, not the constant battle of wills, but the quiet moments, the ones where—every so often—she still fell asleep on his shoulder while they were watching Doc McStuffins.

He squeezed her hand tight as they passed Surrey's Diner. Yep, this was the place to be, a crowd on the square, the chitter chatter of Halloween and the excitement of people finally standing up, being unafraid to stick their heads out. It wasn't Groundhog Day, but damned if it didn't have the feeling of something a hell of a lot worse than winter being put in their rearview mirror.

Chester could feel the excitement of the crowd, even standing on the periphery as he was, backed up against a boarded-up shop front, looking out at the center of the square and the obelisk monument in the middle of it all. He was watching the back and forth as he stood there, no coat as a bulwark against the cool, rising night. The sky was a deep purple all the way to the western horizon, where the glow of orange behind the edge of the square heralded the end of day.

And for these people, the end of all their days.

Chester heard the laughter of children, the excitement. He watched a little boy tell another about his costume, about his Minecraft head, whatever that was. There was a time when he might have cared, when he would have taken the side of this child and his hopes and dreams and enthusiasms over William's quiet despair for the inevitable death of all these people.

But now William was not here to argue against them, and Chester could not find it in himself to argue for them, and so that was that.

All that remained was the cold knowledge that all of these people would die eventually, and that all he was doing was speeding it up, pushing the minecart down the tracks faster than it would otherwise advance toward its natural end. These people had hurt him, and they were mortal. William had not been mortal, but they had brought his end, his and his fellows, even so. It was a crime what they did, a crime for all of them, these horribly detached people, blind and stumbling and stupid to the last of them.

"It is All Hallow's Eve," Chester whispered, standing back at the edge of the square, looking over the crowd, "and I will take all that you hallow." No one heard him except for those still within, and they applauded his resolution.

It was nearly time.

*

Ms. Cherry let them off at the square and then just threw her car into park a half dozen paces away, getting out and joining them, not caring that she'd blocked the road. Horns sounded behind them, and Reeve only glanced back. In retrospect, the madam had done something pretty smart there. That might even save a few lives if this thing went downhill.

"How will we know who we're supposed to take it to?" Cascy asked, keeping his tomahawk low. Reeve glanced back at him, and the taxidermist was showing a sign of nerves that Reeve couldn't recall seeing from the man before. He was a dirty old pervert, but his bravado had been carrying him along pretty nice until now. His head was swiveling, and he was trying to take the whole crowd in.

Reeve did the same, in a hurry, and there was so much noise as they hit the back of the crowd that he didn't know exactly where to look either. Their enemy could have been anywhere, after all, and—

"To hell with these shoes," Ms. Cherry muttered. She kicked them off and climbed barefoot up the nearest lamp post a couple feet. She held up her hand to shield her eyes from the orange glow of the setting sun that fell across her olive skin the minute she was out of the shadow of the buildings on the west side of the square. "Look for the people who are standing like stones in a river. The ones unmoved by what's going on around them—the watchers. Like him!" She pointed out a guy in a black jacket not ten feet away from Reeve.

Reeve frowned. Cherry had a point, and it wasn't like he didn't know what to do here. He eased his way through the crowd up to the guy, his sword in hand, and just leaned forward a little as he went by and poked the tip at the man's ankle.

The reaction was immediate: a gasp, and the guy threw his head back like he was going to howl at a moon that had barely started to rise yet. Reeve came around him in time to see the eyes go wild, demon fire sweeping through and leaving him with baby blues as the darkness fled. He realized it was Scott Karshman, and Karshman fell to his knees, gasping for air.

"Well," Reeve said, looking back to see Casey, Dr. Darlington and Father Nguyen following behind him, the crowd jostling, not even noticing Karshman fall, "that's one."

*

Alison was ready by the time they hit the exit ramp for Midian. Guthrie took it at about sixty, barely slowing to make the turn toward town, shooting past Fast Freddie's and the diner as she accelerated. Alison would have applauded that, but she didn't know where the OOC's motives were sitting and could only hope she was telling the truth about being down with the struggle of kicking the Legion out of Midian. Because that was really all that mattered at the moment.

The town car's horn blared hard as Guthrie swerved into oncoming traffic and then back into her lane, weaving around an old pickup that wasn't going nearly as fast as they needed it to. Alison was down with that offensive driving, too, because she had a feeling it was gonna be a close brush this time.

She'd thought the cow demon was a fucking trip, crazy as hell when she'd scoped it through her rifle. She'd managed to get sights on Gideon the fire-sperm shooter, and the carny of flaming impregnation, too. Kitty Elizabeth and the stupid bikers and the Rog'tausch; she'd taken shots at all of them at various times, cool and dispassionate through her rifle's scope. She'd seen them, seen what needed to be done, and taken it upon herself to act as exterminator, just like if they were any other kind of varmint.

Every one of them had had nasty plans. Death, death, and more death, that was what they'd brought. And when challenged, they hadn't hesitated to try and kill her husband and anyone else who got in the way.

But not even one of them had veered out of their way to lay utter havoc on a gathering of children. Halloween, for fuck's sake. It was the next thing to kid day, except for Christmas. People handing out candy to children, and this sorry fucking asshole Legion was going to get in there and profane the damned thing, and not even to execute some grander plan to end the world or assemble a juggernaut demon, or even to get their fucking rocks off.

They were doing it for petty fucking shitty revenge.

Going after kids was the lowest of the low in her opinion. The others had had plans that would've killed children, but that would have been a by-product. This was targeting, this was the shit she scraped off her boot on a dirty curb next to the other shit already scraped off.

Alison just steamed in silence. She had her holy dagger and a small Glock with a couple mags, and that was it. If she was lucky, that'd be all she'd need. Her rifle wouldn't do a damned thing even if she had it, because there was no damned way she was using it in the town square while it was filled with who knew how many kids, even if she had a decent vantage.

This was up close and personal all the way.

And as they blew through a stop sign with another blaring of the town car horn, Alison just hoped she could get up close and personal enough with the starter of this fucking bullshit, that bastard that had been standing off with them yesterday morning around the front of that panel van. Because she wanted to gut him nice and slow for this, and watch the devil bleed out of his eyes as she sent his ass right back to hell, where he belonged.

*

Lauren had a squirt gun filled with holy water and a letter opener that Father Nguyen had apparently consecrated at some point in the last couple weeks, and that was it. She didn't have her big water tanks with the industrial soaker nozzle, and she would have looked really funny carrying it across the square in any case. That might have been a dead giveaway that something was amiss, at least for the demons of Legion.

She watched Reeve stab Scott Karshman in the back of the ankle, about as gently as she could imagine the thing being done without a scalpel and a careful, one-centimeter incision, and she had a feeling things were gonna get bad pretty quick from here. The less warning they could give, the better off they were going to be.

Ms. Cherry had been a smart addition, she thought. The madam had done a pretty swift bit of thinking, blocking the road and then climbing the lamp post to do spotting. Lauren had a feeling that her incognito state wasn't going to last very long, especially since they had no headsets, no voice communications, and zero coordination. It wasn't a small detail, but they were basically just sitting here in a glut, waiting for shit to go down. All the code names in the world wouldn't help them now, because when it all went south they'd have no way to talk to each other except by shouting across the square, which was sure to be in a panic situation if they were right about what was going to happen here.

And now that Reeve had just vaped Scott Karshman, ridding him of demon possession, Lauren was more sure than ever that this was the place, this was time, and this was the shit that was going to go down.

She halted a few steps back from Reeve, trying to figure out how she could be of best use. Reeve was already retreating, carefully, going sideways through the crowd as Karshman was grunting and getting back to his feet. Nguyen brushed past her in his priest black, clutching that cross mounted on the wooden dowel like it was a walking stick, almost like he was costumed for the occasion. Casey was following the sheriff, and Lauren was left to hang back, clutching the letter opener concealed in one pocket and the squirt gun in the other, keeping her head down as she scanned the crowd.

"Aww, man, what the hell?" Karshman moaned, getting back to his feet. He looked down and moved his foot around to take a look at the spot of pain that appeared to be ailing him. "The hell is going on here?"

"It's Halloween, dumbass!" Keith Drumlin shouted at him, tossing a frown at Karshman. Drumlin was standing there with his kids, not even covering their ears as they listened to him call another guy a dumbass. Lauren couldn't help blinking at the sheer redneckery on display.

"Fuck you, Keith!" Karshman fired back, lifting his left foot up and standing on one leg so he could peek at his little wound. "Something bit me. I feel funny." He looked around. "What the … where are my kids?"

Lauren felt her own blood cool at that. She was trying not to think of Molly, but the fact was … she had to be here, didn't she? If this was where the Legion was making their move, that meant Molly was around somewhere, didn't it?

Lauren broke off and pushed past a couple people who were chuckling at their kids to reach the nearest lamp post. She jumped up on the little ring where the concrete brace at the base met the first metal, and perched there with her foot using the one inch or so of lip to get a leg up and scan the crowd.

It was a bigger crowd than she would have figured for this town, for this moment in their history. There had to be a couple hundred people here, and at least half of them were kids, she thought. There were some others in the brew, too, a few obvious plants of Legion, she thought, but there were also some non-parents that were watching with worried looks, like Chauncey Watson, who had his back to the front window of Surrey's and his arms folded in front of him, his old jacket looking like a relic out of the seventies, if not earlier. He had a couple people with him and they were chatting, showing undisguised looks of concern. One of them was a tall black man that she thought might have been the pastor at the Methodist church—Jones, if she remembered right. She didn't exactly frequent his establishment. She'd heard the others talking about him, though, as a potential member of the watch, and it looked like he might have come with Chauncey and a couple others to support their local sheriff in their own way. She saw a tall guy with a baseball cap on and thought it might have been Mike McInness, but she couldn't be sure.

Lauren turned her attention to the middle of the crowd, where there was a raised dais set up in the middle of the square, just in front of the monument. This thing was put on by County Administrator Pike, yet there was no sign of Pike—nor of Ed Fries, come to think of it. The dais was empty, like high noon before a gunfight. She half expected a tumbleweed to blow across it.

And then, as she started to look away, Lauren caught the flash of long brown hair near the dais. She focused in, saw the girl turn her head, looking around, cold, calculating, scanning the crowd not like a person here to have a good time, but like …

Like a person looking for targets.

Lauren dropped from the lamp post and landed hard, twisting her ankle slightly and ignoring it as she started across the square toward the middle. She limped a little, just pushing past the pain, trying to get through the crowd to the center. Trying to get to …

Molly.

*

Braeden was waiting for somebody to say something, for Pike to stick his head up and make a little speech, as he was probably bound to do given he'd gone to the trouble of setting this whole shindig up. That was fine with Braeden because so far it was looking reasonably successful to him. People were here, people were excited, and the sense of life in this place was infectious. He'd been to Surrey's Diner a few days ago and the square had been dead at midday. Not a good look for the place, not that there weren't already enough boarded-up windows to give it that effect anyway most days. Midian didn't need to lose what little vitality it had left.

He wanted to see this place come up like a boxer knocked down in the eighth round. Like Rocky in the last movie, rising back up with that look in his eyes, telling his opponent, *Your ass ain't knocking me down*. Braeden wasn't much for princess tales, though he watched them obviously, but to him Midian getting back to its feet was a Cinderella story right up there with an underdog winning the World Series. Against the Yankees.

"Daddy, when do we get the candy?" Abi asked, practically vibrating. She stopped and waved, the little pumpkin bucket causing her coat sleeve to slide up as she let it run up her wrist. Braeden looked and saw she was waving to Brenda Matthews, and Braeden nodded stiffly at her. She had a real unpleasant expression, her mouth a thin line, worried and watching, keeping her kid on a short leash in front of her.

"Soon, baby," Braeden said, feeling himself continue to relax. It was a festive atmosphere in the square, and just then the lamps all came on, shedding their light around. How could anything bad happen here?

*

Guthrie brought the car to a screaming stop one intersection away from the square, and Hendricks was about ready to thank a God he didn't believe in and maybe even add a "Hallelujah!" for good measure. Things had gotten pretty bad when they'd gotten off the interstate, and a couple times he had wondered if Guthrie had intended to just kill them now rather than let them get in a rumble with this Legion demon in the square, because her driving suggested that saving lives was about the last damn thing on her mind.

"I would have thought being in a shell-cracking car accident would have made you a safer driver," Hendricks said as he got out of the car, which Guthrie had just left in the middle of the street. She wasn't the only one who'd done this, to be fair; double and triple parking made the block leading up to the square pretty goddamned impassable by anything other than foot traffic.

"It wasn't the car crash that did it," Guthrie said tersely, slamming her door behind her. "It was really the falling off the mountain that made that shit happen." She started striding toward the square with a purpose, and that purpose was starting shit, because she had her baton in hand. She wasn't sparing the horses here, either, leaping up on top of a Jeep Cherokee with a single bound and peering out into the square beyond.

"See anything?" Duncan asked, his own baton in hand. He stopped next to the Jeep, head on a level with Guthrie's shoes, and stared out into the square himself.

"Feel anything?" Arch offered, and Hendricks thought it might have been the big man's version of a joke. It fell flat, of course, like most of his attempts at humor did.

"No," Duncan said, "but I can't feel these things."

"I think I see 'em," Guthrie said, her lips a thin, thin line. "Like islands of pissed-off in the middle of a sea of happy." She glanced down at Alison, Arch, and Hendricks, all lingering a step or two behind Duncan.

"And ...?" Alison asked. She had her knife clutched tight, clearly anticipating the crap coming down.

Guthrie didn't emote much, but it almost looked like she swallowed dramatically. "And ... I think we're gonna need a bigger watch."

*

Arch was not exactly feeling the thrill when Guthrie made her pronouncement. He was already hovering on the edge, trying to figure out what the next move was, ready to charge into a sea of innocent people that were clearly sitting in the midst of the world's biggest trap. The problem was, he couldn't see the jaws, not like Guthrie apparently had, saying they were outnumbered in her own sort of way.

Well, the watch had been outnumbered by demons in this town for quite a while, and though they'd certainly taken their share of shots to the chin lately, Arch didn't consider himself the sort to just lay down and let bad things happen, no matter what the odds against them were. "We need to get in there," he said, resolute as he'd ever been.

"But where in there?" Alison asked. She was a fair bit shorter than him, of course, and was standing up on her tippy toes, trying to see through. She'd been a raw nerve the whole ride, madder than mad, madder than he could recall ever seeing her, but trying to hold it all in.

"I see a few," Duncan said and exchanged a look with Guthrie.

"I got eyes on a few more," Guthrie said, shrugging. "I go this way, you go that?" She pointed right, then left.

"Okay," Duncan said and he headed off to the left.

"I'm going with you," Alison said, veering off after him into the crowd. It was a pretty decent-sized bunch, but it was thin enough that when Duncan started pushing his way through, he didn't have to work too hard at it, and Alison just trailed along in his wake, hands buried under her coat, ready for action.

He thought about going with her, after her, or at least grabbing a kiss before they parted, but she ran off after Duncan and Guthrie grabbed his attention before he could dwell on it. "Where the fuck is the cowboy going?" Guthrie asked, craning her neck to look. She was a fair sight shorter than him too, though taller than Alison.

Arch got his answer the moment he looked right over the heads of the crowd and caught the same thing Hendricks had. "Erin," he said when he saw the flash of blond hair hanging in the middle of a knot of people on the back side of the monument, away from the dais set up on the east side of the square. He watched the cowboy hat moving straight along toward her like he was being pulled on a string. "Do we go after him?" he asked. He looked back to Guthrie to find her cutting through the crowd, heading in the direction she'd told Duncan she was going, not waiting for him to decide.

After a second's thought, Arch came to the conclusion that spreading out and snapping off as many of these Legion demons as he could was a lot more important than involving himself in whatever Hendricks was trying to do. Probably ambush Erin and free her up. With a shake of his head, Arch took off after Guthrie, figuring the veteran demon hunter could probably handle Erin all on his own.

*

Braeden waved at Sam Allen, who was about twenty feet away from him behind a couple groups of teenagers in some pretty half-assed costumes, like they'd just come out the door wearing any old thing for the candy. Sam waved back, smiling thinly, his wife a step behind him and their ten-year-old hanging next to 'em. Braeden remembered the words they'd exchanged at the meeting, and he was gladder than ever he'd backed Pike when it came down to it. The only demons in Midian were the kids dressed like devils.

"Daddy!" Abi said, starting to show impatience. Braeden was feeling a little cool himself, and did wonder just a little when this party was getting started. He reached down to check his cell phone and frowned. They were running about three minutes late, which probably wasn't much to a county employee, but was about six seconds short of infinity to the parent of a four-year-old.

"I know, baby," Braeden said, trying to reassure her. She was tugging on his hand hard, like it was a leash and she was ready to run. She did that sometimes, wanting to break free, and he was tempted to let her go here, let her run a little bit. He knew all the faces he was seeing, after all, but there was just that little bit of nagging residual fear that kept him holding her tight, even though their hands were starting to get slippery from sweating together. "Soon, I think. Just a couple more minutes."

Abi let out a puff of disappointment, then started leaning hard, pulling on his hand and putting her weight against it, using him to keep herself from falling as she started walking at a 45-degree angle. She giggled and went in a little circle around him, pumpkin dragging the green grass beneath their feet as his daughter entertained herself in the only way she had available to her.

*

Chester was watching it all unfold, waiting, feeling the moment draw near. He had seen the sheriff, Reeve, enter from down the street to his left, had watched him come through with some of his associates, including the doctor. Then from his right had come the others—Deputy Stan, his bride Alison, the man in the black cowboy hat and coat, and two OOCs.

Chester hadn't been sure any of them would show up, since he knew the sheriff had been cast out of his job in disgrace and the others had been swept out of town in the aftermath of the last attack. But he considered this a fortunate happening; he'd meant for them all to find out about this later, thinking the agony would be sweet, that he could watch from the eyes of someone innocently delivering the message to them all, that perhaps even he himself would deign to leave this body to tell them—and then, perhaps, kill them all. Or let them live with the knowledge, because that would be a reward of its own.

This, though, was even better.

He counted their numbers and knew he had them beaten before this particular game even began. Even if they stopped him, there was no possible way for them to escape this without horrible cost. Chester had been around for too long, had seen too much, and had too many bodies at his own disposal, united against these little people, wandering in their own directions.

His army was not so divided, not encumbered by their own thoughts and worries and agendas; in this, they were united, and their union was driven by a single purpose.

"CRY HAVOC!" Chester shouted, repeating one of William's favorite lines of Shakespeare at the top of his lungs. The crowd noise died for only a moment as his voice rang out, signaling the start of this battle he had planned carefully—and the end of all things for so many people standing around him even now, basking in the light of hope that he was about to snatch away with their lives.

11.

"Shitballs," Reeve said as the voice echoed across the square, loud as though it had come out of a speaker mounted on the monument. He knew a sign when he heard one bellowed out, and this was sure to be the thing to kick it all off. He waited, frozen, having just nicked Pete Walker in the left buttcheek with his sword tip and watched the man grunt and fall from the poke, sulfur smell kicking up like someone had farted rotten eggs.

It didn't take but a second for Pete Walker's grunt of pain to get drowned out by things in the square going ape shit. Lauren Darlington belted past, nearly knocking over Casey as she made for the center of the square, and a half second after that, her little blitz looked tea party social compared to the chaos that broke out in the square.

*

The crowd noise was the first thing that tipped Alison to all hell breaking loose, at least after that fucking voice yelled, "CRY HAVOC!" from somewhere to her left. She was right behind Duncan and didn't spare a moment in pulling her knife, because she was pretty sure this party was starting in earnest. She wasn't disappointed a second later, either, when Duncan deployed his baton right into Max Thomas's face, breaking his nose and exiling a demon all in one shot.

"Fucking shit!" Alison yelled as two kids screamed next to her. The crowd started pushing as awareness started rippling through that things were not as they were supposed to be, and that gut-check tension was about enough to drown out her panic as a torrent of it rose around her and the first screams reached her ears.

Lauren made it about twenty feet from Molly before damnation came raining down around the square. She'd heard the voice and ignored it, her attention on one thing and one thing only: her daughter. She'd knocked people out of the way without apology, linebackered through a twenty-something man that had wandered into her path at the last second, not giving two shits that she sent him sprawling, and had vaulted over a toddler, barely escaping knocking the kid down on the hard concrete edge of the square's curb. If the kid's parent was upset about her cavalier disregard for personal safety, they didn't manage to get their protest out before the screaming drowned out any chance of conversational argument.

Here on the grass in the middle of the square, where the monument stood in the center of a nice X of concrete sidewalks that led from each of the four corners to the middle, was where the crowd was densest. There were a damned lot of people standing on the roads that lined all four sides of the square, but here was where the speechifying was supposed to happen, where the sheep had come for the feeding … where the slaughter would take place.

The damnedest thing of all was that Lauren knew that an event like this was exactly what Midian had needed to get off its damned back, and yet here they were, about to get their fucking heads driven right into the concrete without mercy.

She didn't bother shouting to people to get out of the way. It wouldn't have mattered anyway because the Legion was here in however many numbers they had, and people were here with an ungodly number of kids in tow, and the fear was spreading even though Lauren hadn't seen one act of violence yet that hadn't been perpetrated by her during her run.

All she could think about was getting to Molly, about stopping Molly before it could begin, about pricking her before these goddamned demons could do another thing with her body that she'd regret later. They may have gotten her mother and used Molly to do it, but she'd be damned if they were gonna—

Lauren locked eyes with Molly as she got to within twenty feet. A guy knocked Lauren back a step as he stumbled into her path. He hit her in the arm with his shoulder and she felt a shock of numbness roll down it; he'd hit her perfectly in the nerve, knocked her off balance a step, and she lurched, equilibrium destroyed as she stumbled to try and keep on her feet. She teetered, losing sight of Molly, and then caught herself and came back down, drawing the bright yellow holy water pistol in her left hand and skipping the letter opener because she couldn't feel her right one.

Someone pressed against her on the side, pushing slightly, from knee to thigh, and she suspected it was a kid but she didn't look down to be sure, because her gaze fell on Molly again, and she stopped in shock as she saw the start of the things she'd dreaded.

The things she'd come here to stop.

The thing she'd hoped she wouldn't have to see again.

Molly's lips and chin were red with blood, and there was a raven-haired teenager with long black eyelashes and glitter sparkles all done up on the sides of her cheeks, clenched in Molly's hands, her neck tilted and open, crimson squirting from where her daughter—no, a demon, goddammit—had done incredible damage to tissue and artery and—

"Oh, God," Lauren whispered as Molly came in for another bite. No gun, no knives, just demon strength given to a human mandible. The world turned red around her as Lauren focused on her daughter, the demon, and the hell she was unleashing.

*

Hendricks was about thirty feet from Erin when she grabbed hold of a guy in his fifties that was standing next to her and just ripped his head off with her bare hands, the sound of skin and muscle and veins tearing lost to the first screams of the crowd. He saw red blossom all over in front of him in the growing dusk, lit by the lamps that colored the square. He ignored all of it in his peripheral vision, though, all except for one about three feet to his left, and he threw his sword out almost blindly and was rewarded with a guttural sound that he barely heard and the smell of sulfur that came in hard over the smell of accumulated humanity that surrounded him.

Erin tossed the head without sentiment or even waiting a second to hold it aloft like a conqueror in a movie, just chucked it and then grabbed a blond lady who was stumbling away from her. Hendricks didn't get a real clear look at the woman before Erin threw her bodily through the air and she smashed into the stone obelisk that stood in the middle of the square. Hendricks suspected there was a sickening sound as pliable skull met unyielding rock, but he couldn't hear a bit of it over the chaos. He did, however, see the woman's body bend unnaturally, her yoga pants accelerating up into her jacket as her bones all lost their fight to stay in their proper places. It was just about as gross a display of demon strength as he could recall seeing, watching that woman disintegrate against the monument in the square like an Empire State Building jumper. He forced himself to ignore the sick feeling it produced in him and fought on, trying to get through the crowd to stop Erin, even as he watched her tear through her next victim's chest like she was cracking open a watermelon on the Fourth of July.

*

Braeden's whole body froze in panic when things started to go wrong. He heard the shout, then the screams, then the shoving started, and he jerked Abi's hand to drag her back to him so fast he didn't even think about how it might hurt her. She squealed but he pulled her to him, unresisting, and folded her against his leg as a whole buffet of crazy opened up around him.

Hugo Barclay, a guy Braeden knew from the automotive department at Wal-Mart, came lurching along with his mouth open, Kool-Aid red smeared all around like he was dressed to be a vampire, except he was just wearing his jeans and work vest. Braeden watched Hugo grab Ellie Larson from behind and just sink his teeth right into her there in front of him. Braeden heard a faint scream and couldn't figure out whether it was someone else or Abi. His brain tried to put what he was seeing together, like pieces from twelve different puzzles that weren't fitting together. First he figured it was a makeup display, something right in line with the spirit of Halloween. But who the hell would do something as scary as this in the middle of a goddamned kids' trick or treating event?

Then Braeden watched as Hugo didn't stop with a simple bite, he ripped and tore with teeth pointier than any fake set of vampire ones he'd ever seen sold in any costume display, tearing Ellie Larson's neck wide open. Braeden could see muscle in there, and bone, and blood squirting as Hugo damned near tore Ellie's fucking head off in front of him before he tossed her aside, screams quieted, head barely hanging on at fucking all.

Braeden didn't even have time to scream "Jesus Christ!" before Hugo grabbed Betty Larson, Ellie's mother, by her grey hair and just ripped it harder than Braeden could have believed possible. The hair came off, and so did a pretty good part of Betty's scalp, and she fell to her knees with her mouth open in a scream lost to the goddamned Armageddon around them. Hugo didn't stop, though, he reared up and kicked Betty right in the side and she just broke like a piñata at a party, her belly ripping open on her side as she whipped into the crowd like a Frisbee, knocking over kids and showering people with guts and shit. Braeden smelled the shit, like someone had taken a giant fucking dump right in front of him, and it gagged him, raw and nasty, and the screaming around him broke into his world again, cracking through the fear and panic that had his heart in a vice grip and stirring him into motion again.

Braeden reached down and grabbed Abi under the arms with his left hand as he fumbled under his shirt and coat with his right for the .38 hidden in his pants. He'd be damned if he knew what was going on, but the only things he was sure of right now were that Sheriff Reeve was fucking right about demons, and he had to get Abi the hell out of here before the hell he was witnessing got hold of her.

*

Reeve found no damned joy at all in being right about demons, even if everybody could see it for themselves right now. The crowd at the Halloween event had dissolved into a panicked orgy of violence in the space of about ten seconds, and it was hell on his eyes watching people he'd known for years and years dying in front of him in mere eye blinks while there was near nothing he could do to stop it.

"FUCK!" Reeve shouted as he tried to shove past Monty Franks, who was staring gape-mouthed at Ben Lawler, a guy who had worked at Rogerson's in the produce section through two decades and a change in ownership. Lawler had his own mouth open, but his was filled with demon teeth about an inch long apiece, and they were descending on Rebecca Crosby's face. They sank in before Reeve could get past Monty to do a goddamned thing about it, and Lawler just ripped her face right off like he was pulling off a mask, leaving scraps of meat and flesh on the bone as Reeve screamed his way through, leading with his sword.

He popped Ben Lawler right in the shoulder, ripping through his t-shirt and triggering an immediate response in the man. Lawler seemed to gag, sulfur bursting out of his mouth as he spat pieces of Rebecca Crosby's face out, bloody flesh mingling with the dark fire in the back of his throat, his demon eyes disappearing in a swirl of darkness as he lurched to the side, hand swinging up to his shoulder wound and a guttural "Owww!" making its way out past the remainder of the gore rolling off his tongue.

Reeve didn't have time to even dwell on what he'd just seen, which would have been enough to give him goddamned nightmares for the rest of his life only a couple weeks ago. There was more, and worse, going on around him. "Motherfucker!" he screamed in impotent anguish, not even looking to see if Casey or Father Nguyen were behind him as he waded through a crowd of kids that were crying and covered in blood as he rushed to try and stop this madness before it killed the town he'd sworn an oath to protect.

*

Arch would have expected more blood at a massacre like this. There was certainly plenty of it, but he would have thought there'd be more once things dissolved into the chaos. It seemed like every fifth person in the crowd had gone wild like a vampire in a terrible horror movie Alison had convinced him to watch when they were in high school.

The demons weren't wasting a second or yielding an ounce of mercy, and in doing so they were proving themselves about the lowest form of devil spawn Arch could have imagined. He'd seen what was left after the massacre on Crosser Street, where cannibal demons had eaten whole families alive and left nothing but the scraps.

This was worse.

So much worse.

His brain was filtering out about as much as it could, trying to focus in on the nearest threat, which was a man in a flannel shirt with a demon face that was tearing Paulina Tomlinson in half with his bare hands, her hands clutching ineffectually at her belly as he ripped her open like she was a bag of candy. There was no danged candy at all coming out, though, just blood and intestines, and Arch watched the scene in front of him like it wasn't even really happening, like he was just seeing a criminal pulling out a knife and waving it at someone instead of the grisly spectacle of a woman who'd once served him punch and pound cake at a school dance getting disemboweled alive in front of him.

Arch led with the sword, popping the "man" in flannel in the back with the point. He knew he'd scored his hit, and though he couldn't hear him scream, the smell of brimstone assured him his aim was true. He had no time to reflect on this success, if he could even call it that, because not five steps beyond that, Anna Quentin had something that looked like a small ham clothed in a little pumpkin suit in her teeth and she was ripping it apart like a dog with a strip of cloth in its teeth.

"Oh, Lord, my Father," Arch breathed, not looking too closely at that thing in Anna Quentin's teeth and instead shoving someone out of the way so he could go low and jab her in the leg, "watch over the innocent and protect them in this hour of need." The screams and the cries didn't provide much assurance that his prayer was being answered, so he just kept on as he caught Anna in the leg, and whirled to deal with the next threat.

*

Hendricks couldn't fucking believe this shit. He'd been through demon parties, seen massacres of a sort before, seen all manner of horror, usually after it had unfolded, but this …

He hadn't ever seen anything like this before.

He tried to keep his eyes glued on Erin but he couldn't because there were at least a half dozen demon-possessed townsfolk between him and her, and there was no way he was gonna turn his back on any of them, not one.

It was like an orgy of violence, staggered waves of panicked people scrambling to get out of the kill box, writhing to try and escape the ambush, panicking, freaking the fuck out, losing their shit—literally, he could smell it—and losing their lives. He was fighting against a decreasing tide as some of the lucky ones made it out, maybe. He didn't want to turn around for more than a second every now and again to make sure he wasn't gonna get bushwhacked from behind in this clusterfuck right outta hell.

Someone ate shit against a nearby lamp post, knocking out the light and getting damned near sheared in two in the process. It was an ugly thing, and blood showered down as the body slid, unhooking itself from where it had been split at the shoulder, plopping soundlessly onto the sidewalk, the noise lost in the melee. Hendricks saw it and jerked his attention toward the origin of the throw.

There was a demon not ten paces away from him having a hell of a time. The nasty teeth were bared in a feral grin, and she had someone in her grip right now, ripping 'em up in ways that Hendricks was shocked by even after his tour in Iraq. The sheer power on display and the constant demonstrations of how weak human flesh was next to demon strength was turning this town square into a vile, disgusting sort of meat grinder. He'd fought these things, after all, and this Legion and their possessed were a fair sight stronger than run-of-the-mill demons.

The demon finished its grim work, and pieces went flying. The head came shooting off at Hendricks with a good bit of steam behind it, and he couldn't dodge it quite in time. It clocked him right in the skull, knocked his hat off and dropped him to the ground, the dusky square and the violence of the attack disappearing in the flash of light and the painful skull-on-skull contact that surged through the bone around his eye.

Hendricks felt his ass hit the grass, his sword falling out of stunned fingers. Someone tripped on his legs and it fucking hurt, but not as bad as the skull shot he'd just taken. It was like a headbutt from hell, and really, that was about what it was, hell chucking a disembodied head right into his kisser. He was just lucky it had hit bone on bone, because if it had hit him in the lips he figured would have been spitting blood and teeth, maybe even gotten knocked out.

He had just pried his eyes open when the fingers wrapped around his neck and dragged him up to his feet. He didn't even have the presence of mind to scramble for his switchblade until his feet were already dangling off the ground. It wouldn't have mattered anyway;

the knife was gone, and so was his hat, just as out of reach as his sword.

"Hello, Lafayette," a harsh, grinding demon voice squeezed its way out from between Erin Harris's lips. She was grinning like he'd never seen Erin grin, not even in all the times they'd screwed. A demon-length tongue flitted between sharp teeth, and Hendricks suddenly had a sinking feeling that he was gonna get screwed by her again pretty soon.

*

Alison wasn't in the worst of it, that she was pretty sure, or else she just wasn't seeing the worst of it, because of her height. The crowd was thinning as this thing dragged on and people either ran or got killed. She'd seen both, sometimes both at the same time. Rob Kinney had caught a demon punch from his wife right to the chest, impaling him. She reckoned based on the rumors it wasn't the first time Sally Kinney had penetrated her husband, but from the way his eyes shut after looking at her in complete disbelief for about five seconds, it was gonna be the last.

The slaughter had been going on for maybe thirty seconds or a minute, she couldn't tell. If someone had told her it had been an hour, she wouldn't have been surprised, because she'd already tripped over three corpses in her scramble to put a halt to this. She didn't want to look down, either, because the first time she did, she saw something nauseating that she couldn't ever unsee, no matter how many years she lived, and it just made her madder and sicker and more ready than ever to gut the fucker responsible for this.

Alison poked Sally Kinney in the back harder than she needed to, getting her right in the shoulder as she went by, and Sally jerked, her husband's corpse still hanging off her arm. She dropped immediately, dragged down by weight her human muscles couldn't hold up now that the demon strength had left her, and underneath the torrent of cries and moans, Alison caught Sally Kinney's very distinct howl of disbelief that seemed a perfect counterpoint to Rob Kinney's look of betrayal as his wife had killed him.

Alison didn't have time to comfort Sally, though, and she damned sure didn't have time to waste. She'd lost sight of Duncan in the opening fracas, and she caught a glimpse of him now as a couple demons came jumping out of the crowd to land on him. She saw his t-shirt, the red one with the Millennium Falcon schematic, get shredded under long fingernails powered by demon strength, and another cry rang out from her left. "Send the OOC back to the inferno!"

Alison snapped her head around and saw him, standing at the edge of the square, up against the boarded up front to the old secondhand clothing store. It was the guy from yesterday morning, the one Reeve had cuffed. Patient zero in this whole contagion, the one who'd brought this shitshow to town. He was the head carnival barker of the damned as far as Alison was concerned, and she peeled off from helping Duncan without a thought. This was her chance to end this fucking disaster, or, failing that, at least put the stop to the bastard responsible for it.

*

Braeden Tarley had never shot another human being before, and as he fired his first round out of his revolver, he wasn't sure whether he still had or not.

The world around him was like a slow-motion dance of death. Abi was screaming under his arm. He had her tucked under tight, his forearm wrapped around her little ribcage as he started forward on quivering legs, his pistol out in front of him. He was looking through the back sights and they seemed comically large, like football goalposts with the front sight somewhere in the distance. Beyond that was a blur of unfocused motion, and the faint outline of a face and yellowed eyes, and Braeden squeezed the trigger without seeing much other than that.

He didn't even hear the shot, but he saw the barrel flash right into someone. He jerked the trigger again, knowing for a fact that his pull wasn't anything close to smooth but so goddamned scared and frantic he couldn't stop it. The barrel flashed again, light in the dusky dark, something flickering around him like streetlights losing power.

Braeden pulled the trigger unevenly again, still staring right down those massive gun sights. They were so small the last time he went to the range, like the size of his pinky finger with a notch between them, and now they were enormous, like two tombstones sticking out of the back of his gun, which suddenly seemed big enough to launch artillery out of.

The world snapped back into normal motion, and Braeden felt wet warmth running down his leg. Whether it was piss or blood, he didn't know and didn't care. He held Abi tight and she was still screaming at the top of her lungs, not even a cogent word coming out of her.

Braeden saw something coming at him from the left, out of the corner of his eye, but he couldn't focus on it. It was almost like his eyes just couldn't snap to, couldn't get on what he was looking at. He whirled and fired, more out of panic than anything, because that was the side Abi was on, and he turned to try and play keep away from whatever the hell it was—

His eyes snapped into focus on gnarled teeth and a face that was unlike anything he'd ever seen before. The eyes were glowing at him, bulging, like they were gonna leap right out and jump into his own. There was a stink in the air like dirty diapers and Braeden's whole body felt like a live wire had dropped on him at some point, he was so damned rigid.

He fired again and didn't even feel the jerk of the revolver. He saw the light at the end of the barrel again and went to squeeze the trigger again but this time there was no flash. He'd lost count of how many shots he'd fired, and that face—

Good God, that face!

—was coming right at him. Braeden threw up his right arm and felt something snap as he took a hit to his forearm. It didn't hurt, but he damned sure knew he'd been hit. It hit again, this time at his elbow, and he saw someone swatting at him with real strength. There was something wrong with the angle of his arm, and he was dimly aware that it didn't normally hang like that. His fingers were numb and the pistol was gone out of them, and he blinked in surprise as he realized all these things—

Jesus.

Abi's screams had faded to a low wailing, and Braeden turned his head to see her sliding through his left arm. Her jacket was all bunched up where gravity had started pulling her through his grip, and he could feel the bare flesh of her belly against his left hand where he was clutching onto her for dear life. Her eyes were wide and her mouth was wide open like the day they'd met, when she'd come out of her mother and greeted the world with top-of-the-lungs screaming, changing his life forever.

Braeden tried to raise that right hand up to defend her again, but it stubbornly refused to move below the elbow. The forearm sagged, broken, out of commission, rips in his sleeve like something with claws had shredded its way through. He hadn't felt a bit of it beyond the impact, but he was bleeding, sure enough, and now that his hand was out of the way he could see that face again—

That fucking face!

—and it was all yellow eyes and bared teeth, and for some reason words from Abi's favorite bedtime book, *Where the Wild Things Are*, came springing out to mind. Braeden scrambled back on weak legs, holding himself between Abi and that thing, that fucking thing—

That Demon.

—so it couldn't get at her. His feet were on solid concrete now, and he didn't even remember getting to the sidewalk or the road around the square, he just remembered that he damned sure needed to get the fuck outta here, back to the truck.

There was a smell like sulfur from somewhere behind him, and Braeden didn't know where it came from, but it beat the hell out of the smell of shit. He looked back and saw Barney Jones, the pastor of the Methodist church with a fire axe in his hands, and he brought it down on someone's arm, taking that sucker right off at the elbow. Braeden would have blinked in surprise, but he need to turn back to the thing that was after him, the thing that was—

Right there.

—following him, except there were three of them now, and if they'd ever had human faces, they were buried under the blood that surrounded the teeth and lingered under the eyes that were yellow as the bees in that book of Abi's where they were learning the alphabet.

Abi's scream found voice again as Braeden stumbled on a curb. He didn't even have time to wonder *Who the fuck put a curb there?* before he twisted, landing hard on his back and keeping Abi from smacking the pavement. He took it all on the right side of his ass and all the way up to the shoulder blade, and the distant pain was enough to loosen his grip on his daughter just a little.

When they landed, she bounced against him, turning so that her forehead bopped Braeden right in the sternum. He felt it, but not as bad as she did, her face scrunching up to cry. Before it had been all red-faced screams, but now it was the welling tears of pain. He felt it, knew it was coming—

I'm sorry, baby doll.

—and something about it reminded him of Jennifer, the way she'd done that same tear-up-before-crying routine one night when he'd thought they were gonna break up but they didn't. It was the first time he saw her cry, but it wasn't near the last.

Abi looked up at him, the glistening droplets of water forming in the corners of her eyes, her face perfectly poised like it always did when she was about to cry, and then—

Dear God.

—it stopped, pain giving way to fear, that lurch of rolling uncertainty that followed a sudden drop. She didn't have time to be scared, not fully, but it flashed across her face in that instant, cradled in his arms—

His baby.

—and pressed against his chest, just like when she was born, just like her mother had done so many times before that, sitting in that perfect place that he'd saved for the two girls in his life—

Oh, Abilene.

—and he felt the first hard jerk against his arms, tugging. And the scream that Abi let out was pain, pure pain firing every nerve in her little body as awareness crashed in around her and she cried in fear and pain—

Oh, God, no.

—Braeden held on, held on tight, his own panic and pain setting in, jerking fast like all his muscles went into knots, and his left arm felt the pressure of resistance as Abi tried to hold on tight as she could, as her armpits made contact with him, something ripping at her, trying to tug her out of his grasp—

Like a reverse birth, dragging her out of his arms, out of the world.

—and he held on tighter, because he had to, he was—

Her daddy.

—outmatched, and he had no strength left in his right arm but he brought it around anyway limply, trying to get hold of her anyway he could. The look on her face as they were tearing her away from him was agonized—

Tearing her apart.

—and he screamed, "ABI!" at the top of his lungs but he couldn't even hear himself in the middle of the tempest in the town square. His daughter's face was white as fresh linens, her little lips frozen open and crying—

I was supposed to protect you. I promised your mother I would ...

Braeden lost her then as she slipped away, just like her momma, except this time he watched her die in front of his eyes, to those yellow eyes, and those nasty teeth, and he couldn't look away, not for one second, as for the second time in Braeden Tarley's life he lost the most important girl in his whole world.

12.

Reeve was losing his goddamned mind, losing track of what was going on around him, and shit was slipping away fast into the realm of un-fucking-salvageable. He was stuck in the corner of the square, a roar of people stampeding back the way he'd come in, a herd thinning by the moment as unspeakable violence was unleashed. Reeve was watching children die by the dozen, adults being torn to pieces by hellspawn, and it was all he could do to keep from throwing up while he was stabbing wildly at every demon he could lay steel on.

He watched a little boy that was probably no older than his eldest grandson, seven or so, get shredded in the teeth of Ryan Flanigan, and Reeve stabbed out as hard as he could, but it was way too goddamned late by the time he got Flanigan in the side. He was dimly aware that he might have caused more damage than he'd intended to, not holding back much as he stabbed, but he had no time to worry or think about that.

Ms. Cherry was still on the lamp post, shouting at people to get their asses over toward her, past her, but he could barely hear her over the clamor. He blinked a couple times when he saw her up there, and then she pointed to something and he lost focus on her.

Lonsdale the demon hunter came screaming into the fray behind him, his sword up over his head, and brought it down on Lisa Melman, splitting her damned head clean in two, driving out the demon but killing the woman, too. Reeve was about to say something when another demon, this one in the form of Dave Klapper, drove a hand right through the back of Lonsdale's head, splattering his goddamned code-speaking brain as he smashed the Brit's skull. Dave Klapper took a hard hit to the side of the head from a shining brass cross mounted on a long wooden rod, and thumped to the ground out of sight under Lonsdale's empty-headed corpse.

"Nicely done, Father Nguyen," Reeve said, not sure whether to be grateful or sorry that Lonsdale had been killed, especially given what he'd done to Lisa Melman. But there wasn't time to think about it. There'd be a time for grieving later, and he knew he'd be drinking his fill of it. For now he spun back around in time to see Casey bring down the sharp end of his tomahawk across Miguel Gallardo's hand, poking straight through tendon and bone and causing the man to scream as he expelled a demon.

The crowd was thinning ahead, through slaughter and retreat, and Reeve could see Duncan with about a mountain of demons on him; five circling him and striking, weaving in and out like sharks, and in the second he took to pause and reflect on it, four more came out of the crowd at the OOC.

That decided it for Reeve, and he headed straight for Duncan, hoping somehow maybe if he could help the expert demon, Duncan just might be able to help him stop this shit once and for all.

*

Lauren was sick watching Molly possessed, like seeing her perform in a school play turned into a slasher monster movie. Her daughter's mouth was dripping red, glistening, gushing it under the flickering lamplight as the scene of hellish chaos unfolded.

Lauren had nothing handy but her squirt gun filled with holy water, and she spritzed Mark Beckwith in the face as he came at her with demon eyes, not even turning to look at the man as he screamed and burst into flames. She didn't dare look to see if the demon was excised, because she was too busy staring at Molly, unable to tear her eyes away as Molly hefted a two-year-old and killed her with one bite in a scream of venomous glee.

"Molly!" Lauren shouted, not intending to tip her hand as she approached but unable to hold it in any more. Part of her was just churning, knowing her daughter was in there somewhere, was inside that thing, watching it commandeer her body and tear apart innocent people.

Molly looked right at her, grinning, blood dribbling down her chin, yellow demon eyes glowing like headlamps but fainter. Molly leapt right at her, coming down only a couple feet away. She swept in behind Lauren before Lauren could even get a squirt off, and suddenly there was a hard yanking pressure on her wrist and Molly had her hand bent up behind her back. The squirt gun tumbled loose to the ground with a faint clatter that was barely audible under the anarchy as Molly spun Lauren back around and then slammed her against a light pole that winked out as Lauren felt the pressure of the metal against her back.

"Hi, Mom," Molly said in a guttural voice, far removed from the normal sweetness or even the occasional snark that she directed at her mother. There was nothing of that here, nothing familiar, nothing decent.

All that was left was a demon, staring into her eyes.

Molly breathed out at her, and blood drooled out down her chin in a little wave, like a tide crashing out and splattering down the front of her dress and all along the flat bit of her upper chest that was exposed. "Do you like what you see? What I've become?"

"You're not ... Molly," Lauren barely got out around the hand clamping her throat. This was all a game to them, to these things. It was revenge in the most painful possible way, infliction of pain for the sake of it. Lauren's right hand was still numb from the hit she'd taken at the start of this, but she could feel her fingers again, and she snaked them into her pocket as she dangled in her daughter's grasp.

"But Mommy," Molly said, mockingly, keeping Lauren pinned in the air, just enough pressure on her collarbone to keep her from getting choked out but not nearly enough to stop her from feeling lightheaded. As if the numbness in her fingers hadn't been enough to work around ... "How can you say that? We're family." Her daughter cackled in way that reminded Lauren of a witch from an old movie. "You know what would make you feel better?" Lauren felt the letter opener there, just inside her pocket, waiting, as Molly sprang the answer on her. "How about some killing—you and me, together? It'd be like a family reunion, and then, when we're done ... you can watch me slit my own throat."

Lauren grunted, her fingers finally closing around the letter opener's handle as Molly cocked her head to listen to Lauren's reply: "Or I could just do it for you right now."

Molly's eyes widened and she brought up a hand, lightning-fast, to block Lauren's path to her neck. It was a funny thing, survival instinct, Lauren thought as she watched the demon move her daughter's body to protect itself. Even shit-stain, worthless demons had it.

Lauren slammed the letter opener tip-first into Molly's wrist, the one attached to the hand anchoring her in place, and heard a whoosh of air before the sulfur smell hit her in the face like someone had crammed a carton of rotten eggs up her nostrils, full force. Lauren dropped and caught herself, barely, knuckles of the hand clutching the letter opener hitting the ground. Molly hit her knees, the black fire roiling as the yellow eyes disappeared back to hell.

Lauren felt her breath come back in a rush as her head bobbed forward uncontrollably as she landed. She took a breath, then another, before she heard a faint "… Mom?"

She looked up and saw the fear and terror in Molly's eyes, the tears already starting, and Lauren didn't hesitate. She pulled her daughter to her and hugged her tight, ignoring the war going on around them.

*

Amanda was getting swarmed by an endless wave of these damned drones, a few fucking essences stacked into a human body and unleashed with blood-spitting rage on these townsfolk. The good news for Amanda was that she hadn't caught the eye of the damned king shit of these things. The bad news was that she knew Duncan had, because she'd heard him scream something about sending the OOC back to the inferno, and doubted it was happy times on the other side of the square.

Hell, there were no happy times anywhere in this square, except maybe for the bastards doing the damage.

"This is not going to be easy to contain," Guthrie muttered as she slammed a baton through the nose of a human, expelling the demon that had just caused him to eat a kid, but probably not doing him any favors in the process. There was no way Home Office was going to be anything but flaming pissed about this fuckup. This was not the simmer they'd sent him back to ensure. This was beyond a boil, and sadly, Guthrie didn't see any way to turn the heat down after a massacre like this.

"How about you lick my snatch, Hendricks?" Erin asked him, yellow eyes full of pissed-off glee, having a grand old fucking time. Hendricks felt his skin crawl, a full-body shudder even as she squeezed him by the neck, hanging him in the air.

The light of day was damned near exhausted, sun well past the horizon line, the lamps around the square flickering on and off like they were suffering from a power shortage. The chaos around him was fading, the numbers of Midian's citizens flagging as some of them got their feet beneath them and took off, and a little from the fact that there seemed to be fewer demons running around than there had been a few minutes ago. Maybe they'd gone to a bar or something, Hendricks didn't know.

All he knew was that he was looking into the face of one right now as it squeezed the fucking life out of him, thumb pressing so hard into his windpipe he couldn't even speak. "I … won't …" It was a labor of all he had just to get that out.

"But you would for another demon girl?" Erin's smile was a sick thing, a twisted distortion of the one from the girl herself, wider and broader somehow, the demon teeth on full display, like she'd gotten a Joker smile at some point in the last day. "You're not making me feel special, Lafayette."

His skin was clammy cold, the sun was setting behind his eyes, and his brain was starting to get hazy. "You're …"

"I can't hear you, Hendricks," she said, pulling him closer. Hot, stinking demon breath washed over him, like Erin hadn't brushed her teeth in a decade. It had a faint trace of sulfur and he gagged from memory and the association. It took him back to lying on the hard ground, staked in place. Erin lowered him down and he felt his knees bump the ground. He looked up into her face, shadowed and shaded by the growing dusk, and for a moment he thought Kitty Elizabeth was standing over him again, and he felt cold as a Wisconsin winter.

There was no fight left in his muscles, no life left in his fingertips. He felt sick, but it was a distant sort of sick, like his stomach was a million miles away and unable to respond. He stared up at Kitty—no, Erin—and she looked down on him with that same maniacal joy that Kitty Elizabeth had shown when she held him down—

—dominated him—
—tortured him—
—broke him—
—and took his will and desire and lust and everything left that had made him feel alive.

The sound of screaming and crying faded around him with the rest of the world, and Hendricks couldn't feel anything but the hand at his throat and his knees against the hard ground. All he could see was that face, that terrible face—

Like the one that killed Renee ...

"I can't hear you, Lafayette," Erin said with that wide, glowing smile, "and no one else will, either, ever again, after you—"

The yellow eyes went wide, and there was a burst of nauseating sulfur that triggered Hendricks's gag reflex. Erin's hand vanished from his throat, jerked away as she herself spun, mouth open, darkness swirling within, threatening to swallow Hendricks whole as he stood there.

Erin hit her knees, falling to his side like she'd been kicked away. He turned as all his weight came down and he caught himself on weak hands, watching Erin drop, watching her curl up on her side. He saw the demon essence swirl out of her as her eyes returned to normal.

"... Hendricks?" Erin said, voice hoarse and scratchy. Her mouth looked back to ordinary, and the gap between her front teeth was between human teeth now, not demon ones.

He stared at her, afraid to trust his eyes. He was toast, dead, about to get the life squeezed out of him at the hands of a goddamned sick, torturous demon. Who would ...?

He turned his head and looked up, and there she stood, her hair all aglow like a raging fire, watching over him like an avenging angel—hell, maybe she really was—and when she offered him a hand, he took it, and she pulled him to his feet.

"Thanks ..." Hendricks said, barely getting it out around his throat, which felt like someone had pounded it with a wooden dowel for a week after he'd had a long drink of broken glass, "... Starling."

Starling regarded him with care and nodded, then a second later she was gone, leaving Hendricks to fall back on his haunches there in the square, unable to find the strength to get to his feet, the sounds of battle fading with the last of the day.

*

Arch had been stabbing every pair of yellow eyes he could see, pushing his sword point into shoulders and elbows and buttocks and every other place he could sneak in and lay one on these suckers. The smell of sulfur was a constant now, and he'd had enough of the devils charge him that he could confidently say he'd done his part in ridding the town of this mess.

But as he looked around him, he saw way too much death and carnage to consider his modest efforts much of a success.

There were dead and dying people everywhere, and of the dying, most of them weren't of the fixable variety. These demons had gone in with more viciousness than Arch would have expected from a pack of rabid wolves and with more strength than a bull elephant. There were a lot of pieces missing from a lot of folks, and his shoes had been sticking with every step, like he was walking on a movie theater floor. This was a little more slick, though, and he didn't want to dwell on the why.

Arch could see Guthrie snaking her way around the square to the far side, following the path she'd agreed on with Duncan to start with. The most he could say about what the OOC was doing was that she was probably lowering the final kill count, but she was leaving a trail of pretty battered people in her wake. Maybe even some dead, though Arch wasn't watching closely and didn't want to know. It wasn't as though he could just drop what he was doing and have a throwdown with her right now. That would have been suicide for both of them, given that there were still more than a few Legion drones zipping around, trying to get fresh blood.

Arch spun to look back in the direction Alison had headed, and the crowd had cleared enough that he saw a couple funny things. One was Hendricks and Erin, the cowboy kneeling and Erin down on all fours, looking like she was working hard to come up. They were a little away from the monument at the center of the square, and he took only a little notice of them because his eyes flew immediately to what he saw beyond them about thirty or forty feet.

Alison.

She was walking with a purpose, heading straight for someone, and it took his eyes a second to adjust in on who she was going after.

When he saw, it took him a moment more to realize who it was.

It was the dadgummed sonofagun who started this all. Arch knew him, because he was the one who'd been there yesterday morning when this whole thing started.

Arch stabbed his sword into the shoulder of a demon coming at him and peeled off in a hurry, breaking into a run as he headed after Alison, meaning to follow his wife to the end of this thing.

*

Reeve figured out pretty quick that Duncan had shit under control. He was swinging his arms and his baton hard enough to crack skulls, and he was laying people out hard. He'd put down a good six or seven demons, but twice that many more were coming for him, the OOC serving as a kind of lightning rod for these shits as they ran out of human prey, what with the crowd in the square thinned by flight and death.

As much as Reeve wanted to wade into that and get him some, he figured that hanging on the perimeter of Duncan's fight was the wiser course, taking a poke at a demon as it darted by, trying to get at the OOC. He expelled that motherfucking squatter from Sheila Nielsen's body and sent her gasping to the ground as the black fire ran through her eyes. He grabbed Sheila by the back of the collar and dragged her away from the fray, trying his level best to protect while he was serving up cold fucking vengeance for these demon motherfuckers.

He was about ready to circle like a shark again when he caught sight of something beyond Duncan's little whirlwind of hell that got him looking. He thought he caught sight of Alison Stan, but she disappeared behind a couple parents running with their kids clutched tight to their chests, screaming as they hurried past. He saw her again as they got away from her and realized she was heading toward the edge of the square beyond, walking right toward some swarthy dude in a flannel shirt. Reeve watched her, perplexed, and then he realized exactly what he was looking at.

It was that monkey fucker he'd cuffed before shit went haywire yesterday and started this shitstorm.

Reeve didn't even hesitate; Alison was just stalking toward the bastard like he was a deer in the woods, and it looked like he was prepared to meet her just the same. Reeve skirted the edge of Duncan's fight, but something that looked like a torso came skidding out at him and took his legs from beneath him, sending him plummeting face first to the road, hard. He caught himself on both hands but felt the pavement give him a road rash on one palm and across his fingers on the other hand, elbows stinging from the impact. That rib he'd fucked up yesterday blazed with pain, and he moaned, low and long, trying to get his wits gathered about him. It took a minute.

When he looked up again, Alison was behind the fight with Duncan, and Reeve started to push to his feet, damned sure he wasn't going to let her get all the satisfaction of ripping apart the motherfucker who'd killed Donna.

*

Alison hadn't been counting the seconds since hell had broken loose in the square, but she had a decent estimate and guessed that all the blood currently covering the streets and grass of the square had been let in less than two minutes' time. It had been a frenzied mass of chaos, like a fight between wild badgers in a telephone booth, but now the streets were clearing, people running the hell away as the last of the demons on this side of the square were congregating on Duncan, trying to get him down.

Alison had faith in Duncan. He was tough; he could take it. And even if he couldn't, he'd distract these bastards long enough for the innocent people that had been stacked up in the square from one side to the other to get a chance to escape. They were running for the exits now, and she'd seen faces filled with terror of the primal sort, like they knew hell was coming two steps behind them.

In the middle of it all, past a street strewn with the corpses of women and men and children, Alison was locked onto the guy who started this fucking mess. She tried not to swear so much around Arch, but it was tough sometimes, especially when she got ornery.

And she was nothing but ornery now.

She stalked up to him with her Glock clenched tight in one hand, her dagger in the other. He was just lingering there, staring at her, knowing she was coming for him and plainly unworried in the least.

"What's your name?" she called out, slowing down so she could give her hands a second to quit shaking. Her hands never shook, not with the rifle, and she had zero room for fear at the moment. But this ... this *motherfucker* ... had her so viscerally angry that her guts were quaking with rage, her hands quivering as she tried to pull back on the wild horses urging her to run up and cap his ass right in the fucking face until the slide locked back, to jab him in the neck a dozen times, just hoping the demon eyes would stick around so he could feel it every time she did.

She wanted to fill the square with his blood the way this fucker had done to her people, her friends. She saw faces staring dead at the dark heavens above, faces she knew from work and around town, the faces of men who smiled at her, women who chatted with her, kids who took the lollipops she gave out at the checkout lanes sometimes.

She saw families lying dead, people bleeding out their life's blood around her, taking their last breaths while trying to reach out with quivering hands to touch their loved ones one last time. Michael Dougherty was crawling, his neck wide open, red sluicing down, trying to shake his eight-year-old son, who was missing ... God, he was missing half his head.

Alison looked away, unable to take even the slight dose it was sending right to her heart. They'd come here to protect these people, they'd assembled to protect this town.

And they'd failed.

"What's your name?" she asked, stopping just shy of the sidewalk where he stood, this colossal bastard, this first-rate demon turd shat out of hell on tongues of the devil's own fire. She'd taken up arms when the demons had come after her, after her husband, but she hadn't taken it as personally as she was this—this—this fucking outrage.

"We are Legion," the man said simply.

Alison stood there, letting her hand shake as she tried to do combat breathing, something Hendricks had taught her to get her heart rate under control. Because right now, she doubted she'd be able to shoot for shit, even if she emptied the mag at him from five feet away. "That's your whole rump state's name. I'm talking about yours, the guy who's talking to me right now." She looked right at him and waited, expectantly.

He smiled faintly. "We speak as one."

"Bullshit," she said. "Go high enough, there's always a fucker at the top of the pyramid."

He stared at her with steely eyes. "My name is Chester."

She kicked herself for not remembering. "Chester," she said slowly. "And your friend's name was ... William."

Chester lost his smile immediately. "We lost many friends—"

"You lost William," she said, driving that arrow deep in the fresh wound she saw.

Chester darkened slightly, bare bones of a scowl popping up on that face of his. She hated that face, wanted to use her knife to carve it off so she could have a bonfire and burn it while she watched the flesh melt. She'd never considered herself a particularly violent person, but that reticence was fading away pretty quick. "I lost William," Chester said, once he'd settled a bit, that dark shroud rolling down over him as he tried to cloak his emotions. "But I was not the only one in this body who lost, and I am not the only one enraged."

"No," she agreed, her breathing nearly under control, "you're damned sure not."

Alison raised the Glock and fired, landing the first shot in right in Chester's belly, driving him back a step. She fired twice more, planting them both in center mass, right inside the ten ring like her daddy taught her. His face showed signs of strain, reddening as his essence took the hits.

Alison strode forward, up onto the curb, firing as she advanced. She didn't get fancy, she didn't go for head shots, because there was no advantage to be had there. The smell of burnt-off gunpowder flooded her nostrils, and she came at him slowly, enjoying every gentle, careful squeeze of the trigger. Chester took the hits with surprise, alarm racing across his face as Alison came closer and closer. She kept her cool, kept her calm, planning to demolish him with efficiency and calculation, not daring to take any chances that might let this snakey fuck slither out of the square to do any more damage.

"Just like you taught me, Daddy," she whispered as she fired again and again, right into his chest. She could see her father in her head, imagine him lying in the bed, like he was tethered to torturous unconsciousness by the mere possibility of Chester's continued existence.

Well, she'd take care of that for him.

She was almost to him, her knife clutched carefully in her hand, ready to deal the final blow. All she needed to do was nick him, that was it, and this nightmare would be over. Chester was staggering, face vacant, writhing from the force of the rounds she'd just emptied into him as she ran the blade forward—

*

Reeve was only about ten steps away as Alison fired into the bastard who started all this. Chester, he'd heard him say, and that was fine a name as Reeve had ever heard for a dead man. His legs were pounding against the concrete and he mounted the curb, coming at the fucker sideways. He wasn't going to make it before Alison struck the final blow, it didn't look like, but he had his sword in hand nonetheless, just in case he'd be able to get a hit in before she sent Chester back to hell.

*

Arch stopped running when he saw Alison had it all sewn up. She was on this demon, Chester, advancing carefully through gunsmoke, not too fast lest she trip herself up. He recognized the cold, vengeful, lizard part of her brain at work, and knew she was calculating every move. She wasn't taking any chances; she was going at him methodically, clearly intent on taking him apart and finish this deal once and for all.

*

Chester had been surprised when Alison Stan had remembered William's name. He'd assumed these worthless bugs were too stupid, too self-involved, too self-centered, to recall much of anything beyond themselves. Years of his experiences working with people like this, lauding them in arguments with William, had been washed away in a single day of rage. He'd defaulted into a state where he'd lost all respect for human ability and cognition, and this was the result: Chester getting shot repeatedly, the essence of all those he still carried in this form washing around hard within him.

The disorientation was akin to be strung upside down and yanked into the air, and Chester's balance was the first thing to go. His back hit against the boarded-up storefront behind him and only barely preserved his ability to keep himself even somewhat upright. She had fired countless rounds into him by this point, the stink of the gunfire filling the air around him, another unfamiliar ingredient in an utterly unfamiliar experience.

Chester watched the world around him slosh to and fro as his senses were addled by her unceasing stream of bullets. Her aim was good, her manner cold, and he knew she meant to end him, no doubt.

She meant to end them all.

Chester watched her close to within range; she stopped less than two feet from them, firing again and again into him without remorse. Without emotion.

This was the way it was supposed to be. This was how he had turned his own people loose to do what they had done in this square. There was no remorse, but he had seen emotion. Vengeful blood lust had run over them, his army, and he had watched from the side as the slaughter turned into chaos. Chester had rage of his own, but he had not partaken in this particular gluttonous buffet of rage. A distant part of it sickened him, he realized now as the world listed hard around him like one of the old ships in which he and William had come to the new world for the first time.

The thought of William was like a hot poker jabbed through his shell, piercing the disorientation of the gunfire and spearing him squarely in the essence. The world went right for a moment, and Chester felt the rage solidify him, turning him in one direction and one only.

Hers.

He lashed out with a single hand, striking almost blindly, aiming for nothing but the form in front of him, sticking a gun in his face and coming at him with a knife, and he heard the cry and knew he'd struck true.

*

The feel of something stabbing her in the side made Alison think at first she'd gotten speared by something from behind. It took her brain a second to process that Chester had been the one to do it, lashing out with a hand as she'd started to bring down the knife on him.

It had hit hard, hard enough that it pushed her back a step, dragging the holy blade away from Chester before she could sink the tip. The force of the impact she felt quickly, the pain of it was something that took a moment to sink in, but when it did she doubled over, unable to stop herself from folding, like all the muscles in her belly had quit at once.

"Shit," she said as she bent hard, firing one last time as she did so. The bastard had got her in the gut. The first thought that ran through was that she hoped, dear God, that he hadn't gotten her in the uterus. The pain brought tears to her eyes and when she got them open again a second later she saw the Glock's slide was locked back, the chamber open.

Out of bullets.

She speared forward blindly with the knife before she even raised her head. It was an instinctive sort of strike, lashing out in the direction of danger. She thrust it out there and felt it catch nothing but air, and a second later something got her good across the neck, like someone backhanded her in the throat or like that time she'd run straight into a volleyball net without seeing it—

When Alison looked down, she could see the blood just dripping out, running down the front of her shirt, and when she tried to raise her head, it didn't come up easy. She labored, lifting up, and watched a little more blood squirt out as she caught sight of Chester's face, staring back at her. She tried to stab at him, but he was too far away, and she sagged, her legs failing, arms feeling so weak she just needed to ... sleep ...

"NOOOOO!" More than one scream rent the air around her as Alison dropped to the concrete sidewalk. She couldn't see anything but Chester's feet, and the sun started setting hard in her head, light fleeing from the corners of her vision.

*

Arch saw it from a distance, not believing it as the horror show unfolded not thirty feet away. Alison had it, she had it in the bag, and then Chester swiped out and caught her right in the side. Arch stood there, stunned, the cold evening air running over him having not a dang thing to do with the chill he felt as she struck at him again and he got her right across the throat, splitting it wide, letting the blood run—

Arch was in motion in a second, was zero to sprinting in that moment, and as she fell to the ground at Chester's feet, the dread spiraled at him like a perfectly thrown football about to hit him in the face, and there was nothing Arch could do to block it.

*

Chester slit her throat for good measure, something he might not have done if she hadn't still been trying with everything in her to kill him. He watched her sink low, falling to her knees, dull eyes not comprehending the damage he'd done to her in his own defense, in the defense of the others that were with him.

His work was not yet done, after all.

This was simply another step on the cold path of vengeance he'd set out on.

Chester spun to deal with Sheriff Reeve, who was coming at him from what the man probably perceived to be his blind side. Chester disabused him of his misperception by slapping away the flat blade of his sword and then slamming a fist into the man's gut, rocking him back. Chester stepped on Reeve's hand just hard enough to deprive him of his weapon, and then stood above the sheriff, whose pained face looked up at him, eyes widening in the knowledge that there was nothing left for him to do to save himself.

*

Reeve's hand ached like a car had run over it, and his sword was so far out of reach that even if his hand hadn't been pinned, stinging, under Chester's foot, he doubted he would have been able to reach it before the demon pummeled him to death with one good punch.

Chester looked down at him with cold indifference, like he was staring at a bug, and Reeve just stared back, trying to pour every last ounce of his defiance at this bastard ... this bastard who'd done more to hurt him than anyone else Reeve had ever met.

"Had enough yet, Sheriff?" Chester asked.

"You ... took every goddamned thing from me," Reeve said. He hadn't meant to answer the man, but it just popped out. "My wife ... my town ... you killed ..."

"You still have your life," Chester said.

"I don't expect you're planning to let me keep that much longer," Reeve said. He could see Arch running at Chester from behind, fury racking his deputy's face, sword held high, but he didn't dare look at him for fear Chester would see it coming. Instead he glanced sideways at Duncan, who still had five of these goddamned assholes on him, though they were falling fast. Off in the distance, toward the other side of the square near Surrey's, he could see Father Nguyen with his cross on a stick held high like a battle standard, a few others rallied around him, fighting their way through a cluster of demons that were coming at them. "I doubt you've got much mercy in your heart or essence or whatever you call that black tar that goes pop out of you assholes when you get exposed to the light of day."

"Is that so?" Chester asked, still staring down at him like he was examining him through a microscope, such a low form of life as to not even merit full attention. "I don't think it would be merciful to let you live, Sheriff." And Chester smiled coldly and spun, slapping Arch Stan's hand so hard his sword flew out of it and hit the boarded-up window behind them. Without missing a beat, Chester reached out and smacked Arch in the sternum, and Reeve heard the pop as Arch went sailing back ten feet and hit the pavement, all the air coming out of him in a rush.

That done, Chester looked right back down at Reeve. "And I am not feeling merciful anyway, Sheriff ... so now you can live with the knowledge that not only did you cost your wife her life ... but that you prompted the suffering that has ravaged this town."

And with that, Chester spread his arms wide, wide enough to encompass the square and all the destruction within it. There were more dead here than Reeve could count, even if he'd wanted to look around and actually assess the damage. "Look upon your good works, Sheriff Reeve. I had not killed a human being in over a hundred years, and then only in self-defense. Less than a day in your town and I cast aside those ways and claimed the lives of those you held dear because you and yours made your war upon me." Chester's face was dark again, his rage seething and bubbling up to the surface. "I did not strike the first blow in this, remember. You did." He folded his arms in front of him, and there was a dark satisfaction on his face. "Remember that, as you lie here." His eyes grew angrier. "Remember that, as my servants fetch people from this town, house by house, and slaughter them in front of you and your friends. Watch your community die, piece by piece, and realize—"

Chester's eye went from spiteful to wide in a half-second, and his head jerked around and down, snapping with the force of the sudden turn. His mouth flew open mid-speech, and darkness whirled inside him, a vortex of black that heralded his departure from this world and return to the other one, to the place that Reeve hoped had a lot of fire and torment, though he was fairly certain however much of it there was, it wasn't near enough for the atrocity he'd seen committed in this square.

*

Chester felt the sting and turned, looking down, down at the heel of his shoe, where a dagger rested, its blade sunk in beneath the leather and he watched it, dumbfounded, in shock, as the first tuggings broke loose within him and he felt himself becoming unmoored from this body he had held for so long.

His gaze drifted to where Alison Stan lay, staring up at him, lips in a muted smile that was not half as wide as the darker one on her neck that he had cut out of her very flesh. "I bruise your ... heel," she whispered nonsensically, her hand still on the blade that had struck him.

Chester wanted to say something in reply, something about how she had done no good, that she had not saved herself, nor anyone else, but the vortex ripped and tore at him, dragging some of his fellows ahead of him. He held on a moment longer and then remembered ...

William is on the other side.
To hell with these people.

Chester let go of the earth, let go of the body that he and William had shared for so long, and departed, leaving behind him his revenge and all that he had done in its service, not caring what he might face on the other side, knowing that William would at least be there, waiting.

*

Hendricks saw it just as he was coming back to his feet, the fall of Alison Stan. He heard Arch shout, "NOOOO!" and go running, get whacked around by the demon godfather of all this misery, but he couldn't get there nearly in time, so he settled for hobbling past Erin, ignoring her, and going straight for Arch, but by the time he got to the man, he was just about on his feet, though staggering, and Chester was headed straight back to hell, courtesy of Alison.

"Arch, you all right?" Hendricks asked lamely, grabbing him by the arm and trying to haul him up but failing to do much other than latch on just as the big man was getting his balance to go forward again. He would have smacked himself for asking such a stupid question, but it was done in the heat of a pretty dire moment.

"No, I am not all right," Arch said, shaking off Hendricks's arm like he was shrugging right out of a half-assed tackle. He didn't even look back as he broke into a shambling run straight for his wife, who was just lying there with her throat slit, hand still clinging to the knife she'd just jabbed into the archdemon's heel.

*

Amanda was on the other side of the square, helping a small cluster of idiots finish up their fight when she heard the scream. She batoned some doofus in a muscle shirt in the back of the head as he charged at the priest with the cross staff, cold-cocking him hard enough to send his chin right to the bloody street. She didn't have much use for these makeshift demon hunters, or the real kind, those fucking losers, but she had to admit they'd done a decent job of sweeping the square clean of most of the shit that was soiling it.

"NOOOOO!" Most of the yelling and screaming had died down, so when Amanda heard that, she was able to turn her head and look. Just past the big monument in the middle of everything she saw the shit going down, Duncan up to his elbows in this plague of a Legion, and past that ...

Alison Stan looked like she was about to take a dirt nap.

"Well, that's a real shame," Amanda said and whipped the baton into the face of another one of the demons, this one with blood dripping down her chin. Amanda had actually liked Alison. That was too bad.

*

Lauren was clutching Molly tight to her when the scream crackled through the air. She couldn't see who had let it out, because the dais and the monument were right in the way, but she turned her head in time to see Reeve go down under the assault of some demon, who was holding him. She started to get up, pulling a resisting Molly with her, but something happened, and the demon dropped to his feet. Someone happened to him, Lauren realized, finally starting to shake herself out of the daze that had settled when she'd gotten her hands on Molly again.

The square was getting damned near close to quiet, and the only fighting she could see was Duncan throwing down with about three or four demons, and maybe five more going behind her with Mike McInness from the Charnel House, Pastor Jones, Father Nguyen, and Casey. It looked like they were wrapping things up pretty good, taking apart their bloodthirsty opponents with nasty, angry precision.

Lauren pulled Molly close as she peered across the square at where Reeve was sitting, freed from the demon who'd been stepping on him. He was sagging, shaking his head as he looked past the fallen demon to—

It hit Lauren in an instant that Alison Stan was who that happened to the demon. She couldn't see her real well, but she could tell the blond lady was prone, a knife in her hand.

"Oh my God," Molly breathed into Lauren's ear, and Lauren couldn't tell if she was talking about how Alison looked or was just taking in the scene in the square in general. From what she could see of Mrs. Stan as she ambled into motion, her doctor's training coming back to the fore ... either fit.

*

Arch ran until he was almost upon her, legs wobbling as he slowed only a few feet away. His eyes took her in, her jeans soiled and darkened, the denim almost black from the blood they'd soaked up during her fall. He swept his gaze up, slow, almost afraid to look right at her, at her face. She had a piece missing out of her side, an extra curve that was foreign to him, and he was the expert on her body if anyone was. He took the last few steps as his eyes made their way up to her neck, where her fingers were planted, trying to hold back a tide of red that was still blossoming out between her digits, running bright crimson down her shaking hand.

"Alison," he said quietly as he sank to his knees at her side. His eyes met hers finally, his survey done, and he swallowed hard as about a million different feelings welled up inside him and he tried to keep every last one of them down.

"Arch," she said, barely a whisper, and she reached up for him. He grabbed her left hand with both of his, an impulse reaction. She was holding her throat with the other, not that it was doing a lick of good. "He ... he killed 'em, Arch ..." She turned her head and a little blood rolled out the side.

He dropped her hand and tried to get her to steady herself. "You just ... you just hold still," he said, the desperation leaking out faster than the blood between her fingers. "Help is ... it'll be on the way ..."

She looked back up at him, but her irises were getting glassy. "He killed 'em, Arch. Killed our ..." She blinked, and a little tear ran down the side of her cheek, "... our kids."

Her lips stopped moving, and Arch's hands shook as he touched her pale, cold cheeks. "Alison? Stay with me, baby." She did not respond, and the breath left her body softly, almost a sigh. The red liquid running out of her neck went down to a trickle, all its force expelled, and he stared into eyes that stared back into his, but they were empty of all the life that he'd known in his wife's.

"Alison?" Arch asked, voice quivering. The air was still and quiet around them, and there was a grunt to his right. Lauren Darlington came down right next to him, her hands stained with red as well, her breath hot next to his face. She looked at Alison, ran her hands over his wife's skin, touched her neck, pulled Alison's hand away, and after a moment, she let out a quiet breath of her own.

"I'm sorry, Arch," Dr. Darlington said, and the quiet emptiness settled into him like Midian had died around him. "She's ... she's dead."

Arch stared down at her, into those eyes. Words bubbled up and out, quiet ones that replaced the desperate feel that was clamoring to get out. "Who ... can find a virtuous woman? For her price *is* far above rubies. The heart of her husband doth safely trust in her, so that he shall have no need of spoil. She will do him good and not evil all the days of her ..."

He choked on the last word, and his shoulders heaved, and everything he'd been holding back came out in a terrible howl that split the quiet around him, and Archibald Stan dissolved into sobs, not giving a damn who saw.

13.

Hendricks had followed behind Arch, watching, not wanting to intrude on the man's grief, or on his words with Alison. He was listening, though, and he caught what she said, his mind leaping around a few places with it. It didn't take him anywhere he particularly wanted to go.

"What ... the fuck?" Erin's voice came from behind him. He turned to see her there, holding her head, blood trickling down her sleeve, a little pressed into the part of her palm he could see. Blood seemed to be the theme for today, because goddamn if it wasn't fucking everywhere in this place.

"You were possessed," Hendricks said matter-of-factly, turning his back on her to watch Alison take a last breath before she jerked lightly, once. He didn't want to believe it, but there it was; she was gone, gone in a second, and Arch hadn't even said goodbye, really.

"What ... happened?" Erin asked, her soft footsteps clicking against the road as she came up on him, drawing nearer.

"I fucking told you already," Hendricks growled, and he stalked away from her toward Arch, who was down on his knees, khakis completely stained through with dark liquid. He wandered closer to the man as Dr. Darlington, dressed in some bloody clothes, pulled back and put an arm around her daughter's shoulder. She looked like she'd been through it today, too, which didn't surprise him given what had happened before he'd left for the hospital with the others.

There were a few people moaning and grasping at themselves in the square, but mostly there was just death. He could see another group working their way around, Father Nguyen and Casey Meacham among them, and Amanda Guthrie snaking the long way around, probably hunting any strays. There were still screams in the distance, but other than that, the town was quiet. The lack of sirens gave the air a colder feel to Hendricks, as he stared out across a bloody spectacle of dead kids and parents so gruesome that it would have looked out of place in the war zone he'd been to.

"God damn it," Hendricks said.

"Don't you go blaming Him for this," Arch said, out of nowhere. Hendricks had seen the big man's shoulders shaking and mentally wrote him off. He sure as shit didn't remember himself as functional enough to answer anything after Renee died, not for a while, anyway. Arch looked up at him. Tears had streaked their way down from the corners of his eyes, but the black man's voice was strong as he spoke out in a voice that rang across the square. "It wasn't His doing."

Hendricks was about to let loose with a response that likely would have blistered the air, but one look at Arch's face shut him down. He remembered that feeling, what he saw there, and he couldn't find it in him to deny the man even a fool's ounce of solace. So Hendricks just closed his mouth and he watched as Arch slumped back down to mourn his dead wife.

*

Reeve had watched it all go down to hell from a few feet away, watched his deputy lose his wife right in front of his eyes, and it froze his ass so still he didn't even move for minutes and minutes. He just sat there, on the ground, ass against the cold, blood-stained concrete, and watched the world swirl around him, watch everything happen slowly, painfully slowly.

It was almost like losing Donna all over again.

He started to come out of it a little bit after Hendricks said his thing and Arch snapped back at him. Reeve expected more out of them both, was about ready to get up and get in there if they needed separating, but the cowboy just left it off, with a pretty curious look on his face. Hendricks had ghosts of his own, that much Reeve knew, and every single one of them was apparent on his face in that moment.

Reeve got to his feet real slow, hand and ribs aching like a demon had smashed 'em. He took up his sword in the other hand, mainly afraid if he left it here, it'd be gone for good, swept up for evidence or something by whoever came to clean up this mess.

And looking over it all ... goddamn. Who was going to clean up this mess, anyway?

There was no sound of sirens, no impending ambulances, no Ed Fries rolling up in his car, not even a hint that the volunteer fire department was on its way.

Midian had gone to hell, all right. There was no help coming, either.

"Sheriff?" Duncan's cool voice broke Reeve out of that toxic prison train, and he realized the OOC had no shirt on, his bare chest so glowing white he might as well have applied fluorescent body spray. "We should see to these people."

Reeve blinked at him, and he swept the square once. There were survivors; some wounded, some people clutching at parts of their bodies that might have been hit by holy weapons ... others crying and holding onto family members that hadn't made it. Those who could walk looked like they'd gotten out of Dodge, but there was damned sure no shortage of those left behind.

"Right," Reeve said, nodding once, hard. Maybe the law said he wasn't sheriff anymore, but he didn't see much evidence of the damned law around here, not right now. "Erin?" He called her over and she came, still holding the back of her head and trotting past Hendricks with a sour look. "Dr. Darlington?" She was holding onto Molly tight, standing right next to Alison and Arch, but she turned around to look at him when he called. "There's people here that still need our help." He could see Father Nguyen and some of the others working their way over, stopping and helping where they could. Barney Jones, Casey Meacham, Chauncey Watson, Mike McInness—a few others. Melina Cherry was just down the row from him as well, and she looked like she had a few people she was tending to.

Donna was dead. And even though Reeve had failed in every way, Alison Stan had risen up from certain death and sent the bastard that did the job right back to hell, like a gift-wrapped package for him and a reminder all in one.

This town wasn't dead, not yet.

"We got a lot to do here," Reeve said and went to lead the way.

Braeden Tarley didn't even realize he was sitting until an older black man came up to him and asked him in a soft voice, "Are you all right?"

Braeden blinked, like he was waking up from a long-ass sleep, coming out of the worst nightmare he'd ever fucking had, and he looked up at the man who spoke to him. He knew him, vaguely, as the pastor of one of the churches in town. He was looking down at Braeden with warm eyes, rimmed with concern. He'd extended a hand and it came down right on Braeden's shoulder as the pastor squatted down next to him. "You hear me?"

"I hear you," Braeden said, his voice all rough, like he hadn't used it before. Or maybe he'd used it too much. He looked at the man, the pastor, blinking a few times hard. His throat was raw, Braeden finally realized, like he'd taken a sip of acid. "I hear you all right."

"You okay, then?" the pastor asked, trying to look him in the eye.

Braeden looked back at him, and brought a hand up, itching at his nose with the back of his hand. It was wet, soggy, and snot dripped right out onto his wrist, sticking in the arm hairs poking out of his sleeve. His right hand was just numb, the sleeve shredded. "I ... I don't know," Braeden said finally.

"You, uh ..." The pastor looked around. "You here with anyone?"

Braeden just closed his eyes. "I was here with my daughter." He swallowed hard, not a single tear left to cry. "But she's gone now."

*

Amanda wasn't really bothered by blood and gore any more than these humans would have been bothered by the sight of an animal being butchered. Okay, so maybe some of them didn't have the stomach to watch that, but it didn't bother Amanda much. At least, not like it might have before the fiery crucible she'd passed through recently.

She surveyed the aftermath of the battle with a trace of disdain. Human suffering was pretty unappealing to her, way more gross than blood and entrails, and there was plenty of all of that on display. The milk of human kindness was tasting a little bitter to her at this point, and so she just stood back and tried not to let either the blood or the humanity get on her.

"You could be of some use," Duncan said, finally coming over to her long after night had fallen, and after they'd gotten the few survivors out of the square in the back of cars driven by volunteers mostly. The fire department had shown up to help with that, Amanda noticed, but that was about it. She suspected the funeral directors of Midian would be along shortly to get the majority of the business here today. Some of the people who'd escaped were returning now that things were all clear, and that was a whole 'nother mess of humanity that Amanda wanted to avoid.

Duncan clearly was having similar thoughts. "No ambulances," he said simply. When she didn't respond, he went on. "No news cameras." Still she said nothing. "Something like a hundred people died here, slaughtered by demons, and there's not a breath of this anywhere, and emergency services beyond the local fire department aren't even responding." He turned his head to look straight at Amanda, like he was accusing her of something.

"How about that." Amanda didn't feel compelled to even pretend to act like it was a question.

Duncan just stared her down. "We've been to hotspots before."

"You think I've forgotten this?"

"Emergency services don't fail to respond," Duncan went on like she hadn't spoken. "They may fall apart if the network gets too strained, but the ambulances from Chattanooga? They never even responded to the 911 calls. Tennessee Highway Patrol? Didn't even show up to help, and they would for this kind of emergency."

Amanda kept herself from rolling her eyes, but only just. "Yep, it's a real head scratcher."

"You don't seem too puzzled."

Amanda turned her head slowly. "You're not puzzled, either. You're just trying to act outraged to draw me out."

"This kind of thing doesn't happen," Duncan said, and Amanda caught a hint of danger, "not even in hotspots."

Amanda just stared back coolly. "Well ... this one's different, I guess."

Duncan's face quivered, his slight jowls getting more pronounced as anger flashed across his face. "Why?"

Amanda kept it cool as she answered. It had about come time to have this part of the conversation anyway. "Let's go back to the hotel. We'll ...

talk about it." When she saw Duncan cast a look around, she headed him off. "There's nothing else you can do here." She fixed her eyes on the same point he did, where a white sheet was draped over the place where Alison Stan had died, and where Arch was still sitting on the curb, next to her, sitting his own little vigil. "Hell," Amanda said, taking it all in again, and not really liking what she was seeing on any level, "there might not be anything else you can do anywhere around here."

*

"Hey, Arch?"

Arch looked up at the sound of Pastor Jones's voice to find the man standing there above him, next to another fellow. Arch started to get up but Jones held out a hand to stay his action, saying, soothingly, "Just hang right where you are, Arch. It's fine."

Arch did as he was told, running hands over his stubbly head as he stared up at Pastor Jones. He had his doubts that everything could be classed as "fine" or even within a hundred zip codes of what he would consider "fine," but he stayed sitting on the curb nonetheless, shaded by the half-darkness of the square. They'd brought in cars and flipped their lights, and that was what was shining in from around him, but it wasn't exactly like daytime around here.

Arch looked up at the man next to Pastor Jones, and felt a tingle of familiarity as he stared at him. The guy had a right sleeve that looked like it had been all torn up and he was holding his arm at a funny angle. "This is Braeden Tarley," Jones said, putting his hands on Tarley's shoulders and steering him down onto the curb right next to Arch. "You mind keeping him company while I go see if I can get him a ride to the hospital? I think his arm might just be broken."

"Sure," Arch said, nodding, staring at the monument straight ahead. He'd already half forgotten about Braeden Tarley, and the man was less than six inches from his shoulder.

"Braeden just lost his little girl, Arch," Jones said softly. When Arch looked over, startled, at the man next to him, Jones went on. "Arch just lost his wife, too. You two hang tight, now." And then Pastor Jones was gone.

"I remember you from school," Braeden Tarley said in a terribly scratchy voice.

"I recall you as well," Arch said. "Not terribly well, but ... I recall you."

"I'm sorry about your wife," Tarley said in a thick voice. "I ... lost mine a couple years back. I know how it feels."

Arch just sat there for a second, until the appropriate response floated down to him, and the memory of what he'd just heard settled on him. "I'm sorry about your daughter, that's ..." He shook his head. "That's just awful."

"All of this is," Tarley agreed in that same hollow voice. "And the worst part is ..." his voice crackled a little, "... you warned us what was out there. Reeve ... he ..." Tarley broke it off, his neck sagging.

"There was no warning for this," Arch said, keeping his head down. He hadn't looked back behind him to the sheet that was covering over his wife, not for a while. It was like an itch he kept denying himself to scratch, because that wasn't really her, not anymore. "No warning at all." How long had he been sitting here, now? Arch looked around and saw a few of the others moving around here and there. No Duncan, no Guthrie. He wondered idly if they'd survived. Then another question occurred to him, and this one he gave voice to.

"Where's Hendricks?"

*

Brian Longholt was sitting in his dad's hospital room, listening distantly to the sound of the heartbeat monitor beep in a steady rhythm. He was holding his mother's hand, his pain suppressed by the codeine or whatever that the nurse back on his floor had given him when she'd patched him back up. They were sitting in silence, he and his mom, not wanting to discuss what might be happening in Midian, or ... the other thing.

The smell of the hospital reminded Brian of disinfectant or grain alcohol. Maybe more the former than the latter, but either way that, combined with the soft, overly worn hospital gown he was wearing to keep his ass off the cold wheelchair seat was overwhelming his senses a little. He stared out the dark window beyond his father's bed and listened to it creak against the wind.

"Hey," came the soft voice from the door, causing he and his mother both to turn and look. Whatever Brian had been expecting, it wasn't Hendricks the cowboy, and that caused him to frown hard, instantly, as his mother came to her feet and ran over to give the man a hug.

"So good to see you, Hendricks," she said, like she was greeting an old friend, warm and steady. Brian knew that voice and knew it was basically just her trying to contain herself and be the right southern lady she thought she was supposed to be.

"Hendricks," Brian said, watching the cowboy carefully. He hadn't seen the man since he'd rushed off with Arch and Alison to go stop Halloween, and yet here he was, hours later, apparently by himself. There was fresh bruising along the cowboy's neck, Brian noticed, looking like a shadow or smudge of dirt just above his t-shirt's collar.

His mother noticed it, too. "Good heavens," she said, and did the mom thing where she touched it, probably trying to assess whether she was going to need to use mom spit to clean it off or just chide him for being insufficiently careful when fighting for his life with demons. "Are you all right?"

"Fine," Hendricks said tersely, and then nodded to the bed. "How's Bil …"

He didn't even get Brian's father's name out all the way before he must have pieced together his own answer. Brian watched it come to him, the bad news, the ugly truth, that same sinking, sick feeling Brian and his mom had been dealing with for over an hour now.

The respirator was gone, and Brian's dad's eyes were open again, fluttering, responding to the stimuli of Hendricks speaking. He grunted, looking at the wall, like he had since he'd woken up. It was a guttural noise, and it didn't seem to make any kind of sense.

"Is he …?" Hendricks's voice trailed off, looking at Bill in the bed, whose head was cocked to the side, staring at a blank space of wall and making noise like he was conversing with a monkey.

Brian's mother's hands flitted back to her side and she turned away from the cowboy. "Well, now," she said, and that was it, like she couldn't find a polite enough way to say it.

So Brian did. "He's brain damaged," he said simply, just got it out there. *I shot my father in the head and now he's brain damaged, probably a step above a vegetable for the rest of his life, which is likely to be much shorter than the average because he's probably never going to walk again.* He just stared at

Hendricks and basked in his own discomfort and guilt, because he didn't even have the balls to say that out loud, even though he was sure Hendricks was thinking it.

He knew his mom sure was.

"So, Hendricks," Addy said, coming back around, forcing a smile, "what brings you back to us at this hour?"

Brian was watching the cowboy, still stuck on the simple truth rolling in his head, and he almost missed it.

Almost.

Hendricks's face fell, almost imperceptibly, at the asking of the question. He didn't want to be here, Brian realized, and his mind made the next leap for him, just as quick, and he said it out loud the way he hadn't had the guts to say the other: "Alison."

Hendricks looked right at him, chalk white, and Brian knew he'd landed on it. The cowboy looked like he was about to pull a knife out of his own gut, pained beyond pain, and he turned his attention to Addy, sympathy coming from him like Brian had never heard from the cowboy, not ever before. "I am so sorry."

Brian watched his mother's face fall, the smile vanishing like it was wiped off with an eraser, it was gone so quick.

How could it have gone like this? He'd figured it out, dammit, what the Legion was going to do! How could it ...?

"Alison," Brian said again, and his father's grunt filled the air, no hint that he understood what was being said, and Brian sagged against his wheelchair back as the second piece of horrible news of the evening hit him harder than anything else ever had.

*

Lauren felt like she should be one of the last to leave, but she didn't want to keep Molly here, in the square, mired in the horror, any longer than she had to. The whole place stank worse than a trauma room after losing a patient, and she suspected it wasn't going to get any better in the daylight.

"You should get out of here," Reeve said to her, passing by on his way through, Mike McInness trailing in his wake. She could see Erin Harris in silhouette on the far side of the square, standing guard by a barricade.

They had a perimeter set up now, and people were manning it with barricades someone had gotten from the sheriff's office. She recognized the faces of those standing around. There weren't too many people trying to get past, really; they'd identified most of the dead already and sent people away in stunned shock and tears. Lauren had heard them while she was treating the wounded, of whom there weren't that many. When she looked up at Reeve in surprise, he went on: "Nothing else you can do here, Doc."

Lauren wasn't so sure about that. She could help scrape the dead off the square, help collect some of the severed limbs and heads, talk to some of the people still grieving outside the perimeter. Arch Stan, for instance, was still just sitting on the curb, another guy next to him, both of them exchanging a word every now and again, but mostly just staring off into space. She could do something about that, maybe.

She turned around and saw Molly standing by the barrier near where she'd come into the square when Ms. Cherry had driven her here with the others. Her feet ached, she realized, and the thought of walking miles and miles to get to an empty home ... where her mother's body was still probably laid out in the bathroom ...

Well, that just didn't sound appealing at all, especially after the day she'd just had.

"Molly," Lauren said easing toward her. There were lights on to replace the lamps that had mostly been knocked out during the fray, headlights of cars casting shadows all over the square. The darkness between high beams made it only slightly easier to tolerate looking around. Personally, Lauren doubted she'd seen this many dead people in her entire med school career, maybe even counting pictures she'd seen of cadavers in textbooks. She for damned sure hadn't seen this many bodies torn up before.

"Mom," Molly said, doing her best not to look into the square. She still had blood smears around her mouth, but they looked like someone had wiped them off, at least in the light of the nearest car's headlamps. Molly quivered as Lauren approached. "Where ... where do we go now?"

Lauren felt a ratcheting tension inside, like someone had planted a corkscrew in her back and twisted it so that every muscle and nerve ending was wrapped around it. With every step it felt like someone was turning it, and everything just got tighter and tighter.

"May I offer you a place to stay?" The soft voice of Melina Cherry came through under the buzz of a few voices Lauren could hear beyond the headlights. She peered past Molly and realized Ms. Cherry was standing there in the darkness. She hadn't even noticed her.

Lauren started to open her mouth to say no, that it was kind of her to offer to put them up in her whore house, but no thanks, and yet she couldn't find the words to say that. Looking at Molly, she found herself seeing something like a spark of hope in her daughter's eyes, a plea that said, *Anywhere but home.*

"Yes, please," Lauren said, and she saw the small quiver of relief in her daughter as that sank in. Lauren hugged Molly close, and without a word, Ms. Cherry lifted her arm and put it around both of them. They sandwiched Molly between the two of them as Lauren followed the local madam to her car.

*

It was getting close to morning before Reeve felt like the scene of the slaughter was under control, was sorted out enough that he could leave. "There's nothing left to do," Erin had said, and she'd been right. The funeral homes had come and collected the bodies, the pieces of bodies, and all Reeve was left with when they were done were streets slick with blood, barricades keeping people out of a square that had been the site of a bloody slaughter, and not a damned clue what was going on.

He hadn't word one back from the THP, nor from the ambulance dispatch. No one had shown up but the volunteer fire department. They really were Midian's Finest, in Reeve's opinion, and to a man every last one of them had taken countless people to the local hospitals. The worst had gone to Chattanooga, but there weren't many of those. Most had gone to Calhoun County's hospital, a half-assed operation if Reeve had ever seen one, but they could stitch and suture adequately enough, and Reeve had been all out of operational thoughts to give on that side of things by the time the question had come up, so he'd deferred to the firemen. They knew this shit better than he did, anyway.

Then there was also the matter of that one John Doe, too. The one who wasn't saying a damned thing, whom you could lead around by the hand but that was about it.

The one who wore a face that Reeve would always know as "Chester." He'd sent that fellow along with the boys to the hospital, too, once he'd poked him a couple times himself for good measure. Whoever that guy had been before Chester had gotten ahold of him, if he was in there, he was buried pretty deep. Reeve had his doubts that the man would ever speak again, but then, that wasn't his problem at the moment, and he certainly had enough of his own to be getting on with.

He got that cold and lonely feeling on his drive back to the sheriff's station, though, the one that told him that his ass was hanging out in the wind, exposed. Ed Fries's fat ass hadn't even shown up, and to his knowledge, Pike hadn't either, which made him wonder real hard if Pike had been possessed some time between when Alison Stan had poked him with her knife and tonight, because this little Halloween nightmare had seemed awfully damned convenient for the Legion and their revenge plans.

Something was going to have to be done, and he had a few ideas about that.

The sun was coming up as Reeve turned onto Old Jackson Highway, and he didn't think he had the mental acuity to examine the options too deep and pick one just yet. He was holding himself back from going on over to Ed's place or tracking down Pike and kicking down doors, marching in with gun and holy sword, but it was only because he was hellaciously tired, and he recognized his judgment might just be suspect at the moment.

That was all right, though, because had another idea, but he'd need some rest before he could even think about executing it.

He turned into the sheriff's office parking lot with a pretty small sketch of a plan to solve his rest conundrum. He had an extra key that Pike didn't know about, and there was a refrigerator with some food, a cot in the back room, a few extra pistols inside, and he meant to make use of all of them, probably in that order. If Ed Fries hadn't been at the scene of the square, Reeve doubted he'd find him here now, but as he started to pull in, the sight of a car there just about made him think he was wrong.

The rising sun glared off its windshield as he drove in and parked next to it, behind the wheel of Braeden Tarley's Ford pickup, which he'd taken from a couple blocks away from the scene of the crime. That fella wasn't going to be needing it anyhow; he'd gone off with Barney Jones and Arch, and would probably be bedding down at the parsonage for the evening, after he got taken care of at the hospital. Reeve doubted there'd be much sleeping between those two, but the idea of Tarley driving after what he'd been through had been frightening enough that Reeve had asked the man for his keys and the mechanic had acquiesced without so much as a word of protest.

Reeve stared at the car parked next to him. Now this was a bit of a puzzle to him, because he was expecting Ed Fries and his ratty old Toyota, but instead, gleaming in the sunlight, was a Porsche. He couldn't see who was behind the wheel, but he could tell there was someone in there, and he had a damned sinking feeling, because he only knew one person who drove a car like that.

When Reeve got out of the pickup, the driver of the Porsche got out, too, and it turned he'd been right. Usually, the mere sight of her would have spoiled his whole day, but there wasn't a damned thing left to spoil, so he just said, "Morning, Lex. What brings you to my humble doorstep on this gawdawful, shit-ass morning?"

Lex Deivrel cocked an eyebrow at him. The woman was already made up, had a cup of coffee in her hand, steaming out the little sipping hole, and the expression she wore was pure amusement. "Why, I'm here for you, Sheriff."

Reeve felt that old, familiar sense that a safe was about to drop on his head. "Oh, yeah? What the fuck did I do now?" He answered that question for himself a moment later—got his wife killed, presided over the slaughter of more people than he could count—and waited to see what answer she'd give.

"You didn't do anything," Deivrel said, smiling smugly. "I'm here to help you—for once." She offered him the coffee, which he took, regarding it like it was poisoned, but as soon as it was out of her hand, she rummaged in her briefcase and came out with some papers. She offered them to him, and he took them as she took possession of her coffee once more and sipped it.

"What the hell is this?" Reeve asked. The sun was in his eyes, and he couldn't but barely see the legalese on the pages in his hand.

"That is me shredding the hell out of County Administrator Pike's temporary restraining order that removed you from office," she said sweetly. She talked like that almost all the time, and it sounded fucking patronizing every second. "Congratulations. You're sheriff again, at least until this recall election happens."

He stared at her blankly. "I ... thank you, I guess?"

"Don't thank me," she said with a passive shrug. "Thank Bill Longholt. He's the one who hired me."

Reeve tingled with a chill. "Bill ... hired you?" She nodded. "Before he was shot, I assume?"

She frowned. "He was shot? Is he all right?"

"I don't know for sure, but I don't think it was looking too good."

She made a disturbed noise. "Glad I already charged his credit card."

Reeve just stared at her. "You ... you really don't know what's happened in this town, do you?"

She stared right back at him, unflappable. "Other than them trying to eject you as sheriff? And hookers being burned up from the inside? And one of your deputies walking away from an immense and near-certain windfall from your sad employment practices?" She shook her head. "No, I don't. And frankly, I'm not sure I want to know." She started back to her car.

"Wait a second," Reeve said, calling after her. She paused, dutifully, and looked back. "I ... depending on how things go these next few days ... I might need a lawyer."

Lex Deivrel's forehead moved subtly. Reeve realized for the first time she Botoxed, and this was her version of surprise. "You mean for something other than what I just did for you?"

"Yeah," Reeve said, a little thickly, and Deivrel came back toward him slowly, showing her version of concern. "Why don't we ... go inside ... and I'll tell you the whole story." He waited for her to nod once, and he turned to go in, the bright morning sun glaring back at him from the Plexiglas window of the sheriff's station.

*

Duncan stared at Amanda. She'd known him long enough to know what he was thinking, what he was feeling, even though he was barely showing a thing. "Is that it?" he asked, into the still quiet of her hotel room.

She looked back at him implacably, knowing it was driving him nuts. "No," she said, "but it's all I'm allowed to tell you."

Yep, she knew Duncan pretty well after a century. She certainly knew him well enough to tell when he was scared. She couldn't blame him, though. If she'd been sitting where he was, feeling what he was ... she would have been scared shitless too.

*

Hendricks pulled into the Sinbad just after sunup, behind the wheel of another borrowed car. He was missing the SUV because this one was a small car that Reeve had gotten for him when he'd told the sheriff what he'd meant to do. Stony-faced Reeve hadn't even blinked, he'd just gone to work and five minutes later there were keys in Hendricks's hand and the sheriff told him what vehicle he was looking for. He didn't point him in a direction, but it hadn't taken but a quick circle of the streets around the square to find what he was looking for. And the blood on the key ring? Well, Hendricks just ignored that as the price of doing business.

He put the car in park and got out, stretching slowly. Mrs. Longholt and her baby boy had taken the news like champs. He couldn't decide if it was worse than the idea of Bill being a goddamned vegetable for the rest of his life, but he couldn't help feel that just maybe Alison had drawn the lucky straw on that bargain.

Hendricks didn't want to think about Arch or what he was going through at the moment, either. He remembered the feelings, what it was like when Renee had died, and didn't exactly relish the thought of having to open up and share one damned word of it. He was probably going to, at some point real soon, or at least try, for Arch's sake, but now wasn't that moment. The wound was still open and bleeding, and Hendricks didn't feel up to salting up his finger and pushing it inside right now.

He opened the door and came in, closing it behind him. He locked it without turning on the light, his breathing long and slow in the darkened room. Sunlight was shining in around the curtains again, and he thought maybe, just maybe he was right ...

"You here?" he asked, and the pause after he asked felt unduly long.

"I am here," Starling answered, and he clicked the light.

There was a strange rush of relief seeing her there, standing in the orange lamplight, her red hair shining and lustrous. Part of him wanted to yell at her, but he wrote that off to the emotion of the moment. "I wondered if you'd turn up."

She stared right back at him. "And here I am."

"Not here," Hendricks said, taking a couple steps toward her. "At the square. Where ..." He cut himself off because the emotion made it feel like someone had grabbed his voice box and started to squeeze.

She looked back at him. "I came."

"For about five seconds, yeah," Hendricks said, glancing away. He was having a hard time looking at her right now. It was hot in the room, or at least it felt like it to him. He started to peel off his coat, and he could smell the blood. For a fleeting second, he thought, *at least it's not sulfur* ... "But where were you during the rest of the ... the ..." He had a catch in his throat, like someone had put a fingernail clipping in there and it got hung up on the way down.

"I could not be there," she said quietly. "I could only come long enough to save you."

"I guess that's convenient for me," he said, and there was that strange relief again. "Sucks for Alison, though."

Starling just stared back at him. "Many more will die, you know."

"End of the world, yeah," Hendricks said snidely, and now he felt the exhaustion. "I think that generally suggests all of us will die, doesn't it?" He tossed the coat off to the side and kicked off his boots. He'd been wearing them for way, way too long. He peeled off his socks one by one as he stood there in front of her, tossing them and letting his bare feet rub against the thin carpet. It felt pretty good, not that he cared. "So ... why save me, then?" He waited for an answer. "You already told me the end of the world is coming. Hell, you showed me. So why waste your time saving me?"

Her hair fluttered and suddenly she was next to him, looking up at him with those dusky eyes. "Because I need you."

"Need me for what?" He held himself back from her, but he couldn't help feel the strange sense of heat between them. He remembered when she'd kissed him before, before ...

... Before Kitty.

His hand came up to his lips, feeling them self-consciously, like she could smell the taint of that cunt on him. It had driven him these last weeks, made him ache, made him alone. He couldn't wash the smell of shame off himself no matter how many times he showered, and he hadn't had a desire to touch himself once since then, not even when he woke up hard.

There was a churning in Hendricks's belly as he stood there, face to face with Starling and she stared out at him from behind those dusky eyes. "I need you," she said again, and leaned forward, bringing her lips to his slowly, slower than he'd ever seen her move.

He took the kiss, soft lips against his, not really sure what to do at first. It felt surprisingly warm and tingly, and when her fingers touched his cheek it surprised him that she was not cold to the touch, not at all. Quite the opposite, actually.

He leaned in, returning the kiss, and he smelled something faintly sweet in her hair, something he'd never caught from her before. She parted his lips gently and put her tongue in his mouth, her left hand coming up and running through his hair, knocking his cowboy hat to the floor.

He put his hand around her thin waist and it felt good sitting there. He crept it a little lower as they kept going, and felt her snug blue jeans beneath his palms, beneath his fingertips. That sense of burning shame was gone, washed away with her kiss, a faint memory that twinged him in the back of the head and stopped him for just a second. "Wait ... I ..." he said, but she kissed him again and he did not want to stop.

She pulled his shirt off, unbuckling his belt and nearly ripping his jeans off. She was out of her clothes so fast that he didn't even see her do it, and his dick was hard and poking her in her flat stomach before he'd even finished stepping out of his pants legs. She kissed down his chest and belly and found the promised land, and goddamn he was hard as a rock when she put his dick in her mouth. She moved her lips up and down a few times and it was like wet silk rubbing up and down his shaft. When she stopped, he felt like the world was ending right there, no shit.

She pushed him gently back onto the bed and his ass hit the rough comforter. He didn't even have time to squirm his way up the bed before she was atop him, kissing him as she came astride him. He didn't warm her up at all, but she was wet and ready when she slid down his pole. It happened so fast he didn't even expect it, and she started to ride him, up and down in a perfect rhythm, her hands on his chest, slipping him almost out of her and then all the way back in again.

It took him less than thirty seconds to cum, overwhelmed by the feeling. It came almost as a surprise, but it was such a thick and rich orgasm that he could feel himself tense and squirt all the way from the bottom of the shaft up to the tip. She stiffened as he ejaculated, tilting her head back and thrusting her breasts out as he climaxed. He had his hands on her hips and just held her there, held her until he was done cumming, and then she slumped down to lay her head on his chest.

His legs were still hanging half off the bed as she curled up against him. In the afterglow, that sense of shame, of unexplainable guilt started creeping up on Hendricks again. He felt a little sick, but he didn't know why. Instead he just held the redhead against him, stroking the back of her head where it lay against his chest, breathing slowly and steadily in the cheap motel room until he fell asleep.

When he woke to the sound of the phone ringing a few hours later, she was already gone.

14.

The meeting room in the municipal building was dead quiet this time around, and Reeve was grateful for it. He almost felt like he was a couple blocks away, in the town square, sitting with the dead among them instead of in a packed room of living people. There were actually more faces in attendance this time than there had been for the one a few days prior; standing room only, and there was no shouting, no yelling, just sad and lonely faces staring up at him as he said, "I call this meeting to order." He could have whispered and they all still would have heard it.

"I'm sorry to have to convene this under the circumstances," he said, looking at the darkness visible out the windows behind the standing room only crowd, "especially so soon after what happened last night, in the square. I'd like to have given us all time to breathe, time to grieve ..." He felt a pinch, because damn if he wasn't thinking about Donna again. "... Time to mourn.

"But we ain't got time for that right now," Reeve said, and his eyes swept the room. Dr. Darlington was in the front row, with her daughter Molly next to her, the girl's head on her mother's shoulder. They'd come in with Ms. Cherry, and Reeve had a strong suspicion based on the perfume smell he'd caught a whiff of on the doctor as they'd talked for a minute before the start that they were probably staying with the madam. He didn't much care. It sounded better to him than sleeping in the sheriff's office on a cot.

"What do we do, Nick?" Barney Jones asked the question right on cue. Reeve hadn't wanted to go into this meeting as unprepared as the last, even though he was hoping it would take a different shape entirely.

"We've known each other a long time," Reeve said, looking at Jones, who sat in the middle of a small cluster of people he'd seen take up the mantle of the watch last night. Arch was there, looking a little more alive, and Braeden Tarley was nodding faintly next to him. "Midian ... Calhoun County ... this place is our home." He scanned past them and saw Father Nguyen and Casey Meacham, as improbable a couple as ever he'd seen, nodding along. "These people in this room ... we're like family.

"And last night ... our Midian family got their damned teeth kicked in." He didn't spare the image, because the reality of what happened was a hell of a lot worse, and everybody in this room knew it. Just looking around he could tell that there wasn't a person here who hadn't been hit by a personal loss last night—spouse, child, friend, parent. He caught sight of Keith Drumlin in the front row, pale and shaking, and he knew the man had lost all of those.

"But that's not the end for us," Reeve went on, admiring what a difference a couple days made in the silence as the entire room hung on his every word. "We lost people last night. Friends. People we loved. People we were supposed to ..." he swallowed hard, "... protect. But this town ... it ain't over. And those people died ... but we aren't dead. We're still here." He caught a glimpse of Duncan in the back row, standing tall, wearing a suit again, black with a white shirt, and staring down at the ground, that new black lady at his side watching Reeve as he spoke. "We're still here," Reeve said again, a little harder this time. "And what we do ... is we fight for our home. We fight for our family here. We fight for our town, the way a bunch of us did last night when everything went wrong."

Reeve straightened, clutching tight to the podium, and drew a slow, ragged breath. No one shouted in, no one interjected. This was the sticky part, the one he'd about had a nightmare over only a couple days prior. He swallowed hard, preparing himself for the worst. No matter how it went, it couldn't be as bad as the last meeting. "Now I want to ask y'all the same thing I asked you the other night, and I'm just hoping ... after everything that happened ... we get a different answer this time around."

He took a deep breath, and said, "Are any of y'all ready to believe me now ... and ready to fight ... and help to save this town any way you can?"

The next moment was like an eternity of waiting. He had a flash, thinking it was going to be worse than last time, that everyone would just sit there silently, like an audience of stones, judging him, before it all came apart.

But that didn't happen.

Barney Jones raised his hand first, but only by a little. Arch Stan had his up there just after, and so did Braeden Tarley. Hendricks in the back, shuffling around, raised his, too, though he was covered over a moment later by other hands, rising all over the meeting room, a few at a time.

Reeve stood there as they went up one by one until he couldn't see anyone sitting in the room without at least one hand in the air. He looked out over the townsfolk and felt a hard pang of regret. If only it had gone like this last time, maybe ... maybe Donna would still have been there.

Reeve put that thought out of his mind until later; he knew he was gonna be thinking about her a lot for the near future. Probably the far future, too, because damn if he could ever see himself forgetting about her. But she wouldn't have wanted him to dwell, not now. Not while there was this work to be done.

Because this was her home, too. And even if he couldn't save her ... he'd do this in her memory.

He stared out at the hands raised in front of him, and gave them all a quick nod. "All right, then." In spite of all that had happened, and all the bitter, stinging losses that had lashed him hard as a whip over the last few days, there was suddenly just a hint of hope shining through, like a beam of sun on a damned cloudy, autumn day. "Let's get to work."

Return to Midian in

STARLING

Southern Watch
Book Six

Coming Late 2016!

Author's Note

If you want to know immediately when future books become available, take sixty seconds and sign up for my NEW RELEASE EMAIL ALERTS by visiting my website at www.robertjcrane.com. I don't sell your information and I only send out emails when I have a new book out. The reason you should sign up for this is because I don't always set release dates, and even if you're following me on Facebook (robertJcrane (Author)) or Twitter (@robertJcrane), it's easy to miss my book announcements because…well, because social media is an imprecise thing.

Come join the discussion on my website: http://www.robertjcrane.com

Cheers,
Robert J. Crane

ACKNOWLEDGMENTS

Editorial/Literary Janitorial duties performed by Sarah Barbour and Jeffrey Bryan. Final proofing was handle by Jo Evans. Any errors you see in the text, however, are the result of me rejecting changes. Because I'm a special snowflake, obviously, and the rules of spelling and grammar mean fuck-all to me. I'm trying to tell a story here, people, don't let this petty bullshit get in my way. (I'm mostly joking about that.)

The cover was masterfully designed (as always) by Karri Klawiter from photographs taken by Taria Reed of The Reed Files.

Heidi Schweizer did the first read on this one, and muchas gracias to her! Nicolette Solomita also gave it a read, assuring me that after this particular book, I am guaranteed a prime fireside manor in hell.

Once more, thanks to my parents, my kids and my wife, for helping me keep things together.

Other Works by Robert J. Crane

The Sanctuary Series
Epic Fantasy

Defender: The Sanctuary Series, Volume One
Avenger: The Sanctuary Series, Volume Two
Champion: The Sanctuary Series, Volume Three
Crusader: The Sanctuary Series, Volume Four
Sanctuary Tales, Volume One - A Short Story Collection
Thy Father's Shadow: The Sanctuary Series, Volume 4.5
Master: The Sanctuary Series, Volume Five
Fated in Darkness: The Sanctuary Series, Volume 5.5
Warlord: The Sanctuary Series, Volume Six
Heretic: The Sanctuary Series, Volume Seven
Legend: The Sanctuary Series, Volume Eight* (Coming June 14, 2016!)

The Girl in the Box
and
Out of the Box
Contemporary Urban Fantasy

Alone: The Girl in the Box, Book 1
Untouched: The Girl in the Box, Book 2
Soulless: The Girl in the Box, Book 3
Family: The Girl in the Box, Book 4
Omega: The Girl in the Box, Book 5
Broken: The Girl in the Box, Book 6
Enemies: The Girl in the Box, Book 7
Legacy: The Girl in the Box, Book 8
Destiny: The Girl in the Box, Book 9
Power: The Girl in the Box, Book 10

Limitless: Out of the Box, Book 1
In the Wind: Out of the Box, Book 2
Ruthless: Out of the Box, Book 3
Grounded: Out of the Box, Book 4
Tormented: Out of the Box, Book 5
Vengeful: Out of the Box, Book 6
Sea Change: Out of the Box, Book 7
Painkiller: Out of the Box, Book 8
Masks: Out of the Box, Book 9* (Coming July 12, 2016!)
Prisoners: Out of the Box, Book 10* (Coming September 27, 2016!)

Southern Watch
Contemporary Urban Fantasy

Called: Southern Watch, Book 1
Depths: Southern Watch, Book 2
Corrupted: Southern Watch, Book 3
Unearthed: Southern Watch, Book 4
Legion: Southern Watch, Book 5
Starling: Southern Watch, Book 6* (Coming in August 2016 – Tentatively)
Forsaken: Southern Watch, Book 7* (Coming Late 2016/Early 2017!)

* Forthcoming and subject to change

Printed in Great Britain
by Amazon